TALES OF THE
SHADOWMEN

Volume 4: Lords of Terror

TALES OF THE
SHADOWMEN

Volume 4: Lords of Terror

edited by
Jean-Marc & Randy Lofficier

stories by
**Matthew Baugh, Bill Cunningham,
Win Scott Eckert, Micah Harris,
Travis Hiltz, Rick Lai, Roman Leary,
Jean-Marc Lofficier, Randy Lofficier,
Xavier Mauméjean, Jess Nevins,
Kim Newman, John Peel,
Steven A. Roman, John Shirley**
and **Brian Stableford**

cover by
Ladrönn

A Black Coat Press Book

Acknowledgements: I am indebted to David McDonnell for proofreading the typescript.

Visit our website at www.blackcoatpress.com

ISBN 978-1-934543-02-3. First Printing. January 2008. Published by Black Coat Press, an imprint of Hollywood Comics.com, LLC, P.O. Box 17270, Encino, CA 91416.

Table of Contents

Fathers of the Shadowmen 7
Matthew Baugh: *Captain Future and the Lunar Peril* 11
Bill Cunningham: *Fool Me Once...* 25
Win Scott Eckert: *The Atomos Affair* 39
Micah Harris: *The Anti-Pope of Avignon* 42
Travis Hiltz: *Three Men, A Martian and a Baby* 61
Rick Lai: *Corridors of Deceit* 67
Roman Leary: *The Evils Against Which We Strive* 90
Jean-Marc Lofficier: *Madame Atomos' Christmas* 104
Randy Lofficier: *The Reluctant Princess* 106
Xavier Mauméjean: *A Wooster Christmas* 109
Jess Nevins: *Red in Tooth and Claw* 127
Kim Newman: *The Mark of Kane* 139
John Peel: *Twenty Thousand Years Under The Sea* 172
Steven A. Roman: *Night's Children* 183
John Shirley: *Cyrano and the Two Plumes* 201
Brian Stableford: *The Return of Frankenstein* 216
Credits 287

Ladrönn's cover rough (2007)

Fathers of the Shadowmen

There are 12 of them, just like the Apostles. And one of them turned bad as well. How is that for analogies?

The time has come, in our fourth anthology of stories paying homage to the creations of the great French writers of popular literature, to acknowledge our debt to those who, often before their English or American counterparts, paved the way for the crimefighters, the detectives, the journalists, the magicians, the scientists (mad or otherwise), the monsters and all the superheroes and supervillains of pulp fiction.

Eugène Sue – Paul Féval – Alexandre Dumas

1. *Eugène Sue* (1804-1857). Sue represents the transition between Gothic literature, which was very popular in France at the onset of the 19th century, and modern popular fiction. His bestselling *The Mysteries de Paris* (1842) still contained the traditional elements of Gothic, such as tearful orphans, cackling villains, handsome heroes and mysterious inheritances waiting to be stolen, but gone were the haunted castles, the windswept moors and the evil monks; they were replaced, instead, by an uncompromisingly sordid description of contemporary Paris. Sue's breakthough is the avenging Prince Rodolphe, the Bruce Wayne of his day, minus the bat symbol: a wealthy dandy by day, a merciless avenger by night. His foes, the crimelord known as the Schoolmaster and his cackling crone, The Owl, are pure evil. In *The Wandering Jew* (1844), Sue topped himself with the scheming, ruthless, charismatic Jesuit Father Rodin,

whose plans to rule the world were eventually swiped by lesser writers to serve as the thrice-removed inspiration for the abominable *Protocols of the Elders of Zion*.

2. *Paul Féval* (1816-1887). Féval is the man with the golden pen, the one who created all the modern archetypes. His White Wolf (1843) was a Briton Zorro hiding under a wolf mask and his Rio Santo (1844) anticipated Monte-Cristo by a full year. His gallery of heroes included the warrior-monk Malo de Treguern (1852), Paris Morgue supervisor Severin (1856), the prodigious swordsman Lagardère (1858), the Scotland Yard detective (the first time the word was ever used) Gregory Temple (1862), the superheroic Wandering Jew and his ethereal daughter (1863), the *Buffy*-like Ann Radcliffe and her merry band of fearless vampire killers (1867), the street urchin Pistolet, who grew up to head the Sûreté (1868), the investigative magistrate Remy d'Arx (1869) and more. His villains were even more formidable: Dowager Le Brec, a witch who married the Devil (1852), the vampiric Countess Addhema (1856) and Baron Iscariot (1867), the shape-shifting brothers Ténèbre (1860), John Devil, the uncatchable hero-villain of a thousand faces who dreamed of reshaping the world (1862), and lording over them all, the virtually immortal Colonel Bozzo, leader of the Black Coats, the greatest criminal conspiracy ever spawned on Earth (1844-1875).

3. *Alexandre Dumas* (1802-1870). Féval may have broken new ground, but ultimately, it is Dumas who reaped all the glory. In the space of three years, 1844 to 1846, he penned two unforgettable classics: *The Three Musketeers* and *The Count of Monte-Cristo*, plus the lesser-known *Joseph Balsamo*, a proto-Illuminati novel which proved very influential. He also gave us Lord Ruthven (1851), the nefarious Monsieur Jackal (1854), and the lycanthropic Wolf Leader (1857). Dumas didn't just invent history; he made it more real than real: at the Château d'If in Marseilles, tourists still visit the cell of Edmond Dantès.

P.-A. Ponson du Terrail – Emile Gaboriau – Jules Verne

4. *Pierre-Alexis Ponson du Terrail* (1829-1871). His evolving creation of the indomitable Rocambole (1857-1871) carried on where Féval had left off with Pistolet, and became the template for a legion of future charismatic, adventuring do-gooders who are on the wrong side of the law. He left us the word *rocambolesque*, still used today to describe any feat of derring-do.

5. *Emile Gaboriau* (1832-1874). Once Féval's secretary, Gaboriau, too, carried on his former employer's work with the creation of Sûreté detective Monsieur Lecoq and his armchair sleuth friend, Père Tabaret (1866), heralding the advent of the modern detective novel and ancestors of Sherlock Holmes and Nero Wolfe. A lesser-known character of his was private detective Victor Chupin, who has appeared in our anthology.

6. *Jules Verne* (1828-1905). There is little that can be said about Verne that hasn't been written a million times before, but we shall single him out here for his creation of three immortal characters of popular fiction: the fearless space explorer Michel Ardan, who went where no man (with the possible exception of Cyrano de Bergerac!) had gone before (1865), and two renegade scientist adventurers, Captain Nemo (1870) and Robur the Conqueror (1876).

Gustave Le Rouge – Maurice Leblanc – Gaston Leroux

7. *Gustave Le Rouge* (1867-1938). Le Rouge took Verne's characters and injected them with madness and superhuman emotions. His best-known novels featured a secret society of American billionaires bent on destroying Europe through the use of the first robots and psychic powers (1899), Mars ruled by a Giant Brain (1908) and, his crowning achievement, mad Dr. Cornelius Kramm, leader of the world-spanning Red Hand, who could reshape men like clay (1912).

8. *Maurice Leblanc* (1864-1941). Leblanc took Rocambole and real-life anarchist Marius Jacob and came up with Arsène Lupin (1905), a thief and a gentleman, gifted with the intellectual prowess of his perennial rival, Sherlock Holmes. Like Sir Arthur Conan Dyle, no matter how hard he tried, Leblanc could thereafter never escape from his creation.

9. *Gaston Leroux* (1868-1927). Had Leroux, a journalist, only created Erik, the Phantom of the Opera (1910), his fame would live forever. But with the character of Joseph Rouletabille (1908), his young *alter ego*, Leroux broadened the range of detective novels, from locked room mysteries to spy fiction. Lest we forget, he also created the ape-man Balaoo (1911), the convict Cheri-Bibi (1913) and the cyborg Benedict Masson whose brain lived on inside the robotic Gabriel (1923).

9

Maurice Renard – Pierre Souvestre – Jean de La Hire

10. *Maurice Renard* (1875-1939). Influenced by H.G. Wells, Renard had his mad scientist, Dr. Lerne, graft men onto machines (1908); then introduced us to the notion of superintelligences from outer space abducting men like fish (1912) and created a modern myth, that of the transplanted hands of a killer, in *The Hands of Orlac* (1920).

11. *Pierre Souvestre* (1874-1914). With his writing partner, *Marcel Allain* (1885-1970), Souvestre co-created the sociopathic Fantômas (1911). More sadistic than John Devil, more psychotic than Lupin, Fantômas is the first "heroic" fictional serial killer of the 20th century.

12. *Jean de La Hire* (1878-1956). Walking in the footsteps of both Verne and Le Rouge, La Hire created the first, true superhero, Leo Saint-Clair, the Nyctalope (1911). Leo went on to embody the best and the worst of Colonial France, until he, like his creator, succumbed to the temptation of collaboration with the occupying Nazis and, ultimately, vanished in the fog of war.

These, then, are the fathers of the Shadowmen whom we celebrate for a fourth time in this volume. Join us now and meet the villainous cast who grace these pages, spreading evil from the underworld of London to the seedy taverns of Mars, from the banks of the Seine to New York's Hell Kitchen: Fantômas, Countess Cagliostro, Victor Frankenstein, Irma Vep, Count Orlock, Erik, Madame Atomos, the Black Coats, Charles Foster Kane, Captain Nemo, Cthulhu... Dare meet–the Lords of Terror!

Jean-Marc Lofficier

René Barjavel (1911-1985) is rightly considered to be one of France's greatest modern science fiction writers. Some of his classic novels include Ravage (*1943; transl. as* Ashes, Ashes), *about a world suddenly deprived of electricity,* Le Voyageur Imprudent (*1943; transl. as* Future Times Three), *a seminal time travel story, and* La Nuit des Temps (*1968; transl., as* The Ice People), *the moving tale of the downfall of the civilization that preceded ours. Matthew Baugh chose to use Barjavel's melancholy protagonist of* Future Times Three *and propel him in a rollercoaster of a tale taking place in the planetary romances of Edmond Hamilton, Leigh Brackett and Catherine L. Moore, while at the same time, paying homage to a story published in last year's* Tales of the Shadowmen...

Matthew Baugh: *Captain Future and the Lunar Peril*

New York City, 2021

The green man seemed to come out of nowhere.

The dark-uniformed Planet Patrol Officers were startled, but only for a moment. Their training took over and they moved in on the man, atomic flare pistols ready. He raised his goggles and blinked at them amiably.

The man wasn't actually green, not the way a native of Jupiter, or a four-armed giant Martian, or one of the sea-people of Venus is green. He was wearing an outlandish green costume that covered every inch of him except for his face. It looked like the woolen suits old deep-sea divers once wore. The face was youthful with plain features and the expression of a perennial dreamer. It seemed a harmless face, but harmless people don't often materialize from thin air in front of the Manhattan headquarters of Earth's government.

"Keep your hands away from your body!" a guard barked. "Don't move!"

The green man looked at the guns around him with mild alarm and disobeyed the instructions. His finger stabbed a button on the chest of the suit and he disappeared. An instant later, half a dozen flashes of light seared through the air where the man had been standing.

The guard commander swore under his breath and pulled out his televisor.

"Code red!" he shouted into the unit. "Intruder is an Earthman, approximately 200 centimeters tall and very thin. He is dressed in a baggy green coverall with a hood. Secure the building at once and get the President to safety!"

The green man reappeared in an office on the top floor of the Government Tower. There was only one person in the room, a distinguished-looking man with silver hair. He was Daniel Crewe, the President of Earth and the de facto head of the solar system.

"What is the meaning of this?" he demanded.

The green man held up a hand to fend off questions. He produced a small can and sprayed the door with it.

"What are you doing?" Crewe repeated.

"Forgive me sir," the green man answered. "There is something I have to tell you and I could not let your policemen stop me."

Crewe nodded agreeably. It would be only a matter of seconds before his security team came crashing through the door. It was best to keep this intruder calm until then.

"You have an unorthodox way of starting a conversation," he said, "but you have my full attention. What is it that you want?"

"Sir," the young man swallowed nervously. "I know that in three days you are scheduled to dedicate a museum on the Moon."

Crewe nodded. The whole world knew about the event. It commemorated the landing in the Sea of Tranquility 50 years earlier. That mission had been the beginning of the rush of space exploration that had left colonies on all the worlds of the system. The museum was to be built at Tranquility Base. Soon the glassite dome would be filled with air so that all could visit the monument to human achievement.

"You must destroy the landing craft!" the young man said. "Blast it or bomb it! Use your most powerful weapons. Nothing must remain."

The sound of flare pistols erupted in the corridor as the guards attempted to blast through the office door. The atomic bursts should have cut through the heavy wood with ease, but nothing happened.

"Why?" Crewe asked. "In the name of all that's sane, why would I want to destroy something so valuable?"

"If you don't destroy the landing site, billions will die!"

A bolt of red flame shot across the room and the green man fell. Daniel Crewe spun towards the source of the shot. It was one of his guards. The man had used magnetic clamps to cling to the side of the building and had fired through the window. The blast had grazed the green man, leaving an ugly burn across his forearm.

"Don't kill him!" Crewe cried.

The green man had an expression of terror on his face. His hand shot to a switch on the chest of his costume. The guard fired again but the bolt of atomic flame passed through empty air. The green man had vanished.

It was evening in Paris and the young man sat in a café wearing a nervous expression. He had exchanged the green costume for an inconspicuous synth-silk zippersuit. It fit him reasonably well, though the sleeves and legs were too short.

"Monsieur St. Menoux?"

The man sprang to his feet at the sound of his name. The speaker was a big man, not as tall as he was, but more heavily muscled. His pale eyes stood out vividly in a face that was nearly as dark as his black hair. The man was dressed in a spacer's leather pants and a shirt of iridescent Venusian spider silk.

"I am St. Menoux!" he replied. "Are you the man who..." he trailed off and looked around nervously.

"I'm Stark," the big man said. "Don't worry, we aren't being watched."

St. Menoux could feel the controlled power in Stark's grip as they shook hands. The dark man's face was intelligent and his expression calm, but there was something barbaric hiding in those eyes. He made St. Menoux think of a trained tiger, friendly but in no way safe.

A waitress appeared and took their order. She was very pretty, but her skin was covered with short, tawny fur and her eyes had vertical pupils. Stark said something to her in a strange, guttural language and her face brightened. She took their order for drinks and walked away with cat-like grace.

"I've never seen such a girl," St. Menoux said. "Is she an alien?"

Stark gave him an odd look.

"She's from Mercury." He shook his head. "I'll never get used to seeing lightsiders in human clothing."

"You spoke her language?"

"My parents were prospectors on Mercury," the big man replied. "I grew up there."

The drinks came. St. Menoux had a brandy and Stark had a blood-colored liquor.

"Segir," he said at the other's unspoken question. "It comes from Sha-Ardol."

"Sha-Ardol?"

Stark's pale eyes narrowed.

"I often use the old names for the planets," he said. "I hope you don't have a problem with that."

"Please," St. Menoux stammered. "It's only that I had never heard any of these 'old names.' "

"Vulcan is uninhabited, and the people of Mercury have no name for their world. The other planets, in the names of their own people, are Sha-Ardol, Barsoom, Eurobus, Cykranosh, L'gy'hx, Yaksh and Yuggoth."

"Vulcan?" St. Menoux was perplexed. "I only know of nine planets."

"Then you've led a sheltered life, friend. In addition to those ten, there are the wandering worlds of Rhea and Mongo. Their orbits are so eccentric that thousands of years pass between each visit they make to the inner system. That makes an even dozen planets, and 30 moons."

St. Menoux shook his head in wonder.

"These things are new to me," he said. "I am a time traveler from the last century."

"Can you prove that?"

St. Menoux held out a small capsule.

"Take this and you will see."

The door to the President's office was still in the same place it had been when St. Menoux had vanished. If the Living Brain were right, it would always remain there.

"How can that be, Simon?" Captain Future asked.

"The door is frozen in time," the Brain responded.

The organ was suspended in a transparent glassite case that floated a meter and a half above the floor. It spoke from an electronic voice box attached to the outside of the case. The Brain had once been a human scientist named Simon Wright. When his body failed, he had his brain transplanted to its present home so he could continue his scientific research.

"If that's true, we could blast the building to atoms and it would still be there, hanging in the air," the young scientist continued.

"That's right Curtis," the Brain replied. "All physical change is four-dimensional in nature. Suspend time and no change is possible."

The tall Earthman ran his fingers through his unruly mane of red hair. It was rare that Curt Newton, better known through the solar system as Captain Future, ran into something outside his experience.

"That makes sense," he said. "A man who could alter his own relationship to the time stream could seem to appear and disappear as the intruder did. But what technology could he be using?"

"Many years ago, when I was still human, there was a discovery that could explain it," the Brain answered. "A French scientist named Noël Essaillon invented something that he called *noelite* and claimed it had such properties."

"I remember the name," Curt said. "Didn't he disappear mysteriously?"

"He did," the Brain replied. "There were rumors that his government tested a weapon using noelite. Shortly after that, he vanished from sight. I always assumed that he had been taking into hiding for reasons of national security."

"The man who did this wasn't working for the Earth Government," the third man in the room said. He was Halk Anders, the head of the Planet Police. "If he'd been a part of any legitimate national government, we'd have a record of it."

"Do you have any leads?" Curt asked.

"There have been several groups who've threatened the opening of the museum," Anders answered. "It's a prime target because so many planetary leaders will be in attendance. We've had threats from the Venusian Neo-Zani's, a Martian separatist group called the Sons of the Two Moons, and Dr. Ku Sui's organization, just to name a few."

"Whoever this man is, he seems to be a terrorist," Curt said. "Tell the President that the Futuremen will make certain he doesn't succeed."

Erik John Stark reappeared in his chair with a look of wonder on his face.

"How long was I gone?"

"Only an instant," St. Menoux replied.

"I relived three years," he shook his head. "You say that it is possible to go into the future too?"

"Yes."

"Then you've seen what will happen?"

"It's complicated," St. Menoux said. "Time is shaped like a fan. The present is the fulcrum from which all possible timelines radiate. Any time I travel to the future, I move down the most likely of an infinite number of timelines. I can always return to the point I left, but my next trip will take me to a different future."

"Why are you here?" Stark asked.

"I recently traveled to the 23rd century. I found civilization in ruins there. I checked the records as thoroughly as I could and discovered that there was an interplanetary war that began this year. Many of the leaders of the Triangle planets, Venus, Earth and Mars, were killed at the opening of the Moon Museum. Accusations and rumors went wild until the war broke out. It was only years later that they discovered that the deaths had been caused by an old trap."

Stark said nothing. His blue eyes were fixed on the time traveler's face with a fierce intensity. St. Menoux swallowed and continued.

"In the 20th century there lived a Japanese woman named Madame Atomos. She had sworn vengeance for the use of the atom bomb on Hiroshima and Nagasaki. This woman had a trap planted on the first vessel to land on the Moon." [1]

"What sort of trap?"

"A bomb of some sort," St. Menoux said bitterly. "I had hoped to persuade the President of Earth to abort the opening and destroy the landing craft. Unfortunately, our meeting didn't go very well."

Stark nodded.

"There's a terrorist alert since you popped up in the President's office. All ships leaving the planet will be searched and there's no traffic to the Moon except on official business. To make matters worse, the Moon is Captain Future's home."

"Then there is no hope?"

"You could just use your time travel device to go there, couldn't you?" Stark asked. "I don't see how even Future could stop that."

---

[1] See "Au Vent Mauvais..." by François Darnaudet & Jean-Marc Lofficier in *Tales of the Shadowmen 3*.

"I can't pass between the planets," St. Menoux answered. "There may be a way but I haven't found it."

"In that case," Stark said, "I know just the man to help us."

Tranquility Base was well named. No wind had disturbed the flag since it had been planted midway through the last century. No rust had formed on the landing craft, no rot had set in to the fabric of the flag. The airless lunar surface had preserved everything better than an Earth museum could have. It was fortunate that the craft had landed in an area where there were no Moon wolves. The bizarre silicon-based creatures would have feasted on its refined metals.

A huge glassite dome had been erected over the landing site, but had not yet been pressurized. Curt Newton gazed at the sight. He had been born on the Moon, so this place held even more meaning for him than for most Earth people. He had mixed feelings about this new tourist site on the world that he had almost to himself for so long.

Curt's parents had been scientists on Earth, working to develop artificial beings as servants for humanity. They and their friend Simon Wright had fled to the Moon, seeking a hiding place to finish their experiments. Luna wasn't far from Earth but, of all the moons and planets of the system, it was one of the few places where life had never taken hold.

That was to say, there was almost no life on the surface of the Moon. Michel Ardan's 1865 orbit of the satellite had spotted the ruins of ancient buildings. Professor Selwyn Cavor's ill-fated expedition to Luna's surface in 1901 had discovered a strange inhuman civilization in the vast caverns beneath. Curt had been in those caverns and suspected that there might be an entire living world deep inside the satellite. Perhaps the descendants of the ruined surface cities of Baloise, Ingala and Nial lived there still.

In any case, Curt's parents had their seclusion. At Simon's request, they transferred his brain from his dying body to the serum case that still housed it. Then they had completed their experiments. Their first triumph had been Grag, a towering metal robot of matchless strength. Not satisfied, they constructed Otho, a pale synthetic man who looked and acted nearly human.

Unfortunately, the Newtons' enemies managed to track them to their new home. They murdered the young couple only to be killed in turn by Grag and Otho. Curt had been raised on that lonely orb by android, robot and disembodied brain. They had trained his mind and body to the peak of human perfection and now shared his strange vocation of seeking adventures and righting wrongs.

"Master," Grag's voice came through the spacesuit's radio. "All my tests on the landing craft are negative."

"It's the same with the flag and the stray equipment," Otho added. "If there's anything odd here, I sure can't find it."

"Then we have to assume the green man's statement is a terrorist threat," Curt said grimly. "Well, if he wants to destroy this place, he'll have to deal with the Futuremen first!"

St. Menoux was sitting at the bar in an ancient city on the low canals of Mars. Getting off of Earth had been fairly simple. Stark had bribed their way on an Interplanetary Corporation freighter that had brought them to the red planet.

He sipped his drink and glanced around anxiously. Stark had referred to Jekkara as a wretched hive of scum and villainy and it lived up to its reputation. There was a spaceport nearby and a few of the braver off-worlders mingled with the fierce Martian crowd. *Madame Kan's* was famous for its beautiful dancing girls, its getak tables, and thil, an exquisitely prepared cactus brandy.

St. Menoux was sampling a glass of the exotic liquor as a Martian girl whispered in his ear. She dressed in the local custom, which meant that she was naked to the waist. The tiny bells on her skirt tinkled wickedly as she moved.

"I can promise you pleasures such as you've never known, Earthman," she breathed. "I can find you a pipe of ming if you like, or the forbidden shanga, or perhaps the new drug from Pluto."

The traveler shook his head again, wishing he were somewhere else. He was relieved when he saw Stark signal him from across the room. He rose and moved to join his companion where he sat with another Earthman.

"St. Menoux," Stark said, "this is Northwest Smith. He'll get us where we need to go."

The man called Smith was tall and lean with space-bronzed skin and cold grey eyes. He wore black spacer's leathers and had a heat ray strapped to his right thigh, gunfighter style. If Stark seemed like a tiger in human form, then Northwest Smith was a wolf. St. Menoux shuddered at his need to associate with such men.

"I said I can get you there," Smith said with a thin smile. "We're still working on whether I will."

"Our money's good," Stark replied.

"That's not the issue. You want to land in the Sea of Tranquility. That's Captain Future's backyard. His home is somewhere in Tycho Crater and he keeps an eye on everything that happens on the bright side of the Moon. Getting in there is more dangerous than trying to raid Black Pharol's tomb."

"True," Stark countered. "But you've done that, haven't you, Northwest?"

Smith smiled crookedly.

"My point is, for a job this dangerous I need to know the reason."

"If we don't do this, there will be an explosion that will kill a lot of prominent leaders from Earth, Venus and Mars," St. Menoux said.

Smith looked startled.

"You're kidding, right, Stark? Why in Shar's name would you want to stop that? You hate those government types."

"It leads to a war," St. Menoux continued. "Billions will die, civilization will fall into ruin."

"How could you know that?" Smith demanded. "You couldn't unless..."

"He's a time traveler," Stark supplied.

"Seven hells!" the pilot swore. "I promised myself I wasn't going to get involved with one of those again!"

"There's no other way," Stark said.

Smith scowled and tossed back a shot of thil.

"Fine," he said. "I suppose if I have to go out, making a fool out of Captain Future's as good a way as any."

Gerry Carlyle ran a hand absently through her reddish gold hair as she watched the Planet Patrol cruisers. After a moment, they broke off and she guided the Ark from lunar orbit towards the bright lights of Hollywood-on-the-Moon. Gerry let out a breath of relief and reached for the intercom button.

"Smith, the coast is clear."

"Thanks, sweetheart!" a voice answered. "Any problems?"

"No problems, aside from you calling me 'sweetheart.' "

"I knew there wouldn't be. There isn't a man breathing who could say 'no' to you."

"It had more to do with the fact that I have a hold full of Plutonian ice-tigers," Gerry said. "One look at those brutes and the cops didn't want to inspect the ship too closely."

"I'd meant to ask about that," Smith asked.

"Nine Planets Studios wants them for a remake of *Scott of the South Pole*," she said.

"Isn't that a historical Earth story? What do they want ice tigers for?"

"I just catch the animals," Gerry replied. "I leave the details like that to Van Zorn and his writers."

"Well, I owe you for this sweetheart!"

"Listen, Smith," Gerry's voice took on an edge. "I was never your sweetheart and that goes double now that I'm engaged. As far as I'm concerned, you and I are quits."

"Hey," Smith said. "Where's all this hostility coming from?"

"You'd better be telling me the truth about what you're up to, Northwest," she replied. "If anyone gets hurt in whatever you're planning, I'll hunt you down myself!"

A moment later, a small, camouflaged vessel detached from the underside of the Ark. It was the *Maid*, an Edsel class transport that Northwest Smith had used for years. The battered exterior hid an engine that could outrun or outmaneuver anything the authorities could send after her.

"Are you sure she's a friend?" St. Menoux asked.

The time traveler, and a Venusian co-pilot named Yarol, shared the *Maid*'s small bridge with Smith. Erik John Stark, who hated confining spaces, was in the hold.

"A very good friend," Smith answered, "and you sure as Pharol don't want her as an enemy."

"Mr. Stark said the same thing about Captain Future."

"Curt Newton isn't the kind of person many folks would care to cross," Smith agreed. "But I think our barbarian friend is actually looking forward to it."

"But why?" St. Menoux asked.

"The two of them are about as opposite as can be. Some native Mercurians took Stark in after his parents died. He was just in his teens when the human colonists slaughtered his tribe and 'rescued' him. He's had a hate for human development ever since. You can always count on him to take the side of the oppressed planetary 'primitives.' "

"And Captain Future is on the side of the corporations?"

"Not exactly." Smith replied. "Future is a genuine idealist. He hates to see the people of the planets abused or cheated, and he's come down hard on the worst violators, but he's strictly a law and order type. It's Earthmen who write the laws these days, so he puts Earth's interests ahead of anyone else's. Plus, he believes that Earth has the burden of spreading its culture and technology to benefit backwards worlds. Erik believes that type of idealism is as dangerous as the worst of the corporate land-grabbers."

"Do you share his sympathies?"

"I'll miss the old Martian ways when they're gone," Smith answered. "I'll miss the decadence of Venus too, but they're on their way out with or without me."

"What do you believe in then?" St. Menoux asked.

"Money."

St. Menoux shook his head. He had defended his country from the Nazis, but that had been a duty expected of him. He was a mathematician, not a man of causes. He knew that if his mentor, Noël Essaillon, were still alive he would chide him for this foolish adventure. A scientist's job was to observe and experiment. A little tampering here and there to study the effect on the timestream was justified, but trying to "set things right" was unscientific folly.

St. Menoux thought about going back and asking Essaillon's opinion. Talking to the dead was a simple matter for a time traveler. He decided against it. He knew what the answer would be and, this one time, he very much wanted to change history. He wasn't sure why, but this situation had captured his heart.

An alarm began to sound in the cabin.

"What is it?" St. Menoux cried.

"It's Captain Future's ship, the *Comet*," Smith replied. "Hold on while I try to give him the slip.

The *Maid* began to dodge across the moonscape with amazing agility. The motion was too much for St. Menoux, who became violently space-sick. Fortunately, Stark had come forward and was able to get the traveler strapped in.

It swiftly became apparent that, despite Northwest Smith's uncanny piloting skills, the teardrop-shaped *Comet* outmatched his vessel.

"He's hailing us, NW," the Venusian announced.

Curt Newton's iron-jawed face appeared on the screen. His fiery hair was more unkempt than usual.

"Northwest Smith," he said. "We've identified your craft and we know that you're carrying two terrorists. Land at once or I'll blast you out of space!"

"You think you can?" Smith taunted.

In response a brilliant blue ray of coherent protons slashed past the *Maid*'s bow.

"I'm not bluffing," Newton said grimly. "Land now!"

Smith's shoulders slumped in defeat.

"Do as the man says, Yarol."

Curt Newton stood in the dome, now filled with air. The dignitaries were starting to fill the place. The delegation from Earth was here, as were representatives of Mercury and Jupiter. Several of the many races of Mars from stilt-limbed Aihais to tiny, great-headed Macrocephalites were present. The Emperor of Venus was there, his milk-white skin and pale gold hair stood out vividly against a silken black robe. His cherubic face showed none of the depredations for which he was known. Two stunning Venusian women attended him and Curt knew by their beauty that they must be some of the famous Minga maids. One had the milky skin and bronze hair of Ednes and the other the dark hair and skin of Vejap. Both wore elegant velvet gowns that left one shoulder bare and the distinctive triangular caps of the high-caste women of Venus.

Curt turned away. The daughters of the Minga might be privileged, but they were still slaves. It disgusted him that there were planetary rulers who still condoned such things. Besides, the loveliness of the women was almost tangible and his strange upbringing had not prepared him for such things. Aside from his sweetheart, Joan, he preferred to give beautiful women a comfortable berth.

He turned away and nearly collided with President Crewe, who had a stunning Martian woman on his arm. She had the reddish complexion of her planet, but there seemed to be a touch of Earth in her face. Her silken costume, conservative by Martian standards, made the young adventurer blush.

"Curtis," the President said, "allow me to introduce Ambassador Tara from Helium City."

"*Kaor Jeddara*, Tara," Curt said.

"I'm honored to meet the famous Captain Future," the woman replied. "Where did you learn Martian? Your accent is flawless."

Curt nodded politely and made small talk for a few moments. He was relieved when his televisor chimed. He made his excuses and moved to an isolated section of the dome. The face that greeted him on the screen was an exact replica of his own.

"I've got the ship in custody, Chief," Curt's double said. "The Venusian was the only one on board."

"What about when you hailed them?" Curt asked.

"I got a glimpse of Smith, Stark and the Green Man. I also made sure they all got a good look at me."

Curt nodded. Otho had molded his synthetic flesh into an exact replica of Curt's features and then applied special dyes to his eyes and skin. His normal appearance was that of a pale, hairless human with wild green eyes. The android's synthetic nature made him the solar system's greatest master of disguise.

"Good job, Otho," Curt said. "If they think I'm there, they'll strike here any second. You and Simon head back as quickly as you can. Grag and I will prepare a surprise for our visitors."

Curt flashed a hand signal to Grag, then pressed a button on his belt and vanished from sight.

The green man and his two companions seemed to appear from nowhere. St. Menoux had metal object the size of a small suitcase in his hand. Stark and Smith carried heat ray pistols that they used to menace the crowd.

"Please, stay calm!" Stark called out. "We're not here to harm anyone but we have a bomb. If the police attempt to stop us, we will set it off immediately and everyone here will be killed. To prevent this, we want you to evacuate the dome immediately."

"Stark!" Halk Anders bellowed. "You know that the government doesn't negotiate with terrorists."

"Are you saying that you refuse to take these people to safety?" the big man demanded.

Anders frowned. After a moment, he barked an order to his men.

"Evacuate the dome! We can deal with these men when the diplomats are safe."

Suddenly, a thin blue beam came from nowhere to strike St. Menoux in the chest. The tall man gasped and collapsed gracelessly into a pile of jutting knees and elbows. Stark swore and leaped at the source of the blast. He collided with something and began to thrash around on the ground.

"What is it?" Smith cried.

Stark didn't answer as he continued to grapple with an unseen foe. A moment later, Curt Newton's muscular form shimmered into view. He had used an invention of his own, a light bending device, to lay an ambush. It had been difficult, for the device also kept any light from reaching his eyes. The shot that had stunned St. Menoux had been calculated using his highly trained sense of hearing.

"This is all going to Hell," Northwest Smith gritted. "I have to set off the bomb!"

As he turned back towards St. Menoux, he saw a seven-foot man of metal charging him. He raised his heat-ray and fired, striking the robot in the torso. The metal of Grag's body began to glow but he continued to press forward.

"That was enough to roast a Neptunian ursal!" Smith exclaimed.

"My body is made of inertite!" Grag's voice boomed. "Your puny weapon cannot harm me!"

The robot reached out and crushed Smith's gun with one hand. He let loose a devastating punch with the other, but the outlaw managed to dodge the blow. He ducked past the giant automaton, trying desperately to stay away from the killing power of those hands.

Nearby, Curt Newton was trying every super-jujitsu trick he had ever learned. The big adventurer had mastered a dozen fighting arts from boxing to Venusian aikido, but in Erik John Stark he had met an equal. Stark's massive muscles were a match for his own and his civilized veneer had slipped away, leaving an unrelenting savage.

Both men had lost their pistols in their struggle. They made no attempt to recover them as they rose to their feet. Curt parried a powerful punch and countered by chopping at a nerve center on his opponent's neck. Stark shifted slightly so that his big shoulder muscles absorbed the blow. He rammed his fist into Curt's stomach, causing the Earthman to fall back a step.

Captain Future fell back, matching cool strategy against his opponent's savage cunning. There weren't many openings in Stark's defenses but he was to slip in a jab here and there. The blows weren't very damaging but, little by little, he was scientifically picking the man apart.

Curt landed a stinging shot on his opponent's solar plexus. Stark staggered and his hands went down to guard his body. It was the chance Captain Future had been waiting for and his leg shot up for a disabling kick to the head.

The blow never landed. Stark slipped under it and swept Curt Newton's standing leg. The next instant, they were on the ground with the outlaw's cabled forearm locked around Curt's neck.

Then it happened.

The flag began to change. Its colors and patterns shifted into words. They spelled out: *Hiroshima! Nagasaki! With the compliments of Madame Atomos.*

Curt Newton and Erik John Stark, locked in their deathgrip, didn't see the change. But Northwest Smith did. He leaped past Grag and grabbed something from St. Menoux's body. He reached the flag and began to spray it with a small can. He heard the robot's heavy footsteps closing on him but he never stopped. He was still spraying when the metal fist came down on his head.

Yards away, Curt struggled with all his might against the choke that was stealing his precious oxygen. It was rare that he underestimated an opponent, but he had this time, and it might be the last. He drove his elbow back into Stark's torso and felt ribs bend, but the terrible pressure never lessened.

"At least, I've delayed him," he thought. "Halk's men will be on him before he can do anything."

Abruptly, the pressure vanished and Stark's powerful body was plucked away. Curt forced his eyes to focus and saw that Grag had the dark man in an unbreakable metal grip.

"Are you all right, Master?" the big robot boomed. "I shall crush him for hurting you!"

Curt shook his head violently. It was a moment before he could force words from his bruised throat.

"Just hold him," the young planeteer said. "I don't want any more killing if we can help it."

"As nearly as I can determine, it is a form of micro-technology," the Brain said. "The flag was impregnated with millions of microscopic robots that followed a programmed set of instructions. I can't say if they reacted to the presence of so many people, or if they were simply timed to activate at a set interval after the dome was filled with air."

"But what harm could micro-robots do?" Halk Anders asked.

"Anti-matter," Curt Newton answered. "Each nanometer-long robot carried an atom of anti-deuterium. Together, there was enough to trigger a 22 kiloton explosion. The same force as the Hiroshima bomb." His eyes cut to Smith's unmoving body. "That man saved us all."

"Master, I have done a terrible thing." Grag's mechanical voice sounded mournful.

"We all regret it, Grag," Curt said, "but there was no way you could have known."

"At least, we are alive to regret it," the Brain added. "The anti-matter is frozen in time, hopefully forever. Still, I think this area should remain off-limits until we have more time to better understand the properties of noelite."

"Stark," Curt said. "I'll do everything in my power to gain clemency for you. As far as I'm concerned, you and your friends were the heroes here today."

Erik John Stark stared at Smith's lifeless body. His own hands were bound with magnetic shackles. He raised his head to say something. Then he vanished.

St. Menoux had come to as the men were talking. He wasn't certain what had happened, but he didn't want to take chances. He pressed the device on his chest and the world froze around him. He moved to Erik John Stark and pulled him out of the time stream.

Stark had explained what had happened and the traveler had adjusted his control again. They went back in time a few minutes, to the instant before Grag's metal fist struck Northwest Smith's skull. They snatched the roguish pilot away from a death that had already befallen him.

"The green hills of Earth," Northwest Smith murmured. "It's been a long time since I've seen them."

The three travelers sat in the same café where St. Menoux had first met Stark. Through the miracle of noelite, they had arrived days before their raid on Tranquility Base so the authorities hadn't even begun to look for them.

"I don't understand," Stark said. "Doesn't coming back in time like this undo what we did in the future, the same way you undid Smith's death?"

St. Menoux shook his head.

"One can't change the future," he said. "The timeline in which he is killed still exists. I have only created, or perhaps discovered, a different possible future. I know that idea may be unsettling."

Smith shrugged.

"I'm happy enough with the results that I'm not going to lose any sleep over the metaphysics."

St. Menoux nodded, and wished that he could adopt such a practical view.

"Much as I appreciate being alive, and getting paid, I think it's time for me to go," Smith continued. "I haven't been welcome on Earth for a long time. Can I give you a lift somewhere, Stark?"

"I have business on Venus," the big man answered. "A friend is missing there."

St. Menoux studied them as they planned for the future, then he touched the control on his chest and vanished. He returned home a second after he had left. Annette was there with the same quiet smile he remembered. Through the miracle of noelite, he could revisit that smile as often as he wanted. He would never have to see his lover age, or endure change in his world.

"What did you do?" she asked.

St. Menoux thought back to Tranquility Base. Had Gorham Johnson really landed there in 1971 or had it been Neil Armstrong in 1969? Was the flag supposed to be the United Earth banner, or that of the United States?

"I saved the future," he said, "but I'm just not certain it was the future I meant to save."

"In any case," she said, "I'm glad you did it."

Harry Dickson, sub-titled "The American Sherlock Holmes," is one of the most popular of all European Holmesian pastiches. Created in Germany in 1907, relaunched in Holland in 1927, then recreated in Belgium in 1929, it lasted until 1938 and most of its 178 issues are still in print today. Dickson is a hybrid of Holmes and Nick Carter, and his adventures took a definite turn towards the fantastique *when they started being ghost-written by notorious Flemish author Jean Ray. Our regular contributor Bill Cunningham revisits his first* Tales of the Shadowmen *story, which featured Fascinax, another anonymously-created pulp hero, and continues his bleak narrative of a world hurling along towards the madness and the terror of World War II...*

Bill Cunningham: *Fool Me Once...*

London, 1928

The fog enshrouded the silhouette as he melded with the shadows between the cobblestone street's few remaining gas lamps. His wardrobe was well-suited for this purpose, garbed as he was head to toe in black. His footsteps made barely a tap, muffled by the dripping water of the numerous pipes wrapped around the tenements.

"Would ya' be lookin' fer company there, Guvnor?" came the sickly-sweet, lurid voice from out one of the side alleys that criss-crossed the dodgy London district like arteries. The voice came out of the darkness and presented itself as a young red-headed woman. Pretty, but not overly so, her low-cut blouse and high-cut skirt marking her as one of the street whores who littered this landscape. Her makeup was thick and bold across her face, but her manner bespoke something more than mere prostitution as she stood poised for any potential action from the dark figure.

The silhouette smiled and gentlemanly removed his hat, moving forward into the light to reveal his features.

"As lovely as that prospect may be, young lady, it would keep me from my work. *I have long to go before I sleep.*"

"Oh, it's you, sir. *Lovely night for a stroll.*"

The gentleman nodded, noticing the woman's strong left hand curled around some object she held ready in the dark should he make a wrong move. Nothing like good training.

"*It's a bit too foggy for my taste. I prefer the warmer air of the day,*" he responded. Upon hearing the proper response, the woman relaxed and brought her left hand into the light. There, in her practiced grip, was a shiny stiletto that was no virgin to bloodshed. She flipped the blade, lifted her leg and placed the

25

weapon–what Limehouse denizens would call a *pigsticker*–into her garter. The gentleman smiled again.

"You may also tell your lady friends behind me to relax. The proper code phrase has, after all, been given."

Behind the man, two more girls stepped out of the foggy night wielding more deadly stilettos ready to swarm and sting their gentleman caller. The red-head waived them off, and she dropped her gutter accent, adopting a higher level, yet still public school, mode of speech and manner.

"You'll have to forgive them, sir. It's not every day that you come to call–especially these days. It must be important."

The man smiled again, revealing the same strong-jawed grin the redhead remembered when she "graduated" from the Ministry's training academy–the man who made them agents, who stood for all they trained for–honor, security, Empire.

"Indeed. It is encouraging that you are prepared for just such an event… as always. It speaks to your dedication." The red-head smiled, happy they had earned even that small show of respect from their superior.

"It's all quiet, sir. We're waiting for day shift to come on in a couple of hours."

"Excellent. That should be plenty of time." The gentleman absently tossed his hand back and then forth as if making a point, and with that simple gesture, the ladies' fates were sealed. Thin, finger-sized needle darts flew out of his hand, whistled through the air, hitting all three of his targets in the space of a heartbeat. The trio jerked their heads back in shock as the poison in the needles did its work.

By the time all three ladies felt the sharp points pierce their skin, and then the racing numbness of the poison, the gentleman became one with the shadows along the side of the alley building. In another heartbeat, the trio fell to the ground and shook in seizures.

The gentleman searched the rooftops around him. He could see nothing but the foggy night. Confident of his solitude, he stepped away from the wall and walked through the parade of bodies at his feet to the opposite side of the passage.

He looked down to see the last of his twitching victims, the red-head, her small hands curling and twisting uncontrollably. Her eyes looked up at him, as if to ask "Why?" The silhouette said nothing, but floated past her, his footsteps guiding him to the brick wall of the warehouse. In his eyes, the warehouse was more important business to see to than her inevitable death. As the young woman's hands curled in spasm, the gentleman ran his hands along the bricks.

The alleyway played havoc with Harry Dickson's nostrils. It was bad enough having to be awakened this early in the morning, but to travel across town before breakfast taxed even his sense of curiosity and justice, especially when every sewer grate and rain gutter in the area disgorged such repellent vapors.

However, when the head of British Intelligence calls, you come immediately. Dickson supposed the summons was due to his burgeoning reputation as a "man of action." Unlike other "consulting detectives" who haunted Baker Street, Dickson was one who dove in and "got his hands dirty" to see that a case was handled properly and justice dispensed. Never before had he been asked to prowl these haunts, and certainly not at this early hour.

Dickson knew of these alleys–passages that had seen as much blood and vice as rain. It made him wary of any and all things around him. The detective looked up and saw the occasional figure perched on the rooftops or from an upper story window. They were being watched. It must be a crisis for M to summon him here, and to take this many precautions. Dickson clutched his cane, weighing these variables in his mind. As the messenger from the Ministry led him along the maze of narrow streets and alleys, sometimes backtracking to evade any possible pursuers, Dickson kept his agile eyes busy, and his thin-cheeked mouth shut.

"Hunter! Over here!" The basso voice of M echoed across the dark alley. Dickson looked up to see the head of His Majesty's Secret Service surrounded by several nondescript men. This M (for it was a title, not a name) was dressed in the finest hand-tailored Savile Row, despite the earliness of the hour. *Ever ready*, thought Dickson as he remembered their first meeting, and had sized this M up rather quickly.

M had a sense of entitlement to his manner, no doubt due to his upbringing and family ties, as well as a no-nonsense way of communicating with his subordinates. A gesture, or even a look, were enough to send his agents into action. That entitlement was reflected in his fashion–elegant, yet authoritarian. This M was a spy through and through–a fountain of silence and subtlety, giving Dickson the feeling that he always knew far more than he ever let on. As if by his silence and judging nature, M led him to the conclusion he knew all along, but wanted Dickson to solve on his own.

He thought that's why he and M had gotten along over the years. Dickson liked a good mystery, wrapped in a conundrum–something to hone his skills. M was more than happy to provide, even though the spy master was often forbidden from divulging too much to the "American Sherlock Holmes."

It was the direction of M's gaze that immediately drew Dickson into that mystery. On the ground were three bodies of women twisted at odd angles, as if frozen. Dickson took the scene into his formidable analytical mind. He kneeled down over the bodies, drew a deep breath and he was back in the game, analyzing the minutest detail.

M held out his hand, but Dickson ignored it, preferring instead to peruse the three bodies that lay before him, reconstructing what happened to the three beauties. The men surrounding them took note of the snub, but seeing M's expression, said nothing. That is until Dickson lifted one of the ladies' skirts and looked underneath. "See here, sir!" piped up one of the agents, shocked at such a crude, ungentlemanly display. Dickson looked up at M as if to ask if he could continue. M waved his hand and the agent hushed himself. One of England's keenest detectives was analyzing the crime scene before him, and when that occurred, nothing was allowed to stand in his way.

Dickson pulled down the woman's dress, stood and walked around the corpses. His hand was on his chin as he put the pieces together in his mind, but something puzzled the sleuth. Dickson looked up at M and asked, "What were they protecting? What was so important that it took a highly trained, highly skilled man to murder your three operatives?"

"Excuse me?" said the Minister of Spies without betraying his surprise, and, yes, admiration for Dickson's deductive prowess.

"Quite simple. Follow, please," said Dickson, noting the agents' incredulous eyes. The detective threw a quick glance at M. Though the spymaster said nothing, Dickson could not help but pierce the veil hiding the dread in M's eyes. Dickson added that observation to his analysis of the scene, then gestured to the ladies' corpses.

"These women are dressed as common street prostitutes, and yet, here you are, the head of His Majesty's Secret Service. Despite what the newspapers may print, government officials do not cavort with *common* ladies of ill repute. Likewise, common prostitutes don't carry knives like the one removed from this lady's garters..."

M took notice of Dickson's emphasis on the word *common*, but decided to let it go. The detective's sarcasm would be worth it, if some of his methods and prowess rubbed off on his men.

"Weapons? Removed?" he asked.

"Removed. Note the slight irritation around the skin of the mid-thigh. As if a sheath or a pistol had been there in a custom holster. Pistols draw attention when fired, and attention has always been the last thing an intelligence operative desires. Logic and evidence dictate they carried knives. There was no need for their attacker to disarm them as he..."

"Or she?" inquired M.

"No, *he*. The point of entry of the needle was of a certain angle and force suggesting a man approximately five feet ten inches," finished Dickson. "Their attacker was a man of slightly above-average height and weight who was recognized as an ally by your doubtless well-trained operatives here. That is how he was able to approach and incapacitate them so quickly. He is powerful and precise as evidenced by the accuracy and depth of the needles in their throats."

Dickson paused for a moment and let the evidence sink into their minds. "Your agents, in an effort to protect these ladies' identities from other authorities, have disarmed them, lest their weapons betray the fact they worked for the Crown, more specifically for you."

Dickson continued, "That alone should be sufficient; however, notice the red-haired woman's fingers..." The detective pointed toward the woman's three fingers–the index, middle and third digits. The trio were pointed down while her thumb and "tea finger" were folded underneath her palm. M leaned forward to see the twisted fingers. Underneath the woman's fingernails was a hint of pale blue.

"Poison, a fast acting neuro-toxin," said Dickson. "It works nearly instantly, scrambling, then completely ceasing their bodily functions." He leaned down over the blonde who lay on her back with a silvery needle dart poking directly out of her throat. "Whoever the assassin was, he was skilled, knowledgeable and motivated, but why kill three operatives and simply leave the dead bodies? Since you have summoned me here, and not moved the bodies as yet that means..."

Dickson walked away from the three bodies and studied the cobblestones. The night fog and its clingy dew had not yet been burned away by the morning Sun. Moisture clung to the surface of the path, along with urban grime, revealing various sets of footprints. A quick glance and Dickson matched the footprints to the shoes worn by M's men. The detective then trained his keen eyes further along the path and found a distinct lack of footprints before the brick-walled warehouse.

M followed Dickson's eyes and looked at the wall. Dickson pulled out his small notebook and jotted down some notes. He drew some quick lines, and studied his quick sketch of the crime scene. He looked up and noted the position of the Sun. Then, the detective put away the notebook and stood in the center of the trio of bodies.

"The killer incapacitated the ladies from this position here. He did not remove their weaponry as they were in spasm by the time they hit the ground." Then he walked toward the wall.

"If you had simply walked around the entire area, I might have been thrown off scent," intoned the thoughtful detective. "But, clearly, as your agents removed the women's weapons to hide their true occupations, they have also been very careful to avoid this particular area of the crime scene. Why? Because you wish to hide the true nature of this supposed warehouse."

M's agents stood there, in shock and shame. In mere moments, Harry Dickson had calmly and precisely uncovered their subterfuge through simple observation and deduction. Dickson loosened up and held out his hand to the agent who spoke up earlier. The man shook it, acceding to the detective's superior skill.

"Very good, Hunter," said M, using Dickson's old code-name that he had worn during his days as an operator in Berlin. "You are both an asset and an example for the Service. Please come with me. The rest of my men will learn from your example and tidy up. There is still much for us to do." Dickson again couldn't help but notice the tone of dread in M's voice.

M strode over to the wall next to Dickson. The detective took the hint and inspected the wall more carefully. The brickwork was all in place, except for one small area where there was a slight variation. A casual passerby would never have noticed it, especially when there were more eye-catching distractions like prostitutes haunting the alleyway. Testing his theory, Dickson placed his hand against the brick and pushed. A segment of the wall sprung out revealing a sophisticated combination lock mechanism.

"We haven't the time for you to pick the lock, though I am certain you could do so," said M, loudly enough for his subordinates to hear. He twisted the lock in a manner that indicated he wasn't used to opening it. Finally, as he spun the dial around to the last digit in the series, he pressed the lock inward. A door-sized area of the brick retreated inward with a large mechanical grind of turning gears ending in an ominous *clunk*.

M invited the detective into the darkness and the two men stepped inside. The door reversed itself and became a wall again.

Dickson's keen eyes tried to adjust to the inky black, but even he was blinded by the nearly impenetrable dark.

"Don't move," came M's voice out of the darkness.

Dickson heard another click, from a switch being thrown, and suddenly, an electric lamp came on, lighting the dusty entryway. In front of them was a formidable steel elevator with yet another complex lock on its heavy cage.

"Follow me precisely to the lift," said M, as he walked across the room, carefully stepping on certain tiles in a circuitous path. Dickson held his cane aloft for balance as he stepped. He looked at the tiles as he followed the spymaster, taking note of no disturbance in the light coat of dust along the floor.

The two men arrived at the elevator and M pointed to small jets positioned along the walls. "If you had not followed the precise path, it would have triggered the release of a deadly nerve agent and sounded an alarm at the Ministry. Now let's proceed."

M reached for the combination lock, but Dickson stopped him. He leaned down and studied the mechanism. "I can see no tampering here," he observed. M cautiously twisted the dial and unsealed the elevator.

"What is this place, M?"

"It's where we keep the monsters," M replied with a coldness that chilled the detective to the marrow. "We must discover which of them our intruder has let loose." With that, M ushered Dickson inside the dark womb of the elevator and closed the cage.

M reached for the switch to lower the car and gave the handle several measured twists. The spymaster noticed Dickson's staring at the odd motion and pointed to the ceiling. He twisted the handle again and a series of long spikes shot out of the ceiling with a hiss. The detective ducked and held up his cane. If he hadn't been warned, the razor-sharp spikes would have pierced his skull.

"Carbon steel honed to a razor edge. Dipped in poison. One cut and it's all over."

"Effective," murmured Dickson.

"Not effective enough," retorted M.

The spymaster turned the handle and the blades retreated into the ceiling. He then threw it forward and the car plunged down.

Dickson counted their descent to approximately 20 stories down. Below the sewers and pipes, further down than anyone else had ever excavated. If his estimate was accurate, they were now in the solid bedrock upon which London was built. M noticed his counting, but said nothing as the elevator came to a halt.

The spymaster opened the door and ushered the detective through.

Dickson couldn't see into the darkness, but could feel the cold of their destination against his cheek. The air was stale and silent as a tomb, making it all the more intriguing to the detective. He used his cane as a guide and stepped forward.

M reached around and threw a wall switch. A series of lights came on in sequence, revealing untold rows upon rows of cabinets and displays. Each cabinet qualified as a safe, with its own locking mechanism. The displays were reinforced glass cases lit from below, also protected by sophisticated locking mechanisms. A series of cables fed each cabinet and display, and their pools of light stretched as far as the eye could see.

It was a bunker, a cavern hewn from the solid rock and networked by a series of pipes overhead. Dickson's eyes followed several of the pipes running across the floor to the displays. M simply said, "Gas and other security," and left it at that. The detective didn't push him on any of the details. A quick glance told him that the entire complex was wired for destruction.

"I needn't tell you how important the business of secrets is in our profession," said M flatly. "They are our currency, our stock in trade. Secrets are our weapons. When they are properly deployed, they win wars… like the last one."

"Or they build empires," replied Dickson.

M nodded toward several of the glass displays. "It is exactly why these secrets must never be loosed on the world, Dickson. They become our monsters. We British know what to do with our secrets long before they become monsters."

"You hide them," said Dickson, finishing the thought.

"You know what lurks in the shadows, Hunter. The world has barely crawled out of a World War, the scars of which still blemish many countries. We must be the bulwark, never failing. We cannot allow anyone or anything to prevent that. "

"You can count on my discretion, both as a gentleman and a detective. What lives here, stays buried here."

M sighed, "I thank you for that, my friend. I knew I could count on you. There are others, our intruder I fear, who don't subscribe to that point of view. It is a painful duty, Hunter, one that has taken so much from us already..." M voiced nothing more, knowing the price Dickson paid. Her name had been Irene de Hautefeuille, the sister of his college friend, Antoine.

At one point in his life, Dickson had hoped Mademoiselle de Hautefeuille would become Mrs. Dickson, but Irene (*should he still dare to call her his?*) had married another man, James Oldfeld when it became apparent that Dickson's mistress would always be Lady Justice.

Oldfeld was a good man, kind and gentle and entirely devoted, and the irony of ironies was Dickson knew James was good for Irene. He would rescue her from the dangers of the life Dickson had adopted as one of M's operatives. Oldfeld would keep her out of the shadowy world of espionage, happy and safe, or so they all thought.

A month later, it had been reported in the papers that the Oldfelds had been sailing the Mediterranean on their honeymoon cruise when their schooner had sunk with all aboard. Dickson had been in China when he had heard the news. It tore him apart that the love of his life was dead, and he could not spare the time to shed even a tear. Yes, Justice was his harsh mistress indeed.

The detective walked over to the first display case. It did not seem, in any way, to be disturbed. Inside, man-sized concentric rings of an unknown alloy rhythmically circled a seat hovering in the center of the spinning wheels. Dickson felt a slight hum emanating from inside the glass. A series of controls, damaged slightly by what appeared to be lava rock, showed the date in years, months, days, hours, seconds and milliseconds.

"Take it all in, Dickson. You must understand the threat to our security. Our agents have been finding these *artifacts* for years. Some of them we understand, others are beyond even our finest scientists' ken. They will provide us the clues to our killer's identity."

Understanding the peril they were in, Dickson continued his examination of the displays. He studied the strength of the glass, the seals and the bases, looking for any signs of any tampering. It was hard to concentrate on the details however, when the artifacts inside were so intriguing. One of the glass cases held the preserved body of what Dickson estimated was a sub-humanoid species–large cranial ridges, hunched back and four digits per hand–one, an opposable thumb.

Another display was labeled *Moon Rocks*, while yet another featured what Dickson could only surmise was a life-support suit for hazardous environments. What made it so extraordinary–beyond its obvious superior technology–was that it was fashioned in the manner of a Mongol warrior's armor. The markings and style were unmistakable.

Another case held what was unmistakably a pistol of some sort, but the likes of which he had never seen. The grip was fashioned not for a human hand, but something not of this world. Dickson quickly realized how little of the universe he actually knew, and how so much more was hidden from view. It was exactly as M had done when they entered the dark chamber–a light was thrown on.

And so it went...

Dickson methodically made his way down the various rows, the metal point of his cane clicking across the floor as he walked; past Dr. Griffin's bandages and spectacles (a case Dickson was aware of), past a sword whose label bore the mark of a US Cavalry officer. Then, the detective stopped. He stood before the locked cabinets of files.

"I can find nothing at this point, M," he stated flatly. He pointed across the chamber with his cane. "I would like to examine the file cabinets."

"As long as you don't open any of them. We must know what's going to be used against King George and the Empire, but I can't have you reading any of the material. I'm sorry, the secrets these file cabinets hold could shake the world apart."

Dickson solemnly said nothing, and went back to work with a renewed vigor.

"You see my dilemma," M continued. "Should I inform the Minister that there is a threat, he will ask me why I am just now informing him, how long have I known of that threat, and how it is that the military or the scientific branches of the government know nothing of these artifacts... Damnable politics. It is a can of worms I must bury." Frustrated, the spymaster balled his hand into a fist. "Who, Hunter? Who could have done this?"

Dickson was alarmed at the sheer emotion in M's outburst. "I will continue my examination as quickly as possible," he said. "Are there any person or persons that, to your knowledge or guesswork, know that this archive exists?"

"Not even my personal agents above know the true nature of this building. Only I and my predecessors have had access. It is a secret that is passed down from one M to the next, bypassing any other step of bureaucracy. Since I took my position, I have been the only man down here. This is beyond the capabilities of any ordinary spy–so who might it be? Belphegor? Blake's damn albino? Or perhaps your own nemesis–Flax?"

"We shall see what the evidence reveals," said the detective. "Perhaps the intruder couldn't gain entry. Certainly, there was no physical evidence on any of the safety devices you employ in the elevator."

"And yet, he knew enough to know the archive was here, which in itself is a security breach of the highest order. Find the fiend who has broken in–his motives and agenda. The Empire is counting on you."

Dickson proceeded with his investigations, taking off his jacket and leaving it with his cane. M retreated to another area of the cavernous chamber and sat down. It was going to be a long wait...

Later, Dickson's shouts echoed throughout the cavern, rousing M from his seat. The head of British intelligence raced through the rows of files until he found the detective leaning against one of the cabinets marked "F." The seal of the cabinet was broken.

M pushed Dickson away and pulled open the drawer, pouring through the files like a madman. Dickson stood back a moment and studied the cabinet as the spymaster worked himself into a panic. Never had Dickson seen M so emotional, pulling files this way and that.

"I think I have it," said the detective.

"What? You know who did this?" asked M, pulled out of his frenzy.

Dickson, his face pale, said, "Yes. Now hurry, we must get topside. There's not a moment to lose." Dickson grabbed his jacket and the two men took off.

They arrived in the foyer after the long ride up the elevator. Dickson said nothing, but ran the clues through his mind. M looked at Dickson and saw such a desperate pain there—as if he had been kicked in the gut.

"Hunter, who is it? Tell me," ordered the spymaster. His no-nonsense air of authority cut through the emotion they were both feeling.

"You know who. We've been betrayed by one of our own." Dickson could scarcely get the words out—they left such a bitter taste as he said them. "No more, until I speak with your agents. We will have little time to stop him."

As the pair retraced the proper steps across the floor to the brick wall door, Dickson nearly stumbled and relied on a helping hand from M to make it through. The spymaster's mind raced—what had the detective found that shocked him so? M ran the evidence back through his mind, shuddered then hurried Dickson for the door.

In the meantime, outside, the agents had made arrangements for the bodies of the three women to be picked up. As M and the detective sealed the brick door shut behind them, the corpses were being loaded onto a milk lorry.

Dickson stood beside M as the bodies were covered and ready for travel. M addressed his agents.

"Men, gather round. Hunter has uncovered the identity of our assassin... So tell me, Dickson, what did you find? Who did this?" asked the spymaster.

Dickson cleared his throat and looked directly into M's eyes. The agents stopped their actions and gathered near their superior. "The man we're dealing with is the most vicious kind of fiend. One without scruples, nor code of honor. He is totally ruthless. He is clever and manipulative and cloaks himself with deception. I have not known his like in some time... I used to call him friend..." Dickson's voice trailed off.

"Oh damn," whispered M. "Fascinax–I knew it. He's the only one who could have done it. He could kill these women quickly and efficiently as he knew them from the academy. He knows poisons and his heightened senses could pierce the security measures. He's gone rogue."

Dickson looked around at the agents. All young and unspoiled. He held their gaze as he spoke. He hesitated to do this for it would change everything they had been taught. Everything they believed.

"No, M. It wasn't Fascinax, old friend. It was you."

M arched back a bit. He looked first at his agents, then at his accuser.

"Listen, Dickson," he chuckled, "this is no time for jokes."

But Harry Dickson wasn't laughing. His face was cold and calculated, grim beyond measure.

"The evidence is right before us. This location is secret, known only to those who have held, or now hold, the title of M. None of you have ever been here before today, correct?" the detective asked the agents. He studied their faces. No, none of them had. They began to look at M, who grew more frustrated.

"Dickson, this is preposterous. Recant before this turns into a bad serial cliché," said M. "There's no reason for me to steal anything. I already am the only one with access."

"Yes, but unless this was done stealthily, you would have been accompanied here, as proper procedure requires, and there would have been witnesses to your arriving here, and more inconveniently, to your removing whatever it was that you removed."

"I removed nothing!" shouted M.

"Correction, you removed nothing *last night*. By means of stealth and guile, you came here and made it appear that someone with unique abilities had indeed penetrated your security. You murdered your operatives with efficiency as they had no reason to fear harm from their leader."

The agents said nothing but closed any chance of escape.

"This gave you legitimate cause to enter the archive *today*, in plain sight, to investigate the break-in, and complete your scheme with the perfect alibi. A perfect gambit for treason." The words launched from Dickson like knives from a circus performer. Deadly accurate.

"You dare accuse *me* of treason?" roared the spymaster. "Hunter, I will see to it that you are jailed for this! No, you will be thrown in Seward's Sanitarium and never heard from again!"

The detective reached and pulled open M's overcoat. He grabbed the lining and ripped it open, revealing two files nestled inside. "Gentlemen, I believe this is the evidence we seek."

M's agents immediately moved in and held their superior in place as Dickson grabbed the files.

"I followed you inside because I needed convincing proof, though there was already sufficient circumstantial evidence to launch an inquiry," Dickson stated flatly. "You remember the tall, red-headed girl whose hand was twisted in spasm? The girl you murdered? She named you with her dying breath–three fingers twisted–forming a perfect M."

Dickson laughed a heartless laugh as his eyes bore into M's. "I saw it at once, but had to confirm my suspicions. That's why I shook your man's hand." The agent came forward and held open his hand. In it was a piece of paper with the words: M GUILTY. STAND BY.

"You bastard!" M roared. He lunged at Dickson, but the agents held him fast. He lashed out with his fists, but the detective stepped into the fray and punched him squarely in the face, sending him reeling.

Dickson followed with another punch to the solar plexus, sending the spymaster to the floor. The detective picked him up by the lapels and ever so softly, so coldly whispered into the spymaster's ear, "You won't fool us any longer. I have found you out, and soon, I will find your master."

M stopped struggling and looked into Dickson's piercing eyes, and, for the first time in a long time, the spymaster knew true fear. What he saw in the detective's eyes wasn't justice served, but revenge.

"Hunter?" he cried. "No, you're not..."

"Take him away. I'll see to it these files get to the Ministry," ordered Dickson. "Get out of here before we attract attention." The agents quickly latched onto M and quickly wrapped a rag over his screaming mouth as the chloroform took him to slumber. Dickson stepped out of their way as the agents hustled him into the lorry and closed the door.

Dickson watched as the truck disappeared down the maze. He grinned, then turned away and hurried toward the opposite end of the alleyway. Things were going perfectly.

At the corner of the main thoroughfare, a long black Daimler pulled up. Dickson stepped inside and closed the sedan door. He was greeted by a mirror image of himself. Same manner, features and dress, but somehow paralyzed and lying across the long black leather seat of the automobile.

Dickson leaned over the face of his doppelganger who lay rigid. Only the man's eyes indicated he was wide awake, yet somehow unable to move an inch.

"You will be glad to know that I was successful," said the detective to his paralyzed double. "After all, am I not Harry Dickson, the American Sherlock Holmes?" Dickson, or the man who appeared to be Dickson, loosened his collar and reached for his throat. The detective ripped the latex mask off his face, revealing the equally handsome, yet dark features of Dr. George Leicester–known to the world at large as Fascinax!

Fascinax tapped the pane of glass separating them from his driver. The Daimler pulled away from the curb and wound its way down the streets.

The true Harry Dickson stared out the darkened windows, not daring to meet Fascinax's gaze. Fascinax removed the last vestiges of his disguise, wiped his face and looked at the detective.

"Don't look that way, Harry. I couldn't take a chance." Fascinax studied Dickson's eyes as if his very thoughts somehow spoke to him. "I could not allow you to get your hands dirty, Harry. I owe you that for what you did for me in China. If I had failed, it would be on my head alone."

Fascinax reached into his coat and pulled out the files he had appropriated from M. He opened them and quickly began flipping through the pages. Fascinax read the reports while listening to Dickson's racing heartbeat with his super-sensitive ears.

Fascinax quickly read one page then another, his unique mind checking facts and correlating the data at ultra speed. As the sedan slowly cruised through London, Dickson watched the pieces of the puzzle form together in Fascinax's mind. He wondered what horrors the files contained.

"Yes, Harry, these files do contain horrors." said Fascinax, who looked up. He reached for a brandy from the sedan's bar. He poured the drink and held it up, toasting Dickson. Then he gulped it down. Finally, the words came from his lips, with cold disgust.

"Yes, Harry. It was as bad as we feared."

Dickson watched Fascinax's countenance go from the warm, confident face of a friend to cold, resolute face of an avenger.

"M sold himself–not to a foreign power, but to a terrorist of the highest order–*Numa Pergyll*," said Fascinax, gathering his anger. "This is the evil we're dealing with, Dickson–an evil that doesn't play by the *Marquis de Queensberry* rules, like our old sparring partners. An evil far greater than that of Zenith, Fantômas or even our old friend, Professor Flax. This is evil on a global scale, organized and institutionalized. Evil that revels then profits in mayhem and destruction, Evil that takes no prisoners–not my Françoise, nor your Irene."

Fascinax moved over on the seat and placed his hands on Dickson's neck and head. He adjusted his fingers until his ultra-sensitive fingers found their mark. He pressed hard, and suddenly Dickson relaxed. His fingers twitched and he slowly began to flex each muscle as it came out of its paralysis.

"You asked me for proof, Harry. Now, I have delivered that proof to you. Who do you think followed orders and killed James and Irene Oldfeld?"

Fascinax refilled the brandy glass and held it out to Dickson who took it into his shaking hands, and downed it. He was still in shock–not only from the paralysis visited upon him by Fascinax, but by the news he was hearing. He downed the brandy.

"The names are all in there. The games are over now, Dickson. Your days of chasing after petty thieves, mad doctors, thuggees and bored aristocrats are over. The stakes that are much higher and greater than ever–this is war."

Disgusted, Fascinax tossed the files to Dickson, having already committed them to memory. Dickson studied the files. He could hardly bring himself to believe it, but the clues were all there, pointing toward the most bitter poison–the truth.

M was a traitor. Intelligence reports that would have led to Numa Pergyll's capture were buried in that archive. Alongside Pergyll, there were others, perhaps even more fearsome, even more bloodthirsty. The new Lords of Chaos. Leonid Zattan. Dorje. Benedict Stark. Dr. Natas. Dr. Mabuse. Roxor... working together, building a new, secret empire that crossed all borders.

The sedan pulled to a stop. Fascinax reached for the door handle and opened the door for his friend. Dickson, still on shaky feet stood by the car. "What will you do?" he asked his friend.

Fascinax's blue eyes projected his hurt for the burden he was about to lay at his friend's feet. "Like you. Prepare for Armageddon. First I must deal with Numa. He will fool us no longer."

Dickson froze as the words plunged daggers through his heart. Understanding, he simply nodded, turned and walked away in the fog.

The dark sedan had barely turned the corner when the fiery explosion went off in the archive.

Fascinax had made sure the monsters stayed buried.

In the sixth Madame Atomos *novel, which takes place in early 1966, author André Caroff threw out a casual reference to the infamous East Coast blackout of November 9, 1965, attributing it, of course, to his nefarious heroine, but without providing any further details. Our regular contributor, Win Scott Eckert, takes a closer look at that incident and throws new light, no pun intended, on the subject in a report he had to entitle...*

Win Scott Eckert: *The Atomos Affair*

New York City, November 1965

The city was in darkness. An eerie silence pervaded the decaying brownstones on a block somewhere in the East Forties. At one end of the block was a public parking garage. At the other, a three-story apartment building. No electric lights came from any of the buildings, although candlelight flickered from behind some curtains and shutters. Streetlights were out. The only noise came from the occasional automobile or stray dog.

In the middle of the deserted block was a small, ordinary tailor shop.

Or was it ordinary?

Madame Atomos and her two black-clad underlings swept into the darkened storefront of Del Floria's Tailor Shop, one floor below street level. She and one man went into the fitting booth and turned the coat hook on the back wall. The other man activated a mechanism on the pressing machine, releasing the back wall of the fitting booth. He settled back to await his mistress' return.

The wall swung inwards, admitting Madame Atomos and her confederate to the high-tech lobby. Two guards went down quickly under her knockout darts, and the interlopers entered the headquarters of U.N.C.L.E.

Due to the power outage, the agency was running a skeleton crew tonight, as she had anticipated.

Madame Atomos had caused the blackout, of course. The entire Eastern Seaboard was down, but her concern was this particular building. Reaching the control room was a cakewalk. Only four more agents barred their way, and were easily dispatched.

The lights in the control room were out, although glowing switches and indicators from large computer banks along the wall twinkled and reflected off a Plexiglas dome in the center of the room. Underneath the glass was a blurred shape hidden in the shadows.

Madame Atomos' man went to a control panel, flipping switches and knobs, raising the Plexiglas. He aimed a small penlight into the center area.

Madame Atomos raised her hand, revealing a dart gun. The Plexiglas rose to the top and she called, "Come out! Show yourself!"

"Indeed, indeed I shall," came the British-accented reply. Emergency lights flared, and a weathered, avuncular gentleman wearing a tweed jacket stood up. He shuffled forward into the light, a pipe clenched firmly between his teeth.

Madame Atomos was astounded. "You!" she exclaimed.

"Hmm, what? Ah, yes. Me. Gentlemen, if you please?"

Two agents stepped out of the shadows created by the emergency spotlights, covering Madame Atomos and her guard with modified Walther P-38s. One was a dark-haired man in a neat grey suit and dark tie. The other was blonde and wore a black turtleneck sweater.

The latter spoke briefly: "Don't move," he said in a Russian accent, and relieved them of their weapons.

Ignoring the two agents, Madame Atomos spoke to the intelligence chief. "What are you doing here?"

"I work here, of course. Number One, Section One. In charge of this, our New York headquarters." He paused. "You're here to kill me. A final seal of your alliance with the self-styled 'Technological Hierarchy for the Removal of Undesirables and the Subjugation of Humanity.' "

"And how do you know that?"

"Hmm? Well, it's obviously not a friendly social call, but beyond that, this is an intelligence agency, after all. We've known for several days."

"It *was* too easy, then. The opportunity to cause the blackout, breaking in here... All too simple. You planned all of it."

"Ah yes, well, my top enforcement agent here did the planning, but yes. Although you were only supposed to cut power to this city block, not the–ahem– entire East Coast." The chief turned to the black-haired man. "Too simple, she says. You'll do better next time."

The agent nodded, embarrassed. "Yes, sir."

Madame Atomos smiled triumphantly. "So, you were not expecting such a widespread power failure. Very interesting. Such a lapse could leave the United States... what is the word I am searching for? 'Vulnerable.' Yes, extremely vulnerable to an attack. Is that not so?"

The chief faced Madame Atomos once more. "Yes, that is so. Kanoto Yoshimuta... You were a young woman in '45, when I pulled you from the wreckage in Nagasaki. It's a bit personal, I suppose, but I feel somewhat responsible. In saving your life, back when I was with Z5, I unleashed you on the world. Now you are 'Madame Atomos,' criminal mastermind. What shall we do with you, Madame Atomos? We appear to have a stalemate."

"What do you propose?"

"The organization you're dallying with will not treat you honorably. You still care about such things as honor, Madame Atomos?"

She nodded, stiffly.

"Then you acknowledge your debt of honor to me."

"What do you require?"

"Firstly, sever your alliance with THRUSH. Secondly, abandon any further plans to… ahem… assassinate me, or any of my agents. And third, withdraw your plans to attack the United States."

"Done," Madame Atomos replied, and fired three paralyzing darts from her false fingernails. The drug in the darts took effect within seconds, rendering the men conscious, but unable to move.

Madame Atomos spoke once more to the intelligence chief. "I do recall you, of course. I could not forget. You were kind to me 20 years ago, Mr. Waverly, and so I shall not kill you and your men tonight, or any other night. You may consider there to exist a permanent state of truce between your organization and mine.

"However," she continued, "do not fool yourself that honor has been satisfied. You may feel that a balance has been restored, that your…*error* in saving my life has been rectified. In this, you overlook the larger imbalance, the wanton destruction visited upon my homeland by your Western powers. Honor must also be satisfied for this atrocity, and I shall continue to pursue it."

"Honor… or revenge?" the older man managed to grit out.

"That is, in this case, a distinction that hardly matters."

With that, Madame Atomos bade them good evening, and disappeared into the blackout.

Michel Zevaco (1860-1918) is somewhat forgotten, even in France. He was a journalist, a publisher, a film director and a well-known anarchist who passionately defended public figures such as Captain Dreyfus and Ravachol. But it is for his prodigious swashbuckling saga pitting the indomitable Chevalier de Pardaillan against the Milady-inspired Fausta that he might still be remembered today. The Pardaillan novels span from the 1550s to the 1610s. They were first published in serialized form in La Petite République, *starting in 1902, and eventually collected as ten volumes*: Les Pardaillan (*1907*), L'épopée d'amour (*1907*), La Fausta (*1908*), Fausta vaincue (*1908*), Pardaillan et Fausta (*1913*), Les amours de Chico (*1913*), Le fils de Pardaillan (*1913*), Le trésor de Fausta (*1913*), La fin de Pardaillan (*posth. 1926*) *and* La fin de Fausta (*1926*). *Micah Harris selected Zevaco's anti-heroine as a worthy enemy (and perhaps more) for Robert E. Howard's nototorious Puritan Solomon Kane in a historical tale of political intrigue and clash of civilizations over…*

Micah Harris: *The Anti-Pope of Avignon*

Avignon, 1576

The tall, gaunt man in simple black, girded by a heavy chain, sat on the stone floor of his cell in the old Papal palace of Avignon. For centuries, the fortress-like edifice had been a rumored haunt for unclean spirits. But now *other* shades were seen to stir through windows once again lit at night. The people of Avignon were perplexed by what these omens meant, but not the man in black. His intent in coming to this place had been to abort a malevolent scheme while yet inchoate. Unfortunately, events had developed far past what he had been led to believe.

Down the corridor sounded the torpid grate of long disused metal hinges, and he was aware of slippered feet whispering toward him, along with the scratch of rougher garments. A small procession soon appeared. The man in the lead wore a cowl and robe. Though first in order, he was not the leader of the group, for in service of another he bore delicacies on a golden salver: strawberries and honey along with the more mundane foodstuffs of milk, bread and wine.

The Puritan knew such fare was not for him, but for whom? Was he, then, not alone in this dungeon? But what prisoner would be so feted? He did not attempt to ask the cowled man, for he was immediately distracted by the young woman who followed. Hers were the slippers he had heard. Her gown clung to a voluptuously curved figure, full breasts lifted to meet the low neckline, and about her bare shoulders hung luxuriant, jetty locks.

This vision of ripe pulchritude, which would have stirred desire in most men, struck the Puritan with distaste... followed immediately by an abject sense of failure. For this woman was the one he had come to Avignon to carry away across the Rhone River and back to La Rochelle. This was Fausta, she of the blood of Pope Alexander VI and Cesare Borgia.

She turned on him her dark eyes, wet flakes of coal already as hard as diamonds, then turned aside to pause at the barred entrance of his cell. The man in the cowl paused and looked back toward her uncertainly. She beckoned him on with an imperious flick of her wrist and the lackey obeyed. Now she parted full, painted lips and showed perfect white teeth.

"I am told you are he who came here in the interests of those Huguenot settlements so near Avignon, those doomed first to fall when I make this city again a Papal stronghold. But 'twas a fool's errand, unworthy of the rumored acumen of the one known as *the* Puritan. *Are* you truly Solomon Kane?"

"You have said," the man in black responded, his craggy countenance as pale and impassive as the face of the chalk cliffs which lift the city of Avignon above the Rhone.

Kane had entered France through the harbor city of La Rochelle to offer his sword arm to the Huguenot cause, no more or less than many other English Calvinists had done. Before long, his prodigious abilities as a battle strategist set him apart, and friend and enemy alike spoke of him with distinction as *the* Puritan. Rumors of the effects of his designs troubled King Henri III on the throne of a divided land, and even reached distant Rome, giving the Mitered brow of Pope Gregory XIII cause to furrow.

Fausta tossed her head back, black locks gamboling over her bare shoulders, and laughed. The sound was like the rustle and peal of tiny bells. She leveled her gaze to meet his own. "Are you in the place of Christ, then, that you answer me as he did Pilate?"

"I make no claim to be in the stead of Christ; t'would be blasphemy. But my Lord has schooled me how I should answer, and that I resist not evil."

"Hypocrite!" Fausta rejoined, the tip of her tongue flicking scorn with each syllable. "Was it not 'resistance' that brought you here to seize *me*?"

"My attempt against you was not in regards to my own interests, but those of God's cause. I resist the oppression of those whose blood has flowed since Saint Bartholomew's Day because they desire religious freedom. My Lord himself took up a whip of cords to banish by force those who obstructed worship in his Father's house and has thus set me an example."

"But the Galilean did not repeatedly dip a sword in human blood as you have done. Did he not warn you that he who lives by the sword will die by it? In that you should have heeded him as well."

"My soul is made clean by Christ's righteousness; I am ready to depart."

Fausta laughed mockingly. "But *I* am not yet ready for your departure. Your capture will advance my campaign when I make claim to the Papal throne.

While Gregory remains in distant Rome, ineffectual in dealing with your opposition of the Catholic Church, I have come to Avignon, to the very threshold of France and the Huguenot threat, and captured their master strategist."

"Are you mad, woman?" the Puritan asked, his jaw slack in the face of such unmitigated egotism. "Do you truly think to seize the Papacy from Gregory? Have you forgotten your *sex*?"

Fausta drew up her slim shoulders and stiffened primly. "I am the inheritor of Pope Joan who was called 'John,' she who was Vicar of Christ before childbirth betrayed her. Further, I am a blood descendent of Pope Alexander, through my ancestress, Lucrezia Borgia. Joan's office and title have been passed down by succession to Lucrezia's female descendants, a secret alternative to the Papal line. Though none before me who has received this office has been so bold as to come forward and make claim.

"Until I have replaced Gregory as Pope and Avignon is again the site of the Holy See, you are a valuable political prisoner to me. I use you as you would have used me, though not as rudely as you might think. You are kept in the Low Treasury beneath my own apartments in the Papal palace. 'Twas here the Popes of old stored their most precious acquisitions, and *you* are most precious to me."

With a sardonic smile, Fausta resumed her journey down the corridor. Only then did Kane see the third party of her procession, for he had been obscured by Fausta herself. At sight of him, the Puritan's eyes narrowed and a momentary, small tremor shook one craggy cheek, but by sheer will he returned his whole face to the stillness of stone. His eyes remained narrow. "Gaston..." he hissed through clinched lips.

"Ho, great Puritan!" the swarthy complexioned man with curled, black mustachios said. "You were right in warning the council of La Rochelle to never trust a traitor, eh? But I think in time, over the course of our journey, I won even *your* confidence. The *petite affaire* of the boar, who would have gored you but for my well-trained arrow? Of course, that you survive to enter Avignon was paramount to my true mission."

"And from the moment you saved my life, Gaston, have you rehearsed in your heart how you would taunt me with that fact as you do now?"

" 'Rehearse?'–no. 'Relish'–would be a better way to put it. And now, Solomon, *do* I have your love? Do not your scriptures say that you must forgive me, on penalty of eternal fire?"

"Aye. I do forgive you."

The mustachios twitched higher on Gaston de Rochefort's cheeks as he smiled. "From the heart? I believe 'tis written you must forgive from the heart."

"Aye. I bear you no malice for your deceit toward me. Christ was also betrayed, and Christ schools me that the servant is not greater than his master."

"Yes, but Judas did not live to receive forgiveness, did he?"

"He brought his own destruction down upon his head, for he could not live with the consequences of his actions."

"I will have no trouble living with mine," de Rochefort said. His eyes were suddenly cruel and dour and there was no longer any mirth in his voice. "And I dare say my life will be much longer and fuller than yours."

He turned curtly to go.

"Gaston?"

Fausta's agent drew back to the barred cell, hoping for an imploring for mercy.

"Yes, great Puritan?"

"I forgive you on my own account, but there is *he* whom you did not give a chance to offer *his* forgiveness. I do not revenge myself for deeds done against me, but avenging the evil deeds against an innocent... Ah, in that lesson I am also well-schooled, and have applied myself assiduously... one might say... with *relish*. Pray to Satan that God does not unbind me. For then I will be free to execute on you judgment for the life of one who proved my most faithful friend."

Gaston de Rochefort cocked his head, his dark pupils rapidly oscillating inside slit lids as though at a loss as to whom Solomon referred. Then he drew in a deep breath and expelled it with a laugh. "That... egg? 'Twas not on my account that he valued so little his own life..."

So intense was Solomon's gaze, so quick was his lunge, like an iron-tethered panther, that de Rochefort forgot the cell's bars for a moment, and sprang away. Except for those bars, Kane would have constricted his length of chain around the Frenchman's neck until the flesh of his throat squeezed through the links.

Gaston's face blanched, but his color quickly restored, and, chagrined that his defeated enemy had humiliated him, he stabbed his forefinger at the imprisoned Puritan.

"My man motioned for the boy to be silent! You see that you are yet alive. And so would he yet be, had he not opened his mouth to give you warning! He did not suffer. 'Twas quickly done."

"Aye, I *saw* how it was done! I heard the beginning of his cry ere you silenced him. I saw young Hezekiah's body piling at your feet, your blade scarlet with his life. If your lackey's pommel had not struck me from behind, your blood would have mingled with Hezekiah's, and tonight, though conscious of my own imprisonment, I would be satisfied that *you* were conscious in Hell!"

"Hell may be my final place, but I dare say you will precede me there," Gaston snarled. "Are you not also 'Cain?' You have slain those whom you should call 'brother,' good Christian men, just as convinced of their righteousness as you, who fear the heresies of Calvin shall surely place souls in Hell! I am a mercenary and a rogue, but the sin of hypocrisy cannot be laid to my charge!"

With that, Gaston de Rochefort departed in the direction that Fausta and her lackey with the salver had taken. And Solomon Kane, the momentum of his rage expired, dropped back to his cell's floor.

Sleep finally overtook him, and it was only his preternatural sense, strong even when his natural force was abated, that awoke Kane to a delicate clink and scrape. At first, he struggled to lift the lids of his eyes against the gravity of slumber, but once he apprehended the strange sight before him, he was immediately alert.

A cowled and cloaked figure held out the golden salver, empty now but for the wine and bread.

"You are the monk who carried the salver before Fausta earlier," Kane said. "Did your mistress send you?"

"I answer to no mistress. I am not he whom you suppose. Think of me as... your Grand Inquisitor."

Kane rose to his feet before this ultimate mortal enemy of his faith. Links of his chain dully chimed as they dropped behind him, falling back upon one another. Steady in the face of possible torture, he still could not suppress an involuntary chill at the voice of this Grand Inquisitor. It possessed that aural quality of glasses filled to different measures, when teasing fingers coax their lips so that they murmur forth in sonic effulgence, as if the air spoke in ecstasy of itself.

"Do men of your exalted office now stoop to serve dainties to heretics?" Kane asked.

"The occupant next to you left these foodstuffs. She thought they might satisfy your hunger. Indeed they might–if it pleased me to give them to you."

Kane ignored the taunt. " 'She?' Who is *she*, and why is *she* in this place?"

"Look to your own affairs! Why are *you* here?"

" 'Twas to combat heresy that I came hence. To carry away she who would by force of arms compel men to embrace spiritual harlotry on pain of their lives! Who would put women and children to the rack and screw to compel them into eternal torment of Hell!"

"And do those you Huguenots slay suffer no pain? Yet those you kill say they fight to save men's souls from Hell as well." Here the robed figure indicated the tray and what lay upon it. "These... doctrinal issues. Do you truly believe it pleases your God that men slay one another over this grape and wheat? Is it truly such a great matter?"

Kane frowned.

" 'Inquisitor,' " he said, "verily, you are a sounding brass and a tinkling cymbal! 'No great matter?' Did not your own Council of Trent affirm that all who deny the sacramental bread and wine transubstantiate into the flesh and blood of Christ are accursed from God? There is nothing less at stake than an eternity of abject bliss or loss for each soul of mankind. There are not many paths to salvation, all of which one may pursue at his pleasure, but there is the one true way which my Lord schools me is both straight and narrow!"

The robe of the Grand Inquisitor rustled like a hiss of contempt. "Salvation? There shall come an age when men struggle no more over the way of salvation, when they will learn it has always lain elsewhere, and then they will lay down their arms. To end all striving I have come, though long delayed, and I will begin with the conflict at hand. In this cause, you shall serve me, Solomon Kane.

"I am of the Horla. Soon, my brothers will join me, and the age of the Horla shall begin. Already the whole Earth is out of joint at our coming–hours, days, and seasons moved out of place–though our herald is only now appearing unto men."

Kane coolly stepped back into the shadow of his cell, his chain scraping along the floor. "You speak madness, Horla. Neither would I serve you were I free."

"Deliverance is closer than you think. Where you are bound was not at first a cell for prisoners, but the old subterranean palace treasury. When the last Pope left Avignon, he made it a secret archive, storing precious documents and artifacts and walling over doorways to conceal them. Fausta somehow learned some of this–but not *all*."

"You're saying there is another door to my cell, one walled over?" Kane asked. "What matter? Should I break through it, I am yet chained. Nor would I take the key to my bonds if you offered it to me, for I will not be indebted to you."

"Chained here, you serve me not, but neither do you serve your own cause. Your mission does not have to end a failure, Solomon Kane. You may yet return with your prize to La Rochelle. Serve me, and I will give you Fausta. Aye, say the word and tonight you will feast, not on the meager fare upon this salver, but on venison and champagne from Fausta's own larder!"

"I trust you not, Inquisitor," replied Kane, "for I perceive you have no authority here at all. It is a desperate man who seeks an ally in one who is locked and bound."

"Desperate, Solomon? *You* shall come to know desperation in this place, and when we speak again, I shall find you more agreeable. That I promise you."

With that, the hooded, robed figure withdrew into the deeper shadows and was gone. To Kane, it all seemed a strange dream. Though as he tried to return to sleep, he found his mind much occupied with what the mysterious figure had said: what had he meant that time was already out of joint, and when would this "Age of the Horla" come to pass?

Kane would have doubted the reality of the encounter, save that, the next morning, the golden salver with the untouched wine and bread set outside his cell. When Fausta returned that evening to visit again Kane's neighboring cell, the monk before her struck his foot against the tray, sending the wine splashing over the floor and the bread crumbling underfoot. Further, the fresh foodstuffs flew from the salver the monk now bore and joined the stale bread and wine on the ground.

Fausta cuffed the man's ear. "Fool!" she snapped. Then she grabbed the ear she had stung and twisted it, the monk grimacing in pain. "Why did you leave the salver from last night here in the corridor? Clean this mess–after you fetch fresh victuals from above. And she obviously does not savor the bread and wine–why did you bring them again tonight? Return only with milk, honey and fresh strawberries! I go to commune with her."

"And where is Gaston de Rochefort tonight?" Kane asked Fausta as the monk scurried away.

"He came last night only by my special dispensation, granted because he was instrumental in capturing you," she answered. "I allowed him his moment to gloat, but I will not subject you to his repeated jeering. I heard him–how his man took you from behind; more, how he murdered a boy when the lad sought to warn you. Gaston's actions were without honor. I have never heard that Solomon Kane ever met a foe but face to face. You, in turn, deserved no less."

"And yet, lass," he answered, "you consented to his scheme of deception."

"I did *not*," Fausta said. "He was recommended to me as one who could deliver you. I did not know precisely how he would accomplish the deed."

Kane grinned mirthlessly: "I believe there is very little that Fausta does not know, that she *desires* to know."

At this, Fausta drew up her slim shoulders imperiously, but clearly Kane's words left her abashed. Without answering, she continued to the next chamber.

Afterwards, she did not acknowledge him when she passed his cell en route to the neighboring room.

From the first of his captivity, Kane's chain had chafed the skin of his waist through his clothes, and when he unbuttoned his shirt to examine himself, he discovered a section of flesh scraped raw. Long inured to hardship, he endured the discomfort stoically, as he did all physical unpleasantness of his current living conditions.

Still, Kane was a man of action, and his previous environments, no matter how harsh, usually had been of his choosing, whether under the high boughs of a forest or jungle, or on the deck of a ship from which horizons never failed to yield fresh revelations of diverse wonders. This had proven true as an inkling he first felt as a lad in Devonshire, a sense that the familiar woods and marshes of his hometown were but the far outposts of something that might ever go on and on, world without end.

The loss of free access to that world chafed his soul more than the chain afflicted his flesh. He wondered how went the war. Fausta had yet to take him bound from his cell and exhibit him as her spoil, so her longed-for hour was not yet come. Still, he ached for some knowledge that would extend his view beyond these walls whose mere monotony began to raise them to monolithic heights about him.

It was then that the rapping began on the other side of the wall connecting his chamber with that of the mysterious occupant next door.

In response, Kane lifted his chain, made his way across his room and rapped his fist against the stone from where the sound had emanated.

Immediately, there was a rapid-fire tattoo against a lower part of the wall. Kane's eyes dropped to that spot: there, a block of masonry–Kane blinked and dropped to his knees before it to be certain–was slightly wriggling, as though being pushed from the other side!

He immediately began to work his fingertips to find purchase on the elusive, slight edges of the brick that seemed intent to tortuously writhe free of the mortar that had held it in place for centuries.

The ends of his fingers were quickly scraped, and still the brick had yet to progress. Kane looked about his cell for some tool with which to work. His eyes fixed on a dingy, metal spoon he had been given to eat the occasional bowl of gruel. Rising hastily, hefting the heavy chain behind him, he crossed his cell floor, snatched it up, and returned to the wall. There, he dropped on his knees and descended upon the squirming brick with the spoon handle's end.

He chipped at the mortar. Digging a fourth of an inch deep on the right side of the brick, he then dug a similar trench on its left. Then he scraped along its top and bottom.

Meanwhile, as though the person on the other side sensed what Kane was doing and took heart from his efforts added to hers, the brick began to squirm about more vigorously. Finally, he tossed the spoon aside and once again dug the ends of his fingers into the shallow troughs he had made in the mortar. Now, he had purchase, now he pulled...

The brick tugged free, and he let it fall. Kane immediately peered inside, but the chamber beyond was dark. Dust particles swarmed in the air that issued in: a stale, sepulchral air, redolent of a long-sealed charnel house. Kane flinched at the offending odor.

His mind was tossed between Fausta's irreconcilable dealings with his fellow captive. Why did Fausta feed her a princess's dainties and house her in conditions so foul? Some exquisite torture of that witch, he was certain.

The rapping was now a frantic scratching from the floor on the other side of the opening, a sound like the scurrying of a rat's tiny, scaly talons over slate.

"Can you hear me? Who are you?" he called into the hole. No response. He placed his mouth to the opening in the wall, calling out again. The dust of unsettled ancient masonry coated his tongue and the back of his throat. Kane coughed, recoiling.

The scratching receded into the further reaches of the chamber and he was certain now that rats were indeed its source. The woman who had knocked so eagerly before must have swooned, and he shuddered at the thought of her unconscious person vulnerable to such vermin. He reached with both hands into the opening he had made, and, grasping the brick above it, pulled with all his strength and tore it free.

When he had removed a few more in this manner, he lay on his back before the small breach, and powered by the force of thighs strengthened through years of travel over rough terrain, he repeatedly thrust his boot heels against those bricks surrounding the aperture.

They quickly gave way, and now Kane had ingress large enough to slide his body through. First, he thrust his arm into the opening to find how deep it was, and was soon up to his shoulder. He withdrew.

This, then, looked to be the bricked-up doorway of which the Horla told him. Undoubtedly, his fellow prisoner had discovered this as well, which is why her knocking had directed him to this spot. He hesitated now, on his side of what would have been the threshold, feeling a sudden sense of foreboding. He shook it off contemptuously. A woman needed his aid! Lying on his stomach, facing the opening, he slid through, dragging his heavy chain with him.

In a moment he was inside the chamber, one not much larger than his own.

And one without occupant.

Kane scowled. Had someone become alerted to his efforts in reaching his fellow prisoner and ushered her away before he could establish contact? As his eyes began to adjust to the dark, he pulled himself free of the opening and stood aright. A door, not bars, had been restored to this chamber's hallway entrance. He stepped forward, and then the slack of his chain became taut and he was firmly tethered.

The room was coated with dust, of which the initial opening of the wall had been harbinger. Its walls were lined with bookshelves that reached to the ceiling. Various texts, bound volumes and parchments, were strewn about a reading table, where the dust appeared recently disturbed. He snatched up a book at random, a copy of *Translation of Secretum* by Petrarch. Opening it, and bringing it close to his eyes, Kane read, *Often have I wondered with much curiosity as to our coming into this world and what will follow our departure.*

Such idle speculation baffled him. This world was made by God for man—what, then, could possibly *follow* mankind? With a contemptuous expulsion of breath, he tossed this record of an exercise in futility back to the table.

Then his eyes scanned the other texts that lay there. There was a copy of Ovid's *Ars Amatoria* and a handwritten manuscript with the heading "The Miller's Tale" from the depraved *Canterbury Tales*. While still a boy, he had been warned away from Chaucer by his village parson. And he remembered the discovery of a young woman in Devonshire reading Ovid—she had been marked with the Scarlet Letter ever afterward, at least in the eyes of the villagers.

Nearby lay a painting depicting Mary and the infant Jesus, surrounded by an admiring Heavenly Host. Though the Madonna with Child smacked to Kane's Puritan sensibilities of Catholic idolatry, he found strangely more disconcerting how something held sacred was now casually profaned by its proximity to Ovid's and Chaucer's texts.

There was another painting, this of a fair-skinned woman with a breast exposed. Kane could not know that this was a portrait of none other than Fausta's esteemed ancestress, Lucrezia Borgia, nor did he linger over what was to him an image of the coarsest wanton. By this portrait, spread out in a fan over the table, was a hand of upturned Tarot cards, the *Papessa* raised above the others.

His now fully accustomed eyes gleaned from the gloom of the room a draped altar before a crowned woman whose outstretched arms invitingly exposed her multiple rows of breasts. This was a statue of Diana, brought to Avignon when it was a Phoenician outpost and dug from the ground on which the Papal palace now stood.

" 'Tis an idol of pagan harlotry, preserved in this wretched place, beckoning me to embrace her rows of witch's dugs," he spoke aloud and spat. What had brought him to this room, and why, he knew not, but he would return to his cell, seal the wall, and never return.

It was then that he noticed the hanging of the altar's drapery suggested a human being underneath it...

He called. No response. He stretched toward the altar, finding his chain heavier than before. Still he reached out, leaning forward on the balls of his feet... and the effort cost him–sweat beaded his forehead.

Now that wretched scratching of scaly talons sounded all about him, though no rats scampered into view–

–as he snatched away the draping veil, let it pile in silken folds at the base of the altar–

–to reveal a human skeleton, the pelvis unmistakably that of a *woman*.

The sweat drenched him now, and the rodent scratching increased in magnitude from the walls, the ceiling...

He remembered now: it was the same he had heard back in Devonshire, when he was a boy, in the home of Goody Cloyse, whom some said had fled to the New England colonies when she was warned she would be brought to the council for consorting with demons–

And Avignon had ever been the occult Mecca for the necromancer, the alchemist and the astrologer. It had never ceased to be, even in the days of the Papacy. Avignon–the "city of the winds," and Scripture schooled Kane that Satan was the power of the air. Here, then, was where those powers found crags to roost.

"I am prisoner in Babylon, *the habitation of devils, the hold of every foul spirit, and a cage for every unclean and hateful bird*!" Kane cried out the words of John the Divine as he swooned against the table of books and sent fluttering the divination cards. "If I can make it back," he said, focusing on the hole through which he had passed.

The chain weighed him down, and falling prone, he crawled for the egress. And now he heard the aerial tones of the Horla.

"You are sick, Solomon. It was set that you should be so once you breathed the air of this chamber. I can control this contagion, on the level of your coarse cells, that it not damage irreparably your tissues, for I am aerie and of more subtle stuff. Take me in, I implore you, and serve my cause!"

"I will not serve you. Bowed though I am, I still do not bow to you, Horla."

"Then you have nothing, and you will die."

"I have faith in God," Kane said as he inched for the opening, dragging his belly over the floor. "Aye, and I have a will, a will that God has granted me authority to hold inviolate. And I will not bring it under your yoke!"

Sweat blurring his vision, Kane became aware that, despite his efforts, he was moving not at all. Still his hand beckoned out, even as his consciousness passed.

He came to on a soft pallet of satin pillows, feeling the first sun he had in days. Sweet fragrances, fresh air, sounds of birds from boughs bobbing with the wind which blew through the large, open windows and billowed the tapestry of one wall...

His eyes were clinched against the light. A rustle of gown and slippers, and then, lowering herself to her knees by his side, Fausta, now lifting and placing his head on her silken lap. Kane's eyes opened on the beauty of her exotic oval face, which floated against her black, diamond-braided hair like a starry sky. Her lush scarlet lips parted eagerly to reveal her white teeth

"A flock of sheep, all evenly shorn," a feverish Kane spoke in Puritan bliss, then his gaze dropped to her low-cut bodice. " 'Breasts like twin roes...' "

"Why, is that the Song of Solomon, I hear?" Fausta asked as her mouth resolved into a beautiful smile, tainted by the slight peal of mockery in her voice. "Are you wooing me, Kane?"

Kane was distracted from his appreciative contemplation when a filmy veil seemed to drop from a full length mirror visible over Fausta's shoulder, and his own ugliness shocked him, as though his craggy countenance had been revealed to him for the first time. He suddenly felt poignantly aware of her thin gown, and that more than the dress's silken fabric, his head rested on Fausta's silky thighs.

He moved to rise, but found himself too weak, sweat suddenly sheathing his face and body.

"Shhh," Fausta said, passing her hand over his wet brow. "Your fever is breaking. Take more rest, Solomon. Rest..."

He yielded to the gentle pressure of the small hand now against his chest, relaxed, and closed his eyes. Soon, he slept again.

When he awoke, a golden salver had been placed by his pallet, with milk, bread, wine and strawberries. He sat up, grabbed the foodstuffs by the handfuls, cramming them into his mouth, then taking deep draughts of the milk. The wine, he purposefully did not touch, for he wished full command of his faculties.

Suddenly aware of a flurry of silk coming from behind him, he looked to see Fausta moving to lower herself by his side. The sudden reddening of Solomon's ears and cheeks heralded that he had not forgotten where his head had rested when last he awoke.

"Good morning, Puritan. Yes, eat your fill. You must needs be strong for the work to which I shall set your hand."

He lay the remaining bit of bread back on the salver and sought to rise to his feet, feeling keenly Fausta's red lacquered fingertips pressing to restrain him. Her touch was like tiny daggers of ice-laced fire, tantalizingly cold and hot at the same time.

He did not attempt to rise further, feeling yet unsure of his legs, but molding his features into pious scorn he looked at her and said: "Serve you? You are the scarlet woman riding the unclean beast that is the Papal palace of Avignon."

"The beast, alas, has lost its legs, Solomon," Fausta said, her expression bitter yet wistful. "My contingent has deserted me, and without the support of men and arms, my plan to replace Gregory has failed ere it began."

Kane's eyes narrowed. "Why desert you?"

"You carry in your own body the cause. Your illness is not isolated. 'Twas a plague that invaded the whole palace. Before news of the contagion could spread and the palace could be quarantined, my entourage fled."

"I find it difficult to believe that you did not do likewise," Kane said, as he struggled to look beyond the beauty of the face to see if a lie lay incarnate there.

"Alas, I was one of the first to succumb. It seems this pestilence slept in one of the sealed rooms below, and when I opened it, 'twas awakened and released to do its worst. When I was no longer the imperious Fausta of the blood of Popes, but a woman weak and near death as any other, I was deserted."

"Yet you have recovered splendidly. Enough to tend me. Did no one nurse you?"

There fell on him then a leaden gaze from Fausta as she resolutely drew up her shoulders: "I am Fausta; my will is iron and resolute. 'Twas all I needed to raise myself from my sick bed."

Suddenly, her gaze was soft again. "Your will is also strong, Solomon Kane."

"So is my faith in God. The same, I think, cannot be said of you."

"Yet we were both stricken, and both recovered. Is it not odd, this indifference?"

"My Lord schools me that he sends his rain on both the just and the unjust. Your healing is, perhaps, his graciousness toward you, that you should have time to repent and not perish. Aye, and I find myself grateful for his kindness toward you."

Fausta smiled again and pressed close to Kane. "I think you have come to love me, Kane, you who came to take me captive."

"You have ministered to me in my need, but you have so done without just cause, and that, lass, troubles me."

"I owed you. You were right. I was not innocent of how you were dealt with by Rochefort. But I think your discomfort is not that of being dealt with kindly by a mind you perceive to be villainous. Nay, I think it is the nearness of my young body, my ripe lips, to your own and the knowledge that you might take me now and know that lushness of woman for which you secretly ache. You only have to act, Solomon. Besides, we are already more intimate than you know. Who do you think bathed and put fresh clothing on you? Rochefort?"

At this, she grabbed his head, pulling it toward her own. Kane fell back, crying out: "Woman, do you think to mount me as you did the scarlet beast?"

In response, Fausta pressed her leverage and fell atop him, bringing her lips close to his ear and hissing:

"That is exactly what I intend, you pious fool! If you want to live, do not resist me. I promise you, maiden, that your virtue shall remain intact. 'Tis the Horla I seek to beguile, not you."

Kane started to speak, but Fausta laid a slender finger across his mouth. Then she slowly slid it over his lips as her own descended to meet his. Kane was awkward as her lips plied his, but the ungainly clinch seemed to satisfy Fausta. She withdrew, rose, smiled at him, then seemed to float in her gown across the floor to the door of the chamber. She opened it, paused to look back at him, still smiling, then stepped outside, closing the door behind her.

Without Fausta to restrain him, Kane decided to try his legs again. He swayed a bit once he had risen to his full height, but he had had to gain sea legs before, and found the sensation similar. He looked about the chamber for his weapons, though he had little hope of finding them there.

His search was interrupted by the sound of the door opening and closing behind him, and he turned to see Fausta returned. From under a satin draped divan, she produced his sword, dagger and slouch hat. She glided to him within an arm's length of distance. Kane stepped back.

"No, no, my Puritan," she said. "You have nothing to fear from me. Certainly, no more love-making. I had to convince the Horla that I was too self-conscious with his presence in this room to complete my seduction. Yes, he was here, observing all. If I could compromise you to venture outside God's grace, then you would be given over to the Horla. And he much desires you as his vessel."

Kane's expression soured. " 'Tis a creature of the pit."

"Thanks to your natural awkwardness, he saw that that my work was cut out for me, and agreed to give us privacy. But we shan't have it for long, so take these your weapons and listen."

"Speak, then," Kane said as he donned his hat, strapped his sword to his waist and his dagger to his calf.

"I came to the palace of Avignon, as I told you before, because it gave me proximity to the Catholic-Huguenot conflict. But there was another reason. An... occult reason. Avignon has a rich history in the dark arts, something that was not unknown to the Popes during their time here. Certain artifacts and writings were collected–but not destroyed. Strange, is it not, that good men allow this foothold to darkness? Visitation was allowed by dispensation to this secret archive in the Pope's treasury, and it was thus allowed to wield its influence over the minds of monks and scribes. Other texts were added to it over the years before Pope Gregory XI left Avignon and the Papacy returned to Rome. The occult archive was secreted, sealed and forgotten... intentionally so.

"But, as you pointed out to me, dear Solomon, there is little that Fausta does not know that she *desires* to know."

"You have yet to say why, lass: why open that accursed crypt?"

"Necromancy, Kane," she answered curtly. "Aye, I see your countenance darken at the word. Would that mine had as well. But I had found the bones of she to whom I am inheritor. These earthly remains, I was told, in a place of dark power, could draw forth her soul; more, here her spirit would enter me, filling me with the wisdom of Pope Joan."

"But the delicacies on the salver–those were for a *skeleton*?"

"For Joan's *spirit,* when she inhabited my flesh. They were to give her pleasure. But it was not Joan who took possession of me–or savored my dainties."

"The Horla," Kane said, the name seeming to simmer on his tongue.

"He had been imprisoned in the archive as well. No doubt the last Pope of Avignon saw to that before he left. I believe the pestilence was placed in the cell to finish the Horla. The contagion did not, for he was resilient beyond human kind. Like a hellish locust, the Horla lingered, waiting until his time came.

"Then, I opened the archive. It seems the pestilence had also lingered. The men who unwalled the chamber were first to succumb, but it was I who spread it among my own people. When the Horla was inside me, he kept my body whole, yet I breathed out the plague on those who were not so protected.

"Kane, we have both passed through that sickness and are now impervious to its foul touch. But it lives on in the raiment we wore while ill and can thus still be passed on to others. If the Horla could take possession of you, he will have you and I bear this contagion to La Rochelle and other Huguenot settlements, all of whom will gladly receive you with me in tow as the prize. And so would Pope Gregory, who would take you into the Vatican itself when he heard you came bearing a would-be Anti-Pope whose bid in Avignon you had aborted. For Fausta and her lineage are known to him."

"Yet the Horla left your body, allowing the plague to overtake you. He risked your death, and a putrefying corpse in my train would gain me admittance nowhere," Kane said.

Fausta smiled. " 'Twas a risk, true, but he knew the strength of my young body and also my will, for he had been in my mind. But *I* was also in *his*.

"Kane, the Horla believes when the plague strikes indiscriminately–strikes even the Pope–Catholics and Huguenots alike will accept that there is only indifferent Nature and lose faith in a Divine Order of good and evil. Then men will readily lay down the swords they have raised for religious cause and willingly receive the type of kingdom the Horla offers."

"Truly, we wrestle not against mere flesh and blood," Kane said. "It seems, then, that we two who have passed through this pestilence must burn this palace, purge the disease by fire and destroy this demon's arsenal."

"Such a conflagration is not needed. Under the Horla's control, I charged Rochefort to seal again the occult archives–and your own cell, where the pestilence spread when you broke through the wall. The Horla wants to conceal he has been freed; perhaps his cell is not hidden and what it holds forgotten to *all*."

"But–will not the pestilence have taken root in Rochefort's own body?"

"We cannot risk otherwise. He must not leave the palace alive." Fausta smiled. "I believe that is in accordance with your own will, Master Kane?"

"Then, he has remained here? Why–?"

Kane cut off his question, for his eye noticed again the mirror he had observed when his head lay on Fausta's lap. Her back was to it as before. Again, it seemed draped with the filmy veil. Now, however, he could focus on this odd *mise en scène* and see that the veil was not, in fact, hanging over the mirror but hovering *in* it, shifting and shimmering, and this amorphous shape did not allow Fausta's reflection to pass through.

"*Down*, girl!" he shouted, his hand descending toward the long knife strapped to his calf. In an instant, the hilt was in his grasp and the blade whirling end over end toward the shape in the mirror behind Fausta.

Her eyes wide, Fausta was only momentarily perplexed at Kane's command and the sight of him going for his blade. Then her keen instinct for preservation kicked in, and she dropped face down, just as the knife was flipping through the air toward her. It careened harmlessly overhead, and, as the knife shattered the mirror into a silvered hail, she heard an inhuman screech of rage.

"The Horla!" she gasped out, even as she felt herself grabbed from behind and hefted into the air. She fought, flailing about in the Horla's grasp but unable to land a blow. Though the entity found her a snared lioness, he was unwilling to release her. In her struggle, Fausta's fine gown was soon ripping and tearing into silken shreds dangling from her slim limbs.

Kane had drawn his sword while his knife was still flying through the air, yet while Fausta levitated in demonic rapture, writhing about wildly, he could not strike at the invisible Horla without risking wounding her.

The door to the chamber flew open, and Kane whirled, sword at the ready, to find Gaston de Rochefort there, grinning, his own long blade raised.

"Ho, great Puritan!" he said, crooning in mock salutation. "Shall we now cross swords or do you surrender since I have you at a disadvantage?"

"You'll find my sword arm far more seasoned than your own," Kane answered.

"What of it?" Gaston asked, nonchalant. "Are you not yet too weak from your illness for the exertions of battle?"

Kane smiled. "I daresay you have not been the picture of health yourself of late, Gaston. If you truly thought yourself my better, you would have already pressed your steel to your advantage instead of assailing me with your worm's tongue!"

Gaston regarded his own blade admiringly, and Kane noticed for the first time a rust color along its edge. "Beware, Monsieur Kane," Gaston said, "for this worm is a *viper*. I have treated my sword with a preparation which is fatal, should it enter the slightest wound. I have a new friend, you see, one who has thus armed me. More, he has entered my body and kept it whole against the pestilence to which, in his service, I was exposed. And now, yes *now*, I feel him entering me again–"

Kane looked back toward Fausta. He found her nearly naked from the Horla's assault, lashed with silken cords harvested from the chamber to a pillar supporting the roof. She looked imploringly toward him, and Kane was startled to see fear on bold Fausta's face.

"Yes!" Gaston shouted, and Kane turned to his enemy. "My every sense is heightened! I am transformed!"

Gaston's face smoothed into the bland mask of an inhuman consciousness; a cold light seemed to descend over his features. Then spoke the Horla:

"Kane, I offered you Fausta and your life. Now you shall have neither, and Gaston de Rochefort will perform my will concerning you both."

Kane smiled in response and raised his sword, trying not to betray that Gaston had spoken true of his weakness. Already his weapon weigh heavily in his hand, and a thin perspiration glazed his face and body, all from what would normally have been but minor exertions.

And only now did the decisive battle begin.

Gaston attacked. Kane thrust his sword forward, and the sound of steel on steel sounded dully against the cushioned acoustics of Fausta's chamber. The noon Sun slithered along Gaston's blade as though flame ushered forth from its hilt to strike his nemesis. Remembering the fatal consequences should Gaston make a *touche*, Kane adroitly dodged the strike, but his brow furrowed: the miss had only been *just*.

He rallied, his sword cleaving the air with its precision-honed edge and shaving away the left shoulder of Gaston's shirt along with a layer of skin. The Frenchman swore at the sting; still, it was but a scratch compared to the beheading Kane had intended.

Gaston feinted, Kane moved to counter and was momentarily left open. In an instant, his enemy immediately followed through, driving the blade hard at Kane's left breast. Reflexively, Kane started, raised and drew back his left arm. This move saved his life, for it shifted the intended target ever so slightly so that Gaston's blade pierced not the Puritan, but merely his shirt and snared there.

Kane whirled away, the sword ripping free of his shirt as he escaped the perilous proximity of the poisoned blade to his flesh. Gaston fell back, swiping the sword left and right in the air to discard the bits of cloth that stuck there.

Kane took the moment to regain his composure. He pushed back from his face his cloying hair, damp from exertion and sickness, taking some relief from the breeze that rhythmically moved the tapestry that ran the length of the wall behind him. Still, torturous rivulets of perspiration ran down his forehead and stung his eyes. He could not help but repeatedly blink, knowing that a fraction of a second of blindness was the only opening his enemy would need.

Gaston's blade was now free of the shirt shreds, and Kane noted that, where they had been, the poison was wiped clean. Gaston charged, his battle cry the unnerving wail of the Horla.

Kane bolted behind the tapestry as the breeze lifted it out from the wall. Gaston plunged his sword through the woven hanging, just missing Kane, as he continued to move behind the covering. The Frenchman withdrew and started to pursue, ready to stab through the fabric again. Then the Horla realized what Kane was about: more poison was now wiped from the edge of Gaston's blade.

He waited for Kane to emerge at the other end of the wall, and then Gaston renewed his charge. The words of the Apostle passed Kane's lips a second time that day: "*We wrestle not against flesh and blood alone.*" At least while Gaston was its host, he knew where the Horla *was*. If he could decisively end their battle while the threat was combined into one, his disadvantage could be turned in his favor. But what could defeat both man and demon simultaneously, as he would need to do?

Then his sight touched on the salver Fausta had left on the floor by his pallet. He raised his gaze back to de Rochefort, a smile easing his grim features, which in turn caused the hitherto arrogant countenance of Gaston to slip and his pace to slow.

"The sword of the Lord and his servant, Solomon Kane!" the Puritan cried out in rally and charged his foe, ready to strike. Gaston recovered and resumed his rush to meet his nemesis head on.

Blurring steel struck, scraped, scintillated, sparks spewing out as though the air, pregnant with the combatants' intensity, combusted about them. Again, Kane's sword lashed, rasped the side of Gaston's, but his breathing was ragged, competing with the grating of steel. The Horla that watched and waited from behind de Rochefort's eyes took notice; Gaston smiled, and, his confidence restored, renewed the aggression of his assault.

Kane's heart rioting with exertion, he fell back as Gaston put him again on the defensive. Soon he would be routed so far from his goal that his cause would be irredeemably lost.

He prayed under his breath, "Lord Jesus, transcend me; come upon me Spirit of God as you did Samson of old."

Kane's sword slashed down Gaston's face from beneath his left eye to his lower jaw. The French man cried in pain, and balked, for, amazingly, the *Horla* felt the blunt of the wound equally with his host! The entity momentarily loss control of its instrument, and, seeing this, Kane meant to see it never regained complete mastery.

Kane beat him back, back toward the pallet where recently he had lain, where the golden salver still set with the remains of his repast. A quick, defensive parry from Gaston followed, then Kane's crafty feint yielded an opening, and the Puritan thrust through the biceps of de Rochefort's sword arm. He howled in pain and the Horla's wails accompanied its host's. Kane then unsheathed his blade from the Frenchman's muscle with a torturous twist of the steel, causing Gaston's sword to drop numbly from his hand. The pallet's pillows on which he now stood shifted under his boots, tripping him to his knees.

Kane's breath came in deep sobs, and his heart still thrust itself wildly against his ribs. He was almost faint, but he had to strike in this instant while the entity was still too stunned by the pain it shared with its host to abandon it. The Horla bleated desperately, "Fool! I have not come to bring a sword but *peace* unto the Earth!"

In response, Kane suddenly flicked his wrist down so that he brought the tip of his blade to the salver immediately by Gaston. Spearing through a crust of bread, he dipped it quickly into the goblet of wine, then thrust his sword upward, piercing the Frenchman's throat and driving the sacramental sop directly into his gullet.

His expression austere, Kane held transfixed with the consecrated point of his sword both de Rochefort and Horla. It was the latter he addressed:

"You never partook of the bread and wine when Fausta was your host, when she *thought* she fed her ancestress' spirit. For this wheat and grape signify the communion of the saints with the God you forsook. Aye, unworthy wretch, in receiving this, you enter unbidden the holy congregation of the Lord of Sabaoth! You affront his Holy Majesty, and shall you not receive due recompense? Begone into the abyss that is held for your ilk!"

Gaston's straining eyes erupted in twin, bloody geysers. A great wind howled outward from his convulsing person, blasting Kane back as a darkness at midday descended over the chamber.

Fausta's head recoiled as though from a powerful slap, clinching her eyes protectively against the maelstrom's force. Windows shattered and shards reeled about the room. Feeling the surrender to unconsciousness he had so far managed to resist fully coming upon him, Kane launched himself across the room, landing against Fausta's nearly unclothed body to shield it with his own against the glass projectiles. Locking his arms around the pillar against which she was helplessly bound, his head drooped at last, his chin coming to rest on Fausta's round, smooth shoulder.

Two days later, Kane was ready to depart Avignon for the Huguenot settlement across the river. Boot in the stirrup of the strong, tall horse that was Fausta's gift, he raised himself above her who stood, once again opulently robed, by the steed's side. He wore his slouch hat, his sword was in its sheath, and his long knife on his calf. Saddlebags were generously loaded with provisions Fausta had also secured for his trip across France back to La Rochelle, but he would not be bearing her with him. He would report to those to whom he must give account the truth: the bid of the Anti-Pope of Avignon had failed. She no longer posed a threat to their religious freedom.

During his recovery, Kane had thought much upon his enemy from the occult archive in the old Papal palace. "He was held in that unclean place until his appointed hour, but your machinations brought him forth before his time," he told Fausta. "It was God who led me here, lass, not to abort your threat, but that of the Horla."

Still, one of the Horla's more arcane statements puzzled him. As he prepared to take his leave, he now asked Fausta if she understood what the Horla meant when he said that the whole Earth was already out of joint at his coming; that hours, days and seasons were moved out of place, though men had only now recognized that it was so.

Fausta's dark brows knit as she considered this saying. Then she answered: "In Rome, Gregory seeks to redress the straying of the vernal equinox by readjusting the calendar year. His learned men say 'twas due to a slight mistake Sosigenes of Alexandria made in calculating the Julian calendar. If what the Horla spoke was true, this resulted, not by human error, but from some catastrophe to the Earth attending the Horla's arrival."

"He *and* his ilk," Kane said. "He claimed there were others, and they, no doubt, shall attempt to fulfill where he fell short." Kane brooded. "I wonder, when shall that day come upon the Earth? When, according to the Horla's vile gospel, truth is no longer valued as a matter over which men should strive?"

Fausta smiled pensively, a trace of melancholy in her voice. "'Twould be a world with no place for Solomon Kane," she said.

The Sun had now slanted shadows lengthy and cool and choice for travel, and as he made for the river, for France beyond it, and a war he understood, Solomon Kane did not deign to look back at Avignon, the city of the winds.

Travis Hiltz returns to Tales of the Shadowmen *with a light-hearted tale featuring Arnould Galopin's space-time traveler, Doctor Omega. This story, which segues directly from the original 1906 novel (available from Black Coat Press), sees the Doctor's path cross that of another cosmic wanderer in...*

Travis Hiltz: *Three Men, A Martian and A Baby*

Space, 1917

We drifted along, the crew of that most wondrous craft, the *Cosmos*, through the vast ocean of the aetheric space-time continuum. In every direction there stretched out a canvas of swirling colors, some of which I did not even have names for.

"Enjoying the view, Denis?"

Turning from the breathtaking panorama, I faced my host, the mysterious savant, Doctor Omega.

He was tall and elderly. His white hair slicked back, except for one rebellious tuft. His attire was a black frock coat, several years behind the current fashion, black trousers and polished-to-a-shine shoes, the characteristics of an educated gentleman.

"Amazing as always, Doctor," I told him. "I could stare at it forever."

"Forever is quite a long time, my boy," he said, patting my shoulder. "And there is still so much more yet to see. Besides, you'd miss lunch. Ah, look there!"

I glanced in the direction he pointed and watched as what looked like a mountain went floating past the porthole. It was bigger than any earthly mountain and tiered, like some enormous wedding cake.

"What is it?" I asked in breathless awe.

"Hard to say at this distance. Could be a planet that follows its own natural laws, the relic of some alien civilization or merely a misplaced mountain," he said, with a shrug, as we watched the behemoth drift away. "There is no end of odd items drifting about."

Hours passed and I was to learn first hand that the tiered planet was one of the more mundane objects drifting through space-time. An army of metal men tumbled past the porthole, like snowflakes glittering in the otherworldly light. We were passed by another spacecraft, shaped like an improbably large white running shoe and then a man, dressed in a soldier's garb, holding on for dear life to the flying carpet upon which he rode.

My eyebrows had shot up in surprise so many times that the muscles in my forehead began to ache. The fabulous soon became the norm and I was able to pull myself away from the porthole as my brain tried to process the endless parade of wonders that I witnessed.

"Is there much danger of collision?" I asked, remembering from past travels that there was peril as well as wonders in the aether.

"The dimensions that we travel through are indeed full of flotsam and jetsam," Doctor Omega informed me, not looking up from his book. He had grown tired of the view and retired to an armchair in the far corner of the room. "But it is also of such infinite size that the odds of collision are..."

I was never to hear what the odds were, as the ship shuddered and echoed like some enormous bell. Both the Doctor and I tumbled to the metal floor and slid about, like dice in a Parcheesi cup.

Doctor Omega managed to wedge himself into the corner, between his chair and the wall, while I was only successful at acquiring a collection of bruises and bumps, before grabbing hold of a table that has been bolted to the floor.

The ship groaned and tumbled for what seemed like ages, until suddenly there was quiet; I experienced a sharp falling sensation in the pit of my stomach.

"I'm guessing our landing will not be a gentle one," Doctor Omega announced. "Brace yourself!"

A bone-wrenching impact followed and all movement stopped. The lights flickered and the room was cast into darkness.

"Denis?" Doctor Omega asked. "Are you injured?"

"Not beyond repair," I replied, wincing, and then climbing unsteadily to my feet. My body ached, reminding me of an unfortunate term at school when I joined (and then quickly resigned from) the rugby team. "Am I to guess that, against all odds, we did collide with something?"

"Most likely a meteor or some form of energy helix," the Doctor mused, amazingly unruffled by the excitement. He had been traveling in the *Cosmos* long enough, before I joined her crew, that he had no doubt grown accustomed to the occasional incident such as this.

I fumbled in the dark to reach Doctor Omega's side, helped him back into his chair and then limped over to a cabinet. Finding a lantern, we soon had enough light to see. Nearly all the furniture was bolted to the metal floor, so there was little mess to worry about. A spilled cup of coffee, some scattered books and writing implements, and a large tear in the left knee of my trousers were the extent of the damage.

Leaving the elderly Doctor to recover, I made my way to a circular hatch set into the floor. As I reached for it, the hatch flew open and a large, bearded face poked through the opening.

"We've crashed!" he bellowed.

"Thank you, Fred," Doctor Omega said. "It had come to our attention."

"You gentlemen are all right?" Fred asked, climbing up into the room. Tiziraou, the last member of our crew, soon followed him.

He was a tiny creature, standing waist-high to myself, with an oversized round head and arms and legs that were floppy to the point of appearing boneless. His thin body was smooth skinned and pale.

Coming from the temperate climate of ancient Mars, his macrocephalic people had seen little need for anything beyond basic clothing. Sympathetic to his more modest traveling companions, Tiziraou was dressed in a hand-me down plaid bathrobe. One of the sleeves was torn and there was a large, fresh food stain down the front of the garment. He held a thin, three-fingered hand to his pumpkin-like head and walked unsteadily as he joined us, muttering in his native tongue.

"There's a burst pipe in the galley and the time rotor has stopped," Fred said, wiping at a cut on his cheek with a large red handkerchief. "Tiziraou and I are going to see about getting the engines back in order. You gentlemen might want to have a look outside. Check for damage to the hull."

Doctor Omega nodded and the four of us climbed down through the hatch, Fred and our Martian companion to the lower levels of our craft, the Doctor and I to the exit hatch.

Ensuring that the air was breathable, we exited the craft.

The *Cosmos* was lying on its side, in the center of a rather sizable pit, no doubt caused by our unplanned landing.

A barren landscape stretched all around us. The ground was a dry, white crust, which our every footstep broke through, raising tiny plumes of dust. The vegetation consisted of a few tiny, gnarled trees, patches of lichen and grey moss.

"It would appear," Doctor Omega mused, adapting a lecturer's pose, hands clutching his lapels, "that the collision knocked us out of the aether into 'normal' space, forcing us to make this rather ungraceful landing. Hmm... Curious."

We carefully made our way around the *Cosmos*, scouting for signs of damage. Aside from a rather sizable dent in the stellite plating, just below the tip of the craft's bullet body, it appeared unharmed.

"That'll cause us to wobble a bit," Doctor Omega said, thoughtfully. "I'll leave it to Fred to decide if it can be banged back into shape or if that plate will need replacing."

I left him to ponder the damage and made my way up the side of the pit to see if I could spot whatever had caused our impromptu landing. The crunching of my footsteps echoed in the still air. Despite my artistic nature, I am not without athletic prowess, but found myself feeling a bit winded upon reaching the top of the crater. The air felt thin and stale in my lungs.

"Doctor!" I called down. "Have a look at this!"

Leaning heavily upon his cane and grumbling as he made his way up, the elderly scientist soon joined me. He paused at the lip of the crater to catch his breath and dab at his forehead with a threadbare checkered handkerchief.

I pointed out a groove in the ground, roughly three feet wide, trailing off into the distance.

"While my mental capacity does not rival yours, Doctor, I would hazard a guess that we'll find whatever we collided with at the end of that rut."

His expression told me he did not share my light-hearted view of the situation, nor relish the thought of more walking. Several hundred yards later, we arrived at the end of the rut, where lay a craft nearly as wondrous as our own.

It was a projectile, roughly six feet long, sleeker and smaller than the *Cosmos*, made of a blue metal that glimmered in the faint sunlight like polished ceramic. One of its red tail fins was bent.

"A shell of some kind?" was my first thought, but Doctor Omega shook his head and pushed at an indentation on the object, with the end of his cane. We heard a hum and a panel slid open.

The Doctor and I both instinctively took several steps backwards. In my travels with him, I had quickly discovered that the universe was full of hazards as well as wonders, and it paid to be careful while you sorted out which was which.

"Bub. Ba-hah," a voice babbled from the opening.

We took a hesitant step forward and peered inside.

An infant lay in the compartment, wrapped up in blankets of red and blue.

"A child! Who would be so heartless to shoot a child off into space...?" I asked.

Doctor Omega tapped at his chin, then taking a much-used notebook and the stub of a pencil from his pocket, peered up into the starry sky. Occasionally, he would jot something down.

The child looked up at me with wide, curious eyes. I reached into the craft gingerly, as the exterior was still warm from its descent, and lifted the child, a boy, up.

"Hello there," I said, in what I hoped was a reassuring tone. "Why would someone abandon a fine boy like you?"

I have no children of my own, but a rather large and fertile crowd of cousins has allowed me to spend a goodly bit of time with infants and I have found that, for short intervals, I rather like the little fellows and seem to have a knack for bonding with them. This unusual foundling was proving to be no exception. He gave me a smile and took hold of my finger.

"Quite a grip," I winced, swearing I could hear the cracking of bone over the boy's gurgling laugh. I struggled to retrieve my finger. "Grow up to be a strong boy, no doubt." I shifted my hold on the child so I could attempt to shake some feeling back into my injured digit.

"Remarkable," Doctor Omega said, looking over my shoulder at the child.

"I find the whole thing rather beastly. Treating him like a... laboratory rat or something."

"No, my boy, I rather think we are seeing the galactic equivalent of leaving a baby on the doorstep of an orphanage," he said.

"What? It's inhuman! We must return him to his home."

"Well, since, appearances aside, the child is most likely not human, that's neither here nor there," the Doctor said, pressing his fingers against the child's skin at several spots. "Hmm, dense musculature. Raised in a high gravity environment. Yes, now I see..." He nodded to himself, smiled briefly at the child, then glanced back my way. "According to my understandably hasty calculations, I would guess the craft came from there."

He pointed into the night sky, to a spark of green, far off in the distance.

"That light, if memory serves, is the last trace of a once proud world. An advanced race of scientists. There's no point trying to get him back home, you see, as there's no longer a home for him to return to."

"His world is gone?" I muttered, sadly peering at the boy. "So, this little rocket was a lifeboat?"

"Exactly. His being sent into space was an act of parental love," the Doctor said, chucking the baby under the chin.

"If he's the last of his people, what will happen to him?"

"I think that was thought of already. Rough calculations of the course he was on when we collided, I believe he soon would have arrived... let's see... ah-ha!"

The Doctor's thin finger now pointed towards a familiar blue-green planet.

"Earth!" I breathed, holding the baby up to see the Earth. "You're going to Earth, little fellow!"

"Yes," Doctor Omega said, looking over his calculations. "Most likely, the United States."

"America?" I said, to the child. "Well, I imagine you'll turn out all right despite that. So, do we just send him on his way?"

"Once we have Fred straighten out that guidance fin, he'll be able to continue on his journey. Best thing for the tiny chap. A ship full of bachelors like us would hardly be a suitable home."

Fred, Doctor Omega and I were soon standing on a ridge, watching the repaired rocket and its occupant soar off towards Earth. It had been the work of a hour for Fred to make the craft spaceworthy again.

"Hope he's found by a good family," I said, wistfully.

"I'm sure he'll do you proud," Doctor Omega smiled.

"So, we crashed on the Moon, eh?" Fred said. "In school, they said it was a lifeless world, so we'll have some quiet time, while we get the *Cosmos* back in shape. Should be able to hammer out that dent and have the time rotor humming along by dinner time."

Just then, Tiziraou came running towards us, his thin arms flapping wildly, his robe billowing out behind him, like a cape. The Moon's thin atmosphere and light gravity caused him to bounce several feet into the air with each step.

In close pursuit of our martian traveling companion were a trio of short, bandy legged creatures, encased in leathery armor and wearing goggles with dark lenses. Each held a metallic spear in their tentacle-like hands.

"Selenites," Doctor Omega mused, in happy astonishment. "How interesting. Notice how the muscle structure of their upper bodies...?"

Fred and I each grabbed one of the Doctor's arms and dashed for the safety of the *Cosmos*.

Rick Lai's unfolding saga continues to focus on Josephine Balsamo, Arsène Lupin's arch-enemy whose budding career among the Black Coats is fraught with perils, and her rival, the young detective Irene Chupin (or Tupin), "rescued" from the cult horror film La Residencia *(a.k.a.* The House That Screamed*). While the following tale can be read independently, readers wishing to reacquaint themselves with Irene and her ghastly trials at Madame Fourneau's College for Young Women in Provence, as well as Josephine's role in the Bluebeard Murders in Paris, may find it useful to reread the tales published in our second and third volumes before choosing to enter the...*

Rick Lai: *Corridors of Deceit*

Paris, London, 1896

To the population of London in November 1896, the House of Crafts was merely the headquarters of a reputable fashion company. In reality, the building was the headquarters of the nefarious criminal society known as the Black Coats. Its basement served both as a dungeon and a torture chamber. Presently, a young woman wearing a brown blouse with a black tie and a black skirt was unceremoniously dragged inside a cell.

"Your new abode, Dodger," coolly announced her flamboyant jailer.

She was a woman with short brown hair, brushed from the forehead in a wide stock, giving the impression of a bird-like crest. Her tall, lean body was attired entirely in black. A patch covered her right eye. Her open coat was styled like an Inverness cape. Her outfit also comprised a shirt with a cravat plus pants and boots. A ring of keys dangled from her belt. An amulet in the shape of a cat's head was chained around her neck. Her right hand clutched the back of the captive's chestnut hair.

"Please don't hurt me, Milady," whimpered Dodger.

"I don't intend to. As a talented thief, you're a valuable asset for us. A period of incarceration should cure your stubborn streak, however. You disobeyed my order to steal Baron Gruner's diary."

"I couldn't let you blackmail the man I love!"

"You little fool! You were merely expected to flirt with Gruner. He cares nothing for you."

"That's not true."

"Enough of this nonsense! I let you have the 'Dodger' sobriquet. Your insolence merits a demotion. Remember the nickname of 'B. F.' from our schooldays? It suits you so well!"

Releasing Dodger, Milady secured the door and left the basement. The cell's door had a small window covered with bars. Light from a small lamp poured through it. Dodger removed a folded page from her sleeve and held it to the light. Though she knew the inscription by heart, reading it consoled her:

"*Dearest Berenice, pray for my soul, I will pray for yours...Irene.*"

Dodger knew it was dangerous to hide this paper. Milady would punish her if it was found, but seeing the words reminded Dodger to perform a ritual every day. She did it now.

"Our Father, who art in Heaven...."

The White Lodge, a late-Georgian mansion in the Blackheath district of London, belonged to Noel Moriarty, a leading member of the High Council of the Black Coats. His wife, known to London's high society as Madame Koluchy, never appeared in public with her husband. In fact, most people believed her to be a widow. This majestic woman with black hair and dark blue eyes was presently dining at the White Lodge with her father, Count Corbucci, a heavily built man with a large white mustache. Both father and daughter wore gold rings shaped like snakes. The Count was a patriarch of the Camorra, the Italian secret society which had long ago spawned the *Veste Nere*, a.k.a. the Black Coats. His daughter headed another criminal enterprise known more simply as the Brotherhood.

"Mabuse's Espionage Hotel will need a competent architect, Catarina."

"I would recommend the designer of our headquarters, father. This artisan also worked for Marguerite Chavain and Madame Sara."

"You've reorganized the Brotherhood in preparation for the upcoming meeting of the High Council?"

"Yes, I have a new chief of staff, 'Milady Nevermore.' "

"Wasn't she Antonio's principal assassin? I'm surprised that my foster son let her go."

Corbucci was discussing the Black Coats' head of Asian operations. On a trip to Havana, decades ago, the Count had adopted a homeless waif named Antonio. Before her marriage to Noel, Catarina had been fiancéd to Antonio. Their betrothal had been broken for reasons known only to the Corbucci family.

"She was my operative before she was Antonio's, father. Six years ago, I sent her to Japan to be trained by the Iga ninja clan. Antonio made the arrangements. She was always slated to be in my employ."

"What happened?"

"Just as her training was concluding, the Koga clan attacked the Iga village. Nearly all the Iga ninjas were massacred by a 'Steel-Skin Kung Fu' expert imported by their Koga rivals. Milady survived, but she suffered extreme injuries. Antonio informed me that she would face a prolonged recovery, so I temporarily lost interest in her and Antonio used her in the meantime."

"So he stole one of your own. How charmingly bureaucratic."

"When news of Milady's activities reached me, I forced Antonio to relinquish her back to me."

"What happened to your prior chief of staff?"

"Josephine will now report to Milady."

"Considering her previous failures, I don't understand why you let her live. Your affection for this former classmate of yours is affecting your judgment, daughter."

"Not true, father. I have despised her since our very first encounter."

"And yet, you picked her to be your assistant during your tenure as prefect at that school."

"The headmistress required the performance of certain distasteful duties. Rather than bear the burden myself, I chose a pretentious girl to assume those responsibilities. Since Josephine proved her... expertise, I inducted her into the Brotherhood. But I still relish in tormenting her."

An attractive blonde woman in a green dress entered the House of Crafts. She was ending a short leave of absence that had been granted her to give her time to recover from some injuries she had recently received in Paris. The blonde woman found Milady Nevermore in her private office rubbing her hands together in a smug manner.

"So you are Josephine Balsamo," said Milady to the newcomer. "The situation is somewhat awkward. I understand this used to be your office, but I needed to move in immediately. Your possessions have been temporarily stored downstairs."

"I understand, Milady," said Josephine, looking around, mentally appraising the furniture. "Your taste is exquisite. I notice a Poe collection on your bookshelf. May I look at it?"

Milady handed *Tamerlane and Other Poems* to Josephine. The blonde woman noticed the dedication inside: *To Kaitlin: A great rarity for a great daughter. Love, Father.*

Returning the book, Josephine pondered the inscription. Milady was an enigma to Josephine. This dedication was the only clue to her new supervisor's identity.

"I was told that Madame Koluchy has approved my posting to New Orleans," she said. "When do I leave?"

"Your reassignment has been cancelled, I'm afraid. I've reviewed the Bluebeard Murders case.[2] It was filled with blunders. You wanted Arsène Lupin to *pay the law* for a murder, but instead of simply committing one, you planned six."

"I had sound motives. I wanted to create a public outcry."

"That is a poor excuse," interjected Milady, wagging a finger.

---

[2] See "The Lady in the Black Gloves" in *Tales of the Shadowmen 3*.

"Don't treat me like a schoolgirl!"

"I wouldn't mention schoolgirls here, if I were you. Your pawn killed many schoolgirls."

"I used Luis Fourneau because the crimes required his artistry to be credible."

"You little fool!" screeched Milady. "That monster should never have been born. You should have let him rot in his asylum. And you should know that Madame Koluchy agrees with me."

"Does she now?"

"Many of our female colleagues have attended the Fourneau boarding school. Professor Chavain of the High Council has even formed an Alumni Association."

"I know. I'm a member–unlike you."

"Your membership has been revoked. Professor Chavain was shocked to learn of your involvement with the murderous maniac responsible for the school's closure. Wild rumors circulated after the press publicized your alliance with Luis Fourneau. It was even said that you and Madame Koluchy had plotted the school's destruction together. But she quashed these stories by addressing the Alumni..."

"What did she say?"

"The truth. That you used Luis without her knowledge."

Josephine knew that Koluchy was lying. Certain details of the Bluebeard Murders had been withheld from Milady and the Black Coats.

"I want to talk to the Alumni. I need to explain my conduct."

"Such a meeting has, in fact, been already scheduled. I've taken the liberty to prepare your speech."

Milady handed Josephine a sheet of paper. The blonde woman's features grew darker as she read it.

"But this is a confession! This is a lie."

"This speech will appease Professor Chavain. The High Council plans to debate Madame Koluchy's proposal to rename the Brotherhood the Black Skirts. Such a change would consolidate the increased role of women in our society, but for this measure to pass, the Council's only other female member must support it. Be thankful that Professor Chavain, as a botanist, didn't insist that *a branch be cut*."

In Black Coat parlance, the *cutting of a branch* meant the imposition of the death penalty.

"We need to discuss your attire at the Alumni meeting," resumed Milady. "Our campaign would suffer if you wore your uniform."

"What uniform?"

"Under the Brotherhood's new dress code, uniforms are worn by all female members."

"Ah, yes. I saw them in Paris. Brown blouses, black skirts and ties. They're even sold commercially. But executives are exempt from the dress code."

"Yes, but this exemption applies to me–not you."

"I'm no longer an executive?"

"You're now a mere employee, entrusted with this building's security."

"You mean, I've been demoted to being *a security guard*! Me–Countess Cagliostro!"

Josephine defiantly raised her hand. It bore a ring with the image of a golden ram.

"As far as I know, your title is unverified. I've instructed the other employees to only call you Mademoiselle Balsamo."

"Yet, everyone calls you Milady."

"Have you researched my lineage?"

"No, I haven't."

"Then you spoke without thinking. In my youth, I suffered from the same fault. But I shall cure you of that habit..."

Josephine delivered her humiliating speech that evening. In another act of humiliation devised by Milady, she had been forced to appear naked before the Alumni. After the speech, Milady instructed Josephine to wait in a dressing room for her new uniform. Josephine stared at her shoulders in a mirror. Two "V" had been branded into each shoulder. Even though this disfigurement had been done on Madame Koluchy's orders, Josephine held Irina Putine of the Chupin Detective Agency responsible. Remembering her triumphant adversary from their days together at the boarding school, the blonde woman began to mutter to herself:

"The Furnace letters... Milady de Winter... Kaitlin de Winter... The necklace..."

There was a knock on the door.

"May I come in, Countess?"

"Yes," responded a stunned Josephine.

A brunette carrying a box entered.

"Your uniform, Countess."

"Thank you, Maude. You've always understood proper etiquette."

"I haven't forgotten your generous wedding gift, Countess. Besides, my former mistress, Lady Beltham, instilled in me a proper appreciation for titles."

"Maude" had been born Hendrika Pienaar in Pretoria. Her codename was derived from the British aristocrat whom she had once served as a maid. Maude also liked to mimic Lady Beltham's courtly accent.

"Do you still have access to the personnel files, Maude?" Josephine asked. "I'd like to see Milady's."

"It's too risky, Countess. Anyone caught reading her file would be worse off than B. F."

"B. F.?"

"You might remember her as 'Dodger.' She's a burglar transferred here from Paris. She's in the dungeon now. Milady treats her like dirt. Apparently, they have some prior history together."

"B. F... Those initials are familiar. Can you get me her file instead?"

"That should be easy. I'll get it from Purity."

A week later, two middle-aged ladies from Bristol crossed the English Channel. One had brown hair while the other was a blonde. Arriving at the Chupin Detective Agency in Paris, they requested to see the firm's owner. A secretary informed them that Monsieur Chupin was in Spain. The visitors were instead directed to the office of Irina Putine, his chief assistant.

Irina was 26, tall and slender, with a glossy mane of black hair. A brooch shaped like a pentagram was pinned on the right side of her orange dress. A black tie was tied around her collar. It matched the black silk gloves on her hands. Silver bracelets graced her wrists.

"My name is Rosette Trevor," said the brown-haired lady. "I live in Bristol with my husband and daughter. This is my neighbor, Eva Relli."

"I teach architecture at a local university," said Eva. "I moved with my son to England from Naples after my husband's death."

"Madame Trevor, your maiden name is Morrell," replied Irina. "Your two siblings are deceased. Your brother was a painter. Your sister, Natalie, ran a boarding school in Provence. Two of her three children are dead."

"Why, that's amazing," said Eva. "It's just like Dr. Watson's accounts. Imagine Mademoiselle Putine deducing all that from your appearance, Rosette."

"It's very easy for Mademoiselle Putine to make those statements, Eva. She knows all about my family. A month ago, she killed my nephew, Luis Fourneau."

"I was acting in self-defense," said Irina.

"I don't doubt it. Luis was a fiend."

"Your sister, too, was also somewhat controversial."

"I won't defend Natalie's reputation. The floggings at her school were abhorrent. I'm here about her daughter, Berenice. She and your employer's late niece, Irene Chupin, were close friends."

"Irene's very much alive, Madame Trevor. She told me about Berenice."

"But the newspapers reported Irene's death from shock after my nephew..."

"You were about to say–after your nephew chopped off her hands. The accounts of her death were inaccurate.[3] Irene's relatives wished to protect her from publicity. They never issued a denial."

"May I meet her?" inquired Madame Trevor.

---

[3] See "Dr. Cerral's Patient" in *Tales of the Shadowmen 2*.

"That's impossible, I'm afraid. Irene now lives in complete seclusion. But I have something else to show you..."

Irina went to a large safe in her office. She entered the combination and opened the door. Among shelves of papers, she removed a bundle of letters tied together and handed them to Madame Trevor.

"These are some of Berenice's letters to Irene."

Madame Trevor untied the letters and skimmed through them.

"I recognize my niece's handwriting. How did you get them?"

"During Irene's recuperation, they came into Monsieur Chupin's possession."

"He couldn't know Berenice wrote those letters. She used an assumed name."

" 'Blythe Furnace,' yes. But the French translation of Furnace is Fourneau. Your niece's alias shares the same initials as her real name. Monsieur Chupin astutely uncovered her true identity."

"Your employer never contacted my niece."

"Monsieur Chupin only found the letters after your niece's disappearance. Perhaps you could confirm Berenice's friendship with Irene, if only to verify our own information?"

"My niece was lonely and friendless during her childhood. My sister Natalie doted on her sons, but woefully neglected Berenice. The three children resided in a segregated area at the school. Natalie forbade Berenice to socialize with her students, whom she regarded as the dregs of society. She was, in fact, planning to send Berenice to a proper boarding school in Paris. Berenice, who was then 13, feared that Parisian girls would see her as a graceless provincial..."

"A concise summary, Madame Trevor, but there is one missing fact: Berenice did befriend a student at your sister's school."

"What year was that?" queried Eva.

"It was in August 1885," answered Irina. "But please continue, Madame Trevor."

"Berenice stole a set of keys from her mother. She wandered around the school at night."

"Just like a burglar," observed Eva.

"My niece was a bit of a tomboy, since her only playmates until then had been her brothers. As you noted, Mademoiselle Putine, a new student's arrival changed all that. Her name was Irene. She had been locked in a storeroom while Natalie conferred privately with the girl's guardian..."

" 'Guardian' isn't quite the proper term to describe Henriette d'Andresy," noted Irina. "Her son, a cunning thief, had been nursed by Victoire Chupin, Irene's mother, and when the girl was falsely accused of one of his thefts, Henriette enrolled her son's foster-sister at your sister's school."

"Yes, my niece told me all that. Berenice unlocked the storeroom where Irene had been confined. That's how the friendship between the two girls began.

Irene had a book with her, a novel by Charles Dickens–I don't remember the title..."

"*Oliver Twist,*" said Irina.

"My sister reviled Dickens as a defamer of the French Revolution. Berenice warned Irene that her mother would burn the book if she found it, so Irene gave it to Berenice, and even inscribed it. Over the next few weeks, the girls continued to meet clandestinely. When Natalie eventually enrolled Berenice at the Institution Bachelard in Paris, the girls hoped to correspond, but complications arose in the matter of Irene's surname."

"How was that a problem?" wondered Eva.

"Perhaps I should explain," volunteered Irina. "Natalie Fourneau's pupils were unwanted children. She protected the reputation of the people responsible for her students' confinement by changing the surnames of many girls. Chupin became Tupin."

"So Irene wouldn't be able to receive mail!" said Eva.

"Irene was a special case," said Irina. "Henriette d'Andresy had warned Madame Fourneau that Irene's uncle was Victor Chupin, the private detective. Monsieur Chupin had been deceived about the reasons for his niece's presence at the school, but insisted on writing to her nevertheless. Of course, his letters were addressed to Irene Chupin."

"How did Berenice manage to circumvent this peculiar arrangement?"

"My sister kept meticulous records and Berenice was able to break into Irene's file. Then, using the identity of 'Blythe Furnace,' she pretended to be an old friend who had gotten Irene's address from Monsieur Chupin. This subterfuge was necessary because the mail was also being censored."

"Natalie was reading the mail?" asked Eva.

"My sister delegated that task to her prefect," said Madame Trevor.

"Josephine Balsamo, your nephew's accomplice in the Bluebeard Murders," added Irina.

"My niece's stratagem worked and the correspondence went on for over four years," continued Madame Trevor. "During this time, she was badly harassed by a fellow student, Kaitlin de Winter, the daughter of an English Baron assigned to the Paris Embassy. She gave Berenice vicious nicknames. My niece's initials are meaningless in French, but Kaitlin said they stood for 'Bloody Fool.' In a letter, Irene advised Berenice to fight fire with fire."

"Meaning?" asked Eva.

"Kaitlin professed to be related to the de Winter family from Monsieur Dumas' Musketeers novels. She insisted on being addressed as 'Milady.' Irene pointed out that the proper title of a Baron's daughter is 'Right Honorable,' so Berenice started calling Kaitlin's 'Right Dishonorable.' Kaitlin was also a devotee of Edgar Allen Poe. She liked the nickname of 'Raven' because of the poem, so Irene suggested that Berenice call her 'Craven.' Irene knew how to handle a bully for a simple reason. Because she was a bully herself. She was, in fact, my sister's last prefect."

"But Irene was coerced by Josephine into becoming a prefect," said Irina. "So Berenice was advised on how to fight a bully by a person who had already submitted to another bully's domination."

"Whatever Irene's motives, my niece was very grateful," said Madame Trevor. "She viewed Irene as her best friend. Berenice was later devastated to learn of her mother's death, her brother's incarceration and Irene's alleged demise. I then traveled to Paris in order to take her back to Bristol. Before we could return to England, a horrible event transpired. Berenice returned from Sunday Mass to discover her room vandalized. Irene's letters had been torn to sheds. The pages of Irene's gift, the Dickens book, were ripped out. My niece saw this as a horrible desecration. All the remembrances of her best friend had been destroyed. Neither I nor the Countess could console her."

"What Countess?" said Irina.

"Countess Corbucci, one of my sister's former students. She came to the Institution Bachelard to offer her condolences."

"Was this Countess a blonde?"

"No, a brunette. Soon after the vandalism, Berenice disappeared. Her room showed signs of a struggle. All her clothes and possessions were missing. The same night, Kaitlin also vanished with her belongings. The police couldn't trace either girl. I believe Kaitlin was responsible for both the vandalism and my niece's disappearance."

"Why reopen this case?"

"I received this letter. I didn't want to go to the French police because of their general ineptitude. Eva recommended your Agency because of Berenice's connection to Irene."

Rosette handed a letter to Irina. The sleuth scrutinized it.

"The person who wrote this is a terrible writer," commented Eva. "Several English words are misused. Do you get the gist?"

"Yes, Madame Relli. The writer identifies himself only as 'Parker.' He or she wants 50,000 francs for information about Berenice's whereabouts. Parker desires a meeting at a warehouse along the Seine this Sunday night. The signal will be the playing of a musical instrument."

"I don't have that kind of money," pleaded Madame Trevor.

"It doesn't matter. The Chupin Detective Agency will gladly pay for this information in light of your niece's friendship with Irene. We will also be waiving our customary fee. I will contact you to report on the meeting's results."

"You're very generous," said Madame Trevor. "Thank you."

"Rosette has been very honest, Mademoiselle Putine," said Eva. "Don't you think that you should be equally forthcoming?"

"Eva!" reprimanded Madame Trevor. "You must apologize. Mademoiselle Putine has been extremely kind."

"But not altogether candid with us. She's Irene!"

"What has prompted this absurd conclusion?" asked Irina.

"The similarity of names: Irene Tupin–Irina Putine," said Eva.

"Despite the fact that Madame Trevor mentioned the horrible mutilation that befell Irene."

"You're wearing gloves."

"My hands are normal," said Irina. "You may examine them."

Irina removed her gloves. Eva gently touched her hands, puzzled at first, but then pushed back the silver bracelets.

"There are scars on your wrists! You have much explaining to do, Mademoiselle."

"My scars resulted from a suicide attempt."

"Why did you attempt suicide?" asked Madame Trevor.

"Are you familiar with the Nihilists?" said Irina.

"They're anarchists who murder Russian aristocrats."

"Yes. Years ago, I was in Paris with my Russian mother. The Nihilists murdered her and took me prisoner. Their vicious abuse prompted me to slit my wrists. Monsieur Chupin rescued me and became my legal guardian. I spent years at an English boarding school. Upon my return to France, Monsieur Chupin changed my name to avoid further Nihilist persecution. My alias is derived from his niece's name."

"Nihilists operate in Russia," challenged Eva. "This is France."

"Madame Relli, did you ever hear of Countess Yalta?"

"No, I haven't."

"I remember the case," said Madame Trevor. "The Countess was poisoned by the Nihilists in Paris 16 years ago. A hospital in Avignon was named after her."

"That is correct. Countess Yalta was my mother," said Irina.

"I don't recall any reference to a daughter in the newspapers."

"My parents were unmarried," replied Irina, lowering her head in shame.

"I'm sorry for forcing that admission. Eva, you must apologize to this gracious lady," said Madame Trevor.

After the two women had left, Irina, who was really Irene, mentally rehashed the lies she had just told. She had, in fact, gone to an English nursing home, not a boarding school, after her discharge from the Countess Yalta Memorial Hospital, where a surgeon had surreptitiously given her a new pair of hands.[4]

On Sunday night, Irina went with a satchel of money to the banks of the Seine. She was armed with an umbrella that concealed a sword. The docks were

---

[4] See "Dr. Cerral's Patient" in *Tales of the Shadowmen 2*.

deserted, except for a person playing a harmonica. The musician was a blonde woman whose physique resembled Irina's.

"Ain't you a swell, dearie," complimented the blonde, speaking English with a Cockney accent. "What's pinned to your chest? A pentagon?"

"Are you 'Parker?' "

"Purity Parker. You must work for Mrs. Trevor. Nice umbrella. What's on the handle? Looks like a horny horse."

"It's a unicorn's head."

"That ain't no unicorn, luv. I'm wearing a unicorn. A Black Skirts unicorn. Ain't it pretty?"

Irina experienced an odd feeling looking at Parker's uniform. Madame Fourneau had given her prefects similar dresses as gifts.

"What are the Black Skirts?"

"It's the new name for Madame Koluchy's Brotherhood. Why not call us the Sisterhood, eh? Maybe Koluchy don't want us confused with them Catholic Huns. I'm a personable jerk. I handle files on them that work for the Black Coats."

"You're a personnel clerk."

"Just what I said," concurred Parker pointing to a brown manila folder lying on a crate. "That's B. F.'s personable file. You can take a gander if you hand over the money."

"How did the Brotherhood hire you?" asked Irina.

"My brother Larry got me this job. He's Colonel Moran's chum."

"Your brother is Parker the Garotter?"

"My brother ain't no rotter! He's a strangler."

"My apologies. Why betray the Black Coats now?"

"The bigwigs made the Personable Deportment part of Koluchy's gang. The new boss wants to fire me. Bit of a fancy pants. Calls herself Milady Nevermore."

"Is her real name Kaitlin de Winter?"

"That's right. Kitty Winter. Kitty treats B. F. like trash."

"What's happening to B. F.?"

"Her Nibs locked her in the cellar. Very impotent persons are interested in her, too. Balls-Ammo took a peek at this file."

"Tell me more about Balsamo."

"I hear she's going to America."

"Take the money. Hand me the folder."

The two women made the exchange. Irina opened the file and read it under a lamppost. The contents confirmed all her suspicions. Purity opened the satchel, examined the bills and then closed it.

Absorbed in the file, Irina didn't notice a man moving in the shadows. His head was encased in a white, hood-like mask that formed an implacable face with high cheekbones and thin lips. The mask had slits from which the ears

77

protruded. The figure wore a black coat buttoned over a bare muscular chest. Black pants and gloves completed his costume. His right hand gripped a large sickle.

"Traitor!" yelled the man in black. *"Cut the branch!"*

The bizarre intruder leaped out of the darkness. His sickle made a wide sweep towards Purity. The blow was extremely swift. Irina never saw it make contact. All she saw was the Cockney's blood-soaked hand over her face. Stumbling backward with the satchel, Purity fell into the Seine.

"Murderer!" shouted Irina. Dropping the folder, she unsheathed the sword from her umbrella. Irina and the stranger thrust and parried back and forth. The duo locked blades near the dock's edge.

"Who are you?" demanded Irina.

"I am the Pallid Mask! Be grateful that I have no instructions to kill you!"

Pushing Irina away, the attacker jumped into the river. As the Pallid Mask vanished underneath the waters of the Seine, Irina recalled a play suppressed by the French government. The Pallid Mask had been another title for the Phantom of Truth in *Le Roi en Jaune*. The murderer had modeled his costume on the enigmatic character from the controversial drama.

Victor Chupin was back in Paris. His long Spanish trip had ended in failure. Roger Vollin, the leading French authority on the Spanish Inquisition, owned a torture blade created by the infamous Sebastian Medina in the 16th century. The blade had been stolen in Paris, and the thief's trail had led to Barcelona. Retained by Vollin, Chupin had futilely searched for the stolen artifact.

Inside his office, Chupin, a short man of 47 years, now perused Irina's report on the Berenice Fourneau investigation. Irina was seated in front of his desk.

"I told Madame Trevor that no one arrived for the rendezvous," she said. "She's now convinced that the letter was a hoax. We're fighting the Black Coats. I didn't wish to put her in harm's way."

"Irina, you must drop this inquiry. Berenice's a thief whose family has persecuted you."

"I can't abandon her–notwithstanding our dubious pasts and questionable relatives."

"I just don't understand your sense of obligation to her."

"When we were at school, she confided all her secrets to me. I was like a priest hearing a confession. She even told me her greatest fear."

"We have no hints to Berenice's whereabouts."

"The Black Skirt uniform is the key. It is sold by the House of Crafts, a London fashion firm operated by Madame Koluchy. Josephine Balsamo left the Fourneau school to work for Mrs. Moriarty, a former prefect. Years ago, I read the school's files on all my predecessors. Mrs. Moriarty's maiden name was Corbucci, although she was known at the school as Koluchy. Koluchy has to be

Countess Corbucci. She must be related to Count Corbucci, the Camorra leader. Rumors exist surrounding a daughter named Catarina. He hid her during a civil war inside the Camorra. Her sanctuary must have been the school.

"Berenice's file confirmed that Kaitlin de Winter was also recruited by Koluchy after she left the Institution Bachelard. The two then abducted Berenice and coerced her into thievery. Kaitlin tormented Berenice by stealing her jewelry. Berenice maintained her love of Charles Dickens, for her codename was 'Dodger.' Kaitlin's is 'Milady Nevermore,' a reference to both Dumas and Poe. Berenice is now her prisoner at the House of Crafts in London. She's in danger. I want us to go to London at once to deliver her."

"I'm afraid we can't," said Chupin. "We won't be ready for at least another week. 50,000 francs of our funds are lost at the bottom of the Seine. I must arrange a loan to avoid bankruptcy. If only the police had found the money when they recovered Purity's body."

"Waiting isn't an option. I'll go to London by myself then."

"Someone needs to watch your back. Take another operative with you."

"You know very well we can't spare anyone at the moment."

"We've had this conversation before, Irina. Why are you constantly running alone into danger? Are you punishing yourself for having been Madame Fourneau's prefect? You need to forget about that cursed school."

"I'll always have *these* to remind me," said Irina, extending her hands. "You know why I wear these gloves. It's because I can't stand to see the flesh beneath. Dr. Cerral gave me the hands of a girl whom I persecuted. I'm still haunted by her memories."

"You didn't kill her. In fact, you avenged her death."

"That act alone doesn't wipe the slate clean. I fear that I'll be damned for all eternity. If I rescue Berenice, then maybe God will forgive me."

"Very well," said Chupin. "Go to England alone then. But you must recruit a regular assistant."

"You want me to hire someone in London?"

"Yes. From one of our English competitors. I've tried to make inroads into the British market for years. The Agency needs someone familiar with London. Here's a list of candidates."

"Anna Beringer of Tyler's," said Irina. "I've heard of her. May I hire someone not on this list?"

"Only if it's someone with top credentials."

At the House of Crafts, Madame Koluchy had asked Milady to come to her office.

"Do you know Purity Parker, Milady?"

"A scatterbrain currently on vacation in Paris. We should remove her in the upcoming purge."

"That's no longer necessary. Her recent performance review indicated a potential for betrayal. As a precaution, I had her kept under surveillance. She was caught passing information to Irina Putine of the Chupin Detective Agency and was–terminated."

"Do we know what information she leaked?"

"One file was missing. Fortunately, we keep duplicates. Here it is."

"My old schoolmate's! Why is Putine interested in her?"

"They met at a boarding school in Provence. This is Putine's file."

Milady took the second file and read it. Besides Irina's role in solving the Bluebeard Murders, she had known nothing about the sleuth's past until studying this dossier.

Later, she went to the Archives to find more information about Irina. She returned to her office with a file on Dr. Anatole Cerral of the Countess Yalta Memorial Hospital in Avignon. As she put the file on her desk, she felt something brushing against her boot.

"Apollyon!" cried Milady with delight. She reached down to pick up a black cat. Petting it affectionately, she saw in the doorway a thin figure with dark hair and dark eyes. He wore a ring similar to Count Corbucci's. He had come to London to attend the gathering of the High Council.

"Our mutual friend missed you, but not as much as I," declared Dr. Antonio Nikola.

He had met Milady in 1889. As a favor for Koluchy, Nikola had visited the Institution Bachelard to evaluate a schoolgirl for induction into the Black Coats. He was so infatuated by the future ninja that he had given her a necklace. Koluchy introduced herself to her the following year.

Putting the cat aside, Milady embraced Nikola in a passionate kiss. Some minutes later, they studied Cerral's file while stoking the cat.

"I understand your interest. Cerral could theoretically engineer another limb transplant, but an optic replacement is beyond even his skills."

"I was hoping..." murmured Milady, rubbing her eye-patch.

Nikola touched her cheek affectionately.

"Don't worry about your outer beauty, my love. Nothing will ever mar your inner radiance."

"Excuse me," said Madame Koluchy entering the room. "I need to talk to *my* chief of staff."

Inside Tyler's Investigations in London, Irina met with Anna Beringer, a detective nearly her own age. Irina had enlisted Anna to help rescue Berenice. If she performed well, Irina planned to offer her a permanent job.

"I've been hearing rumors about these Black Skirts," volunteered Anna. "I've seen women wearing the uniform at a local thieves' den, *The Old Fellow*. My informant there, Porky Shinwell, says the women work at the House of Crafts. They even have identification cards."

"One of us needs to sneak inside that building by posing as a Black Skirt. Once we determine the layout, we can rescue Berenice by breaking in during the night."

"Your plan won't work. I'm too well known by the local criminals, and Josephine Balsamo knows you."

"She's probably in America by now. Is it unusual for the Black Skirts to wear gloves?" asked Irina.

"In this autumn weather, it's quite common. Black is the preferred color," Anna replied.

"Do any of the Black Skirts resemble me?"

"Yes, two: Mary Holder and Maude North."

"I must replace someone unimportant. What are their backgrounds?"

"Mary's the cast-off lover of Sir George Burnwell. Some small talent as a thief. A minor underling, at best. Maude, on the other hand, is a versatile impersonator. She instigates complex swindles with her husband. Our decision seems obvious."

"Yes. Clearly Mary."

That night at *The Old Fellow*, Porky Shinwell invited Mary Holder to share a glass of champagne with him in a backroom. When Mary entered the room, she was easily overpowered with chloroform by Anna and Irina. An identification card was found inside her purse. Irina quickly changed into Mary's uniform and immediately left the tavern.

The next morning, the Black Skirts reported for work at the House of Crafts. Scores of employees stood in a long line at the door. A gloved woman, believed to be Mary Holder, was constantly coughing into her handkerchief. The others, afraid to catch what she had, kept a polite distance from her. Irina presented Mary's card to the Black Skirt on duty at the front door. Her face was still largely covered by the handkerchief, but she glanced at the guard. Her eyes widened upon recognizing Josephine Balsamo.

Once inside, Irina wandered around the main floor for a few minutes. She was about to open a door leading to the basement when a hand tapped her shoulder.

"Excuse me, you're in a restricted area," said a harsh voice. "We haven't been properly introduced. I am Milady Nevermore. Show me your identification card!"

Hoping that Milady had never met Mary, Irina complied. Watching the one-eyed woman, Irina felt she was in the presence of a relentless enemy. Milady returned the card.

"Your name is Mary Holder. What were you doing here?"

Before Irena could spin a yarn, Josephine Balsamo surfaced abruptly.

"Mary's eyes are black. Yours are blue. You're–Irina Putine!"

Irina punched Josephine's jaw. The blonde woman fell down. The detective then hit Milady in the left eye, causing her to stagger a few steps back. Irina then twirled around to run, but her neck was quickly grasped from behind by Milady. The detective grabbed the wrists of her attacker, but she couldn't break the Black Skirts' hold.

"Balsamo, are you alright?" asked Milady, as Irina struggled futilely.

"Yes, Milady," answered Josephine rising from the ground.

"Our captive here is squirming. I could render her senseless by pinching a nerve, but a severe punch to the stomach should suffice. Will you oblige?"

"With pleasure," joyfully proclaimed Josephine as she delivered a sharp blow to Irina's stomach.

When Milady released her hands, the detective toppled forward. Milady bent down and patted the slumbering Irina's head in mock affection.

Elsewhere in the House of Crafts, three members of the High Council, Dr. Nikola, Madame Koluchy and Count Corbucci, were being harangued by Dr. Mabuse, a man of indeterminable age with a goatee. Mabuse was outlining his proposal for the Espionage Hotel.

"The hotel will be equipped with secret listening posts. Two-way mirrors will permit the listeners to spy upon the guests. The architect will be here soon."

Milady interrupted the meeting.

"I have captured an intruder–Irina Putine."

Koluchy, dressed in a black gown, extended her hand.

"*Will there be daylight?*" interrogated the matriarch of the Black Skirts.

"*It will be daylight from midnight to noon if it's the will of the Mother,*" answered Milady, ritually.

She then stooped down to kiss Koluchy's ring. An order of execution had been issued against Irina. As Milady left, she passed the architect who had just arrived to join the conference. Eva Relli and Milady exchanged greetings.

Irina regained consciousness in the basement of the House of Crafts. She was lying on a raised slab in the back of a dimly lit dungeon. Her arms and legs were shackled to the slab by her wrists and ankles. Six feet over her neck was an axe-like blade. Approximately 15 inches in width, it was attached to a metal pole leading upward to a series of clockwork-like gears in the ceiling.

"The Medina blade!" uttered Irina.

"You recognize my new toy," said Milady. "I crossed swords with your employer when I stole it. My false clues sent him on a wild goose chase to Barcelona. Medina's creation inspired a famous story by Poe. This blade was an early prototype. A later, larger blade could slice through a person's midriff, but this particular model is most effective at decapitation. I have attached it to a mechanism constructed in the best traditions of Poe."

Milady pointed to a series of levers on the ground.

"The lever near your right foot starts and stops the pendulum. The middle lever restores the blade to its starting position. The far lever opens and closes the shackles."

The farthest level was pointing towards Milady. She gazed at her reflection in a wall mirror.

"I'm very sensitive about my remaining eye. Your death would be more merciful if you hadn't struck me there."

"I merely struck a craven bully, the Right Dishonorable Nevermore."

"You seem familiar with certain exchanges between two schoolgirls. Our files documented your friendship with my other prisoner. No doubt you corresponded with her during her stay at the Institution Bachelard."

Milady pulled the innermost lever toward her. Swinging back and forth, the blade descended with each movement. The one-eyed woman went to a small table and picked up a ball of black yarn with two long needles.

"If you don't mind, Mademoiselle Putine, I'll knit to pass away the time."

"Do I get a last request?" asked Irina.

"I will grant it within reason."

"May I see my friend before I die?"

"Your reunion will be diverting. You probably haven't seen her in over a decade."

Putting the needles and yarn back on the table, Milady marched towards another cell. Opening the door with the keys from her belt, she hauled Dodger out.

"A friend desires your company," mocked Milady. "You're hiding something!"

Milady yanked a page out of Dodger's right sleeve. Throwing her back into the cell, Milady locked the door. She returned to the slab.

"Regrettably, Dodger–B. F.–has broken the rules of her confinement. Her visiting privileges have been revoked. I'm courteous enough to read this paper aloud. Maybe you'll find it entertaining. *Dearest Berenice, pray for my soul, I will... pray...*"

Milady couldn't finish. A tear formed in her eye. She placed the paper gently on the table.

The pendulum was now five feet above Irina. Suddenly, the truth consumed the detective.

"*The prisoner is not Berenice–she's Kaitlin! You're Berenice!* You abducted Kaitlin and forced her to join the Black Coats! You gave her the B. F nickname that she created for you! You called her Dodger! You took her title of Milady! You stole Kaitlin's belongings!"

"Am I supposed to be impressed? You already knew this. Parker gave you Kaitlin's file."

"We've both been fed false information. I never met Kaitlin before in my life."

"You met her at an English boarding school before she moved to Paris."

"I was never at an English boarding school."

"Yes, you were. Victor Chupin sent you there to escape the Nihilists."

"What Nihilists?"

"The Nihilists who murdered your mother."

"My mother?"

"Countess Yalta."

"Countess Yalta is not my mother! My mother's Victoire Chupin! *I'm Irene*!"

Irina felt trapped in a nightmare of her own making. Her own lies were now being used against her. Eva Relli must belong to the Black Coats. She had manipulated Rosette Trevor into contacting Irina to find Berenice, and had reported the cover story the detective had told them.

The pendulum plunged to four feet above Irina. Milady was outraged by Irina's claims.

"You lie! Irene's dead!"

"Compare the names Irina Putine and Irene Tupin."

"Victor Chupin gave you the alias of Irina Putine as a homage to his late niece."

"I know all the contents of your letters to Irene. I can prove it, too. Ask me any question."

"A pointless exercise. My letters must have come into Victor Chupin's possession. He showed them to you after seeing my real name in Kaitlin's file."

"But the letters were signed Blythe Furnace."

"The truth could easily be deduced. The same initials. The surname. Your claims are ludicrous. You have a pair of hands."

"My hands are the result of an experiment by a surgeon named Cerral."

"Most ingenious. I learned of Dr. Cerral while researching your Russian mother. You must have kept abreast of what transpired at the hospital named after your mother and used his theories as part of your ploy."

"Check the scars on my wrists!"

"The result of a suicide attempt during your imprisonment by the Nihilists."

The blade was swinging two feet above Irina.

"Koluchy hated your mother, because she beat her. She secretly loathes you too. She only wants to manipulate you into killing your best friend!"

"Parker must have told you about the false rumor that Madame Koluchy ordered the destruction of my mother's school..."

"She did! She worked in concert with Josephine. They were both beaten by your mother—just as I was! I couldn't tell you that in my letters."

The blade now dangled only a foot above Irina's neck.

"Stop lying about my mother!" screamed Milady.

"At school–in the storeroom–there, you told me things that were not in your letters. Your greatest fear..."

"You're stalling for time!"

The blade was beginning its final descent.

"Be very careful now," hissed Milady. "The blade's even with your chin."

The blade rotated to the right.

"Berenice, your greatest fear was becoming..."

Irina stopped talking as the blade passed over her Adam's apple and swooshed to the left.

"...someone like your mother."

Irina closed her eyes in anticipation of her own death, but it did not come. She opened her eyes. Milady had pressed the switch to stop the blade. Its edge was an inch from slicing the left side of her neck. The shackles sprang open. Moving slowly to her right, Irina rose from the slab.

"Irene," sobbed Milady.

"Yes–Berenice."

"I'm not the girl from the storeroom anymore... I was full of despair when I thought you died. I wanted to strike out at the world. Koluchy offered me power. You wouldn't understand..."

"I understand all too well. Your mother and Josephine made me the same offer."

Milady opened Kaitlin's cell door with her keys.

"Kaitlin de Winter, I grant you your freedom. You know the exits from this building, Please take Irene to safety."

"Kaitlin, why did you keep that dedication page torn from *Oliver Twist*?" asked Irina, helping the other woman to get back to her feet.

"At the Institution Bachelard, Berenice claimed to have proof that I had vandalized her quarters. I went to see her with the page, hoping to trade it in exchange for her silence. But I was overpowered by her and Koluchy. During my years of servitude, my only comfort was prayer. Reading your inscription reminded me to pray."

"You'll soon all be saying your prayers!" said a woman's voice.

The wall mirror had swung open, revealing a secret passage behind it.

Madame Koluchy emerged with a pistol. Following her were Dr. Mabuse and Count Corbucci, both armed with pistols, Josephine Balsamo, Eva Relli, the Pallid Mask, armed with his sickle, and a woman with black hair. She pointed to her uniform.

"My Black Skirt unicorn lured you here," announced the woman in an unmistakable Cockney accent.

"Purity Parker!" said Irina.

"No, I'm Maude North," said the Black Skirt, switching to a cultured voice. "The Pallid Mask is Mr. North. The real Purity accepted my offer to take a joint vacation to Paris and I used a blonde wig to impersonate her. My husband's blade never touched my face. A vial of pig's blood was concealed in my hand. I streaked my face with it before falling into the Seine and swimming to safety with your 50,000 francs. After that, we killed the real Purity, disfigured her and threw her body into the river."

While the others covered the three women with their guns, Josephine strolled over to the pendulum. By manipulating the switches, she retracted the deadly blade back to its original height.

"Dr. Mabuse's concept of an Espionage Hotel came from this prototype," explained Eva, pointing at the mirror. "It's enabled us to see everything."

"Milady, lie down on the slab," said Koluchy. "Maude and Eva, restrain the others."

After Milady had complied, Josephine closed the shackles. Maude held Irina's arms from behind. Eva did the same to Kaitlin.

Josephine pulled out one of the needles from the ball of thread on the table.

"You shouldn't have mocked my title, Berenice. And you not even being a true 'Milady.' But I remembered a letter to Irene, from my days as a censor, describing a necklace in the shape of a cat's head–a gift from an admirer to the writer. Seeing that necklace around your neck, I suspected you were Blythe Furnace. Your prisoner's real personnel file later identified you as Berenice Fourneau."

Irina had also recognized the necklace, but the false personnel file had misled her. It depicted the jewelry as property stolen from Berenice by Kaitlin.

"Josephine came to me after she deduced your identity," said Koluchy. "She warned me that you might betray us if you ever found out that Irina Putine was your best friend, Irene Chupin. For years, Eva Relli had been spying on your aunt. We arranged this affair to test your loyalty. Josephine's title of nobility is hereby restored as reward for her cleverness. Her executive rank is also restored. You're the branch that needs cutting, I'm afraid."

"I'll appeal to the High Council," said Berenice. "Dr. Nikola won't permit this."

"He can speak for himself!" said Count Corbucci. "Antonio, please join us."

Nikola entered from the wall panel.

"Excellency, do I have your permission to speak freely to the condemned?"

Corbucci nodded his head in approval. Nikola treaded slowly towards the woman he had known as Milady. His hand brushed the ball of thread with the remaining needle. He stoked the hair of his shackled lover gently.

"Berenice, I owe everything I am to the Black Coats. They rescued me from starvation in Cuba. I cannot defy them. Not even for you."

Nikola bent down and kissed her on the lips. As he walked away, he spied Irina being held by Maude. Nikola moved in front of the detective. He seized her wrists.

"I curse the day when my precious Milady befriended you."

Nikola spat in Irina's face and then released her hands. He turned to Corbucci.

"I do not need to witness this execution, Excellency. I ask permission to return to my hotel."

Although a ruthless man, Corbucci possessed genuine affection for Nikola. He sensed the younger man's need for solace.

"Your request is granted, Antonio. Furthermore, I shall accompany you."

Corbucci and Nikola left the dungeon.

"I know why you're doing this, Koluchy!" said Berenice. "My mother isn't the only reason. There's Antonio! You couldn't stand the thought of another woman in your ex-fiancé's arms!"

"Countess Cagliostro, perform your duty. *Cut the branch!*" ordered Koluchy.

Standing over Berenice's right side, Josephine raised the needle like a sacrificial knife.

"You will die by the pendulum, but you will only hear the blade. I'm removing your other eye."

While the Black Coats focused their attention on Josephine, another needle dropped from Irina's right sleeve into her hand.

She stabbed Maude's left hand. Crying in pain, the woman let go of her grip on the detective. Irina broke completely free and sprang toward the slab. She pushed the outermost lever forward. Berenice's shackles snapped open. Irina then tackled Josephine.

Berenice whirled off the slab. Mabuse and Koluchy both fired their pistols, but the shots missed. A swift leg kick from the one-eyed woman hit Koluchy in the stomach. She collapsed, overcome by pain. Berenice then delivered a brutal punch to Mabuse's face. He, too, fell unconscious.

Meanwhile, Eva Relli was struggling to restrain Kaitlin. Busting loose, the former schoolgirl had turned around and delivered a devastating series of blows to the blonde woman's body.

The Pallid Mask swung his sickle at Berenice's head, but it passed harmlessly over her as she dropped to the ground. Swinging around, her extended right leg hit the man's feet. He smashed into the ground. Maude's uninjured hand snatched Mabuse's gun from the ground, but Berenice was faster and grabbed her arm. The Pallid Mask got up and sprang forward, lunging with his sickle. Berenice threw Maude in his direction. The blade pierced her stomach.

"Juan..." gasped Maude as she died.

Dropping his sickle, the speechless Pallid Mask let his wife's body slump to the floor. He gripped Berenice's throat with both hands. The one-eyed woman delivered two karate chops to her antagonist's arms. The Mask released his clasp. Plucking the man's right arm, Milady flipped him off his feet. As the chalk-faced assailant was lifting himself up, she kicked him in the jaw. The Pallid Mask crumbled in a senseless heap.

Berenice saw Kaitlin standing above a vanquished Eva. Irina and Josephine, however, were still struggling on the ground. The needles were in each combatant's right hand. Each woman was holding the other's wrist with her free hand.

Berenice seized the back of Josephine's neck and pulled her away from Irina. The blonde woman dropped her needle. Berenice then shoved Josephine into Kaitlin's former cell and locked the door. With Irina and Kaitlin's help, she deposited the other Black Coats in neighboring cells.

"You'll regret sparing my life!" screamed Josephine from her cell. "I know how you escaped. Nikola hid the other needle up his sleeve before kissing you. He then slipped it to Irina and maneuvered Corbucci to safety. Koluchy will figure out everything. Someone will die for this. *Cut the branch*! This time, that *branch* will be your lover!"

"I doubt it. Antonio will question Koluchy's motives in engineering my disgrace. Allegations about her hatred for my mother will be tabled. Koluchy can't afford another fight with the Alumni. You're a more convenient *branch*! This is your third failure! Farewell–Countess!"

"What happened to Kaitlin and Berenice after your escape?" asked Victor Chupin.

Irina was briefing her uncle at the Chupin Detective Agency.

"Kaitlin insisted on being taken to the home of Baron Gruner. He should protect her from any further persecution. Before leaving London, Berenice burglarized Maude's apartment. Here are the 50,000 francs that Maude stole from us. Earlier in the dungeon, Berenice detached the Medina blade from the torture device. We delivered it to the Vollin estate. This is Roger's check for its retrieval. Berenice's staying as a guest of the Vollins for the present."

"Roger has an impressionable 14-year-old son. I hope Berenice doesn't give young Richard any bad ideas. We need to discuss one final matter, your new assistant."

"This employment contract merely needs your signature. My choice wasn't on the list."

"This contract is for Blythe Furnace!"

"Berenice is reviving her old alias."

"But I said it had to be someone with top credentials."

"Besides the skills of an Iga ninja, Blythe possesses a rich knowledge of the London underworld. And she solved a mystery that even stumped you: The Case of the Purloined Pendulum."

"This isn't funny, Irina! The woman's a homicidal lunatic. She nearly beheaded you."

"A clear misunderstanding–atoned for by her subsequent actions."

"Not in my eyes! Let her seeks atonement in a nunnery or an asylum."

"If you persist, I might resign and open a competing agency with her."

Victor Chupin sighed. He couldn't bear the thought of a separation from his niece. Reluctantly signing the contract, he silently prayed that this document wasn't her death warrant.

Like Harry Dickson and Fascinax, the Sâr Dubnotal is another anonymously-created hero from the French pre-World War I pulps. Some have credited writer Norbert Sevestre for the creation of this early master of the mystic arts, but that is very much in doubt. Roman Leary, who is new to Tales of the Shadowmen, *has chosen to co-star this supernatural defender with another crime-fighter, also forged amongst the Tibetan snows. It is in New York's notorious Hell's Kitchen district that the two meet in a tale entitled...*

Roman Leary: *The Evils Against Which We Strive*

New York, 1927

I will never forget the day I saw the stranger standing outside Miss Nolan's door. I have made many memories since that distant summer day in 1927, but few are as vivid as the sight of that extraordinary man. His stylish morning coat would have been enough to mark him as a man apart in the Hell's Kitchen tenement where I lived, but it was merely incidental compared to the multicolored sash he wore about his waist, or the immaculate white turban that crowned his head. His angular features were framed by a neatly trimmed beard which was only a few shades darker than his deeply-tanned skin.

I was only nine years old, and I had never seen such a man outside of the illustrations in a copy of *Arabian Nights*. I was watching him nervously through a crack in my own front door and wondering what he could possibly want with Miss Nolan, when he suddenly turned and looked directly at me. I felt an ice pick stab of panic, but something kept me from slamming the door and shooting the bolt. Instead, I simply peered back at the man and we regarded one another for a long, silent moment. Slowly, the corners of his mouth turned up in a smile.

"It is all right, lad," he said. "You can come out if you like. I am a friend."

His English was flawless, but heavy with an accent that I was too provincial and inexperienced to recognize. I could only imagine what my father would say if he caught me speaking to this man, one of the "dam' foreigners" he sometimes ranted about in his drunken tirades. Fortunately, Da was passed out on our tattered sofa and I knew from long experience that he wouldn't be awake for many hours yet. So, curiosity overpowering my fear, I stepped into the hallway.

"Allow me to introduce myself," said the man. "I am the Sâr Dubnotal, the Great Psychagogue, called by some the Napoleon of the Intangible." He gave a deep bow and then, to my great relief, he added, "But you can call me *Doctor*."

He gazed at me expectantly with his piercing green eyes. I knew I should say something, but I was in such a state of awe that I could only stand and gape.

For an awful moment, I almost ran back into my apartment, but then I thought of Miss Nolan and how disgusted she would be if I behaved in such a cowardly way. She had been very impatient with me lately, and I didn't want the stranger to tell her I had been rude to him. I forced myself to stand up straight and hold out my hand.

"It's very nice to meet you, Doctor," I said. "I'm Nick."

"It is an honor to make your acquaintance, Nick," said the Doctor, and he shook my hand as if I were another splendid gentleman like himself, rather than a pale, sickly boy dressed in rags.

Emboldened by his friendliness, I asked, "Where are you from, sir?"

"Many places," he said, "but France is the country I call my home."

I brightened considerably. "I know about France! Miss Nolan gave me a copy of *The Three Musketeers*. It was a hard book, but when I finished it, she took me to the zoo. Do you know Miss Nolan?"

"Should I?"

"I thought you were getting ready to knock on her door."

"Ah," said the Doctor. "As it happens, I do not know Miss Nolan, but I would very much like to meet her. Do you know if she is at home?"

"No, sir, she's at her bookshop."

"*Her* bookshop? She is the proprietor?"

"She used to just work there, but the old lady who owned it died, and she left it to Miss Nolan in her will."

"Remarkable," said the Doctor. "Do you know the name of this bookshop, Nick? Or where I can find it?"

I was about to answer, and then I caught myself. Why was I telling so much to this strange man? What if he wanted to hurt Miss Nolan?

"I promise I do not mean any harm to Miss Nolan," the Doctor said.

I gasped. "How did you know I was thinking that?" I whispered. I was frankly terrified, but too fascinated to turn away. "Are you a genie?"

"Hardly," he said with a smile. "And I did not read your mind. Your thoughts were plainly evident upon your face."

I frowned, and felt the face in question flush with embarrassment. At this, he favored me with a look of mild rebuke. "Come, now," he said. "Do not look so abashed. You are right to be cautious. You are old enough to know there is evil in this world."

I thought of my Da, and then buried that shameful thought before the Doctor could read that on my face as well. "So how can I know that you're a good guy?" I asked. "Why are you looking for Miss Nolan anyway?"

"Those are fair questions," the Doctor said. He gestured toward the nearby stairwell. "Why don't we sit down for a moment and discuss it?"

"OK," I said, and we did just that. I can hardly convey how strange it was to be sitting there with the Sâr Dubnotal. Regal though he was, he seemed perfectly at ease in those shabby surroundings, and I could almost imagine that we were sitting together in some exclusive club for wealthy tycoons, instead of on the top step of a filthy stairwell.

"Nick, I am very concerned about Miss Nolan," the Doctor said. "I think that she may need my help."

"How can you know that? You didn't even know her name until I told it to you."

"I will explain." His eyes fixed on a point in the middle distance. "I am here in New York to visit a friend with whom I have been corresponding, a certain Judge Pursuivant. I was meditating in my hotel room when I sensed a disturbance in the astral plane which..."

"The *what*?" I interrupted, thoroughly confused and wondering what Miss Nolan had to do with airplanes.

The Doctor sighed. "Of course," he said, mostly to himself, "silly of me." He looked me squarely in the eye. "Nick," he said in a quiet voice, "last night I had a feeling that something very bad was happening, and my feelings with regard to such things are never, *ever* wrong. Just as one can follow smoke to a fire, I have followed that feeling to this building," he pointed down the hall, "to that apartment. Do you understand?"

"Yes," I whispered, and though it sounded a little crazy, even to the ears of a child, the Doctor was so grave and assured that it was impossible to disbelieve him.

"Excellent," he said. "Now, tell me, do you care for Miss Nolan?"

"She's my best friend in the whole world."

"Do you spend a lot of time with her?"

"She lets me stay with her when my Da..."

"Yes?"

I tore my eyes away from his penetrating gaze. "I visit her a lot."

"I see," he said, and I am sure that he did. "I want you to think very carefully about what I am going to ask you now. Has Miss Nolan done or said anything recently that seemed strange to you?"

"Well...she won't play checkers anymore."

"Really?"

"Yes, sir. She used to love it, but now she says it's..." my brow furrowed as I tried to find the word. "*Infantile*, that's it. She's been showing me how to play chess."

The Doctor raised a single eyebrow. "And how are you progressing?" he asked.

"I'm not very good. She yells at me a lot."

"Did she ever do that before?"

"No," I said, and I thought I sounded very small and weak. I looked down at the steps.

"Is there anything else?" the Doctor asked. In my mind, I could hear a faint echo of Miss Nolan's voice, icy with rage: *You insolent whelp!*

"Nick?" the Doctor asked, as gentle and persuasive as a caring father.

You insignificant maggot!

"Please look at me, Nick."

I clenched my teeth and stared resolutely at the floor. Inside me there was a sudden rush of anger toward the Sâr Dubnotal. Why was he making me talk about these things? Why wouldn't he just leave me alone? I felt the curses I had learned from my Da curling on my tongue, eager to be spit into his face. Snarling in defiance, I turned to him…and I was immediately struck dumb by what I saw.

The Doctor, his eyes glittering like emeralds, was casually walking a gold dollar to and fro across the knuckles of his right hand. Suddenly, he clenched his fist and the coin disappeared. Then he turned his wrist, slowly opened his hand, and the coin was sitting up on its edge, perfectly balanced in his palm.

I was dazzled by this sleight of hand, and in my amazement I momentarily forgot my anger and pain. My reprieve, however, was short-lived.

"Nick," the Doctor said, "I know it hurts you to discuss these things, but I'm afraid it's necessary. I cannot help if I am not privy to all the facts. However, there is a way you can give me the information I need without having to actually talk about it."

"There is?"

"Yes. Unfortunately, you still have to *remember* it. It will not be a very pleasant experience, but it will be of invaluable assistance to me."

"Assist you how?" I asked, a petulant whine creeping into my voice. "What exactly do you want to know?"

"I want to know why Miss Nolan doesn't like checkers anymore," he said, without a hint of irony or sarcasm. "Will you help me?"

I considered it for a moment. He was such a strange man, but everything about him inspired feelings of confidence and trust. Of course, I knew from my books that all the best villains did the same thing, but I couldn't persuade myself that he was bad. I glanced at the coin, still steady and straight on its edge in the center of his hand, and I made my decision. "What do you want me to do?" I asked.

"Keep your eyes on the coin," he whispered.

Slowly at first, then with increasing rapidity, the coin began to spin. I felt a chill despite the summer heat.

"How are you doing that?" I asked, and my voice seemed to come from some distance far outside of myself.

"I am the Great Psychagogue," he replied, as if that explained it. "Concentrate on the coin. See how it reflects the light. Let everything else around you fall away…"

As he said these words, I felt a sudden lightness, and my surroundings seemed to grow hazy and indistinct. I felt as if I were slipping into a fever dream.

"Do not be frightened by what you are feeling," the Doctor said. "I will be with you on every step of this journey."

The stairs completely disappeared into a dark, grey mist. The air was cool and dry, and I could no longer feel the floor beneath me. All the while, floating before my eyes, the coin continued to spin, flickering like a golden star.

Then, there came a sense of gentle descent, and I could once again feel the wood of the steps. The flickering light began to slow, then ceased. The hall re-formed, but retained a certain dim, artificial quality, as if it were an imperfect reproduction constructed from someone's flawed and fading…memory.

I felt a shock of realization. I heard the Doctor's voice, not with my ears but with my mind. *That is correct, Nick*, he said. *We are within your memories.*

There was a creaking on the steps. I looked down and saw Miss Nolan, bundled in a heavy coat and brushing flakes of snow from her shoulders. There was a package with a red bow in the crook of her arm, and I recognized it as a gift she had given me at Christmas, a used copy of *The Book of a Hundred Games.*

She was then, and remains to this day, my ideal not only of feminine beauty, but of Beauty itself. Petite, red-haired and freckled, she was the very archetype of the fair Irish colleen, and seeing her filled me with such love that my heart ached.

She looked up and saw me, and her blue eyes narrowed with concern. "Nick!" she exclaimed. "What are doing out here? You're going to catch your death of cold!"

I wanted to answer, but I couldn't. Startled, I tried to stand up, but my body wouldn't respond. *Do not be alarmed*, I heard the Doctor say. *You are a dreamer, conscious of the fact you are dreaming, but powerless to control your actions. Relax, and let yourself be pulled by the strings of memory.*

Miss Nolan knelt in front of me. "So," she said, "in his cups again, is he?" I slowly nodded. "Oh, well," she sighed, "may as well be mad at the sky for being blue. Maybe if your Ma hadn't died so young…" She shook her head, and then her expression of dismay vanished with a mischievous wink. "Tell you what, why don't we have some hot chocolate?"

At last I spoke. "Can we? With whipped cream?"

She gave an exaggerated scowl. "What do you think this is, my boy, the Waldorf-Astoria?" She laughed and tousled my hair. "Come along, Master Rockefeller. I hope you'll forgive us for not having cream tonight."

Suddenly, the scene changed and we were in Miss Nolan's apartment. I was sitting with her on a couch, a steaming cup of cocoa in my hand. "Have you made any progress on *Robinson Crusoe*?" she asked.

"It's too hard," I whined. "Why can't I keep reading *Tom Swift*?"

"You can, but I want you to read other things, too. I want you to challenge yourself, Nick." She reached over and tapped my forehead. "You have a good mind, so I want to see you use it. I want you to be living better than this when you get to be my age."

"You're not doing so bad," I assured her.

"Think so, do you? Twenty-four years old with no decent man to speak of? Barely scraping by working as a clerk in some old lady's bookshop? And a haunted one at that?"

"Haunted?" I asked. "By a ghost?"

"Well, what else, silly? I've heard it a couple of times coming from the cellar."

"What does it sound like?"

She frowned. "It sounds like a crying child. I've gone down there to look, but I can never find anything. I asked Mrs. Bishop about it, and she says she hears it all the time. 'Pay it no heed,' says she. 'It's just another lost and forgotten soul.' Pretty spooky, eh?" I nodded vigorously, and then the cocoa was gone and Miss Nolan had her arm around me, holding me close. I felt myself drifting into sleep, lulled by her warmth and the sound of her heartbeat against my ear. "I want you to listen to me, Nick," she said. "I'm going to give you a key. Anytime that I'm not here and your old man gets to be a bit too much, you can come over and stay, OK?"

"Yes, ma'am," I said in a drowsy whisper.

"That's a good boy," she said.

Then I was awake again, sitting on the couch alone, reading by a feeble ray of spring sunshine. I was on the last chapter of *Robinson Crusoe*, and consumed with elation at being so near to the end. There was a rattle at the door, and Miss Nolan stepped into the room. "Now there's a handsome man to come home to," she said with a grin. "I was hoping you'd be here. You can help me celebrate!"

"You got a new job?" I said.

"Oh, better than that! Nick, my boy, I deserve a good swift kick for every time I ever complained about dear, sweet, lovable Mrs. Emily Bishop, God rest her soul!"

"What do you mean? You always said she was nasty. When she died two weeks ago, you said..."

"Bite your tongue, my lad! That wonderful lady, that *angel*, has reached out from the grave and delivered me into a better life!"

"How did she do that?"

"She left me everything, Nick! Do you understand? She wrote a will and left me everything she owned!" Laughing, she took my hands and led me in a little victory dance. Then a disturbing thought occurred to me, and I gave it voice: "Does this mean you're going to move away?"

Miss Nolan sat down on the couch and pulled me down with her. "Now, Nick," she said, "sometimes a person's circumstances can change and they...and they..." A far-away look came into her eyes, and then she winced as if in pain.

"Are you all right?" I asked, leaning in close. She roughly pushed me away.

"Yes," she said sharply. "Yes, I'm perfectly fine. It's just my head... Sometimes it hurts." She started rubbing her temples. "It started about a month ago, right after Mrs. Bishop got sick. It always goes away after a few minutes. I just have to... Oh...God..." She gasped and curled into a fetal ball. For a moment I was panic-stricken. She was clearly in agony and I had no idea what to do. I was even considering going to Da for help, when she suddenly sat upright. She looked at me for a moment as if she were surprised to see me, then gave me a peculiar little half-smile.

"Distressed, boy?" she asked. It seemed like such an odd thing to say, and was said in such a mocking tone, that I wasn't sure how to respond. I waited for her to say more, but she just kept staring at me with that strange, impish look. Her eyes, normally so gentle, began to burn with a predatory cruelty. She was scaring me, and must have sensed this, because she blinked a few times and appeared normal again...almost.

"I'm sorry, child," she said. "You must forgive my behavior. It's these dreadful headaches. They can really be quite debilitating. Now, as I was saying, you are clearly concerned that I will be leaving you to your own devices in this...place." She looked around with a sneer, then seemed to force herself to smile. "But you must not trouble yourself. You are very important to me, you see."

"I am?" I said, and my misgivings disappeared at the pleasure of hearing her say this.

"Oh, yes!" she exclaimed. "In fact, I don't think I could live without you."

No one—not even Miss Nolan—had ever said something like that to me before, and I was over the Moon. I rushed forward and hugged her, barely noticing the stiffness and hesitation of her returned embrace. Then she softened and some of the familiar warmth and affection returned to her arms.

"Steady on, Nick," she said with a laugh. "What's brought all this on?"

"You're the nicest person in the world," I said.

"Am I? Well, I suppose I'd be foolish to argue with a thing like that."

I looked up at her, and the strange and unpleasant light that had danced in her eyes was gone. "Is your head better?" I asked.

"My head?" Her eyes narrowed in confusion. "It *was* hurting again, wasn't it?" She brightened a little. "But it's all gone now, thank the Lord."

There was a sudden stillness, and everything around me seemed to freeze; a moment trapped in amber. I couldn't understand what was happening. I felt a rising panic as I gazed into Miss Nolan's now vacant eyes.

We have to go forward, Nick. I heard the Doctor say. *Please release us from this memory.*

But I'm not doing this! I cried out to him, but even as I thought the words, I realized I was wrong. In fact, I was doing it, and I knew why. *Please bring me out*, I implored. *Just let it all stop here.*

I will not force you to continue, Nick. But let me ask you this, do you believe I have seen all I need to see?

I did not respond.

This is the last pleasant memory you have of Miss Nolan, isn't it?

I let my silence stand for a yes, and I refused to say anything more. I expected the Doctor to grow angry at me for my obstinacy, but all I could sense from him was pity, which was somehow worse. *Very well*, he said, and I thought I could hear him sigh. *I will count down from...*

No! I interrupted. *I'll show you the rest. I'll show you everything.* I concentrated...and entered a kaleidoscope of pain.

– I sit, nervous and bewildered, staring at a chessboard while Miss Nolan berates me for an obtuse clod.

– I feel her cuff me on the back of the head. *Cocoa?! Impertinent brat! Am I your serving wench?*

– I see her on the floor, holding her head, writhing in pain. *What's happening to me? Why is this happening to me?* I go to her and looks up at me, frightened and imploring. *I'm losing me! I'm...I'm... Away from me, boy! I don't need your help! Go back to your sot of a father!*

I cried out, whether aloud or only in my mind I cannot say. I felt myself plunging into the black abyss where I had buried the worst moments of my young life. I rushed headlong through the death of my mother; through a hundred beatings from Da; through a thousand cuts of Miss Nolan's increasing and unaccountable cruelties...

...I am standing outside of Miss Nolan's door. On the other side, I can hear a low, guttural chanting, punctuated by a series of small cries. In my hand, I hold the key that she gave me, and I resolve to use it. I quietly step into the apartment. The room is saturated with a dull, yellow glow coming from some indeterminate source. Miss Nolan is sitting on the floor, her back turned to me. She is naked, but her body is covered with symbols and writing I cannot understand. The chanting and the crying is emanating from her, but it does not sound like her voice. She falls silent, and sees me over her shoulder. *You dare?* she says, low and dangerous. *You dare disturb me now?*

My mouth moves but no sounds come out. I want to run, but I am rooted to the spot.

Nothing to say? She rises to her feet and turns to face me. The strange runes and foreign script cover her from head to toe. *Tell me boy, do you like to see me this way?*

I shake my head. I don't like it at all.

No? Why is that?

My mouth feels as if it is full of sand, but I force myself to answer. *Because this isn't you,* I whisper.

She laughs. *That is an interesting observation. Perhaps you are more intelligent than I presumed. If so, then you won't have any difficulty learning this lesson.* She steps forward and strikes my face with the back of her hand. *Look at me, you insignificant maggot!* She grasps my chin and forces me to look into her eyes. They were once blue, those eyes, but now they have darkened to black. *If you ever again come unbidden into my presence,* she says, *I will thrash you until you bleed. Do you understand?* I say that I do, and she strikes me again, hard enough to send me to my knees. *You do not weep,* she observes, standing over me.

It never does any good, I reply.

There is a long silence, and then she is helping me to my feet. *Go,* she says, *and remember your lesson.* She slams the door behind me and...

Please, Doctor...

She slams the door behind me...

Please bring me back...

She slams the door...

Please...

...I was once again sitting at the top of the stairs, staring at a spinning coin in the hand of the Sâr Dubnotal. For a moment I could not move or speak. The thought occurred to me that I was still trapped in the labyrinth of my memories. I felt a rising horror at the possibility I would have to travel those dark corridors again, but then the Doctor's hand closed. "It's over, Nick," he said. "You have done well."

Relieved beyond measure, I closed my eyes and took a deep, shuddering breath. "Did you find out what you needed to know?" I asked.

"Yes," he said. "I was able to see things through your eyes which were very telling." He turned his head and pointed to the side of his face. It was red and inflamed as if he had been struck. "I felt things, too."

"I'm sorry," I said.

"You have nothing to apologize for. I made you relive those memories. It is right that I should share your pain." He stood up and brushed off his pants. "Now, my lad," he said, "I have to see about some things. I have a very good idea what is happening here, and who is responsible for it. But I need to confirm my suspicions."

I stood up too. "What about Miss Nolan?" I asked, and I could barely keep myself from clutching at his coat like some desperate beggar. "Can you help her? I mean, can you make her...be like she used to be?"

"I do not know, Nick," he said, and my heart fell. "However," he added, "I give you my word that I shall do my best, and the Sâr Dubnotal always keeps his word." He held out his hand, and I shook it. "We will see each other again," he said, and he went down the stairs.

I waited until I could no longer hear his footfalls, then sank back to the floor. I was still sitting there, exhausted and consumed with an inexpressible sadness, when I became aware of an object in my right pocket. I reached into it, and when my hand emerged, it was holding the Sâr Dubnotal's golden coin. In spite of all I had endured that afternoon, I found myself smiling.

Many hours later, after Da had gone out for his nightly prowls, I sat alone in the apartment listening to the warm wind rattle our single windowpane. There was an occasional flash of lightning, and the rumble of approaching thunder held the promise of a summer storm that, hopefully, would break the suffering heat.

I was staring with listless disinterest at a copy of *Tom Swift and the Land of Wonders*. Ordinarily, I could always count on good old Tom to take me away from my troubles, but that night I couldn't think of anything but Miss Nolan and the Sâr Dubnotal. Every few minutes I found myself reaching for the gold dollar in my pocket, holding it up to the light, reminding myself that it was real. In fact, I was doing that very thing when I heard a tapping at the door. I opened it a crack, and saw Miss Nolan smiling at me.

"I owe you an apology, boy," she said sweetly. "I'm afraid I've been quite hard on you lately. Why don't you come over and allow me to make amends?"

I wanted to run to her, but the devastating memories dredged up by the Doctor were still fresh in my mind. I hesitated, remembering the sting of her hand against my cheek.

Miss Nolan kneeled, making her eyes level with my own. "Afraid?" she whispered. "There's no need. Come with me, and all of your pain will end. I promise."

Even at that age I knew that was a vow no one could keep, but I didn't care. All that mattered was the kindness I thought I could hear in her voice. For a smile and some kindness, I would have forgiven her of a thousand false promises. I opened the door and rushed into her arms. I could have cheerfully stayed in her embrace forever, but she quickly pulled away from me and led me to her apartment. We stepped inside and, to my surprise, I saw that the room was illuminated solely by an arrangement of candles spread out over the floor.

"I'm going to show you a new game tonight, boy," she said as she closed the door.

"Is it as hard as chess?" I asked, filled with a sudden foreboding.

"Oh, no," she said with a laugh. "You'll find these rules to be very simple." I gave a sigh of relief, which turned to a gasp as my eyes adjusted to the gloom.

Drawn on the floor were a series of large, interlocking circles, each containing a mad jumble of letters and symbols, which, with horror, I immediately recognized. They were the same ones I had seen painted on Miss Nolan's body.

I turned in time to see her bolting the door. She was still wore a smile, but now it was little more than a thin, red slash across her pallid face. In her right hand she was holding a knife. She walked toward me, and I stepped back until I was in the center of the pattern of circles.

"What are you doing?" I asked, frightened and confused.

"She intends to kill you," said a voice behind me, and the smile disappeared from Miss Nolan's face.

I turned, and saw a patch of darkness shaped like a man detach itself from the shadows. It wore a slouch hat pulled low over its face, and a long black cloak, which, as it moved, revealed a flash of crimson lining.

"Hello, murderess," it said to Miss Nolan, and its voice was like a whisper of wind between forgotten graves.

"Who are you?" Miss Nolan asked in a fearful whisper.

There was a thoughtful silence, followed by a low chuckle. "My enemies once called me *Der Schwarze Adler*," said the living shadow, "The Black Eagle."

Miss Nolan visibly struggled to gather her nerve. She crossed her arms, hiding the wicked gleam of her knife. "Boy," she said, never taking her eyes from the Eagle, "come here to me."

I didn't move.

"Do as I say, boy! This man is dangerous! Get over here, now!"

I looked at the dangerous man. Beneath the brim of his hat burned a pair of black eyes that seemed to smolder like coals. He was the living personification of every night terror I had ever known, but somehow I did not fear him. "Why did you say she was going to kill me?" I asked.

"She has killed many children," he replied, "most of them even younger than you."

"You lie!" Miss Nolan shouted.

The room filled with a hollow, mocking laugh. "Do not waste your breath," the Black Eagle snarled. "I have been to your little bookshop, and I have stood in the charnel house you have hidden behind the walls of the cellar."

There was a flash of lightning outside the window, and Miss Nolan looked as if it had struck her between the eyes.

"Oh, yes," hissed the menacing man in black. "I have seen their bones. In life they were poor, homeless, forgotten. You looked at them and saw the perfect victims for your perverse rituals. You thought you could pluck them from the streets and no one would notice. No one would care. But you were wrong."

The cloak rustled, and a pair of automatic pistols appeared in the Black Eagle's hands.

"*I* noticed," he said. "*I* cared. And tonight I have come for a reckoning."

"No!" I cried out. I stepped in front of Miss Nolan and held up my arms in an attempt to shield her. "You're wrong! She'd never do anything like that! It must have been the old lady, Mrs. Bishop! She told Miss Nolan not to listen to the sounds in the cellar! She said it was ghosts! She was..."

I was interrupted by Miss Nolan, who suddenly lifted me in her arms–and pressed the edge of her knife to my throat.

"Leave us!" she commanded the Shadow.

The Black Eagle laughed. His guns were steady, unwavering. Outside the window, there was a tremendous crack of thunder and the rain began to fall.

I could feel Miss Nolan trembling. "If you shoot, you will hit the boy!"

"No, I won't," the Shadow said, and I closed my eyes.

There was a deafening crash...but not of gunfire. I opened my eyes and there, standing over the shattered remains of Miss Nolan's door, was the Sâr Dubnotal.

"Stay your hand, my friend," he said to the Black Eagle, "lest you take the life of an innocent woman."

If the Eagle was surprised by this interruption, he did not let it show. "Hello, *El Tebib*," he said. "Shouldn't you be having dinner with Judge Pursuivant?"

"I informed him that I might be late. Please lower your guns."

"Yes!" Miss Nolan said through clenched teeth. "Listen to him! Or this boy's blood is on your hands!"

The Doctor slowly turned until his eyes met mine. "Have courage, Nick," he said. "This nightmare is almost over." Then he looked at Miss Nolan, and a darkness came into his expression that I had not seen before. "I demand that you release Mary Nolan," he said.

Miss Nolan's arms tightened around me. "What are talking about, you fool?" she said. "I *am* Mary Nolan."

"No, you are not," the Doctor said. "Nor are you Emily Bishop, though you called yourself that for many years while you occupied her body."

Miss Nolan gasped. "How can you possibly know that?"

"It is not for nothing that I am called the Conqueror of the Invisible."

There was a giggling in my ear, and I knew that Miss Nolan was on the brink of hysteria. "You arrogant poseur," she said. "Do you think you impress me? I have conquered death itself, many times over, with only the power of my own indomitable will!"

"Indeed," the Doctor said. "The will to do unspeakable deeds in the service of abominable gods. The will to destroy innocent lives in order to unnaturally extend your own." His lip curled into a sneer. "I stand in awe of your will... *Lady Ligeia*."

Miss Nolan–Ligeia–said nothing. The edge of the blade bit into my neck, and I could feel a warm trickle of blood run down my skin.

"You told Nick that you couldn't live without him," the Doctor said, "and you were correct. Your...sacrifices...were sufficient to give you the power to invade Mary Nolan's body, but your possession could not be complete until you spilled the blood of a child who loved her."

Incredibly, despite the dire peril I was in, I felt an enormous weight lift from my heart. It really wasn't Miss Nolan who had been so cruel these last weeks! It was some evil imposter!

"It is over, Ligeia," said the Sâr Dubnotal. "You cannot complete the final ritual."

"I can!" Ligeia shouted. "I will!"

"I think not," said the Black Eagle. "These vile ceremonies take time, do they not, *El Tebib*?"

"Indeed, they do, old friend, time that we will not allow."

Ligeia growled like an animal.

"The game has ended, sorceress," the Doctor said. "Put down the boy. Release the woman. Go to your final judgment. Who knows? Perhaps there is mercy even for the likes of you."

"You know that isn't true," Ligeia snapped. "Even now I can feel Hell's hot arms, opening to embrace me. But I tell you this! If I must go to the flames, I'll go knowing that I defeated you!"

She was going to kill me then, of that I am certain, but she was interrupted by an explosion of gunfire. Screaming, she dropped me to the floor and tumbled against the wall, clutching at her head.

I looked up at the Black Eagle, his eyes blazing behind a plume of gun smoke. "The bullet only grazed her temple," he said. "She will be fine."

I heard Ligeia cry out in rage. I turned to see her holding the knife to her own neck. "You may have saved the pup," she screamed, "but I still claim the bitch!"

I have often wondered if there was anything the Doctor or the Eagle could have done to stop her. They were men of incredible abilities, and it is certainly possible that they could have somehow prevented Ligeia from slashing Miss Nolan's throat, ending both of their lives in a final act of cruelty and spite. But, as fate would have it, I was the one closest to her, and I was the one who acted first.

I leapt forward and closed one of my hands around Ligeia's wrist, and the other around the blade. I felt it cut deep into my fingers, but I ignored the pain and held the knife with all the strength I could muster. Her eyes locked with mine, and I stared into those bottomless black pools of hate.

"You're...not...strong...enough," she hissed. "My will–"

"Has been thwarted once and for all," the Doctor interrupted. He grabbed Ligeia's arm and pulled, adding his strength to my own. By now, the blood was flowing freely from my lacerated hand.

"Blood!" Ligeia cried in a voice choked with panic. "No! Not without the proper–"

Some of the drops landed on her chest, and she cried out as if they were acid.

"No," she whimpered. "It can't end like this...it can't...it..."

"Behold, Nick," said the Doctor. "The storm clouds fade."

The blackness in Ligeia's eyes dissipated and lightened...and turned to a crystal blue. The pressure on the knife eased, and I was easily able to wrest it away from her.

"Nick?" Miss Nolan said. "What's happening? What on Earth...?"

"Sleep," said the Sâr Dubnotal. He pressed his forefinger against Miss Nolan's brow and she immediately fell into a swoon. "It's over," he said. "The evil that lurked in her heart is gone."

"I know," said the Shadow. He swept his cloak through the air and the candles went out, plunging the room into darkness.

I could hear voices in the hall, and I realized that some of the neighbors were probably coming to investigate the noise. Then there was the distinct click of chain being pulled on a light, and a policeman was standing in the apartment. He was tall, with a prominent nose and a pair of piercing eyes set deep in a pale, mask-like face.

"Tend to them," the patrolman said to the Doctor, and then he stepped over to the door. "This is the police!" he shouted down the hall. "Some thieves broke into this apartment and attacked a woman and a child, but they fled when I arrived. Everything is under control! Please go back to your rooms and remain there!"

The Doctor chuckled. For the next few minutes, he ministered to the wounds suffered by me and Miss Nolan. "I am very sorry for what you have been through, Nick," he said as he finished applying my bandages. "Miss Nolan will not remember any of these events. I think perhaps it would be best if you didn't either. Look into my eyes and I will–"

"No," said the policeman. "The boy was brave tonight. He deserves to remember that."

The Doctor considered this, then nodded. "My friend is very wise, as usual."

"But I wasn't brave," I protested. "I was scared to death!"

The policeman looked at me. "You stepped in front of two loaded guns to protect someone's life," he said. "That is not the act of a coward."

"He is right, Nick," the Doctor said, gently placing his hands on my shoulders. "There are many evils against which we strive. No man's life is ever completely free of them. As you contend with them in the years to come, remember your courage on this night."

He stood up and went to the door. "I believe our work here is done," he said to the policeman. The officer gave him a curt nod, then disappeared into the night.

The Doctor hesitated in the door for a moment, then looked back at me, "You have the heart of a lion, my son," he said, "and you have earned the respect of the Sâr Dubnotal."

And then he, too, was gone.

This tale takes place eight months after André Caroff's first Madame Atomos novel and three months before the second. The deadly Japanese mastermind has tasted defeat for the first time, but she nevertheless has succeeded in inflicting unprecedented damage upon the United States. Now, she is relaxing, waiting for her next doomsday scheme to mature. And, in the meantime, she decides to have a little fun, as only Madame Atomos can...

Jean-Marc Lofficier: *Madame Atomos' Christmas*

Dallas, November 1963

Winter had come early that year and, with the approach of Thanksgiving, consumers' thoughts had already turned towards Christmas.

Dallas had hung its traditional season's decorations across its boulevards and avenues, and the department stores on Market Street had begun to decorate their windows accordingly.

There was enough of a chill in the air to easily conjure up images of turkey and roasted chestnuts.

Madame Atomos was dejectedly watching the efforts of a clumsy department store employee, promoted to decorator for the occasion, to hang a red plastic Santa Claus above an impressive pile of newly-arrived color televisions.

It was the hour of the local news broadcast.

Only a few months before, her first attack against the country she hated so much had failed miserably. However, she had succeeded in inflicting thousands of deaths upon her sworn enemy: the United States of America. Still, all that had happened on the East Coast and the few Texans who knew the truth, despite the news blackout arranged by the FBI, were used to their Eastern colleagues' exaggerations. In fact, the good citizens of the Lone Star State took the whole thing with a hefty grain of salt. Wasn't New York where a giant ape had allegedly once climbed the Empire State Building? Hadn't they been told about a flying saucer and a giant silver robot paralyzing Washington DC? And what about that bronze fella and all his gimmicks? No, really, a good Texan couldn't very well believe in all the tall tales that one read in Eastern papers.

The store employee had just failed to hook the Santa Claus for the third time. Madame Atomos sighed. She had stopped there to look at the local news to see if they reported any suspicious troop movements or special security measures being taken locally. Her next plan would start with the destruction of Texas and her latest discovery, a virtually indestructible plasmoid substance, was slowly maturing at her secret base, located not far away, near the property of a trusting rancher named Calvin Pooley.

Despite her scientific knowledge, Madame Atomos had a poor understanding of American society, much of which left her perplexed. Yet, she realized that, in order to destroy America, she had to gain a better understanding of it. That's why she forced herself, whenever she could, to watch the news–she favored CBS–and, especially, the local news which was often full of revealing details.

But today, this stupid, clumsy man was disturbing her concentration.

Madame Atomos turned the stone of her ring, which looked like a large ruby in a gold setting. It emitted a thin red beam, no thicker than a human hair, which went through the glass and pierced the employee's skull. The man's brain, suddenly subjected to incredibly high temperatures, exploded. He dropped to the floor, where he remained still. A few rivulets of bloodied brain matter began to seep from his nose and ears.

Madame Atomos sighed again and walked off into the night. As she crossed Elm Street, she realized she was bored.

Suddenly, a bit of news she had just watched on television gave her an idea. A magnificent idea. A smile appeared fleetingly on her razor-thin lips. A diabolical plan was already forming inside her prodigious mind. It wouldn't take much more than ten days to execute it, she thought. And her plasmoid wouldn't be ready, in any event, before the new year.

Ten days... Why not twelve days? As in that insipid song, *The Twelve Days of Christmas* that some stores had already begun to play.

The Twelve Days of Christmas, indeed! Why, it would be her own Christmas gift to herself!

Twelve days later exactly–Madame Atomos prided herself on punctuality!–the guinea pig whom she had personally selected and who had just been subjected to an intensive nuclear treatment, was, for the last time, sitting attached to a metal chair in an underground base located near Calvin Pooley's ranch.

Everything was ready. But Madame Atomos left nothing to chance. She had to have the man repeat her instructions one last time.

"Tell me again what you're supposed to do, Mr. Lee Harvey Oswald," whispered the deadly Madame Atomos.[5]

---

[5] According to several reliable witnesses, Lee Harvey Oswald, during the last months of his life, when some of his whereabouts remain unknown to this day, had changed physically, experiencing unexplained hair loss and premature aging.

Doctor Francis Ardan is that French proto-Doc Savage hero created in 1928 by Guy d'Armen in City of Gold and Lepers *(available from Black Coat Press). In Randy Lofficier's tale, Doc Ardan, who already had a brief meeting with Antoine de Saint Exupéry's Little Prince in our second volume, makes here a no less extraordinary encounter in...*

Randy Lofficier: *The Reluctant Princess*

Southern France, The 1920s

Doctor Francis Ardan (as he was known in France) was hacking his way through a massive forest of thorns on the side of a mountain in the Pyrénées. He felt as if he had no sooner chopped a pathway than a new batch was growing almost before his eyes. He would never get to the other side of the forest at the rate he was going. He was starting to feel discouraged.

He sat down to take a breather and to think about what had brought him on his strange quest. He had returned from his travels in the Far East, planning to take a well-deserved rest while doing some research on the Cathars of Montségur. But that research had awakened a curiosity he could not quench.

While reading about legends of lost treasures in France, he had come across a strange story. It was said that a young Noblewoman had been enchanted more than 400 years earlier in a village named Perceforest, somewhere in the mountains along the border between Spain and France. The legend had it that she would sleep forever, unless awakened by a stranger willing to brave the many enchantments which held her prisoner.

At first, Ardan had dismissed it all as mere fantasy; after all, it had to be a fairy tale. But something about the legend continued to eat away at him and he began to do further research. In the end, it seemed that there was clearly some truth to the whole thing. He was unable to let it rest and decided he had no choice but to set off to find the answer.

The difficulty of his quest had at least helped him to decide that it was true; but he was still unable to reach what he presumed was his goal: the other side of the enchanted forest. The explorer was no quitter; he knew there had to be an answer. If this was a "magic" forest, perhaps he needed to fight his way through it by unconventional means. Rather than using brute force, he decided to use some of the eastern methods he had learned on his journey through Tibet. He centered his thoughts and tried to feel himself becoming one with the forces of nature; in his mind's eye, he pictured a path opening up through the tangle of plants, leading him to his goal. As he gently breathed in and out, he felt a change in the air around him. Cautiously, he opened his eyes and saw that a path had mysteriously appeared directly in front of him.

Still breathing in a set pattern, he began to walk through the forest of thorns.

The path curved and twisted until Ardan no longer had a sense of the direction he traveled. But his meditative breathing enabled him to remain calm and not focus on his fear of becoming lost. Eventually, after walking for what seemed like hours, but which had in reality only been mere minutes, the young adventurer found himself standing in front of a stone tower in the midst of a clearing. As he circled it, he was unable to see any opening in its rough surface. Without a doubt, this was another challenge.

He again tried Eastern meditation, but this time it had no effect. He thought about the legends he had read and tried to recall if there was anything in them that might give him an answer to how to enter the tower. Then he remembered a passage he had read that had talked about an event said to occur just before the mysterious enchantment had overtaken the young noblewoman. He looked at the tower and repeated a phrase supposedly spoken by her.

Immediately, a wooden door appeared in the wall right before his eyes. He turned the massive iron handle that held it closed, and as if it had been oiled the day before, it gently swung open on its hinges.

To Ardan's surprise, the corridors inside the tower were brightly lit with glowing torches. He had no idea where to find the object of his search, but simply walked forward, certain that he would find her as this was now clearly meant to be.

The corridor spiraled around like the shell of a snail, and eventually the adventurer reached a chamber in what he perceived was its center. There, in a large canopied bed, was a beautiful young woman. She had cascading, golden hair and alabaster skin. Ardan felt mesmerized by her beauty. She lay motionless on the bed, but it was clear that she was not dead, merely in some state of suspended animation.

The young man circled the chamber, looking at the young woman from every angle as he tried to determine what he needed to do to awaken her. Finally, he decided that he would follow the blueprint laid out in every fairy story he had ever read or studied; he approached the beautiful Princess (for he was sure she must be a Princess) and bent over her to kiss her.

As his warm breath touched her face, her dark golden eyelashes fluttered and she opened her astonishingly beautiful sapphire-colored eyes. Ardan was shocked when she reached up a delicate hand and slapped him in the face!

He stepped back as the Princess sat up in her bed. "How dare you!" she exclaimed. "Just what do you think you're doing?"

"I... I..." Ardan felt himself at a loss for words, something unusual for the sophisticated scientist. Finally, he was able to speak, "I'm sorry, your Highness. But you have been under a charm for many centuries. I have fought my way through a series of enchantments to come here to awaken you. I thought I would use a method that has been written about in many stories, and that meant I needed to kiss you for the spell to be broken."

"I don't care about you kissing me, sir," said the beautiful young woman. "I want to know what gives you the right to disturb my peace and quiet!"

"I don't understand. I simply wanted to help you. Weren't you placed under this spell by an evil enchantress?"

"Of course not! I chose to enter this state. It is my sanctuary."

"What reason could you have for such a bizarre thing?"

"You say that centuries have gone by, so perhaps you do not know what life was like for a young woman when I was born, sir. You cannot imagine how hard it was to be a woman with a mind of her own. I wanted to study and walk freely in the forests. I had no desire to be married off to some ugly, old horror of a man because it would gain my family lands and power. Indeed, I am not sure I desired to marry at all.

"If I did not marry, then my only choice was to wall myself off in a convent, and I fear I am not better made for the life of a religious, as I have a rebellious soul and do not take well to being told what to do by anyone, man nor woman.

"Thus, I chose to ask a sorceress of my acquaintance to place me in a state of peace and happiness to forever escape a life I could not bear to contemplate," she looked at Ardan in sadness for what she had lost.

"My Princess," said the explorer, taking her hand, "I think you will find a changed world awaits you! You no longer have to belong to any man if that's your wish."

"Will I be totally free?"

"No. No one is totally free, but I think you will approve of the world outside this place."

"I suppose I can give it a try. But first, tell me how you managed to get inside my tower? I had thought that I was quite clear it was to be a puzzle that no one could solve."

"Ah, that... It was something I read you had said on the day before the enchantment took hold of you."

"And what was that?"

"*No day is so bad that it can't be fixed with a nap!*"

Paris – Yet again we were astonished by an amazing feat of derring-do, as the latest flying ace on the Parisian scene, the amazing Phantom Angel, flew her biplane over the Eiffel Tower and climbed down a rope ladder (while somehow managing to keep the plane circling overhead!) to disarm the notorious anarchist Azzef who was threatening to blow up the radio transmitter at the top. Our City is certainly a better place for having a heroine of her caliber watching over us. – Joseph Rouletabille writing in L'Epoque.

Xavier Mauméjean's contribution to this year's Tales of the Shadowmen *is a delightful parodic romp that brings together two iconic figures of English literature: P. G. Wodehouse's inimitable Bertie Wooster (and his clever factotum, Jeeves) and Agatha Christie's detective Hercule Poirot (with his "little grey cells" and ever-reliable Hastings). Bertie thrives on chaos, while Poirot worships order. When the two meet, expect sparks to fly during...*

Xavier Mauméjean: *A Wooster Christmas*

Worcestershire, Xmas 1921

For a mystery novel, Agatha Christie is certainly the best choice.
Bertram Wilberforce Wooster in *Much Obliged Jeeves*

"*Beanacht...*"

"Indeed, sir. Good morning," said Jeeves.

"Did I say something?"

"It sounded like Welsh."

"Good Lord, did I speak Welsh?"

"Each day provides its share of surprises, sir."

To know me is to know what condition I am in after an evening spent at the Silver Slipper. The foxtrot follows the quickstep, and the gimlet follows the foxtrot, for notwithstanding this new law that prohibits drinking after 11, nothing rehydrates a dancer more than a cocktail with gin, vodka and lime. I went home at exactly the time of the fashionable tune, *Three O'Clock in the Morning*–well before the milkman pops round to perform his listed duties. When I woke up, a migraine was applying a vice to the Wooster noggin, which just goes to show that there is after all more under my night cap than some say–even if I never wear a night cap. That's why Jeeves had shimmered into my room like a benevolent ghost, carrying his miracle medicine.

"My head feels like... that strange vegetable that begins with a P?"

"A pumpkin, sir?" he said, putting his concoction on the nightstand.

"Always the right word, Jeeves."

"Thank you, sir."

"How is the weather this morning?"

"Snowy, sir, but with a wintry Sun."

"Bright light, then? Wasn't it Plato who said that Truth is like something thingummy noodlethwap?"

"Precisely, sir. Like the Sun, one cannot stare at it directly."

"A quote that suits my present condition."

"Entirely apposite, sir."

With the solicitude which is the pride of a devoted servant, Jeeves took care to leave the curtains closed. I leaned back against the pillows, staring at the glass on the nightstand. At first glance, and even looking at it twice, I didn't trust Jeeves' hangover cure. Yet, Jeeves' creation is worthy of my unquestioning trust, since it is on the basis of its miraculous properties that I initially hired him. I swallowed the egg beaten in Worcester sauce with a dash of red pepper in one gulp. At once, it exploded inside me like a bomb in the days of the Zeppelins. I felt my head burst, my eyes roll like marbles, and then the Sun rose and the bluebirds began to sing.

"Better, sir?"

"I feel like Caesar ready to cross the... dash it all, what was that place?"

"The Rubicon, sir?"

"You may check the map later. Right now, let's pay homage to breakfast. How was your evening, Jeeves?"

"Excellent; thank you, sir, for inquiring."

"Weren't you supposed to go to the theater?"

"Indeed. At the Old Vic."

I used the corner of my toast to doodle in my egg yolk.

"All the papers rave about this new dramatist. What's his name again?"

"Perhaps you are referring to Mr. Chekhov?"

"Tsk, tsk, another poor man forced to flee from these nasty Bolsheviks."

"Chekhov is dead, sir."

"Oh, are you sure?"

"Without a doubt, sir."

"I hope that didn't spoil the play for you. That bacon was perfect, Jeeves. And I'll have a few more cups of that excellent tea."

After two more cups of the life-saving liquid, I went to the bathroom. It is a shame that our scientists ignore the euphoric properties of the average bar of soap. When you hold it under water and let it go, it surfaces in a most thrilling fashion, entirely suited to spread joy in the most discomfited of souls. Sometimes, I think that if Dante had spent more time playing with a bar of soap, his life would have been transformed. Mankind would have gained a great humorist, partygoer and all-around fun person. After 20 minutes of play, I regretfully left the tub, shaved and went back to my room to put on my old rags.

I immediately noticed what passes for Jeeves' frown: a slight upward rise of the eyebrow and an almost imperceptible lowering of the corner of his lips.

"A problem, Jeeves?"

"None at all, sir."

"Family worries?"

"Not as far as I know."

"Your uncle Charlie Silversmith lost his position at Deverill Hall?"

"He would surely have informed me if that were the case."

"So all's well?"

"As well as can be, sir, except for a minor detail."

"Really?" I said, trying to postpone the attack.

"I fear that sir forgot to shave his upper lip."

"Oh, that?" I said, caressing my mustache. "Don't you think it makes me look dashing?"

"No, sir. No more now than on your first attempt. I seem to remember that it was not a fortunate experience."

"Some time has gone by...."

"For everyone, sir."

"*In tempore opportuno....*"

"Indeed, sir, but if I may be so bold, I do not think that the opportune time has yet arrived."

"Yet Douglas Fairbanks..."

"...Is an American, sir, and we cannot merely adopt the customs of the former colonies."

"Will this warrant me another notice in the Junior Ganymede register?"

"Only time will tell, sir."

For those who don't know what I'm referring to, you must know that Jeeves belongs to a club of gentlemen's gentlemen and other people in service, located on Curzon Street. According to Article 11 of the rules of this ancient institution, each member must describe the habits of his employer in a special register. Thus a member seeking employment can learn of the habits of his potential master, whether he rushes to the rescue of widows and orphans or casts stones at them. Ordinarily, an employer only warrants a single notice in the register, but Jeeves had hinted to me that I was the exception.

"How long has it been since the new register was opened?"

"Twelve years, sir."

"You still keep it up to date?"

"Diligently, sir."

"How many pages do I warrant now–two, I believe?"

"Twenty-two, sir."

My surprise was such that I forgot to correctly button my vest. Fortunately, Jeeves was there to fix it.

"And what motivated this further amplification, pray tell?" I asked while Jeeves busied himself.

It was then that the telephone rang. Taking advantage of that diversion, Jeeves glided like a zephyr towards it.

"Your aunt, sir."

Trusting in the Woosters' reliable instinct, I mentally threw myself to the ground, bracing against the storm. I had immediately thought of Lady Worpledon, my Aunt Agatha. For those unfamiliar with my history, I will only say that

Aunt Agatha is married to the execrable Spenser Gregson who made his fortune in Sumatran rubber, that she almost never leaves her lair of Wollam Chesey in Hertfordshire and that she uses barbed wire where other ladies prefer diamond necklaces.

Staring at my mustache, Jeeves handed me the receiver without giving me any more information, a gesture I thought of as petty coming from such an ordinarily noble soul. Fortunately, the screams at the other end of the line dissipated my doubts; it was my Aunt Dahlia. The dear old thing remarried a Tom Travers the year when Blue Bottle won the Grand Prize. I feel a sincere affection for her.

"Hullo, venerable relative!"

"Bertie! I thought you were in America?"

Truth to be told, I had been forced in exile there for a while after a slight disagreement with Sir Roderick Glossop, an eminent specialist in nervous disorders and manager of a nuthouse. During a compulsory stay with Aunt Agatha, a snake in the grass had told Sir Roderick about the incident of the Policeman's Helmet. During the rowing finals between Oxford and Cambridge, in a rash and foolish moment, I had indeed stolen the headgear of a servitor of the Law. Since then, this action haunted me like the ghost of Hamlet's father. Sir Roderick Glossop saw me as a dangerous predator ready to abscond at any time with his precious helmet collection. Fortunately, there had been a silver lining to this incident. Glossop had broken my engagement to his daughter, Honoria, who since childhood had been nudging me toward the bonds of matrimony. Before Sir Roderick could lock me up in a padded cell, I had fled to the other side of the pond.

Suddenly, I asked myself: why had Aunt Dahlia phoned me, when she thought I was still in New York? I remembered a book I'd read recently, one of those mystery novels I devoured at night when the rain makes pinging noises on the windows–*By Order of the Czar*. In it, anarchists conspired with other anarchists, or against them, and none of them were half as smart as Aunt Dahlia.

"In America? Certainly not!" I decided I would wait for her to disclose her hand.

"Excellent, because you'll be able to come tonight for Christmas Eve dinner, then."

"Christmas Eve dinner? What, tonight?" I repeated, a tad naively, I confess, as I twisted my neck to look at the calendar.

"Come on, Bertie, you know it happens every year at the same time."

Indeed, we had reached December 24th. Now I knew why Aunt Dahlia had phoned. Knowing perfectly well that I was back in London, she wanted to make sure I wouldn't miss this old family tradition. Travers was cunning in that way; she would have felt at home inside a wooden horse plotting to take over Troy. But she was right: I had all but forgotten.

"No problem. You can start serving the plum pudding, rehearsing the carols and everything that goes with them."

"You are a dear."

"You know my motto: women and children first."

"Don't forget to bring Jeeves."

Sometimes, I wonder if, in my Aunt's heart, the image of her poor Bertram isn't being slowly erased and replaced by the roman profile of Jeeves carved on one of her ventricles.

"Why? Do you need additional staff to serve eggnog?"

"No, but we have a, shall we say, special guest this year."

Her voice could have been heard as far as Coconut Grove.

"Will you please stop being mysterious and tell me what you are talking about?"

"We've invited a Captain Arthur Hastings. A veteran from the Somme. I met him when I served as a volunteer in the Royal Army Medical Corps when he was wounded. You both love tennis, you should get along."

"Then I fail to see the problem. Do you need Jeeves to keep the score?"

It is worth noting that at this point, Aunt Dahlia paused. Then, after a minute of silence, she barked:

"Listen: Captain Hastings asked me to invite one of his friends. I willingly agreed, of course, you know me, but now I'm having second thoughts. The little Belgian hardly stops chattering. He is getting on your Uncle Tom's nerves, and you know how patient he is. I lost patience long before Tom. But above all, Monsieur Poirot prizes himself on being a deep thinker. That's why I'd like to see Jeeves take him down a peg. Tell me, his brain is as sharp as ever?"

"Not to worry, I feed him a plate of fish every day."

"Very good. Then be here at eight."

"Kind of you to ask me as well."

"Yes, isn't it?" she mooed before hanging up.

I almost felt like dancing the Rite of Spring. Of course, I was happy at the notion of spending Christmas in the Woosters' ancestral home in Market Snodbury, Worcestershire. But I was already salivating at the thought of enjoying Anatole's cooking. Maestro of the cooking pots, gift from the gods to our mortal palates, Aunt Dahlia's chef makes me regret having only one stomach. Even though he is French, Anatole, unlike many of his colleagues, does not cook only French dishes. He is always ready to try some good, old-fashioned English recipe, such as his succulent steak and kidney pie.

My spirits uplifted, I decided to no longer dwell on the register of the Junior Ganymede and leave to Jeeves the responsibility of his entries. I put on a Jacques Fath suit and my best pair of deerskin shoes.

"I would recommend these, sir. It's snowing outside, and your shoes might be damaged," said Jeeves as he offered me a pair of rubber boots.

We Woosters are known for our magnanimity, and I accepted the boots with all the kindness a medieval lord would show to a transgressing vassal. Jeeves showed further concern for the impact of the weather on my delicate constitution by handing me a pair of kidskin gloves. Fully accoutered, I went to the Drones Club to chew the curd in the company of my friend Bingo.

One cannot but love Christmas when one is a Londoner. At this time of the year, the city radiates a festive atmosphere that the worst blows of the Great War could not diminish. Even in Dec. of 1916 the mailmen delivered letters amongst bombed-out ruins, most of any crowd on Regent Street were soldiers out of uni-forms, and every shop proudly displayed a sign reading "Business as usual." Fortunately, that time is gone. I hurried towards the Drones Club, my overcoat collar upturned against the cold. Customers were leaving shops their hands full of presents or gawking at the lavishly decorated windows of Selfridge's. On the ice rink inside, lovers and children were skating to the continuous music of the store's ragtime band. The streets were lit up and sparkling with gold-colored garlands. Every street corner seemed to have a hot chestnut peddler.

I arrived at the club, the entrance of which was decorated with a ball of holly and a tiny Santa Claus made of paper maché. Leaving my boots at the cloakroom, I went to the smoking room where I knew I'd find Bingo Little. With Pongo Twistleton, "Catsmeat" Potter-Pirbright, Boko Fittleworth and Reginald Herring, a.k.a. the "Salted Herring." Bingo is one of the pillars of our club. Besides myself, of course. I have enjoyed a not inconsiderable prestige since the time I crossed the club's swimming pool by grabbing the ceiling's net. At least, I was crossing the pool until a sore loser cut the net. We call ourselves Drones because we make as much noise as real drones, although once a year the senior members ask us to relocate to the Senior Liberal Club in order to straighten up the lampshades, repair the broken furniture, and so on. The exile to the Senior Liberal Club is appreciated differently depending on whether one enjoys being served by, believe it or not, female waiters.

Bingo was in deep conversation with a whisky soda. After the customary exchange of "Hullo!" and "How do you do, old branch?" we began tackling se-rious business, i.e.: the horses in this year's Derby, Pongo's birthday and, espe-cially, our annual dart competition sweepstakes, which at ten shillings a ticket keeps the till full.

"Catsmeat and Boko will join us later this afternoon to discuss it."

I made the sorry expression of a Hun prevented from looting a nunnery.

"I'm afraid I shan't be able to stay. I'm supposed to spend Christmas Eve at Market Snodbury."

"Anyone I know?" asked Bingo, taking a cigarette from his case.

"The usual crew, plus two stowaways: a Captain Hastings and a Monsieur Poirot."

Bingo's mouth dropped and he stayed there, his lighter still on, like a Statue of Liberty afflicted with a toothache.

"Poirot?"

"You heard me."

"*Hercule* Poirot?"

"If you'd like."

"Don't tell me you don't know who he is, Bertie? Ouch!"

Bongo dropped the lighter and began to suck his thumb, waiting for my full confession.

"Not in the least."

"You, who brags about reading murder mysteries and whose manservant has to rush to the nearest bookstore to get the latest Spinoza, you don't know Hercule Poirot?"

He was quickly becoming irritating. Young Bingo, you see, is the type of man who knows everything there is to know about sports cars and male fashions, but when it comes to literature, his knowledge stops with the *Sporting Times*.

"As you can see, I'm as innocent as a new-born lamb."

Bingo Little assumed an educated air. It made him look as if he was giving his admission speech at the Royal Society. "Hercule Poirot is a famous detective whose investigations are often recorded by his friend, Captain Hastings."

"Really?" I said, barely suppressing a yawn.

"That's true," he reply, unnoticing. "And his name is often linked with that of the Queen of Crime, Mrs. A..."

"A...?"

"A..." he repeated, leaning over his whisky soda.

"Almost there, Bingo!"

"I've got it! Mrs. Ariadne Oliver!"

The budding literary critic gave me a list of a few titles, then I went home. Jeeves finished loading the suitcases in the boot of my old sports coupé and we left our cozy headquarters at 3, Berkeley Mansions, Berkeley Square, London, W1, driving towards the divine kitchen of Anatole.

I'm not particularly gifted with descriptions, but suffice it to say that Aunt Dahlia's rustic haven of peace, its gardens and dependencies, were buried under snow. Seppings opened the front door. The icy composure of the old butler seemed reinforced by the weather. I dispensed with the "What ho!" and went straight to the point.

"Where is my aunt?"

"In the salon," replied Banquo's ghost.

You can say what you want about Seppings, but he knows the house. Even if I wouldn't immediately think of asking him to join us for a picnic on Brighton Beach, I trust his directions entirely. While Jeeves was unloading the car, I rushed to join my dear old aunt.

Aunt Dahlia had done things well, as she does every year. Trusting the decoration to no one else, she had pinned bunches of holly everywhere in the salon and stuck knots of red and green crepe on the walls. The huge Christmas tree was topped by a large star, and hung with fake snow garlands and ball ornaments. Under it was a pile of multicolored boxes. How many times as a child I had sought to open them before the appointed time? I confess I still felt that old desire. Suppressing a tear of grateful joy at the memories, I was about to say hello when I noticed the gnomes. There were six of them, tough men wearing wool caps and scarves, methodically crushing the pine needles that had fallen off the trees under their cleat boots. At a signal from their master, Reverend Aubrey Upjohn, the local vicar, they launched themselves into a Christmas carol. At least, I suppose that that's what it was, because it sounded more like a concerto for tortured felines, and indeed the mangled tones scared Augustus, Aunt Dahlia's cat, nearly to death. He came running and hid between my legs and I scratched his ears. Augustus only asked one thing from life: three meals a day and 15 hours' sleep. Otherwise, he gets grumpy and I can't blame him. In fact, I'm a rather okay type of human, from the perspective of cats.

With no mercy for their audience, the choir of evil dwarves finished their number. Reverend Upjohn greeted the polite applause the way a Grand Inquisitor receives apprentice torturers. At Aunt Dahlia's signal, they all rushed to the table to stuff themselves with butterfingers and candied fruits. I didn't dare imagine what they might do if they fell on crackers—they'd use them to give birds heart attacks. Well, that's what Bingo Little would do....

"Bertie! Come here!" shouted Aunt Dahlia, her round face unusually pinkish.

It's funny how my aunts can be so different. Aunt Agatha is tall and bony, while Aunt Dahlia is built like an athlete. I walked around the tree and gave her a hug.

"Glad to be here!" I said while she tried to suffocate me.

"You didn't forget?"

"What?" I said, freeing myself from her death grip.

"I asked you to come with..."

I looked at her uncomprehendingly.

"Good spirits?" I said, helpfully.

"No, you ass! Not that!" Aunt Dahlia replied, winking at me repeatedly.

"Your eye medicine?"

"No!"

"But you do need some! You're batting your eyes like an owl."

The dear old thing took a deep breath, making a visible effort. She was obviously exhausted by all the Christmas preparations.

"Forget it, Bertie," she sighed. "Let me introduce you to a dear friend: Captain Hastings!"

The more easily distracted amongst you would be forgiven if you had assumed that the guests in the room were the carolers. Not at all! In fact, Captain Hastings looked nothing like a gnome. He was a man of good appearance, elegant stature and dressed in a well-tailored suit. He wore a frank smile that inspired immediate confidence.

We shook hands.

"Tennis, said my aunt?" I said.

"Only as an amateur. What about you?"

"The same, since William Tilden won the singles at Wimbledon. And he just did it again at the US championship."

"Tsk! An American!" said Hastings, visibly shocked.

We discussed the case of Miss Suzanne Lenglen, who had won three years in a row in both the Singles and Womens' Doubles at Wimbledon.

"Since I moved to Argentina, I don't follow the fashions closely but I've heard reports that Miss Lenglen appeared with bared forearms and a skirt cut just above the calf?"

I was forced to admit the truth of this appalling image. During our conversation, Aunt Dahlia hadn't stopped glancing nervously towards the kitchen. The appearance of a rather odd-looking gentleman did nothing to diminish her anxiety.

"Monsieur Poirot, I'd like you to meet my nephew!" she bellowed with the delicacy of a Scots Regiment.

Poirot rolled up his eyes like a cat.

"Ah! *La famille*. Nothing is more important than blood ties," he said, shaking my hand.

His exaggerated manners and comical accent indicated right away that he was from the Continent–likely a Frenchman. I learned later that he was, in fact, from Belgium. Jeeves told me they are two different nations, but one thing is certain: there's no one else like Hercule Poirot. We Woosters are generally tall, and I'm not even including Aunt Agatha, whose personality adds six inches to her stature. So I had to bend almost halfway to make eye contact with Monsieur Poirot. He might have been 5'4" but he stood up straight, not conceding an inch. His head was egg-shaped and decorated with a superb moustache. At first, I was sorry that Jeeves wasn't there to look at him, but I soon changed my mind. According to Jeeves, a modest dress style should be inversely proportional to one's height. By studying Poirot and the care he took in his attired I could only conclude that he was something of a dandy. Now, those who know Bertram know that he is in favor of greater simplicity. Following the publication of my "What Elegant Men Must Wear" in *Milady's Boudoir*, perfect strangers have stopped me in the street to ask for my tailor's name. And I of course give it to them, for it is the duty of the enlightened man to spread his wisdom around.

"Monsieur Poirot is a policeman!" shouted Aunt Dahlia.

The little fellow inclined his head to the side.

"A retired policeman, dear Madame. In truth, Hercule Poirot is now a consulting detective. One of the best in England."

His oddly accented statement was delivered with obvious self-satisfaction. He immediately reminded me of Aunt Agatha's husband. Spencer Gregson has the gift to turn the story of one of his days at the Stock Exchange into a Norse saga, and as soon as he begins throwing market prices at me, I start nodding off. We Woosters came to Jolly Old with William the Conqueror and fought alongside Richard the Lionhearted, but the Stock Market positively paralyses us.

Wishing to lighten up the atmosphere, I said:

"Like Nick Carter, eh? Bang! Bang!"

Poirot looked down his nose at my fingers, which I had formed into guns.

"*Non*, not really," he said, balancing on the tips of his feet.

"You have a beautiful moustache."

His face lit up immediately.

"You think so?"

"Waxed?"

"*Parfaitement* ! But you too, it seems…"

"Hello, hello!"

It would have been impossible to mistake that breathy voice. Among the persons I almost married, in addition to the aforementioned Honoria Glossop, was Florence Craye. Florence is the daughter of Lord Parcival Worplesdon, which is enough of a handicap for anyone to bear. At first glance, Florence looks like a divine creature next to whom Ida Lupino is a stunted gargoyle. The mere sight of Florence has led stout men to say things they have regretted later. But her flawless faces hides a tyrannical harpy who would not hesitate to send a Light Brigade into the mouths of Russian cannon. And since we are no longer engaged, Florence bears me all the good will of the iceberg for the *Titanic*.

"Goodness gracious, what a small world!" I said, pulling out my cigarette case.

As a matter of fact, I ought to have guessed that Florence would be here. After all, she is family.

"Bertie?"

I pretended to feel nonchalant, but my hands shook lightly. I couldn't count on Aunt Dahlia for help, because she had removed herself.

"Yes?" I said, quivering.

"Bertram?"

"Hullo! I'm here!"

"You're not going to start smoking now?"

I looked at my cigarette's incandescent tip.

"Not at all. I thought I would chew on it for a while, but I like your idea much better."

Florence looked as if she would gladly have hit my head with a croquet mallet but had to keep her composure in front of the other guests.

"I'm told you're a writer?" she asked Hastings.

The good Captain became as red as the Norton lighthouse. He nodded to his Belgian friend and muttered:

"It's nothing. Just a few accounts..."

"I wrote a novel once," interrupted Florence.

Indeed, and if I add that the novel is entitled *Spiral* and is an introspective drama sporting on its cover a green-faced woman smelling a purple lily, you will understand why Florence and I postponed indefinitely choosing names for our first-born.

I felt the need to remind her that Bertram, too, is an accomplished man of letters. I said loudly, "It's a family gift. Have you seen the latest issue of *Milady's Boudoir*? There is..."

"Oh, stop talking about yourself and let Captain Hastings talk, Bertie!"

Obviously, Aunt Dahlia's guest had lost that Cro-Magnon instinct that leads us to mistrust women, for he was all eyes towards Florence. That fact had not escaped Monsieur Poirot's notice. Standing on the tips of his shiny shoes, the detective smiled.

"My friend, he adores the *beau sexe*. He becomes weak in the knees before a head of pretty auburn hair, or a blonde one, and he bows before every beautiful woman who has the good taste of giving him a smile. But he doesn't really understand women, *non*."

Hastings threw an unkind look at the little Belgian. No doubt that at this moment, the poor Captain would have been happier on the pampas trying to lasso a runaway bull. I felt sorry for him. On the other hand, Hercule Poirot and Florence Craye seemed made for each other. They ignored Hastings and I and began discussing the unconscious motivations of the human mind.

Rescue came in the form of Jeeves. No doubt motivated by a solicitous concern for the health of his master, Jeeves whispered in my ear, "Mr. Travers is waiting for you in the library."

Leaving the unfortunate Hastings, I rushed to see my Uncle Tom.

Those readers who through charity or laziness read my stories know that Aunt Dahlia's husband, my Uncle Tom, is an enthusiastic collector. It is, in fact, his only vice. His habit of wearing a moth-eaten old cardigan? An amusing eccentricity. His appearance, which might be described as that of a crocodile afflicted with consumption? Dyspepsia. His years in the Far East made his fortune but left him with a perturbed digestion. (The only way he'd found to deal with his gastric problems was to hire the incomparable Anatole). All forgivable. But when he begins muttering about a "unique find" or a "rare discovery," I take to my heels. I risked jail several times because of an 18th century silver cream pot that looked like a cow. Its handle, shaped to look like a cow's tail, still haunts my nightmares.

Uncle Tom was waiting for me behind his desk. He had a series of ancient coins spread before him on a velvety indigo tray.

"Come and look at my recent acquisitions, Bertie. A unique find."

My heart sank. Ignoring the magnifying glass he was offering me, I stared at the coins.

"Very nice."

"They'd better be. They're authentic Turgech coins from the Xianfeng era."

"Are they valuable?"

Uncle Tom's heart skipped a beat.

"Of course they are. Why do you ask?"

"Because they all look damaged by these holes in the middle."

The old ghost sighed.

"They were made over a thousand years ago."

I hadn't the heart to tell him, but he'd been sold some old junk. When you turn senile, there are always vultures waiting to take advantage of you. Or so I've been told.

Strangely, the examination of Uncle Tom's newest treasure of the ages didn't proceed any further. I had the feeling Uncle Tom had used the coins as a pretext to draw me aside. The facts soon showed I was right.

"You've got to help us, Bertie!" he said, grabbing my jacket.

"Is it about the detective?"

Uncle Tom's teary eyes shone brighter.

"Ah! You realized it too."

"Not a problem. Just tell me in which wardrobe you stashed the body."

"If only it was murder! At least that would occupy Monsieur Poirot and stop him from boring us with his 'little grey cells' and his delicate stomach. No, we need a plan."

"I'll think about it," I said, playing with the Christmas stockings hanging from the mantelpiece.

"You? No, hardly likely. Fetch your manservant. He'll know what to do."

That exclusive interest amongst my family for Jeeves might seem like an irritant but after several years, I've grown accustomed to it.

"Is he... sound of mind?"

"I haven't seen him try on Sir Reginald Wooster's armor hanging in the hall, if that's what you mean. Why?"

"There was a time when Jeeves would never have let you go out with that hairy slug on your upper lip."

I was going to reply with a well-turned *bon mot* when Seppings entered, lowering the room's temperature by ten degrees.

"Dinner will be served in 20 minutes," he said, frost forming in the air as he spoke.

Which didn't matter, because the very notion of imminently tasting Anatole's food was enough to warm me up.

I rejoined the other guests after changing into dinner clothes. The sight of the red table cloth with white embroidering, the crystal glasses and the silverware tugged at my heart. I remembered a poem I'd read at school about the burning of the yule logs and the spirit of Christmas.

The guests were already sitting at the table. They all wore pinkish paper crowns, tilted except for Poirot who wore his straight up. It made him look like an egg in a cup. I put on my crown and sat in my chair, across the table from the detective. He was sitting erect and looked mildly uncomfortable. With his accent, I couldn't understand what he was muttering about, but I heard the words "crowns" and "symmetry." Perhaps his quasi-French nature remembered the guillotine? But it would take more than that to tarnish my good humor. We each had a menu individually illustrated by Aunt Dahlia. I opened mine and read:

Consommé aux Pommes d'Amour
Sylphide à la crème d'écrevisses
Mignonnettes de Poulet Petit Duc
Pointes d'asperges à la Mistinguett
Suprême de foie gras au champagne
Neige aux perles des Alpes
Timbale de ris de veau toulousain
Salade d'endive et de céleri
Plum-Pudding
L'Etoile du Berger
Bénédictins Blancs
Friandises
Fruits

Several bottles of Chateau d'Yquem and a Cigarini Mercurey were served. Those experienced in the ways of Anatole knew what to expect. To me, it was the taste equivalent of a Cole Porter medley. As for Captain Hastings, he seemed to be in a good mood.

"I like to eat at the *Cheshire Cheese* on Saturdays," he said, "because that's when they serve their famous steak and kidney pie."

"Steak and kidney pie? Isn't that a bit rich?" Florence made a face.

Hastings looked embarrassed and muttered something I couldn't hear. I hadn't followed Poirot's conversation. It was as if he wasn't interested by the menu, at which he had barely glanced.

"Don't you enjoy fine cooking?" I inquired.

"*Au contraire.* I was once in love with a beautiful English young lady, but alas, she didn't know how to cook. *Quel dommage!* Perhaps I should have no regrets. I pay frequent visit to *Chez ma Tante*, a *bistrot* enjoyed by all of London's high society. The wealthy, the handsome and the famous all beg to have reservations, for his chef, Monsieur Gaston Blondin, is not the kind of man to grant such favors lightly. But Hercule Poirot is different. Monsieur Blondin, he says to me: 'But of course, there is always a table for you, Monsieur Poirot! I only wish you made the honor of dining here more often!' "

I began to understand the reactions of Aunt Dahlia and Uncle Tom. But we Woosters are no shrinking violets when it comes to facing enemy fire. I ignored his opening salvo and fired my own volley:

"I have also heard good things about the *Bon Bourgeois*. Pete Wimsey recommended it to me. A good chap, but a bit stuck-up. I remember that at Eton, they called him 'Tadpole.' "

Hastings' face lit up.

"That's funny. That's what we called him too!"

"You know him?"

"Wimsey? Of course! Although I've lost track of him since college."

"His Lordship just solved the mystery of the Attenbury Emeralds. I understand it's given Tadpole the desire to become a consulting detective."

Aunt Dahlia turned towards the Belgian.

"In that case, you wouldn't be unique, Monsieur Poirot." I would never have guessed that Travers possessed such a degree of perfidy.

Florence was about to rush to the Belgian's rescue, and I was mentally preparing myself to sweep up the rubble after her, when Seppings and his staff appeared and served the first course. At a discreet command, the servants placed a salad plate before each guest.

I will repeat myself. A salad plate, at the center of which one could barely distinguish a small puddle of *consommé*.

Aunt Dahlia rose up, like Hamlet's father's ghost on the ramparts of Elsinore. Before she could utter a word, Seppings, observing her ashen complexion, said:

"I received formal instructions from the chef. Monsieur Anatole said he will quit if he is asked to serve anything else."

A deep silence fell upon the room, broken only by the tinkling of my spoon against the plate.

Hercule Poirot expressed the desire we gather in the library. "Even the cat?" I asked, to lighten the atmosphere. Normally, my native wit enables me to rise to the occasion, but this time, I failed miserably. Both Aunt Dahlia and Florence threw me withering glances that would have shriveled any *soufflé* not cooked my Monsieur Anatole. So I sat with the others in a row of chairs arranged in a semi-circular pattern. The only thing missing at this wake was a body.

Poirot was clearly thinking. He was standing up, perfectly motionless except for small but expressive twitches of his eyebrows. He looked like a ventriloquist's dummy from *The Player's*. The detective took his time rearranging the trinkets on the mantelpiece (which made Uncle Tom moan), then after having studied his made-up audience at length like a stage magician, he let out:

"Is Monsieur Anatole the victim of blackmail?"

I almost swallowed my brandy wrong. We all turned to look at Captain Hastings, but he only shrugged, as if to say: "Wait for him to finish."

Pleased with our reaction, the detective continued:

"A recipe he might have purloined from another chef... that of his famous steak and kidney pie, for example... One of you might have found out about it and..."

"I'll stop you right now," said Aunt Dahlia with all the amiability of Lady Macbeth. "How dare you suspect anyone here?"

The detective showed no trace of embarrassment as he replied:

"Please understand, Dear Madame, that it is wise to suspect everyone until the innocence of each is established, rationally and convincingly. And when a crime is committed in a house, everyone is automatically suspect."

For my part, I agreed. To deprive us of the culinary talents of Monsieur Anatole was a crime worthy of Newgate. I was going to say "Hurrah" when the little Belgian pointed his index finger at me:

"Monsieur Wooster, I drew from our conversation that you are well aware of what happens in the world of London's finer restaurants. If such a scandal had happened somewhere, no doubt that you would have learned of it."

"I?"

"You."

"London's finer restaurants?"

"My very words."

"A scandal?"

"*Oui.*"

I had run out of things to say when, unexpectedly, Florence came to my assistance.

"Come on, you don't know Bertie. In order to commit a crime, you must have the will to do something, which makes him *de facto* not guilty."

I felt extremely grateful to the barracuda in an evening dress, with nevertheless a smidgen of a reservation that stopped me from dusting off the old engagement ring.

Hercule Poirot enjoyed the argument as if it had been a piece of candy.

"You too, Mademoiselle Craye, are not above suspicion. When my friend Hastings said he liked the steak and kidney pie served at the *Cheshire Cheese*, which is only on the menu on Saturdays, you remarked that you found it too rich for your tastes. French cuisine, of which Monsieur Anatole is a worthy ambassador, often uses oil or butter, depending whether it is *meridional* or *normand*. Therefore, Mademoiselle Craye, I regret to say, but it is possible, although not necessarily probable, that you somehow coerced Monsieur Anatole to not cook a proper meal in order to, excuse my forthrightness, keep your shape."

There are rare moments in life when the truly unexpected happens. For instance, when a sudden flash of inspiration leads you to bet on a horse no one ever heard of, and it goes in to win the Grand National. I was certain that Florence was going to fall upon the little Belgian and claw out his green eyes, but instead she said:

"I'll have one."

"A steak and kidney pie?"

"No, a cigarette."

Florence began puffing on it with all the energy of the Orient-Express but otherwise stayed silent. Monsieur Poirot was the only man I knew to have ever muzzled that howler monkey, and that inspired respect in everyone present. Even Aunt Dahlia meekly screeched:

"Your notion of blackmail is absurd. In fact, it's Anatole who's constantly been threatening to quit if we don't raise his wages."

Hercule Poirot responded in a tone one generally uses in hospitals when speaking to the insane or terminally ill.

"We shall keep our tempers, *n'est-ce-pas*? Then we shall organize facts in a coherent pattern, and analyze them. Those that prove significant, we shall keep. The others... Poof!"

He pulled a piece of paper out of nowhere much like a magician does with a rabbit. I made a note to ask him how he did it so I could use the trick during our next gala at the Drones Club.

Poirot continued:

"Let us discuss Monsieur Anatole's performance then. I have here a list of the meals he was instructed to cook during the last week. Each follows a strict dietary requirement. Is it possible that this distinguished Chef suffered from being turned into a mere provider of ordinary food and to not be able to enjoy the full practice of his art? In other words, you may have hurt his pride."

"How did you reach such a conclusion?" asked Uncle Tom, who was still watching the trinkets Poirot had rearranged.

"I do not usually explain my methods before I solve a case. But you should know that the solution will be found by the little grey cells," said the detective, tapping his temple with his finger.

I thought that the little Belgian ought to be careful to not repeat his performance before Sir Roderick Glossop, because the latter would soon have him locked up.

I then noticed Jeeves stood behind me. As usual, he had appeared like a genie out of his lamp. I got up and whispered to him:

"Are you up to speed?"

"Reasonably so, sir."

"From the beginning?"

"For the most part."

"Any ideas?"

"Perhaps, sir, but I must first help Seppings."

"Oh, bother Old Stuffy!"

"I beg your pardon, sir, but Mrs. Travers' staff is facing an unforeseen emergency."

"I should say so! We may be forced to eat stale fish food tomorrow, Jeeves. You must untangle this business."

"Certainly, sir."

"I will donate my moustache to the cause." We Woosters are as magnanimous in defeat as in victory.

"Thank you *very* much, sir."

As we spoke, Poirot joined us. The man had the discretion of a cat. It was another thing he had in common with Jeeves.

"Someone mentioned a moustache?" he said, caressing his.

"It must be in fashion," said Hastings.

Until then, the Captain had remained rather discreet. But just right now, I saw a malicious twinkle in his eyes, like a gambler about to cash his prize. He turned towards the others.

"I have observed my friend Poirot during his past investigations," he said, "and I have no doubt that he will solve this mystery. But if Mr. Wooster's gentleman thinks he can do better, I suggest a bet."

That was a jolly good idea, worthy of a true Brit. In less than a minute, I settled the terms with the Captain. Then he announced:

"If Monsieur Poirot wins, Mr. Wooster will keep his moustache. If Mr. Jeeves wins, my friend will shave his."

"And I'll do the same," I added, although no one appeared to care.

The detective looked at Hastings with some concern.

"*Mais enfin, mon ami*, it is unthinkable!"

"Why not? Don't you say that no one is better than you?"

"*Naturellement* but..."

"That you are the greatest detective in the world?"

"*Bien sur*, but..."

"I've never seen you fail since our first meeting in Belgium years ago."

The spectators had begun to circle around. Poirot was cornered. His pride, or the fact that escape was impossible, made him consent reluctantly.

"*Très bien*! My little grey cells are vastly superior to the average. The man who would succeed where I would fail has not been born yet."

" Jeeves?"

Nodding to indicate his agreement, Jeeves emitted a small cough before entering the lion's den.

"When we arrived at Market Snodbury, I first took care of my master's luggage, before meeting with the Chef as is our habit. I believe there are some old family recipes which..."

"The facts, Jeeves!" thundered Aunt Dhalia.

"I beg the your pardon," he said respectfully. "When I came in, I noticed that Monsieur Anatole was involved in a lively conversation with Monsieur Poirot. Both gentlemen were making demonstrative gestures to strengthen their respective points. They seemed to be discussing a matter of *étiquette*...”

All heads turned to look at the detective. I could not resist doing so. Poirot's face was as white as chalk, which contrasted nicely with the inky black of his dyed hair.

Jeeves waited for everyone to regain their composure, then continued:

“Monsieur Anatole was planning to serve his *Consommé aux Pommes d'Amour* in soup bowls. Monsieur Poirot corrected him, using the terminology of soup *plates*. Even though France and Belgium are neighboring nations, each has its own linguistic peculiarities. What the French call soup plates, the Belgians call soup bowls. So Monsieur Poirot was not mistaken when he said that Monsieur Anatole's pride had been hurt. That is why he served the consommé in the salad plates. It was his way of avenging his honor as a Frenchman, which had been severely wounded by Monsieur Poirot.”

I think the San Francisco Earthquake cannot have produced a more resounding silence in its aftermath. The detective eventually broke it by saying:

“I shall honor the terms of the bet, because Hercule Poirot's word is his bond. However, may I solicit a favor? At the request of a high-ranking civil servant, Mr. Jesmond, I must to go to Kings Lacey tomorrow. Would it be permissible to do so unblemished?”

“I will guarantee that my friend will honor the bet before I leave for Argentina,” said Hastings, smiling.

Magnificent in defeat, Hercule Poirot asked Aunt Dahlia to accompany him to the kitchen to present his humblest apologies to Chef Anatole. Captain Hastings offered his arm to Florence and went back to the dining room with Uncle Tom.

Once alone, I said to Jeeves:

“*Rem acu tetigisti?*”

“I believe that I have indeed pricked him with a pin.”

“I was blind, Jeeves. But I believe we shan't see or hear from Monsieur Poirot for a little while.”

“Indeed, the coming year may not offer Monsieur Poirot many opportunities to ply his trade.”

“At least not until his mustache has grown back.”

“Indeed, sir.”

“Yes, Jeeves, *Noblesse oblige*.”

“Of course, sir.”

[*English adaptation by Jess Nevins.*]

Jess Nevins is the author of the World Fantasy Award-nominated Encyclopedia of Fantastic Victoriana, *a delightful compilation of notable and not-so-notable characters from that wonderful age of popular fiction. Among these is the colorful and wily rogue-turned-hero Rocambole, one of the most important characters of French pulp fiction of the late 19th century. Jess' tale takes place early in Rocambole's career, when the still villainous anti-hero had found refuge in London between two French adventures. It is therefore in the proud capital of the British Empire that we find Ponson du Terrail's dashing scoundrel looking for yet another opportunity to feather his nest...*

Jess Nevins: *Red in Tooth and Claw*

London, 1849

Rocambole sat at an outdoor table at the Café Royal, sipping an Amarone and contemplating a relief from boredom. He had been in London for only a week, and already the idea of a day full of nothing but indolence had palled from attractive to tedious.

He knew he ought to be content. He was young, handsome and rich, for he had left France with enough money to make even a de Guéran or d'Ardèche envious. Better still, he was unknown to the English constabularies. He should be happy to live the life of a *flâneur*, spending his days idly shopping for the latest in Savile Row fashions–for if he must be forced to live among the English, he would at least be the best dressed of them–and his nights sampling the pleasures of English women, who were equally charmed by his fine features and his full wallet.

What had he to bother him, really? The cross-Channel voyage on the *Doge of Venice* had been quick and pleasant. His lodgings were comfortable. It was a sunny day, the breeze felt good on his cheeks, his hair was ruffling in a fetching manner, judging from the admiring glances of his toothsome Irish server, and his ascension from child of the streets to member of the idle rich was complete.

And yet he was bored. Infinitely so. His own imp of the perverse, which occasionally had led him to commit rash acts in France, was again whispering in his ear, suggesting he have some light-hearted fun with the so-stuffy, so-proper English. (Rocambole sometimes fancied he could see his imp; he thought it might look like a small black monkey, crouched on his shoulder, its eyes alight with gleeful malice. The notions the monkey murmured to him, though amusing, were hardly shocking to him and rarely remunerative, and so he usually ignored the imp and his suggestions.) But what, then? Something profitable, naturally. While his usual outlets for money-making mischief–theft, murder and arson–were possible, he had grown tired of them in France and felt no compulsion to e possible, he had grown tired of them in France and felt no compulsion to begin again in London.

Such things as manipulation of the stock exchange were always possible, and easily enough carried off; Rocambole had once spoken with an amusing Hohenzollern rogue who had convinced him that buying the stock of arms manufacturers, and then altering the headlines of local newspapers to make it appear that war had been declared–thus spurring a run on arms and driving up the price of the stock–would be simplicity itself.

But that would require long-term planning, and Rocambole lacked the patience for that. He was more interested in something that would only require a few months' work and would have a guaranteed and preferably substantial payday at its end.

Rocambole's musings were interrupted by a rhythmical clanging sound, audible even above the noise of the late afternoon traffic on Gordon Street. Sauntering down the sidewalk on the Café's side, nodding to all those around him with a smiling, genial condescension, was a man unusual enough for even the prematurely jaded Rocambole to stare at. The man wore white leather breeches, a green coat and a scarlet waistcoat with a gold band around his hat and a red belt across his shoulder. The clanging sound came from a set of cast-iron rats suspended from a belt worn crosswise on his body; the rats struck each other as he walked.

Behind him Rocambole heard, "Speed, is that Jack Black?"

"What, haven't you met him?"

"No, how could I? I've only been back from Simla for a week. I haven't been to any of the likely spots or seen any of the quick crowd."

"Ah, right. Well, you're in for a treat. Black not only kills rats for H.M., but he's also got a nice line in rat pits."

Rocambole, who had been taught by life and circumstance to always pay attention to his surroundings, and had learned that lesson well, realized that the two men sitting behind him had begun saying something potentially interesting. Their earlier conversation had led him to dismiss them as coarse, roaring blusterers, of the sort who had made the Jockey Club such a displeasure to frequent, but now he paid closer attention to their words.

"...They say he's never been bitten."

"What, never? But...I thought he was a rat-catcher?"

"He is. Likes to stick his hand into a jar of freshly caught rats, to make the ladies scream. Never gets bitten, though."

"And he's the man who runs the pit fights?"

"Oh yes–who better? Everyone trusts him, too. You know your money's safe with him, and that he'll deal you fair. No doping the rats or anything like that."

Rocambole's interest was piqued. Gambling? On rat fights? This was a wrinkle Rocambole was unfamiliar with. On an impulse, he turned in his chair and looked at the pair. As he had expected, they were members of the flash set: heavy whiskers, silk waistcoats, tall hats and jewel-tipped canes. Fake gems, too, Rocambole's practiced eye informed him. They noticed his movement and glanced at him. He said, "I say, sorry to interrupt, chaps, but–did one of you just mention wagering on rats?"

He knew what they saw when they looked at him: a handsome young man with twinkling eyes and a twisted smile, the kind which appeals to the rogue in men and the whore in women. He was dressed in Treadgold silks. Large black diamond on one ring. Smooth skin, but faded scars on his knuckles. In all, one of the swell mob, on the high end of the economic scale, and, from his accent, French. From his words, interested in gambling.

To these two, he would appear to be either a chum in the making or a particularly downy pigeon waiting to be plucked. Rocambole smiled, the smile that had opened the legs of Lola Montez, and stuck his hand out at the one called Speed, and said, "I'm Louis Froget."

It went as Rocambole expected. The pair–the second introduced himself as John Sinnat–demonstrated a familiarity with the better families of Paris. He idly mentioned his acquaintance with the Countess of Clare. They compared their experiences of the Riviera, Rome and Lisbon. Rocambole had never visited any of those places, but knew that a confident demeanor, an amusing delivery and encouraging sounds at the right time will convince most audiences of even the most ludicrous of stories.

Speed and Sinnat invited Rocambole to White's Club for supper, and the Frenchman repaid them with tittle-tattle and gossip he'd heard in Paris–the origin of the wealth of the Duke of Gerolstein, the true parentage of Emile Benoit and the reason for the messy end of Sten de la Gardie.

By nine, they were strolling down Archipelago Street, well lubricated and old pals, and Speed and Sinnat were insistent that Rocambole join them on their way down Gray's Inn Road to the East End, to what Speed called "the money pit."

"It's where most of us go, don't you know. You can find the like across the City most nights, but it's only once every two weeks that Black and Shaw run theirs."

Rocambole only exhibited moderate interest. (Fishermen: never yank on the line when you've hooked your prey. Ease them on to the boat.) "But Speed, *mon vieux*, what is it?"

Speed smiled, an expression which emphasized the rodent cast to his face. "You'll see."

Rocambole did, almost immediately. The building looked like just another public house, and the sign over the doorway read *J. Shaw, Proprietor*, but once into the building's basement, the Frenchman instantly knew what the money pit was. It was blood sport.

The sights and sounds and smells hit the Frenchman simultaneously. The fetid, humid air in the crowded room. The flickering light; the lanterns only lit the pit and left most of the men in the room partially in shadow. The coppery, harsh smell of blood, but not human blood–dog blood and something else, but blood nonetheless, and lots of it. The cacophony of sounds: the avid and even manic shouts of the men, the barks of triumph and groans of financial ruin, and over them all the snarl of a small dog on the attack and the high, piping squeaks of dying rats. Most of all, the expressions on the faces of the men looking into the pit. They showed all the emotions Rocambole knew best: raw greed, the delight of the voyeur, the sickly exhilaration of a devotee of blood sport on watching an evisceration, hatred from the losers towards the winners, contempt from the winners towards the losers, desperation, guilty satiety, drunkenness and arousal. Damp, moldy stone, slicked with blood. Sweaty, puffy faces. Doughy hands, waving guineas or sovereigns.

Rocambole felt at home and a wave of bonhomie rolled over him. He waited until it passed, and only then looked into the pit. It was large, over ten feet in diameter and five feet deep, with a rough cobblestone floor. Standing in it to one side was Black, still in his costume, and another, younger man, dressed nearly as well as Black and sharing his placid expression. On the other side was a small black terrier, panting and happily wagging its tail as it looked at Black. Its muzzle and paws were soaked with blood. Around it were the torn corpses of 15 rats.

Rocambole was about to ask Speed about the dog when Black raised his right hand. The crowd instantly quieted.

"Time, gentlemen. Those of you what bet hagainst my little Billy finishink these 15 off in a minute, well, I'm hafraid you've lost your money to me, and if you had a private flutter, you owe your neighbor his winninks. Pay up proper and prompt, like."

The crowd groaned, some good-naturedly, many more not so. Rocambole smelled more than sensed the potential for violence. He had always had an exceptional sense of smell and had always associated violence with the smell of roses and wine, since his childhood and the riots following the cholera epidemic. But Black seemed oblivious to the threat. He smiled mildly, kept his left hand tucked into a vest pocket, and nodded at his assistant, who began collecting markers and paying winners their sums. The Frenchman quickly saw that Black's blithe assurance of his own personal immunity, or pretense of same, was somehow rubbing off on the crowd; many of them were furious and clearly contemplating assault on their neighbors, but it obviously didn't occur to them to make Black a target for their ire.

Nor, equally obviously, did it occur to the crowd to not pay what they owed to Black. The sight of the greasy silver and gold passing from one hand to another caught and held Rocambole's attention. So much of it, more than the Frenchman would have dreamed possible from betting on a rat fight.

No one saw the way the light, reflecting from the silver and gold, lit up the grey flecks in Rocambole's eyes, or the grin which spread across his face, or the thoughts and calculations that flew like quicksilver through his mind as he contemplated Black and his terrier, and the rat corpses in the pit, and the faces of the gamblers.

The next day Rocambole got directions to Black's home from some urchins outside his boarding house. The Frenchman took a cab over the Thames to Battersea. Initially, Rocambole had some difficulty in seeing which of the cottages was Black's, but then noticed a bird cage suspended above the doorway of one and, next to it, a square of zinc. On the square were painted the words, *J. Black, Rat Destroyer to Her Majesty*, surmounted by the initials *V.R.* and the painting of a white rat.

Black answered the knock on the door. He was dressed more soberly than he had been the previous day, in a clean but worn black suit, and his expression was friendly enough. As Rocambole mouthed the expected, empty words– "Good day, Mr. Black, may I speak with you for a moment?" and so on–he examined Black. Rough, uncombed black hair, black eyebrows and black whiskers, but a sprinkle of grey across it all, so that it looked as if Black had been dusted with powder. Large, dark eyes, and in them, amused geniality, concealed strength and not a hint of deference or intimidation, despite the obvious difference in social status between the Frenchman, who looked the very embodiment of one of the flash mob, and Black, a mere rat-catcher. *Must be careful with this one*, Rocambole thought. *He's fat now, but he came from the streets and they never left him.*

Black led Rocambole through two rooms in the cottage, filled with the remains of rats and birds and fish, all in glazed boxes and all labeled, and into a large back room filled with bird cages which were inhabited by rats, sometimes two dozen or more, and in more colors and shades and patterns than Rocambole would have dreamed possible, from white to jet black to striped in shades from grey-blue to rust. The smell in the room, rat urine and musk and a peculiar dusty odor, was strong, but Black did not seem to notice it.

Rocambole accepted the tea Black's wife offered, and after enduring the usual exchange of polite, empty phrases, said, "I was at the... do you know, I'm not even sure what to call it. The spectacle, last night, where your terrier killed all those rats."

Black smiled. "Oh, yes, sir. We call it rat-baitink. Don't you have 'em in France?"

Rocambole's smile did not change, but inside he moved Black from the "Be careful" category to "Handle with long tongs." Before he had crossed the Channel, Rocambole had been careful to develop an innocuous and bland City accent for occasions like this one when he needed anonymity. For the rat-catcher to have heard the faint Parisian lilt in Rocambole's voice was worrying.

"No, we've contented ourselves with hanging cats. But tell me–your terrier, does he always kill so many rats?"

"Gracious, no. That was a casual think for my Billy. He's the rummest I've ever had–killed of a thousand in an hour, nearest a toucher, many times. I've been offered a sovereign a-pound for him, and won't sell. Even his sons–he's the father of the greatest portion of the small black tan dogs in London now–go for six or seven bob."

"Heavens. That much?"

Black smiled proudly. "Yes. He's a marvel, my Billy. My partner Jemmy– that's Jemmy Shaw, what you saw at the 'baitink–swears that he's my fortune, and without him I'll be left to rack and ruin."

"Where do you get the rats from?"

"I ketches 'em, sir. I've caught rats for Her Majesty, rats and moles, and 'sterminated..."

Black went on in that vein for quite some time, as Rocambole expected. He made encouraging noises and interjections, and let the rat-catcher ramble on about his past and his exploits as a rat-catcher, until Black came around to the *special* rats he had caught. Then–

"I beg your pardon, but–by *special*, do you mean the rats in the other room, the striped ones?"

Black smiled indulgently, the sort of smile an expert gives an interested amateur who has said something foolish. "What, the piebalds? Oh, no. I've a number of 'em, but I have more...unusual ones as well. For connoisshewers, you understand."

Rocambole made his smile sheepish. "This may be forward, but...do you sell any of them? I've a daughter, Marie-France, who loves unusual animals, and I think she'd love a rat."

"Certainly, sir! I've many that I've sold to gentlemen for their little girls. Even sold a pair–gave, really–to Her Majesty."

"Do people often buy a pair, rather than just one?"

"Yes. Don't want the poor blighters to be lonely, after all. And if you want kits–that is, babies–you'd best buy a breedink pair."

"Do the colors breed true?"

"Generally, generally. But you might surprised by how warious they get. Pieds breed whites, blacks breed pieds or cinnamons. You never can tell."

"What about temperament? I wouldn't want to buy Marie-France something dangerous."

"Oh, some strains are more wicious than others, sir, but my rats are gentled, else I wouldn't sell 'em. No, you raise 'em kindly, they'll be sweet as cream, I give you my word"

"Excellent. But...do you know, I think Marie-France might like something a bit more unusual. I believe you mentioned you had some special rats?"

132

Black led the Frenchman past the cages, pointing out the rarer, stranger breeds and the conditions under which each was caught. Rocambole drew the rat-catcher out about them, listening closely to what Black didn't say. Rocambole finally settled on four. The first was a long, muscular brown rat that Black called an *Albanian Brown*. "Frightful talkative, sir. If you listen too closely to it, you a'most think it's talkink to you. And clever, too. You'll need to be watchink it, and for Heaven's sake, don't leave the cage door open, or it'll be out and you'll never see it again." The second was a smaller black female whose fur shone as if it had been greased. The rat-catcher called it the *Priory Rat* and said that he'd caught it out in the country, in a remote valley in Gloucestershire, and that the rat was perfectly safe. Black repeated that, several times, insistently enough that Rocambole was hard-pressed to pretend not to notice.

The third rat was large enough to require Black to use both hands to pick it up. Its thick fur was the color of slate, and Rocambole saw that the rat-catcher was careful to pick it up by the scruff of its neck and its haunches, holding its head firmly and keeping his hands well away from its mouth. The rat chittered but did not attack Black. "This one, I got it off the *Surprise* after it had to stop at Outer Qwhglm to pick up some shipwrecked sailors. And this bugger," and he gently stroked the rat's head, "had climbed onboard and made itself at home in the stores, and the men were too scared to go after it. They let it be until the ship reached London, and then called me in. I just sang to him, then picked him up like this. He's not so bad as he seems, though. Keep him fed, say him a how-do-ye-do when you pass by his cage, and rub his head just so, and he'll be like a lap dog for your girl."

"So big...will he–can he breed with the others? I think Marie-France might want some babies."

"Can and has, sir. He's pupped three litters by ordinary whites and agoutis with no trouble. Quite potent, this one."

"Now, this blighter," Black said, turning to the last rat Rocambole had chosen, "this one needs some lookink after. He's not...domesticated. Tamed, I saw to that, but not broken, if you take my meanink. Requires a careful hand."

The rat was only ten inches long, excluding its tail, but its body was much thicker and more muscular than the other rats'. Its eyes were set more closely together than was usual with rats and its haunches were unusually large. Its fur was a reddish brown that looked the color of blood if the light hit it just right.

"He's not from around here. Fact is, I've never seen his like before. Neither had that Spanish naturalist from the Royal Society who tried to buy him from me. Offered ten sovereigns for his body after he dies, if you can believe it."

"Where's he from?"

"East, sir. *Far* east. Sumatra, they tell me."

"How did you get him? Did you travel–"

"Bless me, no, sir, I've never been east of Margate. No, I ha' friends abroad who know of my interests and pass on unusual animals now and again. This little bugger I got from those friends. Fan-cy friends."

The Frenchman, mystified, raised his eyebrows.

"Never you mind, sir. Just a little joke, nothink to think about."

Rocambole had Black keep the rats for a day and spent the afternoon inspecting properties. For what the Frenchman had in mind, he would need a large space, but one far away from prying eyes and ears. He eventually settled on a warehouse on the south side of the Thames, one of the stretches of riverfront that had still not recovered from the great fires. The landlord, a squat, unwashed man who reeked of gin, was happy to take Rocambole's money and even happier to be tipped extra to turn a blind eye. Black rented a wagon to fetch the rats, bought cages and food from Black and patiently waited through instructions on feeding and care, and then brought them to the warehouse and began the experiment.

Rocambole paired the rats up, the Albanian with the Sumatran and the Qwhglmian with the Priory. The females were in heat, so after each pair established which rat was dominant, they began mating. After that, matters became routine for the Frenchman. He merely had to make sure they were fed regularly–and the rats would happily eat Rocambole's leftovers, although they needed more than that to prosper. He handled the rats enough for them to recognize him and understand that he was their master–no small feat, as the Sumatran and the Qwhglmian were reluctant to admit that they were not in charge–and wait for the babies to appear.

When they did, three weeks later, in litters of 12 and 14, Rocambole was finally able to begin the experiment proper. He put a series of cages on the floor of the warehouse, and in each cage he put four rats, two from each litter, mixing the bloodlines so that Albanian/Sumatran mixes would be together with the Qwhglmian/Priory mix. The Frenchman made sure that they had just enough food not to starve, but never enough to grow fat or happy or even content, and he touched the rats often enough to maintain their familiarity with him, but otherwise let them alone. As he expected, in two months' time, each cage gave birth to another litter. Rocambole kept the litters in the same cramped cages, continuing to handle them, but keeping their food level low.

As expected, the rats grew savage and desperate for food, and learned that it did not profit them to attack him, but that the other rats in the enclosure could be attacked, killed and eaten. When each cage had killed enough of its excess members to establish an equilibrium, Rocambole began feeding them just enough to make them healthy, then let them breed. When they had given birth to more litters, he altered their food supply yet again, and encouraged their viciousness toward one another. The introduction of starving, feral dogs gave the rats a new target on which to vent their savagery, as well as slake their hunger and to associate dogs in their mind with food.

The end result was much to Rocambole's satisfaction. By Christmas, he had a horde of rats who obeyed him and were willing to be picked up by him, and even placed in a coat pocket, but whose attitude toward anything else, especially dogs, was savage.

As the weeks had passed, Rocambole had been a regular attendee at the rat-baiting, and had carefully watched Black. Fewer and fewer men were willing to gamble with Black when he pitted his terrier against only a dozen rats, so he was forced to put increasing numbers of rats in the pit and wager that the terrier could kill them all within a limited amount of time. He always asked how Marie-France was enjoying her rats, and the Frenchman described the offspring, much to Black's avid interest.

It was the Friday before New Year's when Rocambole was finally able to begin the last part of his plan. He had learned early on that the gamblers loved to send the old year off with one great and final exclamation of a rat-baiting, with Golcondas of wealth being gambled, and the most renowned dogs, the Dragons and Vultures and Snarleyyows, being set to race the clock and then top the records.

On such occasions the usual locales would not do for the crowd, being both too small and, as they thought, beneath their dignity as men of fortune. Instead, Black and Shaw rented for one night a large warehouse in Limehouse and opened it to anyone willing to spend money. Such a gathering would usually attract the attentions of informants, if not Peelers, as large crowds of gamblers, pleasurable ladies and floating money had meant riots since the days of Miss Voyant, Abraham the Gentle and the Theater Troubles.

Rocambole had asked one of the regulars about this. He was a portly, pleasantly cynical Irishman named Coyle in whom the Frenchman a kindred spirit, and so kept a close eye on. Coyle said, "You'd think Limehouse would be trouble, and the Dear knows you'd be right usually, but this spot, this louse-crawling, mouse-infested, dank ill-smelling ill-omened moldy pit of the Devil– and no offense to you, sir–is property of the Red Shadows, yellow-faced spawns of Lucifer that they are–and may your line prosper, sir–and they see to it that the Peelers have their eyes diverted by the gleam of silver."

Rocambole made sure to enter the warehouse later in the evening when the hens would have been plucked by Black and Shaw and only the hardened roosters left to be dealt with. Toward midnight, the higher money matches took place, and while the crowds were fewer, they were more intent on the pit and less on what bystanders, such as Rocambole, might be doing.

The sights and sounds and smells of the rat-baiting were much as usual, greed and desperation and vicariously-satisfied bloodlust so palpable as to be tasted by a mere tongue-lick of the air, but among the satisfied or disappointed cries was a note of tension shading into hysteria which the Frenchman didn't like at all. It didn't portend immediate violence, but it had an edge to it which made him keep in mind the nearest exit at all times.

Rocambole waited until the middle of one match, while all eyes were on the dog, a big, filthy-looking mutt, to stroll to the cage in which the rats were kept before they were emptied into the pit. If Black followed his practice, the next match was Billy's, 24 rats in 90 seconds, or something similar, something to top Billy's previous record–no one being willing to take bets on his 15-in-a-minute.

Rocambole carefully removed 16 rats from the deep pockets of his overcoat and slipped them into the cage. They immediately tried to escape while the other rats in the cage, not liking the arrivals' smell, tried to squirm as far away from them as they could. The 16 were Rocambole's best, combining the size of the Qwhglmian, the viciousness of the Sumatran, the intelligence of the Albanian and the malice of the Priory–and all were hungry but not starving.

That done, he casually positioned himself near to Black and waited for the right moment. When the rat-catcher was done with his offering–24 rats killed in 90 seconds–and the crowd was contemplating whether or not to take his bet, Rocambole said, "A handsome proposition, Mr. Black."

"Thank you, sir." *It's no proposition but a certainty* was unsaid, but clear on his face.

"But…24 in 90? That's coming it a bit high, don't you think?"

Rocambole noted with approval that Black kept his surprise and affront off his face, contenting himself with an amiable smile and a professional, "Not at all, sir. I believe it's a fair wager. Care to take a flutter?"

"I believe I will. Tell me, what's the usual? A few shillings?"

"Yes, sir, although some go as high as–"

Loudly, Rocambole said, "What about 30 pounds?"

Silence, then. Thirty pounds was a year's rent in a good section of London, with enough left over to pay a maid for the year. Thirty pounds was more than most in the warehouse would see in a year.

Black simply stared for a moment. Rocambole was pleased that neither the rat-catcher's color nor expression changed; the Frenchman appreciated players in the Game who carried it off well. Black just stared, eyed Billy, who was wagging his tail expectantly, then smiled. "Very well, sir, 30 quids it is."

After Rocambole handed over the money–and it was silver and gold, not the distrusted and still too-easily-forged bank notes–he caught the eye of the fiercest man in range and said, "What about you, sir? Who do you believe more capable, Black's dog or the rats?"

A gleam of yellowed teeth and a contemptuous grin. "The dog. I'm no strawberry."

"I've got six shillings says the rats."

"Done."

Those close saw that Rocambole was intent on proving the crowd wrong and closed in to get what money they could out of the mob, who obviously didn't know what Billy was capable of. The smarter among them checked out Billy first, but he had been in plain sight the entire night, so there was no chance of Rocambole having drugged or tampered with him.

When all the money was collected, Black was holding over a 150 pounds—much less than Rocambole had earned in the past, but more than enough to live well in London.

Black wasted no time. He marched to the rat cage, reached in and pulled out the first 24 he could grab and then tossed them into the pit with Billy and cried "Go!" As Rocambole had expected, several of the rats he had bred were among those in the pit. Black was sure enough of his own ability not to get bit that he did not look closely at the rats he was grabbing in the cage.

Billy happily leapt at the first rat within reach, expecting the usual—a grab, a head shake, and then tossing them aside and moving on to the next rat, accompanied by the pleased shouts of his master.

Instead, while 17 of the rats fled from him, five, hungry and angry, charged him, going for his belly and throat. He managed to pin one down with his paw and bite a second, but the three others were under him, and as they had done dozens of times before, laid his belly and throat open and began feeding.

Billy's agonizing howls were the only sound audible in the warehouse. Rocambole, enjoying the visible shock on Black's face—so satisfying when your opponent knew he had been mastered, and by whom, and could do nothing about it, and had to bear your gaze without responding—chose that moment to say, "I believe that's 150 pounds, four shillings that you owe me."

Rocambole got to enjoy Black's speechless fury for only a moment. Then, behind him, shouts, a door being kicked open, and police whistles. A phalanx of uniformed men entered the room, starting a stampede of fleeing gamblers. Leading the police were Inspector Bucket, a portly middle-aged gentleman, and Sergeant Cuff, a lean, weathered, grizzled older man. The Inspector shouted, "Hunt, Creegan, you take that door. Fitz, Tennison, you take the rear entrance."

Rocambole had been expecting this ever since he entered the warehouse, since he had tipped them off in advance, and so was ready to move. Quickly and smoothly, the Frenchman drew a pistol from his jacket pocket and smashed it into Black's temple.

Rocambole then took three long steps and kicked over the cage containing the rats, which fled in every direction, occasionally up the pants leg of a gambler or policeman. The Frenchman drew his other pistol from his trousers pocket and then fired them both at the oncoming police. He had made sure to mix fireworks' powder into the gunpowder of his bullets, so that his guns made an extraordinarily loud *bang* and produced a voluminous amount of smoke.

The police were startled by the noise and smoke and were momentarily unsure what they were dealing with, and so stopped, just as Rocambole had planned. He then stepped to the rat-catcher's prone body, found the bag of coins, pocketed it and ran for the nearest exit, cuffing aside gamblers in his way. The last words he heard from inside the warehouse were, "Take the bite victims to Doc Blake, he's got experience with this." The Frenchman grinned. No one had experience with these bites, he had made sure of that.

Rocambole walked several blocks until he found a cab willing to stop for him, and then enjoyed a slow ride to the West End. London was too hot for him now, but that was acceptable. London in December was wretched anyhow. America would hardly be any better, but he'd heard Lola Montez had relocated to some place with the atrocious name of "New Jersey." They had had good times together in the past; perhaps it was time to renew their acquaintance…

One of the highlights of Tales of the Shadowmen 2 *was undoubtedly Kim Newman's "Angels of Music," in which the author of the unparalleled* Anno Dracula *series cleverly combined the myths of* The Phantom of the Opera *and* Charlie's Angels *to create a flamboyant trio of 19th century female crimefighters secretly working for Gaston Leroux's shadowy Erik. Kim returns to this wonderful concept with an even more impressive sequel, in which a new team of Angels face an even greater threat. Your mission, should you decide to accept it, is to read...*

Kim Newman: *The Mark of Kane*
(*Angels of Music II*)

Royale-les-Bains, c. 1900

A ticket had been delivered by *pneumatique*. The "Special Performance" would commence, unusually, at 10:30 a.m.

He entered his box via the trap-door. Plush upholstery matched the velvet curtains, soft and rich in the electric lamplight. A phonograph apparatus stood on a trolley. A program lay on his chair. It was an unfamiliar design–not from the Paris Opéra, but a theater in Chicago.

The half-hour chimed. He cranked the phonograph and raised the needle-arm to the revolving cylinder. After a few seconds' hiss, an anonymous voice issued from the bell.

"Good morning, Monsieur Erik..."

He opened the program as indicated by a tasseled bookmark. A full-page rotogravure portrait showed a plump, smiling, expensively dressed patron.

"The man you are looking at is Charles Foster Kane, the American millionaire and press magnate. Kane believes his financial and political interests, and those of the United States of America, would be served by a war among the Great Powers of Europe. Presently, he is summering at Royale-les-Eaux, a spa town north of Dieppe where he has substantial holdings, ostensibly to acquire works of art for his private collection. In truth, Kane has convened a gathering of powerful, like-minded or simply malign individuals and plans to found a cartel dedicated to bringing about a catastrophic conflict..."

Kane had small, piggy eyes–a ridiculous nose, perhaps artificial–fat, complacent cheeks–and an impertinent double-flick of a moustache.

"Your commission, should you be inclined to accept it, is to ensure this offensive organization does not come into being and that Charles Kane is dissuaded from further meddling in the affairs of sovereign nations other than his own. As usual, should you or any of your 'angelic associates' be apprehended or

139

eliminated, the Minister will profess never to have heard of such fantastical individuals. Long live France. This cylinder will perish within a matter of moments..."

A bar of magnesium fizzed blindingly inside the works of the phonograph. Box No.5 smelled like a burning wax museum. The cylinder resolved into molten residue.

The "Special Performance" was at an end.

The young widow Lachaille, following the Persian's instructions, carefully made her way through the labyrinth beneath the Opéra. She avoided the rat-traps, and negotiated several ingenious devices set to inconvenience mammals somewhat larger than the average sewer rat. From respect for poor Gaston, she wore an ensemble from the dressmaker who made such a success of Hanna Glawari's mourning weeds. She left off the veil because it was dark enough under the streets of Paris. Gilberte did not care to vanish entirely into the shadows–though, it occurred to her, disappearance might be the whole purpose of the invitation from Monsieur Erik.

In the absence of the fortune her late husband's lawyers were withholding, she must find means of making a way in the world. Her hard-earned respectable name counted for little, though it was scarcely her fault–no matter what the Sûreté might imply–that her bridegroom proved incapable of surviving his own honeymoon. Without consulting her, the foolish soul had elected to fortify himself with a philter to put "lead in his pencil." He had misjudged the dosage, to everyone's inconvenience–not least his own. For a reputed man of the world, Gaston turned out to be something of a stiff, in all senses of the term. Aunt Alicia said dead husbands were generally best of the breed, but also conceded that society was liable to be leery of Gilberte for now. In Grandmama's day, you had to bury at least two husbands in mysterious circumstances before being categorized as a "black widow." In this impatient, young, electrified century, a single hasty funeral sufficed.

A skiff waited at the shore of the underground lake. She lifted her skirts and stepped in. No sooner was she settled than the boat began to glide soundlessly across the still surface. It was on a pulley, like a fairground ride.

Gilberte had heard whispers of the masked creature–Monsieur Erik, the Phantom, the Trap-Door Lover, the Trickster–who kept a lair beneath the Opéra and retained the services of unusual, hard-to-place young women. His discreet agency had been in operation for several generations. The diva Christine Daaé, with whom mama had sung, was rumored to have been among Erik's original "angels of music" along with the crown-chaser Irene Adler and the model Trilby O'Ferrall. Many "adventuresses" were said to have worked for the Phantom: the detective Loveday Brooke, the witch Unorna, the anarchist Grunya Constantine, the chilly Marahuna, the *naga* Anna Franklyn, the pawnbroker Hagar Stanley, the leech Geneviève Dieudonné, the swordswoman Yuki Kashima. *Les anges* might be fleeting, but Erik's primary lieutenant was always the Persian. This fellow was known to *le toutParis*. Some believed him the true master of the angels, and Erik not a phantom but a phantasm.

The Persian, age impossible to tell, stood on the jetty to which the skiff was pulled. Erik's assistant wore a heavy coat with a good astrakhan collar, and a fez. Gold dotted his person—rings, stickpin, shirt-studs, cufflinks, spectacles-chain, fez-tassles, watch and fob, two prominent teeth. Courteously, the Persian extended a hand and helped Gilberte ashore. She thanked him, modestly.

He pressed his palm to a stone. A wall parted to give access to a large, comfortably appointed room. Gas-lamps burned, susurrating like serpents. Gilberte stepped in and cast an eye over fine old furniture, assessing values to the *sou*. These were the quarters of a well-off gentleman. The subterranean chamber was naturally bereft of windows and thus oppressive for her taste.

A portion of the room was curtained off by a thick but translucent hanging. A man sat in the antechamber beyond, lit from behind as if in a silhouette theatre. Her eyes went naturally to this figure, whom she took at once for the fabled Phantom. She did not immediately take notice of the two other women in the room.

"Madame Lachaille," said the man beyond the veil, "thank you for joining us this evening."

It was a deep, mellifluous voice, precise and perfect. Through Mama, the contralto Andrée Alvar, she knew many singers. She recognized a musical quality in this voice. An odd catch suggested the speaker was compensating for a defect of the palate. Erik took care with certain consonants. Gilberte recalled the stories of the face some claimed to have glimpsed, and repressed a shudder.

She curtseyed as she had been taught—not submissively, but confidently. Grandmama would be proud. And Aunt Alicia. And Mama.

"Gilberte, you will be working with these women. Mrs. Elizabeth Eynsford Hill…"

Mrs. Eynsford Hill was impeccably—if too simply—dressed, and as blankly beautiful as a couturier's mannequin. The woman shook Gilberte's hand, firmly. She had a steel grip in her good green kidskin glove.

"I am honored to meet you, Madame Lachaille," said Mrs. Eynsford Hill, in English. "I trust we shall become fast friends."

Her diction was classroom perfect, with a musical lilt as if she were hitting notes rather than uttering words.

Gilberte responded, also in English, "that is my hope also."

The woman paused, and repeated "that is my hope also" parrot-fashion. It took Gilberte a moment to realize she had been perfectly imitated. Not just vocally; Mrs. Eynsford Hill's expression had been Gilberte's, down to the trick of lowering the eyes while missing nothing.

"I beg your pardon. For such insolence."

Now Mrs. Eynsford Hill was "doing" Erik. She spoke in masculine French, as if from beyond the curtain. As the Phantom, the Englishwoman pulled back her chin and sucked in her cheeks to create a deeper voice. Even those odd consonants were there.

"Elizabeth is showing off," said Erik. "It is one of her 'tells.' Having discovered the extent of her talents, she needs an audience. Like many of my angels, she has a theatrical inclination."

"You are a widow, I perceive," said Mrs. Eynsford Hill, in what Gilberte now took for own–if not her *original*–voice. "I myself, sadly, am not."

"My condolences."

The other angel cooed for attention.

"This is Riolama," said Erik.

If the Englishwoman was so ordinary she seemed strange for the absence or concealment of lively qualities, this creature was a picture-book fairy come to life.

Riolama might have been taken for a child, though her large, active eyes were adult. Well under five feet tall, she wore a shimmering white-grey shift of fabric unknown to Gilberte (who could list and identify as many dressmaker's fabrics as Sherlock Holmes could tobacco ashes), had a wild but untangled fall of dark hair and did without shoes. Her feet were not dirty.

The girl sprang from a tall stool and bent close to Gilberte, flitting like an inquisitive monkey or a bird. She was making up her mind, apparently. After a few seconds, she pecked a kiss at Gilberte's cheek and darted away, back to her perch, pleased.

"Rima likes you," said Mrs. Eynsford Hill. "She's from Guyana, where the *guano* comes from. Or Venezuela, where various violent volcanoes are venerated. The territory is under dispute."

The bird-girl tucked her head under her arm, then smiled. Gilberte felt a chill–it was her own once-upon-a-time smile, which Grandmama had schooled her out of. For their own good, girls do not show teeth. In this company, evidently, teeth were acceptable. Indeed, perhaps mandatory.

If whispers were true, the lipless Erik had no choice but to smile and smile. Beyond the curtain, behind the mask, was–she had heard–a skull with eyes. The Phantom could take first prize in a grinning contest with the mediaeval mountebank Gwynplaine and the Czech Baron Sardonicus.

Gilberte was struck that the Englishwoman and the exotic girl both resembled her. Might she be reunited with unknown sisters? Her father, rarely mentioned by the female relatives who raised her, could conceivably have sojourned in London or Caracas.

She had an inkling Mrs. Eynsford Hill was not as high-born as her too-correct accent would suggest. In Gilberte's experience, the upper classes were as slovenly as the lower orders in their speech–only their vocal tics and mispronunciations tended to be called mannerisms rather than mistakes. Like Gilberte, the

Englishwoman had been taught how to speak to impress others rather than express herself.

"Ladies," said Erik, "if we might proceed. It is best we talk English. It is not, of course, a musical language, but it is in this instance the tongue of our enemy."

Gilberte had high marks in English.

Curtains parted to reveal a screen. The Persian worked a cinematograph projector and images came to life.

The mode was more Lumiére than Méliès—snatches of actuality caught by the camera, rather than a staged artifice. A fat man in a straw hat grinned next to a half-crated statue twice his size, like a big game hunter proud of his latest bag and eager to gloat among his clubmen.

"This is Charles Foster Kane," said Erik. "He is an American."

"All too plainly," commented Mrs. Eynsford Hill.

In another scene, Kane—in a shiny silk hat and a fur coat that looked like a whole bear—stood outside the ruins of a castle in Spain. Workmen carried away and crated up huge stone blocks.

"Mr. Kane has an acquisitive nature," continued Erik, "and a limitless source of wealth. A gold-mine in Colorado."

Now, the man was in evening dress, squeezed between girls wearing little more than feathers. Gilberte recognized the upstairs rooms at Maxim's. Several of her contemporaries could recount adventures at this locale.

Kane posed with a group of sharp-eyed, ferociously moustached men outside the offices of a newspaper.

"In 1898," said Erik, "a correspondent of the *New York Inquirer* cabled Kane, claiming he could write prose poems about the scenery in Cuba but 'there was no war.' Kane responded, 'You provide the prose poems, I'll provide the war.'"

Kane watched troops in Boy Scout uniforms board a ship. Then, he was laughing with Theodore Roosevelt on a podium draped with flags. They made a matched pair of ferocious little boys.

"Mr. Kane did indeed provide the Spanish-American War. In this new century, his tactics have moderated. At least, he spurred his own country to fight over Cuba. Now he intends to foment an Anglo-French War."

Gilberte exchanged looks with Mrs. Eynsford Hill.

"Why would he wish such a thing?" Gilberte asked.

"Mr. Kane is a patriot," said Erik. "With Europe in flames, America would become the pre-eminent world power. The upstart nation, scarcely more than a century old, would dictate its whims from Nanking to Nantes. A continental war would, not incidentally, sell a great many newspapers."

On the screen, the American was at a zoo alongside a pinch-faced lady Gilberte took for Mrs. Kane. He pointed out a cockatoo, which was dragged by a

keeper–silently screaming and flapping–from a branch. It was shoved into a ca-
nary-cage and presented to the magnate.

"Bad man," said Riolama. "Mean to bird."

Gilberte was surprised the girl could speak.

The cinematograph presentation concluded.

In the last century, Royale-les-Eaux had enjoyed a vogue as a watering place for
the wealthy and listless. Mama had sung a season at the Petit Opéra, attached to
the Grand Hôtel and the Casino. The magpie Théophraste Lupin had lifted jewels and broken hearts among the ladies who flocked from Paris and further afield
to summer balls, concerts and gaming tourneys. Their excuse was the local
springs, reputedly a tonic for intimate diseases. In 1890, the waters ran dry and
nothing could be done to make them flow again. The *Société des Bains de Mers
de Royale*, who governed far more than the baths, suffered a decline reversed
only by the miracle of a Yankee deliverer.

Charles Foster Kane had lighted upon the town, bought it at fire-sale price
from its owner, the banker Favreaux, and made it his European compound. What
could not be bought was leased. A motion was before the *Société* to change the
resort's name to Europa-Xanadu, to further the connection with the magnate's
Florida fiefdom. Royale-les-Eaux was an outpost of Kane's empire, an American colony in the Old World. Having relocated castles from Spain, Hungary and
Scotland to serve as guesthouses, he was filling the halls with works of art pur-
chased or looted from the great collections of the continent. A reserve was
stocked with wild boar (a hardy local breed crossed with Australian razorback)
suitable for stalking, shooting, scoffing and stuffing. An army of cronies, hang-
ers-on and minions easily filled the place. However, showing the democratic
impulse of his peculiar country, Kane decreed his private realm be open to the
general public.

As soon as they alighted from the train at the Gare de Royale-les-Eaux, it
became apparent that apparent madness was founded on solid business practice.
Scrubbed and smiling youths of both sexes, with a stylized K on their tunic
breasts, besieged new arrivals. They offered to carry baggage (for 50 *centimes*),
sell post-cards (for 50 *centimes*), provide ginger beer or *gelati* (for 50 *centimes*),
serve as guides to the town (for 50 *centimes* an hour), secure seats at "exclusive"
high-stakes gaming tables (for 50 *centimes!*), or effect introduction to suitable
temporary companions (for considerably more than 50 *centimes*). It was impossible to take three steps in this town without spending money, as if every franc
in every pocket were magnetically drawn to the millionaire's already-
overflowing coffers.

Such a shame the fellow was inconveniently married. No, that was beyond
consideration. Money was beside the point. One did not marry an American, any
more than an orangutan. There were standards.

The Persian had wisely left all gold accoutrements behind save his teeth (and kept his mouth firmly shut to hide them). He swept licensed, uniformed pick-pockets out of their way and located an elderly railway porter. The fellow wore the K-brand, but had plainly been at his post long before the new regime descended. The Persian extended a handsome bribe to make sure their trunks arrived inviolate at the Grand Hôtel. He whispered something terrifying in the porter's ear—presumably invoking their phantasmal patron—to persuade the man it would be best to follow instructions to the letter.

Outside the station, the tiny town was a Babel. Purple-liveried cowboys cracked whips and held up signs to direct crowds this way and that. Royale-les-Eaux was a combination of Wild West "wide open town," Tartar war camp and storybook enchanted kingdom. Bathhouses and hotels had sprouted towers and castellations, some of stone and some merely wooden stage flats, to become every possible variety of gaming-hall, bordello or museum of curiosities. A bandstand in the Venetian style stood outside the concourse. An orchestra in harlequin costumes played while dancing girls hopped around behind a singer in a striped jacket and jaunty hat. Over and over, they performed the town's new anthem, alternately in French (*C'est Monsieur Kane*) and English (*Oh, Mister Kane*).

When the song came round for the third time, Elizabeth said, "I will find out who wrote that tune, and have Rima drop him in a South American river as food for *piranha*. Then I shall have his bones polished and strung up as an example."

Every fourth or fifth building was a peculiar type of café, surmounted by a wrought iron K inside a circle—the Mark of Kane. Here, patrons queued for thin meat patties and salad leftovers served inside limp circles of bread, along with deep-fried potato peelings unworthy of the name *pommes frites*. This fare was handed over in boxes made of folded newspaper (*New York Inquirer* overruns, Gilberte supposed). No plates or cutlery were involved. Customers fetched their own food and found their own tables, if they could—so waiters need not apply for employment. Cheap trinkets were given as prizes to those who gobbled their "Fatty Feast" within the shortest time. It would take a diamond pendant to make Gilberte *start* a Burgher Kane meal, let alone finish it.

She dreaded to imagine what went on in the kitchens. Rumor was that the cowboys herded animals into giant mechanical pens where many whirling blades rendered them—bones, skin, hooves, eyes, bowel contents and all—into a thick liquid which was splashed onto grills to create the circular patties. The Burgher Kane slogan was "over 22,000 sold." Such cafés were supposedly popular in New York, Chicago and San Francisco. From Royale-les-Eaux, Kane intended to expand across Europe.

With dignity, Elizabeth walked down the street, flanked by Gilberte and Riolama. The Englishwoman ignored everyone who tried to importune her, Gilberte kept an eye out for potential assassins, and the bird girl was nervous in this crowded, cacophonous jungle. Impertinent comments were addressed to the ladies by idlers. The Persian saw to it that every insult was punished with a withering glance or, if appropriate, a cuff.

Gilberte herself had to break a pickpocket's fingers before they reached the Grand Hôtel.

The lobby was dominated by a twice life-size painting–a poor copy of Hals' *The Laughing Cavalier* with Kane's face replacing the original sitter's. The curlicued K was everywhere, on doorknobs and antimacassars and wood-panels and the carpet. Gilberte wondered whether the American insisted employees have his mark tattooed on their shoulders like slaves or branded into their thighs like cattle.

At the front desk, Elizabeth announced herself as "Miss Kathleen Ruston," an English lady whose charitable foundation provided improving literature for bereft children in uncivilized quarters of the world. The little flutter Elizabeth allowed into her voice suggested Miss Ruston found Royale-les-Eaux backward enough to be in need of a tract or two.

A sharp-eyed female receptionist saw through the imposture at once. The real Miss Ruston was detained in Huddersfield by a mystery ailment not unconnected with doctored gin. From her reticule, Elizabeth produced a lacquered oblong, embossed with a gold K–a 1,000 franc board from the Casino. A gilt design on the reverse, resembling an octopus, distinguished it from the ordinary run. The receptionist noted this, and signaled for a superior–a sleek-haired, hollow-eyed young man with a sharp-pointed false beard.

"I am Haghi," he said. He might have been German, or Arab, or any nationality. "Mr. Kane trusts you will enjoy your stay, and extends the invitation to join his other 'special guests' in the private salon this evening. *Okee geluk, dama.*"

"*Dankzegging, mens,*" Elizabeth responded, *sotto voce*.

Their host had arranged that Miss Ruston be indisposed, so her identity could be usurped by a Dutch lady who bore a passing resemblance to the *philanthropiste* but was quite a different character. Edda Van Heemstra–dancer, courtesan, thief, blackmailer and trafficker in government secrets–was not a person to be entrusted with a charitable foundation. Her notion of "improving literature" tended to illustrated volumes with titles like *My Nine Nights in a Harem*. Detained during a stop-over in Paris, Mevrouw Van Heemstra currently enjoyed the hospitality of locked apartments in the sub-basement of the Opéra.

On only a few moments' acquaintance, Elizabeth had Edda off perfectly, though her Dutch vocabulary was limited to pages of common words and phrases torn from a *Baedeker's Guide to the Netherlands*. Gilberte admired the performance. Elizabeth was successfully impersonating a Dutch harlot imperfectly posing as an English prude. No wonder she scarcely remembered who she really was.

Among Kane's "special guests," Edda was high in the magnate's councils. She had been entrusted with procuring documents central to his plans.

The register was presented. Elizabeth signed with a flourish. Forging signatures was another of her talents. Gilberte was beginning to feel Grandmama and Aunt Alicia had neglected vital aspects of her education.

"Eddie, you are a sight for sore eyes," brayed a loud, American voice.

Gilberte tensed. This would be a real test. Someone who knew Edda Van Heemstra.

Assembling a dazzling coquette's smile, Elizabeth turned to greet the man who had addressed her. Gilberte saw in her companion's eyes that she had no idea who the fellow was.

Well dressed but for a shapeless slouch hat which put his face permanently in shadow, the American thrust out a paw, as if expecting "Eddie" to shake it like a man. His hand was several sizes too large for his body, thickly furred, with diamond-shaped horny nails. A malformation of the tendons made the fingers curve claw-like, as if he were perpetually clutching an invisible throat.

The hand was his "tell." While Elizabeth was practicing her Dutch, Gilberte had gone through a flipbook memorizing faces, aliases and histories. Erik had excellent, up-to-date intelligence: Haghi, the deferential hotelier, was–without the goatee–also Nemo the Clown, an expert hypnotist, basket-weaver and revolver shot. Gilberte was a fast learner, too. It was her duty of the day to steer Elizabeth through a crowd of "known associates."

"This must be the famous Perry Bennett," Gilberte announced, extending her own languid, gloved hand to the clutcher. "Edd, you must introduce me."

Elizabeth's eyes focused. She followed Gilberte's lead.

"Mr. Bennett, my companion represents an organization which must be well-known to you, though its name is not spoken even in this company. May I present Mademoiselle 'Pia Verm' of Monmartre."

"I am especially familiar with the *rooftops* of that district," Gilberte claimed.

She was also borrowing an alias, but a shadowier one. "Pia Verm"–whose name shifted from moment to moment–was a thief, or perhaps several thieves, or perhaps just a cast-aside body-stocking and mask anyone might pick up and put on. Gilberte thought the name silly and jokingly suggested she represent herself as "Anna Gram" if anyone asked.

However, the man with the clutching hand was impressed.

Riolama peeked out from behind Elizabeth. She wore a sailor suit and had been persuaded to don oversized workman's boots painted pink. She looked no older than 12.

"This is Rima, an auxiliary member of the, ah..."

Gilberte crooked her forefingers and put them in front of her eye-teeth while opening her eyes wide–the universal underworld sign for the nocturnal band "Pam Rive" worked with.

147

Bennett looked at the waif as if she were an ice cream sundae with a cherry on top. Gilberte knew instantly that he was one of *those*–once a girl turned 13, she was of no interest to him. American rogues in his line often wheedled to be appointed as guardians to underage heiresses and were torn by contradictory impulses. Should they rope in a defrocked clergyman and force the girl into marriage at dead of night, or set the fuse to the dynamite and strand her in an abandoned mine?

"What a gathering of like souls!" Bennett announced, in a high-pitched voice which didn't quite match his sinister looks. "I was on the boat train from London with Madame Sara, Sir Dunston Gryme and Simon Carne. Imagine: the Sorceress of the Strand, the Azrael of Anarchy and the Prince of Swindlers in one place! Dr. Materialismus is here, and Abijah K. Jones, the Devil Bug. Yesterday, I saw Wanda Stielman walking arm in arm with Ballmeyer. If only the crowds out on the promenade knew who was among them? What a cut-up that would be! I daresay many would expire from sheer fright to think their sleeves had been brushed by the likes of Baron Maupertuis or Dr. Quartz or Wizard Whateley! Professor Fate and Sir Cuthbert Ware-Armitage have been delayed, because their motor-cars collided on the road from Dieppe and they are conducting a duel. But the Assassination Bureau, Ltd., has opened a stall disguised as a gypsy fortune-teller's, and is advertising cut-rate offers. The Black Coats are here too, even though the Colonel was heard referring to our host as a mere *parvenu.* "

The hand remained stuck out stiffly, quivering with Bennett's excitement to be in such company. Gilberte judged him a minor villain–he was like several women in Aunt Lucia's circle who were overly eager to list invitations they had received from prominent people and always worked "as I was saying to such-and-such-a-person-far-more-distinguished-than-you" into their chatter. Beneath his hat-brim, Bennett's eyes wandered sideways to see if anyone more famous had come into the lobby. Finally, he fixed on someone.

"You must excuse me," said Bennett, bowing slightly. "I see Raymond Owen–a countryman of mine, with similar interests. We must confer on matters of mutual concern. Tethering to railroad tracks has proved a more unreliable method of solving a problem than those of our stripe might wish."

He hopped off, with a gait that suggested his left leg must suffer from the condition affecting his right arm.

Gilberte looked at Elizabeth and Riolama.

They had passed their first test, and were accepted by at least one of this wicked company.

Haghi struck a bell, summoning a minion to escort the ladies to their suite.

In Xanadu did Kubla Khan a sacred pleasure-dome decree...
The words were written in incandescent bulbs over the doors of the Casino.

Gilberte had learned Coleridge off by heart in her English class. It was supposed to be a *stately* pleasure-dome.

The foyer was lined with peculiar contraptions. Patrons fed them with coins, yanked a crank-handle, and peered through a window as wheels whirred, then ground to a halt displaying miniature playing cards. If the centime-stuffer was fortunate enough to get a winning hand, the machine spat out tokens redeemable only at the bar in the Casino. The machines made a horrid, grinding, clanking sound. Their devotees had an impatient, haggard look she found quite disturbing.

"In America, they automate everything," she mused.

"Not *everything*," said Elizabeth. "There will always be a place for the human touch."

Interspersed with the gaming machines were Mutoscopes, which worked on a similar principle. Coins unlocked a mechanism, and working the handle ran a strip of pictures past a peep-hole. *The Dance of the Nile. The Execution of Marie Antoinette. Madame at her Bath. A Flogging on Île du Diable. A Maiden Surprised by a Satyr.* Gentlemen cranked vigorously, and peered at the tiny, flickering action. Live women could stroll past *au naturel* without distracting these addicts from their chemically-graven images.

"Miep Vrå" and "Edda Van Heemstra" were dressed like a pair of black widows. Riolama was back in the suite, taking one of her bird-naps.

In the main salon of the Casino, fortunes were won and lost the old-fashioned way at baccarat or roulette tables. A hall the size of a railway station was lit by a multi-faceted globe, which was studded with electric bulbs and mirrors. This interior sun revolved slowly, wavering lights over tiers of gambling concourses, probably to the fury of people trying to concentrate on their cards or the wheel. Gilberte trusted the sphere was fixed more securely to the ceiling than the famous chandelier at the Paris Opéra. Otherwise it might prove a temptation to Monsieur Erik.

They passed through the busy hall to the inner sanctum. A brass-bound door, emblazoned with the most elaborate K yet, was guarded by a big-browed, jut-jawed giant in evening dress. He was covered in the flipbook. "Edda" was supposed to know him from a previous exploit.

"Voltaire," Gilberte whispered to Elizabeth. "Strong-arm man for hire. You shot him in the head in New Orleans. He's had metal teeth put in since then."

"*Daa-hling*," said Elizabeth, very loudly, "you've done something marvelous with your mouth."

Voltaire grinned, showing sharpened steel.

"Most ferocious," Elizabeth commented. "And this, of course, is, ah, 'Ema Virp...' "

Elizabeth presented their special board, and the giant–who obviously thought less of being shot in the head than many folks of Gilberte's acquaintance–opened the door to the private salon.

It was theatrically gloomy. Kane had stripped hangings, murals, frescoes and candle-sconces from an abandoned Transylvanian castle and reassembled the décor in this conference room.

A huge oak table, suitable for a Viking feast, already accommodated many masked or veiled men and women. A Neolithic altar, grooved and stained by centuries of ritual murder, was set at the head of the table, like a lectern.

"Edda" and "Vi Marpe" took their allotted seats. Masks nodded at them. Some of the veiled ladies wore enormously feathered hats. A few villains had laid daggers, pistols or exotic devices on their place-settings.

An oversized hairy hand waved at them from the end of the table. Bennett must be pleased to be included in the inner circle. They were near the top of the table. Elizabeth had a corner seat, across from a leonine fellow in a papier-mâché Mr. Punch mask. To Gilberte's left was a ramrod-straight, severe young woman sewn into a tight-fitting gown composed of metallic plates.

A middle-aged, white-haired fellow with arthritic hands stood by the altar. Henry F. Potter, a banker, was associated with Kane in usury and union-busting throughout the American Mid-West. He had a reputation for dispossessing widows–which, since her bereavement, Gilberte took exception to. In vaudeville parlance, Potter was the "warm-up" act.

"Friends," coughed Potter, "now we are all present, I suggest we take off our masks. There should be no need for disguise in this company."

To emphasize the point, the banker slipped off a bandit domino which was useless for concealing his identity. She had thought he was just wearing thick spectacles.

Up and down the table, veils were lifted, hats removed and masks slipped off.

Most of the names Bennett had dropped were present: Madame Sara, Dunston Gryme, Dr. Quartz, Simon Carne, Baron Maupertuis. Gilberte recognized others from the flipbook: William Boltyn, an American patron of science who claimed to be wealthier even than Kane, along with his pet engineer Hattison; Gurn, promising mercenary and murderer; General Guy Sternwood, hero of the Spanish-American War according to the Kane papers but "the Blundering Butcher of Las Guasimas" in every other record of the conflict; sleek young Senator Joseph Harrison Paine, the tycoon's bought-and-paid-for voice in Washington; and Julian Karswell, the English diabolist.

Kane's company took in vastly disparate political interests. The woman in the metal dress was Natasha Natasaevna di Murska, sworn enemy of kings and capital. Her father, the mysterious Natas, was mastermind of an international organization called (unsubtly) The Terrorists. Natasha glared fierce hatred at the plutocrats, robber barons and aristocrats who formed the greater part of Kane's company. Gilberte trusted the Angel of the Revolution hadn't been allowed to bring any of the bombs she famously liked to throw at oppressors of the people into this room.

The fellow opposite Elizabeth took off his Mr. Punch guise to reveal a second mask underneath–a tight-fitting, rough-stitched leather hood with slashes to show his teeth and eyes. He was "the Face," whose page in the agency's flip-book of notable fiends, mercenaries and masterminds was mostly blank. His true features were less frequently seen even than the baleful skull of Monsieur Erik. He put it about that he was so transcendently handsome that normal life was impossible–women and men, equally besotted, would abase themselves in his path wherever he went. Gilberte had heard some good stories in her time, but that one took the madeleine.

Potter rapped the altar with knobby knuckles.

Voltaire wound up a phonograph and that dratted *Oh Mr Kane* tune sounded out, played as pompous fanfare. The already dim room-lights lowered and bright spots flared on the altar. Charles Foster Kane himself appeared, arms outstretched, in a dazzling white suit, grinning like an imbecile, enjoying himself immensely. He swept off his straw hat and waved it. He was at once a politician, a pastor, a song-and-dance man and chairman of the board. Gilberte wondered if they were supposed to applaud.

A glance up and down the table showed most of the company were also skeptical. But they stayed. Kane clearly had a species of magnetism. Money, ignorance and energy were a potent combination and–if what she had seen at Royale-les-Eaux was anything to go on–might soon surge around the world.

"Hiya, fellers–and, especially, feller-esses," said Kane. "Welcome to the Inner Circle of the Most High Order of Xanadu. I just made that up, you know. Most of you folks are used to secret societies and such, stretching back hundreds of years. I reckoned it'd be a comfort to have a new one we can sign up to. I'll have X buttons made up..."

Gilberte suspected there'd be a K on the pommel of the X.

"We've a whole pile of doings to get through today, so I'll try–against my natural instincts–to be brief. I'm a newspaperman, so I ought to know not to waste words gussying up the message with flowery language. We want a war, right?"

A few mumbles, and a little bark of excitement from General Sternwood.

Kane made an exaggerated show of disappointment.

"Come on, Inner Circle, I know you can do better than that? We want a War, *right?*"

"*Right*," shouted all the Americans at the table, in enthusiastic unison.

"I suppose so," conceded the English Carne.

"It is inevitable," decreed the Hungarian Natasha.

"*Eh bien*, maybe," shrugged the Belgian Maupertuis.

"That's more like it," said Kane. "I knew you had it in you. Whoo, this is a tough room. Do you like the room, by the way? The Count had cobwebs and bats and rats–I even found a dead armadillo behind a sideboard–but I've spruced the old rags and stones up. Anyway, to the point, this war... I know you all take the *New York Inquirer*, so I'll hurry through the set-up. Last year, we ran a serial in 32 breathless installments, thrilling our readers with *The European War of the Future*. It was a lulu! Wore out three writers. I had them run around interviewing experts in politics, munitions, naval warfare, airships, finance and all manner of things you wouldn't even think of–like military cuisine and fashions in uniform boots, ladies–then doled out their findings in an exciting, rapidly-paced tale. We presented the serial as if they were reports from an actual, live war. Nations fell under the savage lance, dashing cavalrymen charged at each other like total lunatics, nuns were violated by heathen grenadiers–always a popular line–and the crowned heads of half-a-dozen countries wound up rolling together in a wicker basket..."

Natasha Natasaevna allowed herself half a smile at the thought.

"I don't know why we didn't think of it before! We found readers cared more about this made-up war than real ones in Africa and South America. We had better illustrations and more heart-rending quotes. And white people being massacred. Naturally, the boys and girls in the drugstores and on the streetcars are clamoring for a sequel. What, I hear you ask, could be bigger and better and more popular than an invented *European War of the Future*? That's right, *mes amis* and *amigos*... a real-life, actual European War of Right Now. Which is what we are going to deliver."

General Sternwood–who, of course, wouldn't have to *fight* in this war–applauded. Perry Bennett flapped his normal hand against his clutching one.

"I'm just a sawdust-on-the-floor kind of feller who misses the spittoon as often as he gets a bull's eye," continued Kane, "but I've learned the value of buying the best help there is on the market. I did that with my serial, and I'm doing that with my war. So, I'd like those of you who have already contributed to Plan Thunderbolt to stand up, introduce yourselves and shoot us the low-down on how we're going to pull it off. In case you were worried, I *will* be back later–talking about something I know you'll all be much more interested in than strategic details, *the money*. So long, now."

Kane sat down, and the spotlights–hung from a rail in the ceiling–wandered around the room. A small, monkeylike fellow up in the rigging pulled levers and ropes to get the effect. "Evil" Emeric Belasco, a young man with an especially vile reputation. He had two pages in the flipbook, just listing the *variety* of his crimes.

The light came to rest on Elizabeth.

Gilberte found it hard to breathe, but her companion was perfectly prepared.

She stood up and announced her alias. "You know of my exploits," she said, offhandedly. "The Lavender Hill Gold Caper. The Larrabee Inheritance Swindle. The Tiffany Early Morning Diamond Snatch. The Charles Bonnet Art Forgeries."

Heads nodded. Among murmurs of admiration were a few mutters. Some of these folk only now discovered Edda Van Heemstra had bested them in previous dealings. The Rembrandt in Boltyn's collection had been scarcely dry when sold to him–dashed off by the talented Bonnet, one of several "fathers" Mevrouw Van Heemstra had turned up in her travels.

Elizabeth let the grumbles die, and got to business. "Through the strategic seductions of two junior clerks and one senior forward-planner in the British Ministry of War, I have obtained these documents."

She laid a folder on the table.

"These are photographic copies, of course. But excellent."

The folder was passed to Madame Sara, the designated specialist in forgery of government papers. She also did teeth, Gilberte understood. That would explain why the suspiciously golden-haired Italian-Indian adventuress set up shop in London's Strand–the English were notorious for their teeth. The Madame paged through the documents.

"I have the authentic seals," Elizabeth continued. "And the proper ribbons. The British are, as we know, obsessed with their ribbons."

Madame Sara nodded, satisfied.

"Thank you, Edda," said Kane. "You're a living doll." Elizabeth sat down. "Now," continued Kane, "our expert on the big game of politics, Senator Paine, will explain the *significance* of these purloined papers."

The light fell on the prematurely white-haired American dignitary. He was sitting next to the Sorceress of the Strand.

"In all nations, Ministries of War sit around during periods of prolonged peace, irritably finding projects to justify their existence," began the windy Paine, as if addressing his Senate. "Great Britain, possessed of an Empire, rarely has periods of prolonged peace..."

Gurn grunted. He had begun his murdering in the late South African conflict.

"However, when the British Ministry of War has a spare moment, their armchair generals like nothing more than the drawing-up of *contingency plans*, which is to say imagining what wonderful new wars might be embarked upon. For reasons few can explain, it costs as much to compile a folder such as the one we have here as it does to make a battleship. Thus are military budgets rubber-stamped cheerfully by parliaments and despots alike. Sometimes, as with the Boer War, a conflict might be a long time coming. Plans can be framed well before the outbreak of hostilities. But, there are also nasty surprises. Sudden diplomatic rows get out of hand. An unkind word about an ambassador's wife's hat and the Balkans goes up in flames as the triple alliance of Ruritania, Latveria and Syldavia march against ancient foes in Graustark, Transia and Borduria. From Cleopatra's nose to Jenkin's ear, wars have sprung up from such trifles. So, Ministries play games of 'let's pretend' and *plan* what they would do under certain *contingencies*. 'Let's pretend...' resurgent Viking hordes ravage Scotland! Which regiments would be mobilized, what lines of transport must be kept open, where would artillery be deployed?"

Paine tapped the folder.

"This *contingency plan* is founded upon the 'let's pretend' supposition that France makes a sudden, aggressive move against the British in Egypt, to wrest control of the Suez Canal. Furthermore, the French Navy occupies the Channel Islands while building up the fleet–an armada, if you will–in *la Manche*. An army is landed on the South Coast of England. *Jean-François* strikes towards London and King and Parliament. Of course, France has no such intent, so far as we or the British Ministry of War know. Germany, Russia, Portugal, Switzerland, Japan, Pago-Pago, the planet Mars, Atlantis and Swansea have no thought of waging war on the British Empire–but plans exist to be put in action in the event such attacks are made."

General Sternwood lifted a corner of the folder, took a look at a paragraph, and spat. "Limey crocks couldn't defend a whorehouse from a flock of sheep... Look at how they intend to fortify Andover! And no general in his right mind would set counter-invasion troops ashore on the beaches of goddamn' Normandy. They'd be cut to pieces! No, Cherbourg–that's your Frog weak spot!"

The General caught himself ranting and shut up. Paine gave him a stern look.

"If my colleague, Mr... ah... Mr. the Face ... would take over."

Paine sat down, and the spotlight fell on the Face.

"Senator, thank you," said the masked man, who had a rich, persuasive, unaccented voice. Beneath the leather he might be Quasimodo with the measles, but he was as beautifully spoken as any of the well-mannered gentlemen Grandmama warned Gilberte to be wary of. "The importance of the papers Mevrouw Van Heemstra has obtained lies not in details, General Sternwood, but in their shape and form. Much of the text can carry over into the documents Madame Sara will prepare. It is a simple matter of editing, of slanting the material, so that a *contingency* plan of defense will be transformed into a *definite* plan of attack. When the folder is passed to the French Ministry of War, it will be stained with the blood of many agents. The British will have made, or seem to have made, desperate attempts to get these plans back. Concurrently, strategic explosions will stir up activity in Portsmouth. An astute observer will believe His Majesty's Armed Forces are hurriedly preparing an invasion. Furthermore, barracks in the South of England will receive shipments of pamphlets to be issued to private soldiers..."

The Face laid a specimen on the table, which was passed around. Stamped as a British Armed Services publication, it was an English-French phrasebook.

Flicking through, Gilberte found such useful sentiments as "we are delighted to accept your surrender, Mayor," "how long ago did your officers flee in terror, Private?" and "kindly tell your daughter not to put garlic in the breakfast we have requisitioned." She could imagine the outrage in the French press when–inevitably–a copy fell into their hands.

"When the British war plans are delivered to the French government," said the Face, white spittle flecking the corners of his mouth-slit, "they will be convinced the Coldstream Guards are on the point of marching up the Champs-Elysées. They must believe they have no time for diplomacy, and mobilize at once against perfidious Albion."

"Then," said Natasha, taking over the narrative, "bombs shall fall from the skies. Our air-destroyer *Ariel*, presently moored on the Scots isle of Drumcraig, will strike against targets in England and France, chosen for sentimental or patriotic associations. The White Cliffs of Dover. The square in Rouen where the English burned Joan of Arc. Where the *Ariel* does not reach, we Terrorists shall employ agents willing to sacrifice themselves for the cause. Waterloo Station shall be blown up! The vineyards of Champagne shall burn! There must be War!"

Gilberte thought Natasha might be unhappy in her love life. The armored angel fairly squirmed with delight at the thought of carnage on a global scale as other girls her age warmed at the prospect of an extravagant new hat with ostrich feathers or a small but exquisitely stylish diamond pendant.

"Now," said Kane, reclaiming the spotlight, pausing a moment so that Evil Emeric could fix him in the intersection of two beams, "the small matter of the big bucks. Those of you who are professionals do not come cheap, and those of you who are zealots are in need of operating costs. Miss di Murska, I know to the last gear and strut how much gelt it takes to launch an air-destroyer. Well, I am not complaining. I'm here to buy a war. My friend Mr. Boltyn has thrown in with me, so we can afford all the toys we want. His associate Mr. Hattison is an inventin' fool. Thanks to his ingenuity with electrical wires and levers and trickinesses well beyond my brain-pan, each of you will leave this casino a winner, to the tune of better than a half-million dollars."

"Mira Pev" herself couldn't have thrilled as much at the sound of that as Gilberte did.

"Personally, I'd like nothing better than to hand the money over in sacks right here in this room... but there are official bodies to be placated. My accountants have to fill in their forms and justify all my expenditures. I'm known for spending freely, but even I can't just say I've bought a job-lot of statues and paintings and hope not to answer any more questions. So, you will legitimately win your war chests. I have leased the baccarat, chemin-de-fer and roulette tables from the Bath Water Society. For this season, I am the bank. Tomorrow night, you will collectively break me. You may find this shocking, but every game of chance in this town is rigged. Our good friend Mr. Hattison has made sure of that. Anyone in the gaming business knows you can't run the racket without letting some mug win large from time to time, to keep the rest of the suckers playing. Tomorrow night, my friends, you can't lose. Oh, it won't be obvious–there'll be reversals, early losses to build up the pot, to keep other players in the game. But, at the end of the evening, you'll walk off with your pockets full of chips."

Around the table were happy faces. Even the Face's leather mask seemed to smirk. Only Natasha kept frowning.

"I've laid out bait enough to attract all the high-rollers and big operators in the so-called 'professional gambler' line," said Kane, "and it's my hope the pack will sense blood in the water and bet against you. That smug bastard Johnny Barlowe is here, and you know what he's like, with his 'independent air' and his 'mass of money, linen, silk and starch.' 'The Man Who Broke the Bank at Monte Carlo,' hah! I'm happy to give you good money for services rendered, but I'll be additionally tickled puce if you take what you can from parasites like Barlowe. Not to mention Gaylord 'Riverboat' Ravenal, Sebastian 'Basher' Moran and half a dozen other gussied-up sharks in frilly shirts. Take their rolls as well as mine, and go with my blessing. A superfluity of Fatty Feasts, Meaty Morsels and Vril Grills are about to be express-delivered from the Burgher Kane in the lobby, so anyone who cares to join me in dining heartily is welcome to get their faces in the trough."

Like almost everyone in Kane's company who wasn't American, Gilberte and Elizabeth professed to have dined earlier. They withdrew and tactfully had to detach themselves from Natasha–by telling her an especially oppressive Archduke was playing whist in a private room with a bloated factory-owner, a corrupt cardinal and a brutal chieftain of Cossacks. The Queen of Terror trotted off to investigate, regretting she had not worn a bandolier of dynamite sticks to offset her metal-plate dress.

"That girl needs more fun in her life," Gilberte observed.

It was as Erik had guessed. The casino was the pump of Kane's machine.

Tomorrow night, however things panned out, would be exciting.

In their suite at the Grand Hôtel, the Persian unrolled architectural plans. Rio-lama was at his shoulder, big eyes taking in details. She was a quick study. The bird girl still didn't talk much. Gilberte couldn't imagine her upbringing, but she had a lively mind.

When he "leased the bank," Kane made many alterations. He had openly put in gaming machines, Mutoscopes and a Burgher Kane, stamping his K everywhere. The secret purpose of the work was to turn the Casino into a giant machine. A transparent overlay, initialed by Engineer Hattison, showed electrical wires threading through the building like nerves. The globe of lights in the main salon was hollow, like a diving bell. Using telescopic devices, a small person concealed within could have close-up views of every gaming table in the hall. A

156

panel of switches and levers could dictate each spin of a wheel or turn of the cards. The croupiers were literally hooked up; special garters threaded wires through their shoe-soles to make contact with metal plates–the K motifs in the carpets. The Eye-Ball could apply tiny shocks in coded patterns, conveying instructions to the men on the floor.

Decks of cards, printed and sealed on the premises, arrived at the chemin-de-fer table or the baccarat shoe pre-shuffled to suit the house, backs marked in an ink which showed when viewed through a red lens the controller could slot into the telescopes.

"How did Monsieur Erik obtain these plans?" Gilberte asked. "I'm surprised Kane is careless with such things."

The Persian tapped his long nose. "It's one thing to *pay* for such a system, but another to design it, and quite another again to build it. But a few firms are capable of executing such a commission. Frankly, the fellow who said he didn't care what it cost to have a cathedral-size pipe organ dismantled and reassembled in the catacombs of Paris has more goodwill with the specialists than the Yankee vulgarian who quibbled about every franc spent on installing his wonderful cheating machine. Among other accomplishments, Erik is the greatest secret architect of the age. Who do you think the workmen who built Kane's Europa-Xanadu look to for regular employment? We had these plans from the draughtsmen even before Kane did."

Riolama held up one of the flimsies, looking at it several ways, and made little cooing noises.

"Monsieur Kane is no believer in games of chance," Gilberte observed.

"Americans always brag about how much they love to gamble," said the Persian. "What they mean is that they love to *win*. Kane doesn't even think of this as cheating. He is simply unwilling to play any game where he doesn't make up the rules. He takes undue pride in his own cleverness..."

"The vain in Kane is mainly in the brain," mused Elizabeth.

"I think she's got it," said the Persian. "By George, she's got it. The vain in Kane *is* mainly in the brain, and the bane of Kane is plainly to our gain. So have you seen it?"

Gilberte snapped her fingers.

"Gigi, you've seen it!"

Kane, swelling inside his waistcoat from too many Fatty Feasts, could not personally run his machine. He had paid for a marvelous toy, but someone else blew the whistle and rang the bell.

"He takes one enormous risk," she said. "He must trust whoever sits inside his Eye-Ball."

"Just so," said the Persian, pulling out another plan. "But Kane takes precautions. In the average casino, the heaviest security arrangements–the biggest guards and the thickest doors–are for the vault where the money is kept. In Royale-les-Eaux, the most inaccessible room is directly above the main hall. Kane keeps his newest acquisitions there, paintings and statues and trinkets. The gallery is also the only point of access to the Eye-Ball. The skylight is electrified. The windows have shutters, sharpened like guillotine blades, which slice down if something–say, a burglar's limb–is thrust through. Monsieur Voltaire personally ensures no one even gets up the stairs to the main door, which is also electrified. The American cracksman Jimmy Valentine 'cased' the gallery last month, and decided not to bother. Even the authentic 'Vera Mip' couldn't get in easily."

Gilberte shrugged. "Marie Pv" could take care of her own reputation.

"It is fortunate for us that birds may fly where bats cannot," said the Persian.

Riolama chirruped.

"In myth," said Elizabeth, "the sculptor Pygmalion brought Galatea to life. We must now reverse the process, for only a statue can get into that room."

Her false moustache itched. She had to remember not to scratch, for fear of losing her disguise.

Elizabeth transformed herself without stuck-on whiskers. Even knowing the travesty, Gilberte could not recognize the young sculptor as Mrs. Eynsford Hill. She walked, talked, sweated and smoked like a man.

Voltaire had seen Gilberte and Elizabeth as "Edda Van Heemstra" and "Eva Prim" less than a day before. Now, the giant met "Jacob Epstein" and his apprentice, "Priam Vé." No flicker of suspicion sparked in his eyes.

The Persian had hired some roughs to deliver the crate. Voltaire dismissed them and called on the casino's staff–liveried apes with scraped knuckles from dealing with ungracious, complaining losers–to carry the big box upstairs to the gallery. When they could not exert sufficient lift, the major-domo added his own muscle. Voltaire bent double and the apes hefted the crate onto his shoulders. "Mr. Epstein" insisted he accompany the giant and his burden every step of the way.

Maneuvering the crate up the wide marble staircase was tricky. Gilberte trusted Riolama knew how to keep as quiet, and that the bird girl wouldn't suffer injury through awkward man-handling. Voltaire's collar burst as he strained. The apes assisted, keeping the crate from tipping off his back

The Persian had hoped Kane would be occupied elsewhere on this busy day, but he was in his gallery with Boltyn, Hattison and the capering Emeric Belasco. The mystery of who sat inside the Eye-Ball was solved. Evil Emeric was the likeliest prospect in Kane's Most High Order. Last evening, he had shown how nimbly he could work such contraptions from on high.

Voltaire, sweat pouring from his prehistoric brow, set down the crate.

"What's this?" asked Kane. "I said we weren't to be bothered."

"Bothered?" responded "Epstein," blood rising. "*Bothered*! A mistake has been made. No philistine is worthy of owning Epstein's *Rima*. You shall not even set eyes on her loveliness. Kane, your check will be returned, uncashed. You, Giant-Man, lift up the crate and take it away from this place."

Voltaire's fists opened and closed as if he were crushing melons. The casino apes looked helplessly at each other.

"Hold on, hold on," said Kane, trying to mollify the temperamental artist. "Did I say I didn't want your *Rima*? I have people who advise me on what to buy. They suggest I back you, Mr. Epstein. You will apparently 'appreciate.' "

Elizabeth puffed out, but still glowed with wounded pride.

"I am a sculptor of genius, sir. Not a racehorse or a bond issue. I am not to be backed or invested in. My work has nothing to do with money... which is why it costs so much."

Kane tried to think that through.

"If we could go over the wiring specifications again," interrupted Hattison, who looked as if he hadn't had a full night's sleep in months. "Everything must be checked and tested..."

Kane, not caring to be nagged, ignored the engineer. He considered the large wooden box.

"Open 'er up," he decreed. "Let's have a look at your *Rima*."

"Very well," said Elizabeth. "Great care must be taken."

She tapped at spots on the crate, indicating where nails should be pulled. The apes got to work with crowbars.

The crate fell apart. A quantity of straw came away.

The bird girl was on a heavy plinth, crouching inside a large nest. Her face turned upwards, features exaggerated, eyes blind. Twig-legged birds perched on her hands and shoulders. Metal waves of hair fell down her back.

Riolama was inside a carapace of metal-painted plaster over chickenwire. She seemed to be cast from bronze.

Voltaire looked at the statue as if falling in love at first sight.

"She's naked," observed Boltyn. "What would your mother think, Charlie?"

Kane didn't know what to make of the sculpture, but was vain enough to want not to appear foolish in front of his friend.

"How much did you cough up for this doxy?" asked Boltyn. "I'll wager there are real girls who'd cost a lot less."

Elizabeth shot a withering glance at the millionaire.

"It is very *modern*," said Hattison, trying to toady equally to both his masters. They ignored him.

"I think she's fine," said Kane, warming to his decision. "Yes, I see what Mr. Epstein means to say in this piece. Look at the strength in these limbs. The muscles of a wrestler..."

The statue's legs and arms were thick, to accommodate the slender body within. Gilberte didn't know who Erik had got to run up this "Epstein"–probably one of the scenery-makers at the Opéra. It would look better from the back of the dress circle.

Evil Emeric approached the statue, dragging stiff, withered legs. He ran his tongue over his teeth. The stunted cripple had strong arms and a vicious, street-fighter's reputation. Gilberte hoped Riolama was up to the task of taking–and replacing–the little incubus.

"She's a pip, Mr. Epstein," said Kane. "Leave her where she is. And keep the check. Now, we've got a business meeting, so we'll have to cut this short. Have some chips. Enjoy yourself in the casino. Who knows, you might be a big winner…"

Kane pulled a handful of casino boards from his pockets and gave them to Gilberte and Elizabeth.

Gilberte took a last look at Riolama and followed Elizabeth out.

In the foyer, Natasha Natasaevna di Murska was at a window, handing over bundles of large denomination notes in several currencies in exchange for stacks of boards she needed two minions to carry. The Angel of the Revolution was buying into the evening's play on a large scale.

Had Kane foreseen his comrades in the Most High Order would–given the golden opportunity–try to take him for *much* more money than they needed to carry out their parts in Plan Thunderbolt? The millionaire had a less sure grasp of human nature than Erik.

The Terrorists were not the only faction raiding their treasury to buy into the "sure-thing." Perry Bennett and Raymond Owen passed by, heaving large suitcases she guessed were filled with dollars siphoned from orphans' trust funds.

Madame Sara and Dr. Quartz queued for boards, in matching society-fools-on-a-spree disguises. They seemed to have "clicked" last night, which contra-dicted gossip about the Madame's amorous proclivities among her own sex. It could be that the pair merely had a great deal in common, specifically shared interests in human vivisection and unusual medical procedures.

Outside the Casino, among the crowds drawn to bright lights, they breathed again. Elizabeth dropped "Jacob Epstein." She shook out the hair that had been pinned up under her hat and was her own blank self.

The next moves were down to the bird girl.

A well-dressed, vacant-looking Englishman–half-eaten Vril Grill in one hand and sticky sauce on his chin–bumped into Gilberte. He gabbled an apology and then clapped eyes on Elizabeth.

"Eliza," he gasped, astounded.

"*Stone the bloody crows!*" Elizabeth responded, in an unfamiliar voice.

For the first time, Gilberte saw a real expression on Elizabeth's face. Something close to terror, with an overlay of exasperation.

"Madame Lachaille," she said, recovering her usual poise, "permit me to present my husband, Freddy Eynsford Hill."

"Pleased to meet you, eh what, Madame. Did you know you had face-fluff stuck on your lip. Playin' charades, I suppose. Anythin' to pass the time. Rum do, this. I was just wonderin' where the old ball and chain had got to, and up she pops, large as life and twice as bouncy. Eh what, indeed! Don't suppose you fillies'd like to take a spin round the old gamblin' establishment? I've got a feelin' in me nose that this is my lucky night."

Freddy was plainly an idiot. Handsome, well-mannered, mildly amusing–but an idiot nevertheless. From the cradle, Gilberte had been warned against falling in love with–let alone marrying–such a sorry specimen. Referring to his wife, Freddy had used the English colloquialism "ball and chain," but she was the one shackled to a frightful encumbrance. Gilberte wondered how Elizabeth had got stuck with such a blithering disaster. Then again, her own marriage hadn't turned out as well as expected.

Freddy made a move to kiss his wife in a proprietary manner. She applied her fingertips to his neck and the dull light in his eyes went out.

Now, Elizabeth was supporting a deadweight.

"I saw a Tibetan mystic do that once. I don't know how it works, but Erik does. Freddy will be asleep for an hour or so. Help me dump him somewhere he won't get robbed or hurt."

Gilberte took an arm. They carried Freddy through the crowds.

"Lost the family fortune following a seven with a queen," explained Elizabeth to anyone who paid attention. "Paralyzed by shock, poor fellow."

There were *tuts* of sympathy.

Rima carried her clock within her breast. Inside her rigid cocoon, she counted her heartbeats.

The gentle, arrhythmic drumming–and the other pulses of her body–were like the small, living sounds of the jungle. In her mind, all was green and warm and wet and dangerous.

She had no concept of regret, and so did not miss her native land. Bad things had happened there. Fire, death, pain. Others thought her dead. She knew not whether they were wrong. She might be a ghost. The cruel people had always called her spirit, demon, daughter of the Didi.

How she came here, to these new jungles, did not matter.

She thought of what she must do now, not what was gone.

Rima would do anything for Erik. If she were a ghost, he was Lord of Ghost-Kind. The others were the same, though they might not know it. Eliza and Gigi, from different jungles, were Rima's heart-sisters. Mirror-selves, summoned up from still, reflecting pools

When the Phantom played music for Rima, it was like a thunderstorm, a waterfall, a thousand birds singing in joy and terror. It was worth the crossing of a great ocean, wider than any bird could fly, to hear him play. The cruel people made thin songs, with flutes like twigs. Erik poured music through pipes tall as trees.

Twenty-five thousand heartbeats. Enough time had passed.

She stopped counting and opened her eyes. Through slits in the mask-piece she saw the room. A crowd of other statues. Paintings piled against the walls.

She flexed thin, strong shoulders and arms, straining against her second skin of wire, plaster and paint. Seams split, the shell sundered. She hatched like a chick. Her arms broke free. She pulled the plates over her chest and face apart. Wriggling out of statue, she found the room empty of people.

Careful to make no noise, she stepped off her plinth. Her former shell was exploded and hollow.

Rima, free after confinement, danced—rejoicing as feeling returned to her limbs. She wore only her shift and a leather belt. In its pouches were tools. She had been instructed in the use of some items by the Persian. Other implements she was skilled with of old.

A thick carpet was folded away from a closed metal hatch. A heavy padlock sealed it shut. This too held a volunteer prisoner. She set to work with lock-picks. Her fingers were deft. Soon, the padlock was sprung and set to one side. Silently, she lifted the trap-door.

She found what she expected. A thin perpendicular shaft like the inside of a hollow tree, with rungs set in its side. Twenty feet down, another hatch. Beyond that, the Bad Little Man.

Rima had experience with his kind. Cruel people, who set cunning snares that broke necks. Birds knew to fly away when they were near.

She twisted her hair out of her face and tied it in a knot, then crawled face-first into the hole. She made her way downwards, rung by rung, gripping fast with supple toes. If needs be, she could hang by her feet. About half-way down, she heard noise. Voices, the clatter of many small objects, distorted music. She had passed through the floor, and was in a branch dangling into the great room. At the end of it was the Bad Little Man's nest.

Stout chains hung taut around her, taking the nest's weight. Thick, rubber-coated vines carried the magic lightning.

Rima eased through the narrowing space.

Her face hung over the second hatch, which had a glass window.

She saw the top of the Bad Little Man's head. His thinning black hair was oiled, but white stripes of his scalp showed through. His face was pressed to one of many sets of eyepieces. His hairy hands rested on an array of keys, stops, wheels and levers. The contraption was as intricate as the Phantom's pipe organ.

Hooking her feet on a rung, she took a bundle from her belt, and laid it quietly by the hatch.

The Bad Little Man pulled his face away from the eyepieces. He crooked an ear like a cat, but did not look up.

Rima's breath misted the pane inches above his head.

The Bad Little Man twisted on his chair, and pulled himself to another set of eyepieces. His chair was on wheels, which fit to rails within his nest. He could turn like an owl and see in any direction.

Rima unrolled her bundle, which contained a cigarette holder. She fitted it into her mouth and got a grip with her teeth. The holder was stoppered with a tiny cork. The sliver inside rattled slightly.

This time, the Bad Little Man definitely heard her.

Rima reached for the hatch-handle and aimed her holder.

The Bad Little Man looked up. His face was young but withered, eyes black like caves.

She hauled open the hatch.

The Bad Little Man reached for a magazine pistol, but could not lift it in time.

With her thumb, Rima flipped the cork stopper. She spat out a quick breath.

The dart stuck into the Bad Little Man's neck.

Angry eyes fixed on her, but he could not move. Rima knew he was awake in his skull, but his body would not respond. The dart was tipped in venom derived from the poison frog. She had brought a supply from the jungle.

She reached down and twisted the pistol out of his nerveless grip. The gun dropped to the bottom of the nest, clattering into a chamberpot.

The Bad Little Man's eyes glowed with hatred. His locked teeth ground.

Now came the most difficult stretch. She had to extract the Bad Little Man from his nest and take his place on the wheeled seat. There was scarcely room for one person in this space, let alone two.

Rima hauled the Bad Little Man up by his shoulders. They were closer in the shaft than seeds in a pod. She wriggled, a new-born cuckoo tipping a heavy egg out of a nest or an ant juggling a weight many times its own with its legs. She forced the Bad Little Man's body up as hers inched down. When he was completely above her and out of his nest, he was still a weight. She lifted him into the shaft, crooking his withered legs over a rung. She took off her belt and used it to tie him there, a fly left in a spider's web for a later snack.

The Bad Little Man was strong-willed. He fought the frog-venom, face crimson, spittle on his lips. Inside, he roared with fury. But he was helpless. If he built another nest, it would be less pregnable. With traps for unwary ghost-girls, cuckoos or daughters of Didi.

Rima left him be and settled in his seat. She rolled it this way and that, enjoying the smooth motion. It was a comfortable nest, just her size.

She flexed her fingers and touched the keys. Now, with this building as an organ, she would play her own music.

She looked through a set of eyepieces. A distant view suddenly leaped up at her, close and vivid. She had used binoculars, and knew how they worked. She was seeing down into the big room below.

The Bad Fat Man stood by a long green table. Every other gentleman in the room wore black, but he shone in white.

"Ladies and gentlemen," he said, "place your bets..."

Piles of tokens were assembled on a baize grid. The Bad Fat Man elbowed aside a thin croupier. He would personally start off the evening's play. He bent over a miniature carousel. Rima knew this was a roulette wheel. The Bad Fat Man set the wheel spinning. An ivory ball jumped on the whirring carousel like an insect on fire.

Pinned to the giant keyboard in the nest was a chart. It listed numbers, odds, hands of cards and precise times. Beside the chart was a large white-faced clock. As the wheel spun in the casino below, the second hand shuddered.

Rima checked the numbers and times against those she had learned. She imagined her own chart laid over this one. She would play a different tune.

The roulette wheel slowed. The insect tired, close to death.

Rima's hand darted out over a particular key, hovered for a few ticks, then pressed down.

The ball stopped in a compartment within the wheel.

"*Trente rouge*," said the croupier. "Thirteen red. *La maison gagne*. The house wins..."

"...The house wins."

Gilberte had never seen a man so unhappy with his streak of good luck as Charles Foster Kane. Only Elizabeth–and perhaps a few croupiers–shared her insight. The casino staff continued to obey orders from the Eye-Ball, though.

Everyone else "in the know" remembered his plan–"early losses to build up the pot." The pot was swollen, and growing. A lake of money pooled in the counting-cellars beneath the main salon.

Many of the Most High Order favored the roulette wheel. Dr. Quartz, Madame Sara and Baron Maupertuis had laid fortunes on the baize, and seen their chips swept away. Several initiates had gone to the foyer when their initial outlay was seemingly–indeed, actually–squandered, and returned with freshly-purchased boards.

"...the house wins again," said the chief croupier. Chips clattered in a chute, disappearing below. Monies poured down a plughole.

Natasha, Sir Dunston and Senator Paine, preferring baccarat, sat together. An expressionless, wired-up dealer spun cards from the shoe. Gilberte understood that, in addition to the Terrorists' funds, Natasha was gambling with the Face's money. He could hardly be expected to show his, ahem, *mask* in such company, but would not want to miss out on the evening's profit.

Carne, Gurn and General Sternwood played five-card stud with Potter–who was gloatingly raking in chips he was supposed to lose later.

In an antechamber, Perry Bennett was bent over a hazzard table, rattling dice. His peculiar hand was adapted to *crapauds*-shooting, but the "bones" were not falling his way. His friend Owen was betting heavily on the losing run coming to an end, playing the Martingale System–which, under the circumstances, was a sure way to wind up broke.

All around, takers were being took.

Elizabeth, calm again after the Freddy incident, steered Gilberte around the room. They were themselves this evening–"Edda Van Heemstra" and "Virma Ep" were mysteriously detained. At the moment, none of their co-conspirators minded the absences–more in the pot for everyone else. Later, when smoke cleared, their no-show act would be remembered. By then, the real Edda would be loose and likely in trouble. As for "Ma Viper," Gilberte assumed she'd dance away from blame as she had slipped out of every other trap set for her.

The influx of big money was, as Kane had said, "blood in the water."

The salon stank with a hubbub of greed, fear, excitement and desperation. Usually, a casino came alive when a lucky or ingenious soul began to beat the house. Tonight was contrary. Gamblers rarely considered or cared about streaks if the house benefited. After all, odds were always with the house. But, tonight, a record might be set–the biggest single haul in a casino in an evening's play.

Next year, revues and songs would commemorate "The Bank Who Broke the Men at Royale-les-Eaux."

Elizabeth and Gilberte repaired to a side-bar, to drink champagne and take the edge off all the excitement. This was where the professional gamblers, who knew by instinct that something was more amiss than usual, had retreated. Colonel Sebastian Moran, of London and India, and Bret Maverick, of Natchez and New Orleans, debated the presently standing record for a house win, and whether it was about to fall. The inveterate gaming fiends also remembered a macabre record for the number of casino-related suicides in a single night. The cynical Moran was willing to bet the death toll set at Mother Gin Sling's in Shanghai on Chinese New Year's in '98 would be exceeded by dawn. The more optimistic Maverick considered taking the wager. Both were probably thinking of ways to put a "fix" in.

Maverick caught Gilberte looking at them and raised a glass to her. She turned away from his alarmingly appealing smile, and thought of cool green beds of money.

Engineer Hattison, inventor of the cheating machine, was also at the bar, nursing ginger ale and radiating smugness. He also overheard Maverick and Moran, and offered stakes against the professional gamblers, claiming that at the end of the evening the house would be the *loser*, rattling off spurious mathematical piffle to justify his position. Gilberte saw Hattison was making a novice mistake by offering an apparent sucker bet. A more experienced confidence man set out bait and let the mark raise the notion of a wager. The Colonel withdrew from the conversation and returned to play. If there was a set-up, he was determined to get in on the game and snare a portion of the free money he now believed was on offer. Maverick, however, had an acute sense of the way things were going and mildly took the engineer's bet. Somehow, the Westerner tumbled that a fix was *supposed* to be in but was actually off. Hattison threw a sheaf of his patents in to bulk up his meager cash roll.

Elizabeth and Gilberte finished their drinks and returned to the salon.

Kane, on his podium with the small orchestra, was perspiring badly, and trying to catch Boltyn's attention. His fellow millionaire wasn't supposed to be in this phase of the game, but couldn't resist trying to get one up. He sat by Natasha, matching the Queen of Terror's bets and often laying a meaty hand over her delicate fingers in a manner which might well earn him a cut throat before the end of the night. Unless the girl was one of those queer ducks who rattle about revolution all day but secretly wish to spend the night being grossly pleasured by a bloated plutocrat on silk sheets.

Gilberte looked up at the Eye-Ball. She tapped Elizabeth's shoulder.

Faint cracks appeared in the plaster, damaging a 14th Century cathedral ceiling Kane had stuck up to add class to his gaming hell. Fine dust sifted through the cracks. The Eye-Ball's moorings were precisely calibrated. Adding even Riolama's meager weight was a stress not calculated for in Hattison's plans.

Lights on the globe flashed on and off.

Gilberte whistled silently in admiration. Riolama had mastered the system and was playing it like a virtuoso.

All around the room were cries of exasperation, complaint, despair.

Some of the Most High Order grew irritable, feeling they had fed the pot a little too much. It was time for the great Kane's munificence to be made manifest. Others simply ached for their money back, and their promised money on top of it.

Kane could not make a scene without it becoming generally known that this whole casino was a giant trick. But he knew, even before Bret Maverick, that his crooked path had twisted against him. Finally, he slipped from the podium and waddled with an unaccustomed hurry towards the foyer. The staircase which led to the secure gallery above the Eye-Ball was still guarded. Voltaire stood at his position, suitably resolute, invisibly well-armed. Ironically, Riolama could not have got upstairs without his strength.

Casually, Gilberte and Elizabeth followed the magnate.

In the foyer, just as Kane was about to call out to Voltaire, they caught up with him and, with practiced ease, took an arm apiece.

"Oh, Mr. Kane," said Elizabeth, musically.

"Ladies," he said, not recognizing them but not too far gone in panic to miss their appeal, "ordinarily, I'd be happy to escort you, but..."

"We shan't take refusal kindly," purred Gilberte. "This is a special occasion, and we claim you as our prize."

"We could dance all night," said Elizabeth, tugging on one arm.

"Or drink champagne as if it had just been invented," said Gilberte, tugging on the other.

Kane tried to break free, but–for all his meat and money–was not a strong man.

In the salon, general fury erupted at another huge loss. The chutes to the counting-cellar were choked with boards like clogged-up drains. As usual in such situations, a stink was rising. Kane turned to look, but Gilberte and Elizabeth insisted on his attention, patting his damp cheeks, smoothing his sticky moustache. If pricked with one of Riolama's darts, he would not be more deftly immobilized.

Bennett and Owen, black-faced and broke, stalked out of the salon, towards the main doors.

"Gentlemen... friends," cried out Kane as they passed by.

Bennett gave Kane the evil eye and made a vulgar gesture with his malformed hand. Owen drew his thumb across his throat in an equally eloquent sign.

"Don't mind them," purred Elizabeth. "They're bankrupt. They haven't got two pennies to hire a cosh-boy, let alone funds enough to have you killed."

Kane really saw Gilberte and Elizabeth for the first time.

"Do I know you?" he asked.

A commotion exploded in the salon, and spread through the building.

William Boltyn was on the floor, clothes torn, expertly pinned by the dainty boot-heel of Nastasha Natasaevna. She cursed him as every variety of capitalist exploiter and blood-sucking oppressor of the people. She took a croupier's gathering-stick and knouted the millionaire as if he were a Russian peasant and she a Cossack. His face was striped with red weals. So, he wouldn't be conquering the Angel of the Revolution in his suite this evening. Others of the Most High Order were with her, getting in kicks and blows. Their pockets were empty, Gilberte supposed. Dr. Quartz had actually pulled out his trousers-pockets in a caricature of pennilessness. He had gambled away his custom-made surgical instruments.

"The house wins," announced another croupier, blandly.

A shot rang out and the man was down, wounded in the shoulder. Two hefty guards threw themselves on General Sternwood, who had brought his revolver. Voltaire left his post to see what the trouble was.

Kane was pliable now. It was important he see what was happening, so they steered him back into the salon.

It was pandemonium!

Boards flew like shrapnel on a battlefield. Patrons smashed the furniture. Voltaire and the apes went into action, endeavoring to suppress rowdy behavior. Madame Sara tried to splash a bottle of vitriol into a croupier's face, and was instantly trussed and thrown onto a table. Acid burned the baize. The Inner Circle of the Most High Order of Xanadu, assuming treachery on the part of their

Grand Master, took to quarrelling with each other, flinging accusations and daggers. They had no common cause before Kane gathered them. Old rivalries and enmities bubbled up like marsh gas. Simon Carne and Sir Dunston Gryme fenced with swords, leaping from tier to tier. They fetched up on the podium, cutting through the orchestra. Musicians fled diplomatically, grasping their more valuable instruments. Maupertuis brutally kicked Henry F. Potter, as if determined to put the pleading banker into a wheelchair.

Then, all the croupiers started screaming.

This had the effect of stopping fights and destructive rampages. All the staff were rooted to the carpets, juddering and fizzing, hair standing on end and smoking. Cards spewed from sleeves. Trousers-cuffs caught fire. Crackles of lightning ringed the croupiers' bodies. Riolama had cranked up the electrical devices to their highest setting and thrown all the switches at once. There was a peculiar tart, burned smell. This extraordinary phenomenon lasted only a few seconds, then shut off–along with all the electric lights.

Maverick strolled out of the side-bar, with a fistful of Hattison's paper. He tipped his black hat at the ladies, and his appalled host, and calmly walked out of the building. Back in the bar, Hattison had abjured ginger ale and was thirstily swigging whisky from a bottle.

The hall was dim, but infernal–lit only by a few fires. Yelping staff patted at burning patches of their evening attire. With dreadful curses, they helped each other tear wires out of their shoes.

"Gigi, cover your ears," said Elizabeth. "This is not language you should learn."

Kane was limp now, mumbling about "roses' buds."

There was a great rending sound, as if Plan Thunderbolt were torn in half by the Gods, and the Eye-Ball detached from the ceiling. Wires and chains through tore plaster as the globe crashed 50 feet to the floor. It smashed, throwing broken glass all around.

It was a miracle no one had been underneath it.

Gilberte's heart clutched, but Riolama wasn't in the wreckage. Looking up, she saw the bird-girl dangling from a cluster of wires stuck out of the ceiling. With the agility of a born acrobat, she swung from chandelier to chandelier, then found a column she could climb down as if it were a tree-trunk.

Gilberte and Elizabeth abandoned Kane to his ruin, and made a cradle of their hands. Riolama leaped into their grip. They helped her out of the salon, deftly moving through panicking, rioting, complaining crowds.

Heaps of boards were scattered across the floor. Colonel Moran, on his knees, filled his pockets. Most folks were too afraid the building would collapse to bother with scavenging.

They tried to leave the building in an orderly fashion, along with many less cool heads who were fighting and clawing to get out into the relative safety of the street.

Voltaire stood by the main doors, waiting for them, teeth shining like the family silver. Kane must have summoned him with a silent whistle.

"My good man," began Elizabeth, "if you would be so kind as to step aside. This poor girl has had a trying evening and is on the point of fainting…"

The giant's eyes glittered, like his gnashers. He was skeptical.

"*Move your bloomin' arse!*" shouted Elizabeth, in her original voice.

Disheveled folks streamed past Voltaire, but he stood firm, arms extended.

Now was the time for one of the stratagems they had practiced, under the tutelage of the Persian, in the gymnasium beneath the Opéra. It was Gilberte's call.

"Hi Lily Hi Lily Hi Lo!" she trilled.

Riolama flew as if on wires, taking "Hi Lily" and jamming her toughened heels into Voltaire's metal grin. Elizabeth, the other "Hi Lily," took a discarded parasol and jabbed its point into the giant's midriff. Gilberte, performing "Hi Lo," fell to the floor like the dying swan, braced herself against marble, and swept stiff legs against his stout ankles.

Voltaire shuddered but didn't fall.

The angels recoiled and landed on points, adopting poses of aggression and flirtation. Elizabeth twirled the parasol for distraction. Gilberte opened and closed invisible fans, trying to ignore the pain in her shins. Riolama's arms rose in a crane stance and she stood on one leg.

Even the fleeing guests knew enough to clear a circle.

"Hi Lily Hi Lily Hi Lo" was brute force. For all their delicacy, the trio could fell a tree with it. But Voltaire still stood.

After the Persian had tutored them black and blue, they had suffered under an even more exacting master. To become an angel of music, one had to pass muster with Monsieur Erik. Gilberte hadn't believed her throat could hurt so much, or that such sounds could be torn out of her.

Now, they would put their lessons into practice.

Elizabeth began to tap out a tempo with her parasol.

Gilberte found a discarded croupier's scoop. Riolama, alarmingly, picked up a blooded sword.

They tapped in synchronized time. Voltaire's eyes swiveled between them.

The repertoire for three female voices was limited. *Three Little Maids From School* was too trivial, though perhaps effective in a back-alley brawl. Bizet's *Les Tringles des Sistres Tintaient* was too coarse, and they all thought *Carmen* a stupid slut. So, it must be Mendelssohn. *Lift Thine Eyes To The Mountains*. The *Angels' Trio* from *Elijah*.

Elizabeth, the most naturally skilled, took the lead. Gilberte had counterpoint, and Riolama—whose high-notes turned to bird screeches—fluttered around. Song come from their hearts and lungs. Sound rolled from their larynxes in waves. If Voltaire could hear a dog-whistle, this would hurt.

All around, folks were struck by the beauty, then pricked by the pain. Crystal shattered, and another chandelier fell.

They focused the song on the giant in their way.

Blood trickled from his ears, his nose, his eyes. But he was transfixed.

Riolama took the lead from Elizabeth, and improvised–cockatoo sounds, birdcalls from her jungles. Voltaire felt it in his steel teeth, and clutched his mouth as the sharpened false choppers vibrated.

Gilberte became the dominant voice, and ended the song.

The giant fell to his knees, eyes and mouth red.

Without taking a bow, the trio slipped round him into the street.

A few stunned patrons tried to applaud, then thought better of lingering. More chandeliers would fall tonight.

In song, the angels of music had conquered.

Europa-Xanadu was in ruins. A mob was tearing down the facades of every Burgher Kane in sight. Fellows with sledgehammers smashed gaming machines. Liberated cattle charged down the street, trailing bruised cowboys by their lassos. A circle of small boys filled up a lost ten-gallon hat with piddle. The bandstand was seized. An impromptu barbershop quartet sang *Go Home, Yankees* to the tune of *Good Night, Ladies*.

The European War of the Future was finished before it was begin. The false plans would not be drawn up and passed on, the Terrorists' air-destroyer would not strike, the armies would not march. The Most High Order of Xanadu was set against itself. The most dangerous, vindictive and resourceful people in the world believed Charles Foster Kane had set out to fleece them. The magnate would be lucky to get out of France with his skin. He would have to fortify his Florida fastness against the creatures sure to be set against him by those who felt he owed debts no gold mine could service.

The Persian was waiting with a black motor-carriage and chauffeur.

The three women got into the vehicle. The Persian had champagne on ice for Gilberte and Elizabeth, and chocolate-covered insects for Riolama–her favorite delicacy.

Envelopes were handed to them. In Gilberte's was a notice of a bank account opened in her name in Switzerland, and a generous initial deposit.

"Against a rainy day," Elizabeth explained.

Their commission concluded, expression drained from the Englishwoman's face–as if she were Galatea turned back into a statue, waiting for someone to vivify her again.

Then, briefly, she was animated as she gasped, "Freddy!"

Mr. Eynsford Hill was tied to a lamppost. Children painted as wild Indians danced around this totem, giving out war-whoops.

"I suppose he'll be all right," Elizabeth said as they drove by. "Fickle fortune frequently favors the foolish."

Riolama happily crunched her chocolate bugs.

Elizabeth needed a strong teacher of music and diction to set her course, while Riolama was happy in an eternal present surrounded by winged friends. Gilberte recognized them both as her sisters.

They took the road from Royale-les-Eaux, leaving Kane's colossal schemes behind in irreparable shambles. Gilberte knew they would be in Paris by sunrise, to sleep away the day and emerge fresh the next evening–ready again to take flight.

Two days later, a telegram was delivered to Box No. 5. A simple acknowledgement of success, and the continued gratitude of his country. And, though they knew it not, the other Great Powers of Europe.

There would be no War this year.

More importantly, a dire threat was lifted. A certain American tycoon was no longer in any position to make good on his plan to buy the Paris Opéra outright and ship the building stone by stone to Chicago.

Beneath his mask, Erik really smiled.

In the past, John Peel has regaled us with clever little mysteries, but this time, he has chosen to craft a tale starring none other than Jules Verne's most famous character: Captain Nemo. John, a great fan of Verne's works, remembered the passage in Twenty Thousand Leagues Under The Sea *where the* Nautilus *cruises past the ruins of sunken Atlantis, and wondered what other underwater enigmas Nemo might have encountered during his undersea journeys. He comes up with an answer in this most intriguing tale…*

John Peel: *Twenty Thousand Years Under the Sea*

The Antipodes, 1865

Amongst the papers of the late Professor Arronax, the following pages were discovered. They had evidently been intended to form part of his memoirs but had, at the final moment, been torn from the manuscript that he delivered to his publisher. Upon examining the pages, it is simple to see the reason. Professor Arronax was a dedicated and thorough man of science, and whilst many of the events he described in his memoirs verge upon the fantastic, never do they unduly stretch the credulity. The excised section, however, is of a very different timbre.

The first reason is that the events that they purport to describe were never witnessed by the Professor himself–they are merely reported to him by the late Captain Nemo. Being a sound man of science, the Professor could not therefore verify their veracity. The second reason is that the events related by Nemo are, in and of themselves, quite fantastic. It is more than likely that Professor Arronax himself did not entirely believe the account that was related to him. The only reason, therefore, that the papers were not simply destroyed is the evident high regard the Professor held for Captain Nemo. He was unwilling to have his name associated with this tale while he was still alive; but now that he has died, he would appear to be less concerned. Attached to the pages was a note stating:

"Publish or destroy this account as you see fit."

As his executor of his papers, I have been torn both ways. Allowing the general public to read this fantastical account seemed to me to perhaps jeopardize the high regard that Professor Arronax has deservedly merited to date. And, yet, such is the public interest still in the exploits of the late Captain Nemo and his astonishing craft the *Nautilus* that it appeared to me to be irresponsible to withhold further details of his remarkable life.

I merely note that Professor Arronax did not vouch for the truth of this tale. Nor can I; I can merely present it.

One evening, after another of the splendid repasts that the skillful chef of the *Nautilus* had dreamed up–against consisting solely of creatures and plants found beneath the surface of the ocean–Ned Land and my incomparable Conseil had retired, leaving me alone in the company of Nemo. At this point, the *Nautilus* was traveling at a depth of some 14 fathoms. The ocean around us was teeming with small fish, but no landscapes could be observed within the range of the electrical lamps. Nemo stood at his portal, staring into the waters, apparently lost in thought. I had made some inconsequential remark about the bravery and loyalty of his crew–the former perhaps not so surprising, given the enterprise upon which they were engaged, but the latter I found unusual in that the members of the *Nautilus* were drawn from many different and sometimes antagonistic nations. Yet they all owed allegiance to this mysterious Captain of theirs. I had begun to believe that Nemo had retreated into his own thoughts and started to make my way from the room when his voice halted me.

"It was not always so, Arronax." There was another pause, which I took for an invitation to return and stand beside him. As he spoke, he did not yet look at me; instead he regarded the waters that he loved. "There was a time when their bravery faltered, and when one of their numbers betrayed me. I hesitate to speak of it not because it faults my crew, but because the events that occurred are so strange that a man of science like yourself would be understandably skeptical of my account."

"It would seem to me, Captain," I assured him, "that your regard for the scientific method is as high as my own. The notes you have allowed me to peruse and the facts you have related to me demonstrate a clear mind–even if it is one with which I cannot always agree."

He gave a slight nod. "Fair enough, Professor, fair enough. Then I shall relate my tale, and you may accept or scoff as seems most suitable to your humor. However, I shall simply preface it by stating that the events I speak of happened, and, while I cannot fully explain them myself, I do not believe that they are entirely beyond the boundaries of science to explain–perhaps one day, when our understanding of the Cosmos has increased.

"It was during the early days, when the *Nautilus* was still being tested and proven. I had, as you know, assembled a crew consisting of mariners from a variety of nations. One among them was a man from the United States named Suydam. He was taciturn, and considered odd by his fellows, though not unliked. He was a good mariner, and I had no complaints with his performance–until his final day in my employ. That he might have ulterior motives for voyaging with me did not at any time until that final day occur to me.

"We were voyaging in–no, I shall not tell you the waters, nor give any hint of the location, save to say that it was deep within the Antipodes. I would not have that place discovered again by any human being. The *Nautilus* had descended toward the bed of the sea, and we had on the electrical lamps so that we might study the formations ahead of us. There was nothing extraordinary in any of this, and we were in no hurry, so we meandered somewhat as the fancy took me.

"The area there is rather volcanic, so I was being quite careful. An underwater eruption could well damage my vessel, though I was under no apprehension that we would be unable to flee any lava flows. To the contrary, I was hoping that some vulcanism might be apparent to us in order for me to make a study of how lava flows under the surface of the sea. My only concern was that an underwater eruption might cause some sort of a pressure that might impact the ship. Hence the reason to advance slowly.

"As a result, we came across the artifacts quite slowly, and they were instantly apparent in the gleam of the lights for what they were–artificial constructs, and at considerable depths in the ocean. As you might imagine, I was rather excited by the discovery. At first it was nothing more than a simple wall, but it was of hewn stone, neatly fitted, and progressing in a straight line. It could be nothing but the work of skilled hands, that much was certain from the start. As we progressed, though, the nature of the ruin changed. In the place of a simple wall, pillars began to appear. Some were erect, many were fallen, and none supported anything.

"It was quite obvious that some sort of cataclysm had befallen this place. Plato's description of the casting down of Atlantis immediately sprang to mind, of course, but this was in an ocean far remote from his world. But where one city might have fallen to the fury of the elements, others might also."

"You said that this voyage of yours was in the Antipodes," I objected. "But there have been no city-building nations there until the recent past. And none of those cities, to the best of my recollection, have ever been swallowed by the waves."

"You are quite correct, Professor," Nemo agreed. "There have been none. This was one reason why I was so gripped by excitement–whoever had built this sunken city must have belonged to some civilization that was advanced in mind, and yet unknown to science. As we explored further, it was apparent that we had stumbled upon a major discovery. But it was also a most peculiar one. There was... something... about the architecture.

"Marine organisms had grown all around the stone work–and yet not one had intruded upon the stones themselves. It was almost impossible to judge how old the site was because of this. Why had none of the plants ventured to grow upon the stones? I could not then say, though now I might venture a guess. And then the walls and toppled columns turned into semi-intact and that almost perfect buildings as our floodlights swept across the site. Though I was puzzled by the lack of marine growths on the buildings, I was soon deeply disturbed by the buildings themselves.

"Their architecture was–inhuman. I can think of no other word to describe it. The way that the buildings were constructed was not the product of any sane mind. Overall, the sunken city did not appear so strange–there were buildings that must have been dwellings; some small, some larger. There were open spaces where once markets and meets must have been held. And there were temples and larger public structures. This much was clear and understandable. It was only when one's eyes moved from the general to the particular that the peculiar nature of the place became apparent.

"Walls were not quite straight–not in the sense that they were badly built, you must understand, but that they were deliberately constructed in a fashion that seemed out of keeping with a sane mind. The *intentions* of the unknown builders were to construct the structures precisely the way we viewed them. Windows and doorways were not squared, and floor plans were not straightforward. The problem with describing the city is that it was nothing you could quite put a name to–but it was all clearly warped and twisted from the fabric of a normal life. Looking at the city, we all could tell that whatever had built it and whatever had lived there was not entirely human–and possibly not human at all."

I frowned. "You mean to infer, then, that some lesser species than mankind constructed that city?"

"No; such would be absurd, Professor." Nemo considered for a moment. "Certain insects build homes; beavers dam rivers. But they do not quarry stone and use it in their endeavors. No, not a *lesser* species than man–but certainly *another* species."

I confess that I could not follow his reasoning. "But what could you mean by that?" I asked him.

"I am not entirely certain myself," he confessed. "It is simply that all of us who gazed upon that vast field of ruins had a strong conviction–which we later admitted to one another–that human minds could not have imagined that city, and human hands could not have manufactured it. It had the undeniable stamp of something alien to a human mind about it. And, to be perfectly honest, it unnerved us. As you know, Professor, the men I voyage with are some of the proudest, strongest and bravest that our nations have to offer. Yet through all of our hearts and minds at that moment of discovery, a tremor of fear ran. It was as if the place was drenched in evil, and had been so since time immemorial.

"I said *all*, but that is not true. There was one among us who felt only exultation and a sense of purpose achieved–the mariner Suydam. I did not know it at that time, but when he saw the ruins, his face had changed, showing great satisfaction, and, whilst all other eyes were staring at the astonishing and frightening sight, he hurried away. Looking back later, I realized that Suydam had not been surprised to find the sunken city–that, in fact, he had expected to stumble across it some time in our voyaging. One of his fellows told me later that the man had brought with him some ancient book that he studied at night, with a dim lamp, and that he let no other person see. I can only conjecture that it spoke of ancient and forbidden secrets, including the existence of that terrible place. The book vanished with Suydam, which is probably for the best, so I was never able to be certain of this. But it is logical–as much as anything connected with this event conforms to the rules of logic.

"The first that any of us knew of Suydam's vanishing was when the engines gave a strained sound. I was not then as used to the sounds of the *Nautilus* as I now am, and for a few moments I had no clue what might have occurred. I merely understood that our engines were under some sort of strain. Then the noise became a cacophony, and abruptly ceased after a loud banging noise. The lights flickered for a moment, died, and then returned at a lower level of illumination.

"I forgot about the ruins at that moment, hurrying instead to the ship's engine rooms. There we discovered the engineer insensate, and the main generator inoperable. Clearly this was sabotage, and of a potentially lethal type. Without motive force, the *Nautilus* was sinking slowly toward the bed of the ocean. I hurried back to the viewing chamber and saw that we were, indeed, settling on the floor of the sea, amidst the field of ruins. There was a loud scraping sound as the vessel slid down the exterior wall of a temple or some such. Stones broke free, falling with us, as the *Nautilus* came to rest on the bottom.

"Silence then descended, save for the gentle sound of the electric lighting. The air purifiers, powered as they were from the main generator, had closed off. Without them, we had only the air inside the vessel to breathe. We were in a perilous situation–without the generator our air would not circulate, and we could not move from where we lay. I calculated quickly that we had air enough for almost a full day, and that repairs must be effected within that time.

"Clearly, though, the first thing that needed to be done was to identify and isolate the saboteur. If he had struck once, there was the chance that he had further and even deadlier mischief in mind. Accordingly, I had the crew assembled, and it was at that point that Suydam was discovered to be missing.

"The culprit was clear, but his location was not. I had the ship searched while the engineer was tended to, and I examined the generator.

"Suydam had simply and literally thrown a wrench into the machinery–he was not himself an engineer, and clearly did not know the best way to disable my vessel. He had caused damage, but it was repairable. The only question was whether this could be achieved before our air supply became so fetid as to render us unconscious. My engineer, insisting he was recovered sufficiently to aid us, believed that this could be accomplished, and set about organizing his men to begin temporary repairs. We should certainly need to return to our base for a full overhaul, but he expressed publicly his belief that he could manage to repair the *Nautilus* sufficient for us to return home. Privately, however, he admitted that he was not quite as confident as he seemed. However, he did not wish to depress the crew by an open and honest evaluation. I commended him on his wisdom in avoiding the potential for panic, and set him to work.

"Meanwhile, the men I had sent to search for Suydam reported that he was nowhere to be found. There could be only one explanation for this, and I hurried back to the observation room. Thankfully, the searchlights outside the ship were run from a second generator that was still operable. I directed their movement, and in moments we could see a figure that must be the missing saboteur.

"He was walking purposefully through the ruined city in one of my underwater suits. His motivation was unfathomable–he had stranded us here, on the sea bed, and was now taking a walk into the sunken city alone. Surely he understood that he must perish? Even if we were to succeed in repairing the *Nautilus*, he had to be aware that we would not bother to pick him up. And if we died, he would die also. There could be no haven for him in this city that must have been dead for untold millennia.

"And yet–and yet! Suydam had been withdrawn from his fellows, but he had never shown any signs of palpable insanity. So I could only assume that there was purpose in his actions, no matter how inexplicable they seemed. As we watched, he vanished into one of the buildings–one that seemed to be a cross between a temple and a mausoleum.

"One of the sailors had searched Suydam's berth. The book was discovered to be missing, but there had been left behind a slip of paper on which the man had jotted a few notes, Most made no sense at all, but one line did stand out: *In his house at R'lyeh dead Cthulhu waits dreaming.*

"I was not certain there was any sense in this, either–but the building Suydam had entered had the appearance of a mausoleum–and the line spoke of a person who, though dead, yet dreamed. Was it possible that the man thought he was to awaken some sleeper? It made precious little sense–but, then, nothing made any more sense.

"I was seized with a sudden conviction that stranding us here was not all of the malevolence Suydam had planned for us. And if that were to prove to be true, then he had a purpose in his mission in the dead city. I detailed two of my men to accompany me, and left the engineer to make repairs as speedily as possible. The two men and I then suited up carefully for an underwater expedition. We each took along with us harpoon guns and–almost as an afterthought–a small supply of dynamite. I was not sure that any of these weapons would be of any use, but it was better to be prepared for eventualities.

"We then quit the *Nautilus*, and made our slow, determined way to the sunken city. Close up, the ruins were even more ominous, and their strange aura of inhumanity even more pronounced. I was more convinced than ever that nothing human could have built so unholy a place. The lines of the walls, the cut of the stones, their joints and bracing–all of it was done by the plan of something that thought in a very different way from humanity. It was clear that the buildings were ancient, and the thought came to me that they predated human history. Anything this grand, this awful, would have otherwise been noted by scribes of the antediluvian past. Whose hands–or other appendages–built that ruined city I cannot say–nor would I wish to venture a guess.

"One thing puzzled me, though: no fish crossed those ancient walls. Normally, in places such as these there would be schools of fish, and predatory moray eels or hunting octopi would lurk. But here there were no signs of life at all. The ichthyds avoided the place entirely.

"The building the traitor Suydam had entered was now just ahead of us. It had the vague appearance of a large domed church or mosque–though larger than any I have seen in the world above–and constructed in peculiar and inhuman fashion. As we drew close, we could see that there were large doors that led within. These appeared to be of copper and yet–despite their millennia of immersion–were as gleaming fresh as if they had only just been cast. On the surface of the doors were images–pictures of such grotesque and abominable form that I try not to recall them, and will not attempt to describe them to you. Suffice it to say that they were images that even a madman's nightmares could not surpass. The race that had raised this city must have gloried in unspeakable acts of torture and degradation. Not even a fiend steeped in dope and bred in the gutters of our world's vilest slums could imagine what we saw depicted on those doors. And, as we progressed further, we discovered that the interior doors and walls were similarly adorned with pictograms of acts that are too horrific to repeat.

"But there was science behind all of this, too. The beings who created this city knew their architecture and building, and they planned for the ages. Some of the buildings had been wrecked, true, when the city had sunk below the waves, but many more were still intact, and the temple-mausoleum we entered was in a perfect state of preservation. Its age was unguessable, but there was true skill behind it.

"We opened the main doors, and entered the building. There was a small entranceway, about ten feet deep, and then a second set of doors similar to the first. One of my men attempted to open them, but they would not budge. Were they bolted from within? Suydam might have expected to be followed, and sealed them behind him, after all.

"Then a thought occurred to me–perhaps they were like the entrance to the underwater chamber on the *Nautilus*. Two sets of doors, as you have seen, Professor, to allow passage in and out of my vessel. Perhaps these doors were serving the same purpose, and the inner doors would not open until the outer ones closed. I gestured to my men to close the doors behind us, and, once they were closed I examined them and saw that, indeed, they appeared to be a very tight fit. With the outer doors closed, opening the inner ones proved to be a simple matter. They did serve, as I had wildly guessed, to conserve air within the building. When they opened, the water with us in the entrance drained swiftly down channels set in the floor, and we stepped into a further small room, which was virtually free of water.

"As I have said, I had no idea how long this city had lain on the sea bed. Yet, there appeared to be air within this building–perhaps completely stale after all the centuries. There was no way to estimate it, so I tried the experiment of removing my helmet whilst gesturing to my men to retain theirs, in case the air should prove stagnant.

"To my surprise, it was breathable. The only problem was that there was a rank odor, one I have never known before or since. It had something of the miasma of decomposition about it, and that proved to be the more pleasant component of the stench. But the smell, no matter how putrid, did not prevent the air from being breathed. I gestured to my men and they both removed their own helmets, and immediately made comments about the foulness of the air. I was convinced, however, that there was something vitally important to our safety that we must discover as swiftly as possible, so I ordered the men to leave their helmets beside this door and to accompany me.

"It was not difficult to see the path Suydam had taken. Wet footprints led deeper into the depraved building. As I have already mentioned, the walls and doors were given over to horrendous depictions, all of which served to make the three of us more and more uneasy as we progressed. There was no sign of life, ourselves excepted, and the feeling that these were halls mankind was never intended to enter grew as we moved onward. I am a man of science, but the only word that I could seize upon to describe that building was *haunted*–and haunted not by some specter that might once have been human, but by one that possibly had no idea even what a human being was.

"As you may imagine, we were a highly nervous trio, and we clutched our harpoon guns for whatever protection and comfort they might afford. We moved through the building in silence, none of us wishing to break the cold, dank silence with speech. But then, ahead of us, we heard someone who was not so constrained. It was a voice raised in arrogance and triumph. I have made the study of many of the languages employed by mankind, but I could make out no words in this chanting that sounded at all familiar. The words, indeed, sounded as if they were designed to be uttered by vocal cords very different from ours. *Cthulhu* was mentioned or invoked more than once, along with various deities and beings from ancient mythology. Other than that, the words were completely meaningless to me.

"We came to a final door, which lay open, explaining how we could heard the voice making invocations to blasphemous beings. As I had expected, it was Suydam. He was standing before what I took to be an ancient altar, arms upraised, and a gloating, evil expression on his twisted face. The altar was large, carved from a single stone, with horns jutting from each corner. Pictographs in some ancient language were carved deeply into the stone, and covered the altar. Suydam appeared to be reading from these writings as he chanted.

"I called a warning to the man, and he turned to look at me, an expression of fierce triumph on his face. 'You are too late, Captain,' he coldly informed me. 'The One I came here to raise already stirs. His dreams are ending, and life returns to his body.'

"I grasped his meaning. 'You speak of Cthulhu?' I asked him.

"He nodded. 'None other,' he agreed. 'The Great One awakens, and he will reclaim his own.'

"The man was clearly demented, or so I thought. He spoke of raising the dead, as if this was an action a mere mortal might accomplish. And not merely the dead, but the dead of some inhuman race. I was tempted to simply walk away and leave him to suffer the fate he deserved–death, alone, within this hollow city–but I was prevented from following this thought with action.

"For there was a stirring in the air. The foul smell somehow managed to intensify, to the point where my men and I were almost sick. There also appeared a feeling in the air almost electrical in nature. The air was moving, stirring as it had not stirred in long, abandoned centuries. I was unable to understand what was happening, and I have no way at all to explain what happened next, or words sufficient to convey the events.

"Somehow, it was as if there were a connection between where we stood and some other, eldritch place. I had the feeling that vast centuries were somehow being spun aside, that space and time as we know them to be abruptly were seized and shaken as a dog shakes a toy. Everything that we knew as logical and scientific and possible was wrenched through 180 degrees, and the impossible, the unthinkable, the unknowable was happening.

"As a man of science, I have no means of explaining what then occurred–I can merely state that it did happen, no matter how impossible it may sound. In the space before us, a shape materialized. One moment, the space was empty, and the next it was occupied by this entity, the likes of which I have never seen before–and which I devoutly hope I shall never see again!

"It was large, though I cannot say exactly its size–taller and broader than a man, at least 12 feet high. Like a man, it stood upright, but that was all the resemblance it had to anything upon this world. I knew, instinctively, that nothing like this beast could have evolved upon our wholesome planet. And the stench from it was so strong and sickening that it almost crippled all of us, Suydam included.

"Its head was like the body of a squid–large, unblinking eyes, and tentacles that fringed a gaping maw, extremities that writhed constantly. Below that terrifying head was a body, but one I scarcely saw. I have the impression of limbs and claws, but I can attest to nothing. For those great eyes bore into us, and I knew the malice that the creature held for us and our kind. I knew that, if loosed upon our world, it would stamp with certainty the demise of humanity. Such creatures as this and we ourselves cannot co-exist. Even Suydam, whose incantations must have called this creature from some abyss, was stunned by the awfulness of this sight.

"One of my men fired his weapon at the monstrosity. I know the harpoon hit and sank into whatever flesh that monster had, for there came a scream of inhuman rage and pain. The creature lashed out, catching my man and crushing the life from him. Then, in a moment of horror that I cannot forget, no matter how I try, it drew him into that great mouth, and began to devour the fresh corpse.

"I knew it intended the same fate for all of us. Like fabled Polyphemus, this creature thrived on the flesh of human beings. But the poor man's efforts had shown that, though a harpoon might cause the monstrosity pain, it could not halt it. My actions were those of instinct and not rational thought. I fired my own harpoon–not at Cthulhu, for this was surely the sleeper awakened–but at Suydam, whose infernal tampering with the laws of Nature had raised this leviathan. The bolt proved far more effective on the man than on the monster. With a gasp of shock, Suydam fell to the floor, dead.

"Cthulhu, having finished its grisly feast, sprang upon this fresh corpse, raising it to that terrible mouth. I had taken out the dynamite I carried, and removed it from the waterproof covering. Striking a lucifer, I ignited the sticks, and then threw them into that all-devouring maw. Hurriedly, I shook my remaining companion, who had been struck silent and still by the horrors we were witnessing. Together, we stumbled toward the exit doors. Behind us, the dynamite exploded, and there was a fresh, titanic scream from Cthulhu. I chanced a backward glance, and saw that the explosion appeared to have taken the head off the creature–but if it had, whence came that chilling scream? The mountainous body didn't fall, however, and its several limbs were writhing, claws opening and closing.

"We fled as swiftly as we could, returning to the entrance chamber where we had stashed our breathing apparatus and helmets. We sealed the inner door behind us, and then worked at opening the outer ones. At that moment, we heard the sound of many limbs beating on the inner doors. They would not open, of course, as long as the outer ones stood ajar, but as we moved as swiftly as we could out of the buildings, I saw that the solid metal was starting to buckle under the rain of so strong and ferocious blows. It was only a matter of time before Cthulhu battered down the doors and came after us.

"As you know from experience, Professor, it is impossible to move swiftly under the water. It seemed to take us forever to bridge the distance between that foul city and the safety of my craft. Somehow, though, we did. It was only later that the reason for our escape occurred to me–when Cthulhu broke down those inner doors, water would have poured into the temple, and even a being as strong as it could not fight against the power of the sea. Cthulhu must have been washed backward by the pressure of the inflowing water, allowing us those moments we needed to effect our escape.

"Back in the comforting walls of the *Nautilus*, I was delighted to discover that my engineers had managed to repair the craft sufficiently for us to power up and begin to move. I had no time for explanations–nor could I find the words to explain my actions. Instead, I merely turned my craft toward the forgotten city and called upon all the power of her turbines.

"We crashed into that great dome with the prow of the *Nautilus*. It was designed to penetrate wood and steel, and those stones could not withstand the blow. The entire vessel rang with the sound of the encounter, and then we were past. I had the searchlights turned to our rear, and, as we watched, the dome collapsed, tearing down most of the superstructure with it. It seemed to fall in slow motion, of course, as the dome fell apart, and then inward. My frantic eyes searched for any sign that Cthulhu might have made its escape before the collapse, but I could see nothing of the monstrosity. I could only pray that it had been buried beneath those monumental inhuman blocks, and that the building I had taken for a mausoleum truly was such now.

"We managed to limp home in the damaged *Nautilus*, which was repaired. But the one man and I had memories that could not be erased. The sight of that creature, Professor, is one I shall never forget, no matter how hard I might wish it to be otherwise. And there is one more thing that still troubles me. That one line in Suydam's writing that had made some sort of sense:

"*In his house at R'lyeh dead Cthulhu waits dreaming.*

"Perhaps we did somehow kill that creature. Dynamite and the fall of masonry would have killed any entity that this world has ever spawned. But is it enough to slay the being that we saw? Or is Cthulhu still waiting and dreaming again?"

If Eugène Sue, Paul Féval, Alexandre Dumas and others were the literary fathers of our Shadowmen, Louis Feuillade (1873-1925) was certainly the man who visually defined them. The great writer-director was responsible for the images of the black-clad Fantômas, the cloaked avenger Judex and the alluring femme fatala Irma Vep, paramour of the Vampires gang, played by actress Musidora, whose rubenesque figure gliding over the Paris rooftops made such a memorable image. Steve Roman, who makes his first appearance in Tales of the Shadowmen, *succumbs to Irma Vep's poisonous charms with a moody, Berlin-based tale of the darkest* noir *where two, vastly different creatures of the night meet...*

Steven A. Roman: *Night's Children*

Berlin, 1910

It wasn't the finest painting Irma had ever seen–not in her opinion, anyway–but one look at the title on the little bronze plaque beneath its frame and it became obvious why this particular work had attracted the interest of the criminal mastermind she served. And why she had been sent to Berlin to steal it for him.

Vampire was one of Norwegian artist Edvard Munch's lesser-known paintings, but then that could be said about most of the man's work; although his paintings were critically acclaimed, especially among the elite of Paris, to the public at large, he was simply the artist responsible for the haunting imagery of *The Scream*. In fact, most casual patrons of the arts might have found it difficult to believe that the man whose grotesquely distorted figure work and disturbing crimson sunset had made *The Scream* so well known was the same one who had created the more subdued piece at which she now gazed.

Set against a black background, *Vampire* depicted a dark-haired man and a redheaded woman in what Irma could only think of as a sad embrace. The woman appeared to be seated, with the man kneeling beside her; it was difficult to tell if this was true, given the image only showed them from the waist up. His left arm was wrapped around her waist, his head tucked against her bosom, his features hidden in shadow. The woman's right arm rested on his left, while her left hand caressed his right shoulder. Her nose and mouth nuzzled the back of his neck as her crimson locks lay draped across his head and down his back; Irma imagined she could almost hear the words of comfort being spoken to the man as the woman held him tightly.

There was a sense of great loss to the image, of overwhelming sadness, and perhaps that was what made Irma dislike it so. It reminded her of events, of people, in her old life she thought she had finally forgotten.

Still, personal tastes–and demons–aside, she knew it was exactly the sort of prize one would expect to see hanging in the private collection of the leader of a criminal organization known as the Vampires–especially when that leader called himself "The Great Vampire." He had to have it, he had confessed to her one night, and, he admitted, there was no better thief in his organization to effect its procurement than the alluring, raven-haired Irma Vep.

Well, it was always comforting to have one's talents appreciated. Better yet to be handsomely rewarded for her efforts, as the Great Vampire had promised should she return home successful in her quest–not that there could be any other outcome. For a member of the Vampires, disappointing their leader was tantamount to a death sentence, and there was no place on Earth in which to hide that the Great Vampire could not find if you tried to run. Failure was simply not an option.

Irma, however, was unconcerned about incurring her master's wrath. Her mission was a simple one, the details of which she had worked out during her first visit to the museum five days ago. Once freed from the confines of its gold-leafed mahogany frame, she knew the canvas would be easy enough to spirit away before she left for Paris in the morning. All she needed was a means by which to gain access to it after the exhibition had closed for the night...

"Absolutely stunning," said a male voice beside her.

Irma tensed, then placed a hand to her mouth, as though to hide a gasp at being startled; in reality, she was concealing the deep frown pulling at the corners of her lips. She didn't care for interruptions when she was finalizing a plan, even when the interloper was Wilhelm Schmidt, the handsome, blonde-haired curator of the museum. Oh, yes, she knew who he was, though they had yet to officially meet, but that was only because she had caught him surreptitiously watching her each time she strolled through the museum, eyeing her from behind pillars, peeking at her from around sculptures, then quickly scurrying away whenever she turned to confront him. After three days of such intense scrutiny, she had grown fearful that some German police officer had learned of her connection to the Vampires and surmised that her visits to the Munch exhibition–titled *Frieze of Life: A Poem About Life, Love and Death*–were a method of gathering intelligence on the museum's security procedures. Unable to stand the suspense any longer, she finally asked one of the guards if he knew the man's identity, and breathed a sigh of relief when she learned her fears had been unfounded.

After that, she had taken to ignoring her newfound shadow. For a woman who had acquired a sizable number of silent, bashful admirers from London to Istanbul over the years, adding one more to the list meant little to her. Still, she had to admit that most of them weren't as pleasing to the eye as Herr Schmidt. In his early thirties, standing a few inches above six feet tall, he possessed a strong, clean-shaven jaw and the brightest blue eyes Irma had ever seen. She thought it a pity that a man of such good looks should waste his life as a lowly museum official.

A museum official, she suddenly realized, who must possess a set of keys to every door in the place...

"You *are* referring to the painting, I take it?" she asked, turning to face him with a sly smile.

Schmidt looked confused for a moment by her question; then his eyes widened as he realized what she was really asking. His cheeks reddened from embarrassment. "Oh, yes, yes, of course," he replied quickly. "The painting–it is a stunning piece of work, is it not?"

"I suppose," she replied with a tiny shrug of her shoulders. "I'm still trying to see where the vampire is supposed to be." She leaned forward, as though giving the painted background a closer inspection. From the corner of her eye, she stole a quick glance at his left hand. No wedding band on the third finger, she observed.

Single, then, as she had suspected. All the better.

"Why, it's the woman, of course," he explained, gesturing at the redheaded subject. "She is obviously stealing the life from the poor fellow."

"Is that so?" Irma commented archly. She turned to face him. "I only see a woman giving comfort to a man in great torment." She studied it again for a moment. "Perhaps the piece says more about the artist's attitude towards the female species than any symbolism presented by his subject." She flashed a wry smile. "Perhaps it says something about you as well."

Schmidt smiled. "I certainly hope not, Frau ...?"

"Fraulein," she corrected.

"Ah," he said pleasantly, his interest clearly aroused. "Actually, *Vampire* was not Herr Munch's title for the work," he confided. "That was bestowed upon it by Stanislaw Przybyszewski, a Polish friend of his. It was originally called *Love and Pain*."

"I see. Then I take back what I said earlier. The problems with the female species apparently lie with the friend and not the artist. That pleases me." Irma glanced back at the canvas, and nodded in appreciation. "Herr Munch's is a more fitting title, I think–for is not life itself a mixture of both love and pain?"

Schmidt nodded agreeably. "Indeed. You're quite perceptive, Fraulein."

She smiled demurely, and gently placed a hand on his forearm. "For your information, *mein freund*, I am an extremely perceptive woman–about a great many things."

Schmidt swallowed hard. "Of that, Fraulein, I have no doubt." His gaze locked with hers for a moment or two, then he shook his head as though to clear it. "Forgive me, Fraulein, we have not been properly introduced." He bowed gallantly. "I am Wilhelm Schmidt, curator of the museum. And you are...?"

"Irma," she replied, extending her hand so that he could bend forward to lightly kiss the back of it. "Irma Vep."

His lips lightly brushed her knuckles a split second before his right eyebrow did a slow, intrigued crawl upward. He rose and glanced from the exquisite creature standing before him to the one in the painting, then back. "Irma Vep. Is that not an anagram for–"

"Vampire," she interjected with a soft laugh. "Yes. My mother possessed an extraordinary sense of humor."

"And extraordinary beauty as well, I would imagine," Schmidt offered, "if her offspring is any true indication."

"Take care, *mein herr*," Irma warned playfully, "else you may find your heart stolen away by a real-life vampire."

"A real-life one, but still a magnificent work of art in her own right."

"Such flattery, Wilhelm." She batted her eyelashes and sighed melodramatically. "Perhaps if I am not careful, I may find my *own* heart lost to some handsome museum curator."

"One could only hope," he replied.

Irma grinned. What easy prey was man, she thought. So easily baited, so easily trapped.

"Tell me, Wilhelm," she continued, stepping just a bit closer, "do you spend all your time in this stuffy museum, or are you allowed to go out and enjoy yourself once in awhile?"

"It is *not* a stuffy museum," he said, a slight edge creeping into his voice.

Irma stepped back, laughing softly. "Such a serious curator you are, Wilhelm! Please, I meant no offense." She smiled. "But you have not answered my question."

"Enjoy myself in what way?" he asked. "Could you be more specific?"

"Certainly," she replied. "Have you been to the cabaret of late?"

"The cabaret? Well, not in many months. Why should that–" His eyes widened. "Of course! You are Irma Vep, the famous French singer!" He lightly rapped the side of his head with his knuckles, as though punishing himself for not knowing her identity. "Please accept my apology, Fraulein Vep–"

"Please, call me Irma."

He grinned. "Irma. I should have recognized your name. I saw one of your performances while I was in Paris last year. You were very good."

She pouted playfully. "And yet I failed to make a lasting impression upon you, my curator."

"No, no, no," Schmidt insisted. "It is my fault entirely. I was there on business, to negotiate with your Société Nationale des Beaux-Arts for an exhibition of their members' finest works, to be shown here in Berlin, and my thoughts were elsewhere that night."

"Well, perhaps I can do something that will ensure you remember me," she purred. "When you come to see me tonight."

He started. "I beg your pardon?" he asked, his voice rising slightly.

Irma laughed. "I am ending a one-week singing engagement at the Metropol Theater this evening. You *will* come to see me, won't you? It will be my final appearance in your lovely city for some time; I'm returning to Paris tomorrow." *Accompanied by a new addition to the Great Vampire's gallery,* she thought.

"Well, then, of course I will be there," Schmidt replied. "Seeing you perform tonight would be my greatest pleasure."

"I'm sure it *will* be–in more ways than one, my handsome curator," Irma commented with a devilish grin. "If you are fortunate." She playfully ran the tip of her tongue along the edge of her upper teeth.

She turned on her heel and exited the hall, her footfalls drowned out by the sound of the curator's sputtering cough as the breath caught in his throat. By the time she emerged from the museum, a new plan was already forming in her mind. There were a few preparations she needed to make before darkness fell, if she were to guarantee that Herr Schmidt experienced the memorable evening she had promised.

Yes, Irma thought hungrily, what easy prey was man. So easily baited, so easily trapped.

And how very talented a huntress was she.

Death came to Berlin that night, though no one knew it–not immediately. It arrived not by storm or fire or plague, but in a black carriage drawn by a team of six horses as dark as the shadows that surrounded them. And it came in the form of a man.

But it was not the eyes of a man that gazed out from between black curtains at the sartorially attired men and gaily dressed women strolling the cobblestoned streets, but the red-rimmed, hate-filled orbs of a monster. A creature that must have once dwelled within the deepest, blackest pit of hell long before it rose up to walk the land of mortals. An abomination whose very existence was proof enough to the people of its Transylvanian homeland that Satan's minions truly existed, stalking the Earth in search of souls to destroy–and blood to drink.

Berlin was a city overflowing with both in these early years of the 20th century. Enough, perhaps, to quench even the constant thirst of its newest visitor: an undead horror that called itself Count Orlock.

Seated atop the carriage, the creature's hunchbacked servant directed the horses down a narrow alley, away from prying eyes, and into a mist-shrouded courtyard. The carriage rolled to a halt, and the hunchback clambered down from his seat. Tremulously, he approached the passenger door.

"We have arrived, Master," he croaked. "What would you have me do?"

Orlock inhaled deeply, filling his lungs with the smells of the city: factory smoke and horse offal; ladies' perfumes and the candy-sweet scent of young children; the musky tang of men and the sweat-tinged fear of his servant. So many aromas to draw in, so many spices to savor in this city of cattle, he thought, and rolled his worm-like tongue along the edge of yellowed, misshapen teeth that refused to remain hidden behind thin, bloodless lips. Slowly, he exhaled and closed his eyes, letting the sounds of this metropolis, this new stalking ground, assault his pointed, bat-like ears. There was the clatter of horse hooves on cobblestones, the roar of motorized conveyances, the clanking of machinery, the strains of music from the cabaret down the street, the incessant chatter of humans discussing worthless topics.

And above it all there were the quicksilver currents of blood: flowing along arteries, pulsing in veins, racing through organs. Like the bubbling of a mountain stream that greeted the exhausted traveler, it called to Orlock, enticing him, urging him to drink his fill and be replenished.

The monster smacked its lips and grinned. It had been centuries since he had had occasion to fully quench his thirst, and the trip to Berlin *had* been a particularly throat-parching one...

"M-Master?" the hunchback stuttered.

Orlock frowned at the interruption, and opened his eyes. "Very well, Geist," he growled softly. "You may start by opening the door."

The carriage door flew open, and moonlight flooded into the compartment. Reflexively, Orlock drew back to the safety of the few shadows that remained, then snarled at his foolish reaction. He had nothing to fear from the Moon, his one constant companion through the long years. Unlike the accursed Sun that forced his kind to relinquish their possession of the nighttime world with the approach of each hated dawn, the Moon's light was as cold as the grave, its chill caress just as inviting.

He stretched his pipe cleaner-thin legs, and grasped the doorframe with long, bony fingers–digits that appeared less like parts of a once-human hand and more like the appendages of some enormous, winter-white spider, scrabbling for purchase on the lacquered wood. Orlock pulled himself from the compartment and stepped onto the slick cobblestones, then took a few moments to gaze at his surroundings. The courtyard was surrounded on three sides by a carpenter's shop to the east, a factory to the south, and a boarding house of some sort to the north, and set back far enough from the street that no passersby would take notice of the ghastly blood-drinker–or disturb his plans for the evening.

And yet, Orlock sensed a nearby presence. He paused, and sniffed the air. "Someone is watching us..." he said, and slowly looked over his shoulder at the boarding house behind him.

There was a light on in a window on the third floor. And standing at that window, staring down at the vampire lord, was a young woman. Hair the color of spun gold framed an oval face pale with fear. Hazel eyes, wide as serving platters, locked on the glowing red orbs of the walking corpse. Lips soft as rose petals trembled in soundless terror. But she would not remain silent for long.

Orlock raised a talon-like hand and reached out to the girl. He could hear her heart pounding–almost loud enough, he imagined, for even Geist to take notice. And as the shadow of that cold, dead hand fell across her breast, he closed his spider-leg fingers and seized control of the frantically beating organ, squeezing it, slowing it. Halting it.

The girl's eyelids fluttered, and she swooned against the window frame, then slipped bonelessly to the floor. Orlock slowly opened his hand, just a tiny bit. Enough to allow some flow of blood to continue through her veins; enough to keep her alive. After all, she was worthless to him as the appetizer for this night's sanguinary repast if she was already dead by the time he reached her. To a vampire, the only thing more distasteful than the nauseating stench of garlic was the taste of warm blood gone horribly flat.

The ghoul licked his cracked lips, his black heart beating just a trifle faster in anticipation of the feast to come, then clambered up the wall to claim his luscious prize.

He greeted her with a single rose the color of freshly spilled blood.

Reclining on a zebra-striped settee in one of the Metropol's dressing rooms, Irma graciously accepted Wilhelm's romantic gesture and invited him to take a seat. She fought the urge to laugh when he spied the curve of her bosom above the open neckline of her robe and quickly averted his gaze. It was really quite charming, in a way. So different from the coarse manners and even coarser language displayed by the majority of the ruffians and cutthroats who comprised the Vampires' legions; so exquisitely refined. It made her feel like a real lady, instead of a petty thief who merely acted the part.

"So, did you enjoy the performance as I'd hoped, my curator?" she asked.

"It was magnificent!" he declared enthusiastically. *"You* were magnificent!"

"Thank you," Irma said pleasantly. "Then I trust I've made a suitable enough impression on you this time." She took a tiny sniff of the rose, then lowered the flower until its petals rested on her cleavage. As expected, Wilhelm's eyes followed the path it took, then moved on to glance down at his hands.

"You could say that," he agreed with a shy grin.

"And now it is your turn to impress *me,* dear Wilhelm," she said.

The curator looked up from his hands, his rugged features twisted in obvious confusion. "And how would you propose I do that?" he asked innocently.

Irma smiled wolfishly. So easily baited, she thought. So easily trapped.

He wasn't the finest lover Irma ever had–and unlike painting, the art of lovemaking was an area in which she truly excelled as both gifted artisan and informed critic–but his skills were adequate enough to keep her entertained so she didn't drift off to sleep before he had finished. A difficult task, but thoughts of the reward to come from the Great Vampire helped keep her awake.

Vampire, she reflected as she lay on the bed in her hotel suite and let Wilhelm busy himself. *Such a cruel, ignorant way to describe the image of a woman offering comfort to a lost soul.* "She is obviously stealing the life from the poor fellow," Wilhelm had said at the museum. A wry smile curled the left corner of Irma's mouth as she wrapped her legs around his waist and pulled him closer. *I don't know where a man would get such an idea...*

Above her, Wilhelm groaned in ecstasy; his body shuddered. Taking her cue, Irma focused her wandering thoughts on the task at hand and quickly responded in kind, gasping "Oh, Wilhelm!" for added effect. Then she pushed him off. It was time for the next stage of her plan. There was much to do before the night was over, and wasting even five minutes to spout some meaningless pillow talk about his sexual prowess–or, rather, the lack thereof–would only disrupt her schedule.

"A magnificent performance, my curator," she commented, hoping the words didn't sound as hollow to him as they did to her own ears, and rolled off the bed to stand on the floor.

"*Danke,*" Wilhelm replied with a satisfied grin. If he had detected the bland tone in her voice, he was apparently too much the gentleman to say so. Not that it mattered all that much to Irma. He had taken the bait; now came the moment to spring the trap.

She took a moment to glance seductively over her shoulder at him, her eyes promising only a brief intermission before the next act, then crossed the suite to an oaken chest of drawers, on which lay a silver tray containing an open bottle of champagne and a pair of wine flutes. She poured some of the champagne into a glass and brought it to him. "Here–drink. You must be thirsty after all that exertion."

He nodded in gratitude and raised the glass to his lips. But then he paused, gazing at her above the rim. "Am I to drink alone? Will you not join me?"

"Oh, I never drink... wine," the dark-haired vamp said with a coquettish smile. "It makes my head spin frightfully. But, please, don't let that stop you."

"Very well." He grinned broadly, and raised the glass in a toast. "To love."

And pain, Irma thought with a bitter smile. *For you can never experience one without the presence of the other...*

Wilhelm drained the flute in one gulp, and placed it on the nightstand beside the bed. The powerful sedative with which the champagne had been laced took effect almost immediately. One moment he was reaching out to stroke her face; the next, his hand had flopped limply by his side.

Irma watched him slumber for a few moments, then delicately touched his wrist, checking for a pulse. It was slow but strong and she nodded appreciatively, pleased that the handsome curator possessed a hardy enough constitution that ensured the dosage she had given him wouldn't turn out to be a fatal one. He would sleep for hours and awaken late in the morning with a terrible headache–and no doubt a heart broken by her betrayal.

Well, he would not be the first to realize he had been played the fool by the irresistibly alluring Irma Vep, nor would he be the last. *Love and pain,* Irma

190

thought as she turned from her latest victim. *They are the weapons of my trade— and all I have to offer.*

She stepped lightly over to a mammoth wardrobe and opened its doors. Reaching behind the suitcases and hatboxes that were already packed, she extracted a large rectangular valise, set it on the floor, and flipped open its metal clasps. Inside were two items: a pair of collapsible wings covered with black material, and a black body stocking that, at first glance, would give the appearance that its wearer had been transformed into a living shadow—or a gigantic bat, once the wings were added to the silhouette.

A fitting image, Irma considered, given the anagrammatical nature of her name. She unfolded the garment and began slipping it on. "And so to work..." she said with a hungry smile.

"Exquisite," Orlock muttered with a hungry smile, and wiped his bloodstained lips with the back of his hand. The blood in this latest victim—the third course of his banquet—had been the most satisfying so far: sweet like nectar, rich with life. Superior in every way to the brackish swill that oozed from the throats of the lowborn, working-class trollops on whom he had earlier supped.

He rose from the bed and gazed down at the prone figure lying before him. The woman was in her early 20s, with a shape pleasing to even a dead man's eyes, and tresses so brilliant a shade of red it almost appeared that the white satin pillow on which her head rested was engulfed in flame. Who she might have been in life was unimportant to the vampire lord, though the opulent trappings of her apartment and the quality of her blood suggested aristocracy of some sort. No, all that mattered was the purpose she served in his nocturnal feeding: as a source of nourishment.

Not that he was immune to the charms of the fairer sex, he reflected; far from it. In that regard, he was much like the human males on which he sometimes feasted. Women were his weakness, his passion, his favored choice of victim, for it was their blood that always ran the hottest. But it was not only the waters of life that pulsed through their veins that drew him to them. The sparkle in their eyes when they stared at him in fear, the quickening of their hearts as they felt the chilled hand of death caress their cheek, the tremulous whisper of their honey-sweet voices as they begged for mercy—was it any wonder he could never refuse an opportunity to take his fill of such delectable creatures?

And yet, more often than not, it was those very same creatures that served as the catalyst behind every downfall he had ever suffered these past four centuries. He snarled, recalling the last time he had allowed himself to be lured into a trap by the promise of a slender throat upon which to gnaw...

It was to Bremen, a bustling German city to the West, that Count Orlock had traveled in 1838. Desiring to spread his vampiric influence beyond his Transylvanian homeland, he had chosen Bremen as his new location—and the comely young wife of his real estate agent as his first victim.

Ellen Hutter was a dark-haired beauty whose angelic features had captured the monster's stilled heart the moment he saw the picture of her that was carried by her husband, Johann. The couple had only been married a short time before Herr Knock, Johann's employer, had sent the young man to Orlock's remote castle in the Carpathian Mountains to finalize the Count's purchase of an estate in Bremen, yet not even the great distance separating them could diminish the love Hutter possessed for his bride. The outpouring of affection he showed toward the photographic image, speaking to it late at night as though Ellen were sitting right beside him, had both nauseated the vampire lord–and made him extremely jealous. Never in over a century had he seen so alluring a creature; he had to possess her. And so Orlock vowed then that he, too, would know such unbridled love, even if it meant he would have to make Ellen one of his undead "children" in order to win her heart. He *would* win it; of that he was certain. She would be his bride in death–forever young, forever beautiful, forever faithful. And together they would walk in eternity.

At least, that had been his intention. He started the process shortly after his arrival in Bremen, visiting her bedchamber late at night on a few occasions to nibble at her swan-like neck, but he did not complete the task. His thoughts became occupied with carrying out his other, far greater plan: to establish Bremen as a staging area from which his invasion of Western Europe would begin. The rats and other vermin he had infected with the Black Plague were to be his first line of attack; the human victims he turned into vampires would be the second. There were many preparations to make and, even with the aid of a crazed Herr Knock, who'd come to imagine himself the Count's faithful assistant, laying the groundwork for his proposed subjugation of the human race took precious time. When Orlock finally returned to claim his prize, it was to discover that Johann– whom the Count thought already dead back in Transylvania–had rejoined his bride to protect her from the vampire's unholy attraction. And the cur had gathered friends to help him, including an authority on vampirism named Professor Bulwer. Suddenly, Orlock's relationship with the girl was becoming needlessly, infuriatingly complicated. Something would have to be done to simplify the situation–something involving a number of horrific deaths... and a great deal of bloodletting.

Yet Ellen Hutter was not only a fetching young lass, but an intelligent and resourceful woman as well. She knew it was only a matter of time before her undead admirer tried to force himself upon her once more, and feared for Johann's safety if he tried to interfere. And so she came up with a plan of her own: to lure the vampire lord into a trap, with herself as the bait. Not even the Grim Reaper himself could resist such an invitation.

What Orlock had not known was that Ellen possessed the greatest weapon a mortal could hope to use against a vampire: knowledge. When Johann returned from Transylvania, he brought along a leather-bound tome he had acquired during his frightening adventure: *The Book of the Vampires*. It recounted the legend of the living dead–the creatures known as *nosferatu* to the people of Orlock's land–and provided the sole means to vanquish such a monster: Only a woman pure in heart could defeat the *nosferatu*. A woman who willingly offered herself to the bloodlusting demon and remained at his side until daybreak, when the light of the rising Sun would destroy him. And though she knew that by enticing Orlock to enter her bedchamber she was dooming herself, still Ellen went through with her plan. Better she sacrifice her life, it seemed, than allow any harm to come to Johann.

And Orlock, fool that he was, stepped willingly into the temptress's lair– and paid the ultimate price for allowing his passions to get the best of him.

It took decades for his body to reform after the Sun's rays scattered his atoms across Bremen, but not even death's crushing embrace was strong enough to hold Count Orlock for very long. Still, by the time he returned to corporeal form, more than 60 years had passed. The world had moved on; more importantly, the world had forgotten he ever existed, so that he was now free to hunt without fear of exposure. His enemies were either dead or soon would be. Hutter's copy of *The Book of the Vampires* had likely turned to dust, and the plague that ravaged Bremen had become a distant memory. Most surprisingly, however, was that the word *nosferatu* apparently no longer held the terror it once did–but, as Orlock had concluded some time ago, he now had all the time in the world to restore its horrific reputation...

The vampire's lips peeled back in a wide, lascivious smile as he glanced down at his auburn-haired victim. Her alabaster skin shone brightly in the moonlight streaming through the bedroom window, the pale flesh highlighted by the warm glow of fiery locks that framed her face. At first glance, one could almost believe she was sleeping peacefully–a frost-hued maiden wrapped gently in the arms of Morpheus–were it not for all that blood staining the bed sheets, and the wide-eyed death mask into which her comely features had contorted.

"Such magnificent terror," Orlock whispered. He reached out a bony hand to caress her icy cheek–an albino spider scuttling across a snowy field, yet leaving no trace of its passage. "How I wish I could preserve its beauty." The vampire shrugged, then turned from his cadaverous work of art and slithered toward the open window through which he had entered the apartment–just in time for his bat-like ears to detect the whisper-soft sound of heavy fabric fluttering in the breeze. Curious, he parted the lace curtains and gazed out at the moonlit sky above the slumbering metropolis.

Yellow-tinged eyes widened in astonishment. "What is this?" he croaked.

A giant black bat soared high over the streets of Berlin–or at least that was Orlock's first impression of it. As he looked closer, however, he could make out a human form suspended beneath the wings. Another vampire? he wondered, then shook his head. No, if any of his undead offspring, his victims turned night's children, were in this city, he would have immediately sensed them. This was something else, something unknown. Something to pique the interest of an immortal creature that fancied it had seen just about everything during its two centuries of existence.

And then the bat banked sharply to the right, and the moonlight shone down to expose the monster's true identity.

"A *woman,*" Orlock purred, admiring the soft curves that were accentuated by the tight-fitting garment she wore. "One who plays the role of *nosferatu* this evening, it would appear." He ran his tongue along the edge of his upper teeth, already imagining how hot and sweet her blood would taste as it filled his mouth. "Perhaps she would be interested in dining with the genuine article," he muttered, then cackled hoarsely at his jest.

He crept over the window and quickly crawled down the building's brick façade, making his way to the empty, shadow-draped lane below. Yet before he reached the sidewalk, his body had begun to transform–becoming smaller, more compact, more animal-like in shape. Coarse hair sprouted from the top of his bald pate to his malformed toes. His hawkish nose grew longer, flatter, joining with an increasingly widening mouth to form a muzzle. Hands and feet became paws. Even his funereal attire–black waistcoat and matching slacks–metamorphosed, changing from dark fabric to brownish pelt. When the transformation was complete, it was not a vampire that stood in the middle of the cobblestoned street, but a hyena.

A thrust of powerful leg muscles and the beast was off at a full run, chasing the bat shape that glided toward the center of the city.

The hunt had begun anew.

For Irma, the flight across night-shrouded Berlin had been terrifying and exhilarating and far more stimulating than Wilhelm's awkward attempts at lovemaking. The bracing chill of the night air that prickled her skin, the rush of wind in her ears, the certain knowledge that an errant breeze could collapse her wings and send her plunging to her doom–never had she felt so alive, so carefree, so unfettered. Here in the sky her life was her own, with no one to answer to, whether spurned lover or ego-driven crime lord. Given half a chance, she would have preferred to chase the Moon over the horizon and never set foot on Earth again, mission be damned. She doubted, however, that the Great Vampire would be quite so understanding of her feelings.

Irma smiled wistfully. *Another time, perhaps,* she thought, although she had little doubt that time would be long in coming.

Tilting her body to the left and extending the wings forward, she swooped down and began her approach to the museum... and its unguarded roof. Silent and unobserved, like the proverbial thief in the night. It was just the way she liked to conduct her business... and her affairs, as Wilhelm might willingly attest. Irma shook her head to clear it; best to leave such ruminations for later–or never.

A flash of movement in the street below her caught her eye–a welcome distraction from her darkening thoughts–and she glanced down to see who might be watching. So much for traveling unobserved, she mused. But who could it be at this hour? Some late-night reveler staggering home to bed–or worse, a police officer walking his patrol?

Her heart skipped a beat, waiting for the alarm to be raised. But it was neither inebriate nor constable–nor, in fact, was it anyone human. On closer inspection, she realized she was being followed by what appeared to be a dog–a gangly, coarse-haired mongrel that was not only keeping pace with her, but even racing ahead at times, probably trying to determine where she might come to land. Irma chuckled softly. "You'll have to run much faster than that if you hope to catch *me,* my canine friend," she whispered.

And then the most remarkable–and blood-chilling–thing occurred: without breaking stride, the dog looked up and stared right at her, as though it had heard her comment. Bright-red eyes glowed in the darkness like twin coals, and its muzzle stretched wide from side to side, in a ghastly imitation of a smile.

Irma gasped and instinctively snapped back her head in fright, and in doing so lost control of her gliding apparatus. Her body rolled to the right, and suddenly she was hurtling earthward, like Icarus in the legends of old. But no Sun-warmed ocean waited to receive her, only a devilish animal that eyed her hungrily, its smile growing insanely, impossibly wider as the beast raced toward its prey.

But it would have to find its next meal elsewhere. Once over her initial shock, Irma quickly regained control of her wits, then her wings, and soared away from those slavering jaws and burning eyes; the beast howled in anger. With a stiff breeze again holding her aloft, she soon left the creature far behind and sailed the rest of the way to the museum without further incident. A slight twist of her body to set her feet before her, and she gracefully touched down on the gravel-topped roof.

A pleasant chill ran through Irma's body as she freed herself from the support harness; it took all her willpower to keep from laughing with delight at her aerial adventure. Gazing at the flimsy apparatus that had carried her across the sleeping city, she grinned broadly, eager to take to the skies once more. But the sky would have to wait–first there was a bit of art thievery that required her attention.

From a pocket sewn into the harness she extracted the items she needed for the next step in her plan: tools to remove the painting from its frame, a collapsible tube in which to carry the canvas, and Wilhelm's key ring. It took some trial and error, but eventually she located the key that unlocked an access hatch to reveal a ladder leading down to a catwalk suspended above the main hall. Irma smiled. "Why, I'm halfway there already," she muttered.

She clambered down the ladder, then paused to assess her surroundings. The catwalk was 20 feet above the floor, set back far enough to provide museum workers with an unobstructed view of the hall without distracting visitors from admiring the colorful medieval tapestries that hung beneath the wooden planking. From where Irma crouched, she could see the door leading to the Munch exhibit—and the night watchman seated beside it. He appeared to be in his late sixties, portly and grey-haired, with a great bristling mustache draped over his upper lip; if his relaxed posture was any true indication, he was fast asleep.

Quietly, Irma slipped over the catwalk's railing and climbed down the nearest tapestry, taking care not to shred the centuries-old artwork as she grasped handfuls of the delicate material to slow her descent. Then, with whisper-soft steps, she tiptoed over to the guard. The steady rise and fall of his chest was evidence enough that he still slumbered, and a close look at the metal flask of alcohol loosely clutched in one hand let her know he wouldn't be waking anytime soon.

Dead to the world, she thought, and grinned. She crept past him, taking care to tightly grasp Wilhelm's key ring in both hands, lest the rattling of metal roust the old man from his dreams, and then another round of infuriating selections followed before the right key at last turned the lock. Irma slipped inside, closing the door behind her. With any luck, she would be back at her hotel room long before the museum's trusted guardian slipped free from the comforting embrace of Morpheus and raised the alarm.

She gazed around the darkened room, giving her eyes a few moments to become acclimated to the dim lighting provided by the waning Moon. It didn't take her long to locate her intended prize from among the vast collection of Munch's works on display—*Vampire* was the only one fully illuminated, as though the Moon wished to help her in accomplishing her task.

Rubber soles whispering against the tiled floor, Irma fairly glided across the exhibit hall, then paused to admire the painting anew. Huddled in the dark as they were, the man and woman looked even more forlorn than they had in broad daylight. Irma shook her head. How anyone could ever think a portrait of such intense sorrow represented a far more nefarious purpose was unfathomable.

She sighed, then stepped closer and held up the pouch of tools. "Don't worry," she told the couple. "I promise I'll be gentle."

It was while she was slipping the painting into the protective tube that she noticed the eyes staring at her from the other side of the hall.

Burning like twin coals, they hovered about two feet off the floor—roughly the height of a dog, she realized. A guard dog? Perhaps, but it was unlikely—during her previous visits to the museum she had seen no evidence that dogs were used to patrol the grounds. But if not a guard dog, then what could it be? The beast that had pursued her? Impossible! She had left it far behind in the street; besides, how would it have ever gained entry to the museum?

Fighting the urge to run—if only to prevent damaging the painting during what she knew would be a mad dash for the door—Irma affixed what she hoped looked like a comforting smile on her face and slowly took a step back. "Such a good doggie," she cooed. "So vigilant. Your masters must be very pleased with you." Another step back, then another, the eyes tracking her every movement. "I wish I had a biscuit to reward you with. Would you like that? A tasty biscuit for a good dog?"

"Not when there is something far more delectable on which to feast, my beauteous morsel," the beast growled. Its muzzle pulled back in a familiar, hideous smile.

Irma froze, her eyes widening in shock. "W-what...?"

And then the eyes began to rise, as though the animal was attempting to stand on its hind legs–but then they continued upward, going higher until they towered above her. Beneath the black body stocking, her arms prickled with the sudden rise of goose bumps.

"What... what are you?" she whispered hoarsely.

A man stepped from the shadows–no, Irma considered, not a man. A re-animated corpse–or a monster. Certainly nothing human. Its emaciated body hung loosely within a black velvet frock coat, the sleeves of which ended several inches above slender wrists; the black pants legs, too, did not reach all the way down to cover those pipe cleaner-like lower appendages. It was as though the creature had outgrown its clothing–or stolen them from some shorter, unfortunate victim.

"I am Count Orlock, of Transylvania," it said with a brief, mannerly bow of its head. "And you are the bat-winged girl who soars through the night skies, like those of my kind."

"Y-your kind?" Irma asked. She tensed her leg muscles–priceless painting or no, she was running for the door. One glance into those burning eyes as they lasciviously studied every curve of her body told her all she needed to know: that any punishment The Great Vampire might devise for her failure on this mission paled in comparison to whatever the abomination on the other side of the room no doubt had planned for her.

"Yes. My kind." Moonlight sparkled along the tips of hideously sharpened teeth as it grinned. "*Nosferatu.* The undead."

"Oh. Of course," Irma said flatly. And then she was running for her life, silently admonishing herself for having ever closed the door; now, taking the time to open it would rob her escape of precious seconds.

The vampire, however, was faster. Orlock swept across the hall with such incredible speed that Irma was unable to alter her course as he came to a halt directly in front of her. She ran straight into his arms.

Orlock grasped her firmly in a crushing embrace, driving the air from her lungs. Irma tried to draw breath, only to inhale the stench of the grave–a pervasive, stomach-churning odor that swirled about her captor like a fog. Her senses reeled, yet she forced herself to remain on her feet; she knew that fainting now, like some imperiled heroine in a "penny dreadful" magazine, would only hasten her death. There had to be a way to escape...

She glanced toward the door. "The guard..."

"Dead to the world," the monster replied with an unnerving grin. His worm-like tongue swept across teeth that gleamed with the bloody flecks of his latest meal.

Irma gasped. "No..."

Spider-like fingers scuttled across her face, the cracked, yellow-tinged nails finding purchase in the tight hood covering the top of her head. With a deft turn of his wrist, the vampire tore away the thin material, freeing her dark hair from its confines–and baring her neck. His fingers took hold of her tresses and pulled hard, yanking her head back so that nothing obscured his view of the jugular vein that pulsed so invitingly just below the tender flesh.

"Such a lovely throat," Orlock purred. Then he whispered: "Do not worry. I promise I shall be gentle."

Irma struggled frantically, but his grip was unbreakable, his strength superhuman. And so, as she felt the tips of his fangs brush her neck she closed her eyes and prayed for a quick death.

That was the moment when the door suddenly flew open, with a loud crash that seemed to reverberate throughout the entire museum. Vampire and victim turned to see a man stumble into the room on unsteady legs. He lifted his right arm with great effort, and pointed an accusatory finger toward Irma.

"Vixen! Temptress!" he bellowed in a slurred voice. "I've caught you red-handed!"

It took Irma a moment to recognize him, and to make sense of his words. *"Wilhelm?"* Apparently it was a night for impossibilities–the drug she had given him should have kept him unconscious for hours, yet here he was, his anger at her betrayal obviously helping him to combat the sedative's effects.

He staggered forward, his right arm plummeting weakly back to his side; the sudden movement almost unbalanced him, but somehow he remained upright. "You seduced me against my will, had your way with me, and for what? So you could plunder my museum with your"–a sneer creased his mouth as he glanced at Orlock–"your homely lover?"

The vampire turned back to her, his right eyebrow–a bushy, tangled mess of wire-like hairs–raised in a quizzical fashion. "Who is this fool?"

Irma chose to ignore the question. "Wilhelm, help me!" she pleaded as she renewed her attempts to free herself from Orlock's hold. "He wants to kill me!"

"Kill you?" Wilhelm came to an unsteady halt. "Why should he want to do that? Are you not...? I don't..." The confused expression that contorted his handsome features was clear evidence that his drug-addled brain had become stuck between two choices: aid her, or watch as she quenched the vampire's murderous thirst. But if he waited too long to decide, she would surely die.

Orlock glanced toward the window, and a low growl crawled up from his throat. Irma inclined her head to see what had captured his attention: the waning Moon had moved across the night sky on the latest leg of its eternal flight around the Earth, and in its wake, just above the Berlin rooftops, appeared the first glimmers of a red-streaked dawn.

"The sunrise," Irma whispered. She had heard a little of the vampire legends during her travels across Europe–not that she had paid them any real attention–but now she remembered a passing mention that sunlight was deadly to them. She turned to face her captor, a triumphant smile lighting her eyes. "You are to be denied your feast, monster. Dawn approaches, and now you must flee or be turned to dust."

Orlock chuckled. "Quite true–but there is still time for one small... bite." He opened his mouth wide, then swept his head down toward her neck.

"No!" Wilhelm roared, and launched himself at the Count. Curator and vampire collided, and Irma was sent tumbling to the floor, finally released from that crushing grip.

As she sat up, her gaze fell on the collapsible tube and its valuable prize, and she glanced toward the open door. Irma gnawed on her lower lip for a few moments, weighing her options. With the two combatants occupied, all she had to do was pick up the tube and race out the door–and yet she could not bring herself to abandon her rescuer. But was that because she felt grateful, she wondered, or guilty?

She watched as Wilhelm and Orlock struggled, but the outcome was never in doubt. Though young and virile, Wilhelm was still dazed from the sedative, too weak to put up a proper fight, and Orlock was an unstoppable demon. Wilhelm rained heavy blows upon the creature, but they had no effect; Orlock's strikes, however, drew blood with each swipe of his sharp fingernails. And yet Wilhelm refused to give in; for a man scorned, he was putting his life in jeopardy to protect the very woman who had broken his heart.

Irma looked to the window. The morning sky was lightening, but not fast enough to make Orlock break off his attack. There had to be another way to kill him, otherwise, as Irma well knew, he would come for her as soon as Wilhelm had been removed as an obstacle.

She spotted the disassembled picture frame that had held Munch's masterpiece, its pieces lying on the floor where she had left them, and realized its sharp corners could make for a weapon equally as dangerous to a vampire as sunlight: a wooden stake. She grabbed a lengthy section and moved stealthily toward Orlock, whose attentions were focused on Wilhelm.

Not for long, though. With a backhanded sweep of his claw-like nails, Orlock slashed open the curator's throat; blood spurted across the tiles. With a soft gasp, Wilhelm crashed to the floor, both hands wrapped around his neck as he tried to staunch the fatal wound.

Orlock sniffed haughtily. "Such a waste of good blood..." he muttered–just before Irma's improvised stake pierced his heart from behind.

The vampire staggered forward, then turned to face her. The shocked expression on his grotesque face brought a savage smile to Irma's lips.

"I apologize, my dear Count," she purred. "That wasn't very gentle, was it? But then I never promised you I would be..."

Orlock croaked out a wordless response and reached for her, but Irma made no attempt to flee. Instead, she coolly stood and watched as his fingers closed on air and he stumbled backward, making desperate attempts to remove the piece of framing from his decaying heart. A useless effort, for his hands were slick with Wilhelm's blood and the stake was wedged too tightly in his rib cage. As dawn broke fully above the horizon, the undead nobleman sprawled across the tiled floor and gasped out his final breath. Then the rising Sun finished what Irma had started.

As the ashen remains of the vampire lord swirled about her, Irma turned to look down at Wilhelm, and felt a weight settle in her stomach–and on her heart. An enormous pool of blood had collected around him, and his limp hands had done little to stem the sanguineous flow that only now had slowed to a trickle.

Irma knelt beside him and cradled his head on her lap, then gently ran her fingertips across his brow in an effort to soothe his pain; his skin was ice-cold to the touch. "Thank you, Wilhelm, for saving my life," she said quietly, and forced a tiny smile to curl the corners of her mouth. "I... wish that I could somehow return the favor."

Empty words, she knew, because his spirit had long since departed; she realized that as soon as she had touched his forehead. But they were heartfelt nonetheless.

She leaned forward, her raven tresses draping across his head in an unconscious imitation of the very work of art that had cost the handsome curator his life, and kissed him lightly on the lips. Then she reverently placed his head back on the floor, rose to her feet, and went to retrieve her prize.

What easy prey is man, she considered as she headed back to the museum's roof. So easily baited. So easily trapped.

So easily led to their doom.

She glanced down at the canvas tube in her hand, and remembered Wilhelm's comment from the day before: that the painting known as *Vampire* had originally gone by another title–one consisting of three words with which Irma was intimately familiar.

They are the weapons of my trade, she had thought earlier in the evening, *and all I have to offer.*

"*Love and Pain,*" she whispered. "For you can never experience one without the presence of the other..."

The words weighed heavily upon her conscience, all the way back to Paris.

John Shirley, one of the most important authors in the history of cyberpunk science fiction, is about the last writer from whom one would have expected a swashbuckling story. Yet, John, who lived in Paris for a while, plucked two quintessential French heroes, d'Artagnan and Cyrano de Bergerac, to indulge his fancy in this volume. One will note that the two heroes met briefly in the classic Edmond Rostand play, and Paul Féval fils, the son of Paul Féval, wrote no less than seven novels featuring the two stalwart swordsmen. But none have done it with so much verve and panache as John in...

John Shirley: *Cyrano and the Two Plumes*

Paris, 1655

One thing without stain, unspotted from the world, in spite of doom, mine own!–
And that is...my white plume!
Cyrano, in Edmond Rostand's Cyrano de Bergerac

In the Autumn of the year 1655, two hours after dawn, a sorcerer in a bottle-green coat drifted invisibly over the city of Paris, not far above the rooftops. His body upright, the magician sailed past chimneys, and, once, without pause, right through a steeple. He flew along about as fast a raven flies, when it is in no terrible hurry, traveling wherever his mind chose to take him. When the magician came upon a certain district, he slowed, and descended toward a neglected, winding side-street. Here he stopped, just below the rooftops. The sorcerer hovered, and gazed up at three laborers, climbing a scaffold onto the roof opposite. One of them was a burly man in a long tattered coat, most of his face hidden by beard and matted hair. The burly man carried an oaken beam to the edge of the roof, where he could look down at the street. He stood there, holding the beam in his arms, waiting–just as the magician waited. The other two workmen glanced at the burly man, then looked quizzically at one another. But they were afraid to ask questions.

Well might they be afraid of him. The magician knew this man in the tattered coat to be a murderer. He had murdered in the past, and he had been sent here today to kill again, for a handful of gold.

Perhaps the murderer would succeed, the magician mused. Then again, perhaps not.

The sorcerer descended further, almost to the street. Unseen and nearly unseeable, he drifted just over the cobblestones, where he watched the front door of a tenement in which lived the poet, philosopher and soldier, Cyrano de Bergerac.

Cyrano Hercule-Savinien de Bergerac buckled on his sword, donned his ragged cavalier's hat, with its large white plume–its *panache*–and hurried down the creaking wooden staircase.

He paused in the doorway to gaze out on the narrow street, assessing the late October day–a bit grey, but it was no longer raining, and with his prodigious nose Cyrano savored the multifarious scents of Paris: minerals released by the new rain, wood smoke combined with chamber pot's reek, the smell of meat and pastry cooking; some blossom, somewhere–or was it a woman's perfume? Gardenia?

Ragueneau was to meet him here, in front of the tenement–stout, genial old Ragueneau, the baker and poet. They would gossip over a quick breakfast, before Cyrano went to Roxanne. Most Saturdays, when he was in Paris, Cyrano recited his society news to Roxanne as she did her needlework. Some of his ironic *gazette* he would obtain from Ragueneau; some he would cheerfully fabricate. Anything to please his love–his unrequited love.

He had spent a good deal of time, recently, sequestered with the canon Pierre Gassendi, steeped in the priest's strange coalescence of Epicurianism, Christianity and atomism, and he yearned for the grounding of his old friends and for the forgetfulness he found in gazing upon Roxanne in the garden of the Ladies of the Cross.

He had been warned not to return to Paris, but he had been born here, and Roxanne was here, and he could not be away for long. And if a duel was offered him, so be it. It had been years since he had fought a duel, but–perhaps that was the very reason he needed one. In the world of philosophy one felt distanced from the visceral energies of life. Risk quickened the pulse; only Roxanne made his heart thunder more.

But in a duel, he reflected, as he stepped out onto the narrow lane of rain-wet cobblestones, a man might hope for consummation...

Somewhere close at hand voices were chattering away in gutter French–but not from the gutters, on the contrary the gruff male voices nattered from the rooftops, as if the ghosts of Parisian scoundrels disported on the eaves. Workmen, he remembered, were to replace a decaying section of roof-beam today. So his sour-faced landlady had informed him.

There, to his left, came Ragueneau, walking through a small flock of strutting pigeons, the birds foraging at a heap of garbage; the pigeons took noisily to the air at the baker's approach, fluttering near "the king of Bakers" like courtiers, Cyrano thought, applauding the approach of young Louis XIV.

Ragueneau was still portly, Cyrano observed, though perhaps a bit haggard with some of the ill luck that had dogged the once-wealthy merchant in recent years. His eyes lit up at the sight of Cyrano. The pigeons fluttered and Ragueneau raised a hand–then those same eyes widened, his hand stiffened and he cried out in wordless warning–a shadow crossed Cyrano's eyes and he felt the wind of the wings of death–

And suddenly both Ragueneau and the pigeons froze. The pigeons simply *stopped* in mid-air–yes and in mid-wing-beat. The birds hung there, motionless, wings spread, like ornaments depending from a string on a windless day; Ragueneau was as motionless as the pigeons beside him, his hand upraised in warning, his mouth gaping, mustaches bristling as if to underscore the alarm in his eyes. Even more remarkably, Ragueneau's right foot was raised in the air, had arrested fixedly there as if poised on an invisible stairway. But there was no stairway in the lane. There was just Ragueneau defying gravity–for, as he stood there with one foot lifted for a step that never completed, he should have been falling forward.

"Ragueneau?" Cyrano called, his voice sounding muffled and distant to his own ears, "What ails you? You seem to have gotten yourself stuck." He began to move toward his old friend–and felt a sudden iciness sweep through him; a wrenching, as if he were torn from the fabric of the world.

For a moment Cyrano seemed to drift in the air a few paces, like a dandelion puff. He seemed unable to guide himself in the narrow lane; he turned randomly in the air, like whirling smoke–and, to his considerable shock, saw himself standing at his own front door.

He had left his body. So it seemed: he could see his own body, frozen in place, mouth open to call to Ragueneau; Cyrano frozen in place as Ragueneau was. There was a shadow on the frozen Cyrano's face. It was cast by an object impossibly suspended, supportless, in the air over his head: a large piece of wood, roughly shaped into a short beam. This piece of beam looked to weigh about 60 pounds. But as it had fallen several stories from the roof–doubtless it originated with the workmen up there–its momentum would give it a great deal more force than a mere 60 pounds, Cyrano knew. When it struck him, it would stove in his head.

But it did not strike his body. It stayed motionless in the air, inches over his forehead.

And to see himself like this, so objectively…his mouth open, smiling, his head turned, one hand raising in greeting, the other on the pommel of his sword…He could see saliva glistening in his mouth; could see the oil on his skin, the pores on his nose. The rather large pores on his rather large nose.

Well, now. His nose, seen from this perspective, was not really as big as he had always supposed. The mirrors had perhaps exaggerated. It was rather big, yes. But really…

But that thought was washed away by the fear that swept through him, another internal gust: a keen wind from the highest, coldest mountain peaks. If his mind was torn from his body–surely he was dead!

Dreaming or dead, he thought.

"No," came a sibilant voice "You are not dead. Not yet. You are merely outside the stream of time."

"Who speaks?" Cyrano demanded. He was not himself certain how he spoke himself; with his mind or with some manner of ghostly mouth. "Show yourself!"

"I am behind your psychic perspective. Merely think of turning toward the source of my words and your spirit will respond," said the voice.

Cyrano did so, and found his point of view rotating. He was now staring at the tenuous figure of a compact man in a bottle-green frock coat, a high collar, a leonine face; his hair was a mane of silvered black around his globular forehead; his eyes were small and piercing, seeming more substantial than the rest of his psychic form. The stranger floated a few inches over the cobblestones.

"What you see is a mere projection of my mind," said the stranger. "My body is in a trance state in the south tower of my manse, which is in…ah, let us merely say that it is somewhere in Normandy. As for yourself, I have prodded your spirit out of your body–here in one of the crystallizations of a moment, in the necklace of eternity, a spirit is easily nudged free…although I must admit yours was a bit more tenacious than most. No doubt it was rather wrenching for you."

"It was! And who are you, sir, to interfere with my spirit?" Cyrano demanded. "What impertinence! I insist that you meet me, fully bodied, and give satisfaction! You will choose your weapon, sir, and we will have it out!"

The stranger's voice was all silky condescension. "Do you not see the wooden beam caught in its descent toward your head, you fool? Had I not interfered, you would now be dead! Expired! *Pffft!* And as for my identity, you may know me as Alcandre the Sorcerer; also known as Alcandre the Magnificent, Alcandre the Brilliant and Alcandre the Enviable."

"Your reputation has not preceded you," Cyrano said coldly. "And I do not believe in magic. Nor the soul–I was speaking facetiously a moment ago of my spirit. Nor do I believe in miracles–I have argued against them with devastating logic! Even Gassendi agrees with me, in secret. So I must conclude that I am dreaming–or I have taken opium, and forgotten that I have done so. Or possibly I have been poisoned, occasioning delirium. Each is more probably true than your magical freezing of time."

"I have not said that I have frozen time. It continues. We are merely outside its stream–we are, as it were, *perpendicular* to it, so that we do not observe its passing, but are fixed, temporarily, and temporally, within the crystallization of a single moment. However, we haven't 'time' for the full explanation: a variety of subsidiary time relating to the entropy of our spiritual selves holds sway upon you and me. And so we must proceed apace with our business. I have saved your life, sir, for the moment. But if I but reinsert you into your body and give you another nudge, your destiny will unfold as intended. The murder will proceed. And you will die. Or–you can do my bidding, and live!"

"Hold! What's that you say? A murder? How so? Clearly it is an accident! Or–about to be."

"No, Monsieur. I regret to inform you I came upon the information that you were to be murdered, this morning. A team of workmen repair the roof, yes. But one of them is not a workman–he is unknown to the others. His employer has been bribed by a certain gentleman, who works, in turn, for a–ah, a member of the nobility. I do not know exactly which one. This mysterious nobleman has been desirous of ending your life for a long time. But then–you have many enemies. Many have been insulted by your writings, your declamations, and the, shall we say, insinuation of your sword, which always seems to suggest, without much repudiation, that the nobility is made up of cowards...since they have concluded to run from it. One such has arranged for that oaken beam to be dropped on your head as you emerge."

"I insist you tell me his name! I will confront the coward! I will–"

"I truly do not know his name," the sorcerer interrupted, not very convincingly. "You have so many enemies! Who's to say? I could find out, but it is not important to me. You will find out–after you have done a certain task for me. I will intercede, and prevent gravity's own cudgel from falling on you. Then you will be free to make inquiries. You can then rush to the roof and interrogate the carpenters. But first...if you wish to live, and have your revenge, you will do as I ask."

"And should I make an unsavory deal with an hallucinatory phantasm, sir?" Cyrano said, doing his best to sniff contemptuously. Difficult to do when one is pure spirit. "To have dealings with the excrescence of a dream? I would not so degrade myself. Again I assert the unreality of this event."

"You are not dreaming; and I am no phantasm. I am unbodied, but I am quite real. Oh, you are right about magic: what people *suppose* to be magic is *not* magic. It is all science–all of it! But some is a science unknown to scientists! It will *appear* to be supernatural. As for the soul–some have one, while others have not developed one. The soul grows within a man like fruit in a tree. Most such trees grow in poor soil and are poorly tended, they produce no fruit. A few have a truly great, juicy ripe fruit–a truly developed soul! You sir–I became aware that you have just such a soul. A rare thing! A fairly solid soul that would not melt instantly away, once free of its body. The sort the Higher Beings rejoice in, when it ascends to their plane."

Cyrano made a sound of derision. "Oh you knew I had this 'special soul,' did you? Indeed? And just how did you know that?"

"Why–your plume sir. Your *panache*!"

"My panache? On my hat?"

"No, sir. The other sort. That is what you sometimes call it, no? It is–an expression of your essential being. A summarization that adds up to more than the factors of the equation. A *gestalt* of self expression which expresses far beyond your walk in life, although you are unaware it is doing so. It emanates, sir, because of your nature. It sends out a beam of spiritual light...or more accurately, a plume of light...that acts as a beacon, for those sensitive enough to perceive it. And with the guidance of this beacon, I found you. Thereupon, I saw this murderous event coming–which makes you particularly suitable, since, frankly, it gives me leverage for negotiation, yes?"

"This is all the false conjuration of a mountebank," Cyrano protested, though feeling increasingly less convinced of his own convictions. "I don't know how it's done, but..."

"It is no false conjuration, Monsieur. Look around. Do you not trust the evidence of your senses?"

Gazing again at his statuelike body, Cyrano had to admit to himself that he was in a place beyond his experience–and that it did not have the quality of a dream. It had the ineffable tang of genuineness.

Alcandre the Sorcerer nodded as if he'd read Cyrano's thoughts. "Exactly so. Now heed me: Because of the power of your *panache* I can reintroduce your soul into your body. I will then introduce it into a–shall we say, a 'shortcut' in time and space, which will transport you to the time and the place where you will do the deed. There, a distance in the future–you will kill a tyrant! A tyrant who will be the scourge of the poor! A terrible tyrant the world is better off without! That is another reason I picked you: you are opposed to tyrants. Thus you are triply motivated: you have the chance to save your life, rid the world of a tyrant and seek out he who attempted to murder you. If only you perform this one task–kill the tyrant!"

"What tyrant is this?"

"Does it matter? When we pass beyond the edge of the worlds, and traverse time and space to his sanctuary, I will show you a bit of his wickedness. The wars I have foreseen–they will go on and on! The weighty taxation on the poor to build a guilded nursery for himself and his playmates! He is a monarchical absolutist...the very thing you despise! And he will trample France, the nation you love, under his perfectly formed, exquisitely booted feet!"

"And if you are so powerful, why can you not take this shortcut yourself, stab the fellow yourself, and take the same path to *exeunt*, eh?"

The sorcerer scowled. "I am not the only magician in this land. There is one, secretly engaged by Queen Anne, who still works for the crown–or more specifically, for that scabrous conspirator, Cardinal Mazarin!"

"Mazarin? The *Premier Ministre?* Mazarin is a Jesuit! He would have no truck with a magician!"

"He would prefer it thus, true. But in fact that Italian wretch has become aware of my motions, certain conjurations of mine have come to his attention, and he has become alarmed. His own magician is a dwarf of sorcery, scarcely more than a mere chiromancer, but he stumbled upon a rather effective crystal of time-seeing and in it he saw that I intended to destroy the tyrant. So he set a swordsman to guard the tyrant against me: a lackey, a bootlick for tyrants. But–a great swordsman. I confess I fear him. You see–he, also, has...*panache*. His 'plume,' too, is quite powerful, and I'm not sure I can manipulate him magically...and then again, there is the small matter of a charm, with a certain saintly relic inside; it has been placed about the tyrant's neck by that low-rent alchemist. And that too keeps me at bay. But the charm will have no effect on you. And as for the swordsman–why, Monsieur, you are well known to be the equal of any swordsman!"

"Ah well. In my day, perhaps."

"You are only 36! You are at your prime. Would you have your life ended at a mere 36 by a falling log? The ignominy! A great man like yourself? The author of *The Death of Agrippine* and *The Pedant Imitated*? The hero of the Siege of Arras and the greatest swordsman of Paris? But now, attend: Here is a fourth consideration to compel you: You will learn if you are indeed a more masterful wielder of cold steel than this...this *oaf* sent by the Cardinal to protect the tyrant. Unless...you are afraid?"

"I? I fear no man! I am Cyrano de Bergerac! I am..." His voice trailed off as he became aware of a dull rippling sensation in the vicinity of what had been his head. He was vaguely sensible that some aspect of this proposal was befogged by that rippling sensation. Some bell of warning rang within him: *Beware. Something clouds your mind...*

But he was overwhelmed by what had happened, disoriented by the loss of his body. And how he yearned to be reunited with it! This floating about was not something he understood. He was a man of action–not a wisp to be puffed away like the last exudation of a chimney! It was true, as well, that he did despise tyrants. And there was the matter of the murderer. And the chance to see Roxanne again.

"Yes," Cyrano heard himself say. "I will undertake this mission–if you will return me to my body. Although how you can do it without permitting the unfortunate intrusion of this block of wood, I cannot guess. It would indeed be inappropriate for me to die thus, I who have shown that so many others were block-heads by comparison. And so, if you don't mind, I dislike this vaporous state."

His voice trailed off again as he found himself swirling like a human dust-devil. The figure of the Magus made certain sorcerous passes–and then Cyrano was falling through a spinning tunnel, back into...himself.

A wet reverberation, a metaphysical impact, and he was back in his body, standing, now to one side of his own doorway, staring at the short wooden beam yet hanging in the air over the spot where he had stood.

"But–time is still arrested!" Cyrano exclaimed.

"Yes. Your body now moves freely through the crystallization of this moment. It will also move a short distance into the future...and there it will rejoin the flow of time. Meanwhile, this moment will remain crystallized. You cannot move that beam from its place however hard you try! Later, you will return to this place, and this time. If you destroy the tyrant as I request, I will return you to this spot, but one step to the right of that falling block. Time's flow will resume for you, and the block will strike the ground beside you. You will be unhurt and free to resume your life and hunt down your enemy. Free to see your Roxanne again! Free to live past a mere 36 years, to explore the outer reaches of philosophy! But *if you do not do* as I ask–you will be returned to the exact spot from which you were plucked. And you will be brained by that falling block! Do you understand the choice?"

"I do, Monsieur Magician."

"Very well. Turn and approach the wall. Do you not see the crack there, in the wall? Observe! The crack widens! What was only big enough for an ant now gapes open sufficiently for two men to walk through, side by side! It is a transient opening through space and time…"

It was as Alcandre maintained: a crack in the wall of the building groaned and quivered and expanded, wider and wider. Within it was a churning quagmire of nascent possibilities…

Into which strode Cyrano de Bergerac.

They traveled through material barriers as a man strolls through a ground mist. They passed through thick outer walls, through locked doors; they passed beyond cornices and curtains–and as they came, the Magus showed Cyrano visions of the future. They shimmered through time and space, until Cyrano found that he had fetched up in a high-ceilinged, ornate corridor, outside a large, beautifully carved, closed door.

"Surely this is a *palais*," Cyrano said, looking around at fine tapestries and golden candelabra, as Alcandre appeared at his elbow. "I have never seen quite such splendor, though I have been a guest in some very fine mansions."

"Yes. In our time, just a few years ago, this wing of the palace was still being completed."

"A few years ago? I had thought we were traveling some distance into the future, to some faraway time, but–"

"Silence! Would you go back to submit to that block of hard wood?"

"I have no desire for the Sword of Damocles, wooden sword or no, to descend upon me–but I must know–"

"Bah! Enter and see the tyrannical malefactor for yourself!" And with that Alcandre reached out to the knob in the center of the door, turned it, and pulled the door, creaking, ajar.

Feeling odd and unreal, Cyrano loosened his sword in its scabbard, licked his lips, and stepped through into the chamber. The Magus followed, closing the door behind them.

This was an antechamber to a bedroom, Cyrano supposed–candelabra on wooden tables stood to either side of the doorway to the inner room. But two men in finely figured helmets and cuirasses stood beside the candelabra, each man tall, and neatly bearded, each leaning on a long pike, and each wearing the livery of the king.

They looked at Cyrano with astonishment–then they rushed him, pikes lowering as if to doubly spit him.

"Intruder!" one of them shouted.

Cyrano reacted instinctively. Jumping to the right, he snatched the nearest pike, just under the blade, as it slashed past him, jerked it from the astonished man's hands, and slammed its butt into the guard's forehead. The guard fell over backwards, quite unconscious. With the same motion, Cyrano had blocked the other pike, but now the second guard made as if to rush past him out the door, to cry the alarm.

Cyrano swept the pike under the second guard's feet, and tripped him. The guard's helmet banged to the floor, rolling away, and Cyrano, reversing the pike, slammed the flat side of its blade expertly down on the back of the guard's head.

The man gasped, and went limp, quite unconscious.

Cyrano dropped the pike. "Big cumbersome things. Not a weapon for a real man–a weapon to keep real men at bay!"

"But you used it very well, Monsieur," the sorcerer remarked, sounding impressed. "Your skills have not been exaggerated." He licked his lips. "Perhaps we should take a moment to cut their throats? Just to see that they remain quiet."

"By no means! These are doubtless good, faithful men, only doing their duty!"

Alcandre shrugged. "As you will. And now–we proceed–for there is one who must *undoubtedly* die this night–"

"Who goes there?" interrupted a deep voice, from the inner door to the bedchamber.

Cyrano looked up to see the silhouette of a Musketeer stepping through the doorway. Beyond the Musketeer, in the light from a stub of candle in a silver holder, a slender male figure, of no great size, was visible sleeping in the largest bed Cyrano had ever seen. Stirring restlessly, but still asleep. The Musketeer closed the bedroom door behind him.

"There–you saw the tyrant! He sleeps!" hissed the sorcerer. "Win past this ruffian and kill him and all will be well!"

Cyrano's gaze had fixed on the Musketeer–though he was dressed as a Musketeer, no musket was to hand. The man was armed with a scabbarded sword and dagger. His hat was rather like Cyrano's, white plumed, but far less battered. His breaches and weskit were of blue silk, burnished by the candle-light, and his coat the finest cut; he wore the ribbon of a high officer. At his cuffs and ruffled about his neck was the finest white lace. His face was in the shadow of his hat brim.

"An assassin!" the Musketeer burst out, drawing his sword. Then–he hesitated. "But–do I not know this man? Were we not together at Arras? Did I not see your splendid duel at the *Hotel de Bourgogne*, in which you extemporized perfect rhyme even as your sword sought your enemy? How could I mistake that…profile? Are you not known as Cyrano de Bergerac?"

So speaking, the Musketeer stepped forward into the candlelight. Despite his finery, he had the lean, weathered face of a warrior. The bristling black mustaches and pointed goatee did not conceal two long scars on his face, nor an expression as severe as the beetling clouds of an approaching thunderstorm.

It had been some years, but Cyrano now recognized an old acquaintance: Charles de Batz de Castelmore, Count d'Artagnan. Once the fabled companion of Porthos, Athos and Aramis, d'Artagnan had put aside his roisterer's ways to serve the *Premier Ministre* and the crown.

They had not been friends, Cyrano and this Musketeer–d'Artagnan was not of a literary bent, and had not always appreciated Cyrano's sense of humor nor his notoriety for free-thinking, which d'Artagnan, in his middle years, had come to regard as mere anarchism. Nevertheless, they had a powerful mutual respect, forged at the siege of Arras.

So it was with regret that Cyrano de Bergerac drew his sword.

"Monsieur," Cyrano said formally, standing *en garde.* "I ask you to stand aside. For several good reasons, I am bound to destroy the tyrant who sleeps in yon chamber, and would not destroy you also."

Charles d'Artagnan snorted. "Did you really think I could step aside? You would not think of me in such low terms?"

"Not at all, sir. The request was a matter of form, merely."

"And may I ask who is that who stands in the shadows behind you? What influence does this figure have upon your actions?"

"That is my own affair, Monsieur d'Artagnan. And now…"

Cyrano saluted him with his *épée*, d'Artagnan returned the *salut*–and Cyrano thrust testingly. d'Artagnan parried easily and riposted, with *coup droit*; Cyrano performed a *contre-riposte*, to which the Musketeer returned a *contre-attaque;* Cyrano parried with a false attack that became a feint, then a *coup lance;* d'Artagnan performed a grazing *froissement* and then lunged; Cyrano parried and for a moment they were grappling *corps-à-corps.* Then a *dégagement* initiated by from d'Artagnan and they were apart, again *en garde*, involuntarily grinning at one another.

And then Cyrano lunged. Count d'Artagnan parried…

And so it went, back and forth across the room, faster and faster, swords blurring, crossing with a sound like a percussionist's triangle jangled by a madman; only the occasional minor *touché* was effected, with d'Artagnan getting a few shallow cuts on his upper right arm, Cyrano taking one one just above a nostril, so that blood ran into his mouth, and a scratch over the collarbone; but, equally matched, neither swordsman gained significant ground.

The two duellists became heated, the hilts of the flashing swords slippery with sweat, their eyes glittering like their sword-tips, their teeth bared with feral intensity. The fight was a curious wedding of cerebral tactical intensity and competitive animal fury.

After a particularly furious exchange of sharp steel, d'Artagnan stepped back into one of the tables holding a candelabra, rocking it so that the candle holder fell onto the floor, near a tapestry.

"*Arrête!*" d'Artagnan cried, and Cyrano nodded, stepped back, to give him a moment to smother the flames.

As d'Artagnan succeeded at this, Alcandre slipped from the shadows and hissed, "Cyrano! Now you fool–while his back is turned!"

Cyrano whirled on him with narrowed eyes, shaking with the affront of it. "What do you think I am?"

"*Merci*, Cyrano," d'Artagnan said, turning away from the ashes, the fire now smothered. "And now..." He performed his *salut*, Cyrano returned it, and poised to fight...

But just then the door to the inner room opened and a sleepy, rumpled young sovereign stood there in his silk nightshirt and bare feet, scratching himself. "See here, guards, where is d'Artagnan, he is to sit beside my bed! And what was that great crash that..." Then he stared, blinking, at Cyrano, realizing this was not one of his guards. "But who is this? What has occasioned here?"

The Count d'Artagnan turned instinctively to the young king. "Your Majesty! Go back into the other room and bar the door! I will protect–"

He did not finish the sentence, for the sorcerer had stepped up behind d'Artagnan, and struck him from behind with the fallen candelabra.

And Charles d'Artagnan crumped to his knees, badly stunned.

"What!" Cyrano cried, outraged. "That is a *carton noir!* It is not done, magician! We were engaged in combat between gentlemen!"

"Gentlemen? He is a murderous hireling of that Italian bastard Mazarin– and this pallid little tyrant!"

"*Who's* a tyrant?" asked the young king, blinking in confusion. "And what have you done to my friend! d'Artagnan is quite dazed! Guards!"

"Kill him, Cyrano, before he brings the palace down upon us!" the magician urged.

But Cyrano, gazing at the young man, felt some of the fog that had blurred his mind evaporate. "But–that is my King! This is Louis! The Fourteenth Louis! He is but a boy!"

"Mazarin is to die soon enough–and this boy will take full command of the nation! He will bring upon it wars and poverty! Do you not remember what I showed you?"

Cyrano remembered–as they'd traveled to this place, he'd seen, away in a metaphysical distance, the raveling and unraveling of time: he'd seen the building of Versailles, the self-indulgent glories of the court, and the wars–the Wars of Devolution, the Dutch War, the War of the League of Augsburg, the War of the Spanish Succession...

"Guards!" Louis shouted.

"Kill the tyrant!" urged the magician. "And you will not be struck down! You will live, Cyrano! Refuse and I will return you to your fate!"

The Count d'Artagnan struggled to rise, blood rising from his head. "No...the King..."

"Odd," Cyrano remarked. " 'Struck down' did you say? The worthy d'Artagnan is here struck down, struck on the head by a foul blow–just as I was to be. Such strokes are the signature of villainy! They are struck off by the same diabolical hand! I believe it was *you*, sir, who paid to have me assassinated with a block of wood–so that you could manipulate me to your villainy!" The sorcerer's scowl deepened; his eyes flicked. He did not deny it. Cyrano went on, "No, Magus–I am no marionetted believer in the monarchy, and I am not a floundering abaser before the Church. But I know duty when I see it and I know the diabolic when I smell it! And who is better equipped to smell it? No, sir magus–my eyes are opened! You spoke of some distant tyrant but this is the monarch accepted, for better or worse, by the people of France! It is to them I defer–not the crown. Why should I kill King Louis? And why do you wish it done?"

"Why–in a few years, when he is grown a man he will cleave closer to the church, which will send its agents to hound me, to destroy me! I have seen it! It must be stopped! I will not be persecuted! I have used all my magic to this end! And as for you–kill him...or die yourself, Cyrano!"

"I refuse! He is not even armed! Am I to strike down a youth in his nightshirt? Am I a slinking footpad? No! The fight with my esteemed opponent has cleared my head of your dire influence...Again–no! I will not strike him down!"

The young King looked back and forth between them, puzzled, on the verge of shouting for help again–but falling under the magician's mesmeric influence himself.

"Kill him, Cyrano!" Alcandre persisted. "–and I will give you your Roxanne! She will love you as you always dreamed she would!" the magician crowed, leering. "I will use my magic to bend her will to you!"

"Dog!" Cyrano burst out, scarcely believing his ears. "You expect me to insult her by despoiling her will–her very being? Never!"

"Then, Cyrano, you will die, and–but wait!" The magician's gaze had fixed on the confused young King. "He is not wearing the charm!" "The charm?" Louis muttered dreamily, his hand going to his throat. "It was uncomfortable to sleep with, an angular thing that woke me when I rolled on it, I put it aside–do you mean that it was truly...?"

"Gone!" Alcandre cried. "And I am free to strike him down myself!" He drew a dagger from under his bottle-green coat and lunged at the boy, who shrank back gasping...

Then the sorcerer gave a cry, as Cyrano's *épée* flashed, and drove through the magician's ribcage from the side, to pierce both his lungs.

Skewered, the Magus stood there quivering, mouth agape, eyes wide with surprise, until the dagger fell from his hand. He followed it to the floor, slipping from Cyrano's blade as he fell dying, bleeding copiously on the glossy marble.

"You...!" the magician rasped. "You, Cyrano...will die as fated...the oaken beam will fall on your head...for without my will holding you...holding you here...you will be removed to your destined place...In killing me–you doom yourself!"

"So be it!" Cyrano said. He turned to help d'Artagnan to his feet. "Monsieur, forgive me." He turned to the King and doffed his hat. "Your majesty–I apologize for this disturbance. I..."

He was unable to finish the apology. The room containing the Musketeer, the magician and the King began to recede from him–like a transparent box dropped from a high battlement, to fall away, to spin, to smash into pieces.

And Cyrano, no longer held by the will of the magician, was drawn back; was gripped by destiny and pulled inexorably back to that October, that Saturday, that rain-wet narrow, cobbled street, outside the tenement in which he lived. Back to Ragueneau and that hurtling wooden beam...

He appeared on the street–the beam fell.

But he had forewarning, and there was just a split second in which he was able to move slightly to one side...

The beam struck him. Yet it struck his head more glancingly than it would have, had he not been forewarned. He gave a grunt and fell, flailing, into the street, driven senseless, thinking himself flying headlong into the arms of Death.

Cyrano woke a short time later lying, fully dressed, on his own humble bed. He was aware that some potion for the muting of pain had been forced between his lips, that bandages swathed his head. Waves of pain, dulled but unrelenting, rolled through him from the left side of his head. His vision was haloed, and dim. But he was still alive...for a time.

The doctor, talking in low tones to Ragueneau, confirmed Cyrano's suspicions.

"He is in all probability dying. There is nothing more I can do. Who knows? If he remains in bed, perhaps there is some slight chance of recovery. If he rises...no. Even if he lies quietly, I can hold out little hope...Now, sir, I have no more time for charity cases–I must go."

The doctor departed, and Cyrano closed his eyes. He heard Ragueneau speak to him. "Cyrano–I am going to find our friends. Perhaps we can combine our purses and bring another surgeon. Soup, at least–you have nothing to eat here. I will be back soon! Do you hear me, Cyrano?"

"Yes...yes my friend...my good friend..." Cyrano managed, through cracked lips. "How strange it was–I swear to you, I was carried off by a magician, who wanted me to assassinate the King. If I did the deed, I might live.

But...I could not bring myself to do it. Thank heaven d'Artagnan was there to slow me, till my mind cleared, and...and I knew..."

"Indeed? Yes, Cyrano, it was well that he was there." Clearly Ragueneau did not believe Cyrano. Incredulity was stark in his tone.

Cyrano wasted no more time on the tale. He had told many fantastic tales–his friend would conclude this was another, formed in delirium. "I must go to Roxanne...her *gazette*...I must see her again. Before the Old Fellow comes for me. I must...."

"No, Cyrano! You heard the doctor–you must not move! Do not stir! I will return!"

Then Ragueneau departed. Cyrano felt sick, caved-in within himself. But after a few minutes he managed to turn on the bed. In another minute, he was able to sit, and reach for his old cane. In another, to stand, leaning on the cane...

"She waits for me...Roxanne waits..."

And Cyrano staggered to the door.

At the funeral in the chapel of Our Lady of the Cross, the Count d'Artagnan gazed upon the face, the grotesque and noble face, of Cyrano Hercule-Savinien de Bergerac. Cyrano lay in his coffin, dressed in borrowed finery.

The Count d'Artganan was pondering on a strange dream that had troubled him the night before. In the dream, he had been asked to protect King Louis against a feared, unknown assassin. To his surprise, Cyrano had appeared at the door of the King's bedchamber...and with him was a disagreeable little man in green, who seemed to be a magician. d'Artagnan had the curious impression that the magician had somehow been directing Cyrano, with a combination of guile and will. The magician had threatened to send Cyrano back in time to an appointment with destiny, and death–a falling beam of wood was mentioned. *The oaken beam will fall on your head...*

And then this morning, d'Artagnan had been told by Le Bret that the man who'd fought so bravely at the Siege of Arras was dead. That he had been badly concussed by a falling beam of wood, but might have survived had he not insisted on keeping a date with a woman he had loved, chastely loved, for many years...

That Cyrano had died, in her arms, in the garden of the Ladies of the Cross.

Strange! The concordance of dream and real events. Could it be that in some future time he would in truth have to duel with Cyrano–who now lay dead before him? Preposterous. And yet...

"Monsieur d'Artagnan!" called Ragueneau, joining him beside the open coffin. "Ah–how sad he looks!"

"And how is the Madame Robin–the lady Roxanne?"

"She has done her weeping, and now kneels praying for him at a shrine, just outside, where together they sometimes walked. She insists she feels him near her."

"Perhaps–he was a great soul. I did not like his politics–but what a man!"

"Ah, to think I outlived Cyrano! An injustice. Only yesterday I read his *Agrippine* again. In it, you know, he said, *One hour after death our vanished soul will be that which it was an hour before life.* Yet I cannot but think that *his* soul will go on...journeying through time."

"Through time?" d'Artagnan was startled by Ragueneau's choice of words. The dream still weighed upon him.

"And it's a most peculiar thing, Monsieur," Ragueneau continued, bemused. "But as I approached Cyrano, yesterday morning, just before that chunk of wood struck him, why–I seemed to see him vanish! To completely, vanish, for a moment! It was as if God thought, 'No, I cannot let this great man die thus!' and snatched him away. And then God decided, 'But then, I cannot change the rules of destiny for him alone!' And so, a moment later, he restored him...Cyrano reappeared, and was struck down! Well. Doubtless a trick of the light."

"Yes. Yes, doubtless..."

A young man entered the chapel–the son of one Duke de Guiche. Resplendently dressed in velvets, jewels and silk, he swaggered in, a flagon in his hand, a jeweled sword at his side. He wore a broad gold-stitched hat with a great white flourishing plume. He was quite evidently drunk.

"So!" brayed the young de Guiche. "This is the famous Cyrano! I drink to him! But look–that nose–how will they get the coffin lid shut on that nose, eh? They shall have to crop nose or rebuild the lid! Ha *haa!*"

"Imbecile!" snarled d'Artagnan, drawing his sword. "Apologize–or die!" He flicked the sword, and–snip!–de Guiche's plume fell, cut in two, to the floor.

The young nobleman squeaked in fear, and backed away–he fumbled at his sword, then thought better of it, and threw the flagon clumsily at d'Artagnan. Then he ran like a rabbit from the room.

Whereupon the Count Charles d'Artagnan turned to coffin of Cyrano de Bergerac. He bowed his head. And d'Artagnan wept.

The most Quixotic, and yet the most rewarding, contribution to our Tales of the Shadowmen *series is Brian Stableford's homage to the French feuilletonistes of the 19th century.* The Empire of the Necromancers, *of which this is the third installment, is a masterful continuation and expansion of what might be dubbed the "Févalverse" after writer Paul Féval, whose seminal works Brian is translating for Black Coat Press. Drawing from, and incorporating characters from* John Devil, The Vampire Countess, Revenants, *etc., as well as other contemporary sources, Brian is assembling a compelling saga which grows in subtlety and complexity with each chapter...*

Brian Stableford: *The Return of Frankenstein*

(Being the third part of
The Empire of the Necromancers)

The Story So Far

In Paul Féval's John Devil *(Black Coat Press, 2005) that legendary pseudonym is adopted by Comte Henri de Belcamp in support of his mother's career as a notorious member of London's underworld, where she is known by her maiden name, Helen Brown. After attempting unsuccessfully to rescue her from an Australian prison camp, Henri takes news of her death to his long-estranged father, the Marquis de Belcamp, in the small town of Miremont, and is reconciled with him. Meanwhile, he is secretly engaged in financing the construction of an unprecedentedly powerful steamship with which he intends to rescue Napoleon from St. Helena and conquer India; in pursuit of this plan, he takes over a secret Bonapartist organization, the Knights of the Deliverance. Henri is assisted in this project by his long-term companion, Sarah O'Brien, the daughter of a murdered Irish general.*

When a potential traitor to the Deliverance, the opera singer Constance Bartolozzi, is murdered in London, the case is investigated by Gregory Temple, the senior detective at Scotland Yard, assisted by his junior, James Davy. John Devil is identified as the murderer. Temple strongly suspects that the person behind that name is Helen Brown's son, known to him as Tom Brown, but the accumulated evidence seems to point to Temple's former assistant, Richard Thompson (who is secretly married to Temple's daughter, Suzanne). Actually, James Davy—who is another of Henri de Belcamp's many aliases—has framed his predecessor, exploiting the account of his methods Temple has published in a book on the art of detection. Henri/Davy persuades Thompson to flee to France, where Suzanne is a guest at the Château Belcamp, but he is captured and convicted of the Bartolozzi murder.

When Henri is reconciled with his father, Sarah rents the so-called "new château" on the Belcamp estate under the name of Lady Frances Elphinstone. Henri commissions the murders of his dead mother's wealthy brothers but there is one further obstacle to the fortune he intends to collect by this means, in the name of Tom Brown: Constance Bertolozzi's daughter, Jeanne Herbet, who also lives in Miremont. Jeanne is the designated heir of both brothers, neither of whom knows which of them is her father. Henri falls in love with Jeanne after impulsively saving her life, and decides to marry her fortune rather than murdering her.

Henri eventually marries Jeanne under the alias of an English entrepreneur, Percy Balcomb, in which guise he slips out of the jail where he is supposedly confined. Henri is in prison because the obsessive Temple, having failed to prove that he murdered General O'Brien or Constance Bartolozzi, found out where the bodies of his hired killers were buried. Temple obtained thus information from the drunken mistress of the vertically-challenged petty criminal Ned Knob, who was a witness to the murders and disposed of the bodies. Ned also schooled the false witnesses at Richard Thompson's trial, using members of a troupe of vagabond actors.

On the eve of Thompson's execution, Henri inveigles his way into Newgate Prison, helping him to escape by taking his place. When Temple tries the same trick, Henri confronts his nemesis in the condemned cell, almost driving him insane by telling him that Tom Brown is not, after all, one of his pseudonyms but an actual half-brother, sired by Temple. After escaping in Temple's place, however, Henri finds that everything is going awry. The Deliverance is betrayed, his new steamship is destroyed, and his mother has returned from Australia, accusing him of having abandoned her. He finds it politic to commit suicide–or, at least, to appear to do so.

Part One of The Empire of the Necromancers, "The Grey Men" (in Tales of the Shadowmen 2, Black Coat Press, 2006) picks up the story four years later, in November 1821. Ned Knob, now directing the acting troupe, is unexpectedly confronted with his predecessor in that role, "Sawney" Ross, who has been hanged but now appears to be alive again, though somewhat slow-witted. When the reanimated Ross is collected by a diminutive French physician, Germain Patou,[6] Ned follows them to a boat where they are met by a man in a Quaker hat like the one Henri wore in his guise as John Devil.

After being knocked unconscious, Ned wakes up in Newgate and is interrogated by Gregory Temple, now working for the secret police. Temple is supposed to be investigating a series of body-snatching incidents, but his attention has been caught by a report of the Quaker hat. Following his release, Ned tracks Patou to a house in Purfleet. There he renews his acquaintance with

---

[6] A character introduced in Paul Féval's The Vampire Countess (Black Coat Press, 2003).

Henri and witnesses the resurrection of a man from the dead using an elaborate electrical technique recently discovered by a Swiss scientist.

The demonstration is interrupted when Henri's ship is attacked by a rival group under the command of the only one of the reanimated "Grey Men" to have recovered all his faculties: a person who styles himself "General Mortdieu." Mortdieu's hirelings seize the electrical apparatus from the house, taking it to their own ship, the Outremort. *Ned is arrested again, but makes a deal with Temple.*

As the Outremort *is about to depart from her berth in Greenhithe, a three-cornered battle develops between Mortdieu's hirelings, Henri's followers and Temple's men. The fight eventually arrives at an impasse, but a hastily-contrived treaty permits Mortdieu to sail away, taking Patou with him.*

In Part Two of The Empire of the Necromancers, "The Child-Stealers" (in Tales of the Shadowmen 3, Black Coat Press, 2007), Gregory Temple is woken one night by Henri, who tells him that they must join forces, at least temporarily. Temple's grandson has been kidnapped from the Château Belcamp, where Thompson and Suzanne are now resident, along with two younger children of much richer parents; one is the son of Henri and Jeanne, the other the son of the former Sarah O'Brien, now the widow of a German Count.

Temple and Henri set out to make their separate ways to Miremont, where Temple has to break the news to Jeanne that she is not a widow. Henri is delayed and Temple has to respond to the first ransom note with no one to help him but Ned Knob. He is taken prisoner in his turn. Temple's captors are members of a long-dormant society of heretic monks known as Civitas Solis, *seemingly led by Giuseppe Balsamo, who are more interested in securing the secret of resurrection than in the ransom money that will help finance their exploitation of it.*

Henri's delay has been caused by his traveling under the name George Palmer, in which guise he was involved with a vehm *(a secret society of vigilantes) at the time of General O'Brien's murder, and in whose eyes he is still a wanted man. Having made his peace with the* vehmgerichte, *however, Henri is able to attack* Civitas Solis *and liberate Temple and the captive children before disappearing again, intent on joining forces with* Civitas Solis *in the expectation of using them as he had formerly used the Deliverance.*

Now read on...

Spezia, 1822

Chapter One
Sleepless in Spezia

Having written his report out in longhand on the rickety table in his hotel room, Ned Knob began the tiresome work of translating it into two different ciphers, using two different keywords.

The clear version of the report read: *More laboratory equipment delivered today to house rented by Walton, including Voltaic cells and apothecary's supplies. His companion remains hidden; will continue attempts to confirm identification. Other spy seen watching house not present today. Have identified visitor previously mentioned as Edward Trelawny, temporary resident at Casa Magni, San Terenzo, present home of Percy Shelley and Edward Williams. Town gossip associates Shelley and Williams with larger group including Lord Byron, Tom Medwin, Capt. John Hay, Leigh Hunt, John Taaffe, rumored to be involved in conspiracy. Agenda of conspiracy unknown, but company apparently has enemies. Several members recently involved in conflict; Shelley and Hay injured, their attacker, Stefano Masi, badly wounded; legal investigation proceeding. Will travel San Terenzo tomorrow to make further inquiries.*

Having transcribed this screed twice, in the coded versions, Ned immediately put the original to his candle-flame and made sure that it was thoroughly incinerated. Taking great care not to mix them up, he put the two coded versions into envelopes, addressed them differently and applied two different seals to the wax that secured them. Then he took one of them downstairs, where the courier that would initiate its transmission to Gregory Temple of the King George's Secret Service was waiting to receive it beneath the arch of the coaching entrance.

Having watched the courier ride off into the night on a coal black mare, Ned left the hotel and hurried down the steep hill to the shore, where a second courier was waiting discreetly on the approach to the quays. Ned gave him the second envelope, and watched him hurry away. There was a yacht waiting in the harbor that would bear the courier and the letter away in the direction of Marseilles; thereafter, it would eventually make its way into the safe hands of Henri de Belcamp, wherever he might be and whatever alias he was presently using.

Fortunately for Ned, Henri paid a good deal better for the information he received than the King of England's Secret Service, which expected its operatives to be primarily motivated by patriotism. Ned was not devoid of patriotism, but he was proud to maintain an authentic radical conscience beneath his carefully-turned coat. He had no qualms about accepting the King's secret shilling, but he had no qualms either about accepting Henri de Belcamp's secret half-crown. He did not think of his double-dealing as a mere matter of trade; he obtained a whimsical delight from the knowledge that he was working for two mortal enemies at the same time, owing no particular loyalty to either, but he was also glad to be involved in a sequence of events that had the potential to change the world. His gladness had been redoubled by the discovery, earlier that day, that there was a direct and immediate link between the house he had been set to watch and one of the men he admired most in all the world.

However comical or despicable he might appear to the world, by virtue of his dwarfish stature and his criminal tendencies, Ned Knob saw himself as a giant of sorts, and a Romantic above all else. He thought that working as an agent for Gregory Temple's branch of the secret police was Romantic in itself, and that his casual betrayal of the secrets he collected on Temple's behalf to Henri de Belcamp was more Romantic still, but the fact that his labors in that regard now promised to bring him into contact with Percy Bysshe Shelley, the author of the recent *Prometheus Unbound and Other Poems*, was definitely the icing on his own Romantic cake. Ordinarily, given that Ned's short legs were naturally ill-equipped for such work, the trek back up the hill to the establishment that was known throughout Spezia as "the English hotel" would have been a tedious one, but there as a spring in his step tonight.

When he arrived back at the hotel, Ned ate a little late supper in the hotel's meager dining-room. A party of young Englishmen from Sussex, sent away by their parents to improve themselves by taking the Grand Tour, was drinking wine a little too abundantly, as was their habit. They invited him to join them, partly because of the democratic spirit that comes upon young men in a foreign land, when even the humblest of their countrymen seems nearer in station than a disapproving native, and partly because they found Ned almost as innately amusing as an authentic dwarf, but Ned declined. He had already sucked all the information from them that they had; it was their propensity for eager rumor that had given him the names of Shelley's local acquaintances, although none knew the name of Robert Walton's mysterious companion.

They did not take his refusal gracefully. One of the young aristocrats grabbed his arm as he attempted to leave. "Don't go, Master Knob," he said. "We're going whoring later–I'm sure that we can find you a midget, or a little girl, to suit your stature."

"That's very kind of you, milord," Ned said, speaking with conspicuous mildness, although he met the young man's bleary gaze with a basilisk stare. "But I've been down to the lower town already this evening, and I'm tired."

The fool was too drunk to take the hint provided by Ned's expression. "Hear that, fellows!" he said. "The little chap's already been a-whoring, and he's tired." The young man tightened his grip on Ned's right wrist.

Ned used his left hand to pluck the drunkard's hand away, squeezing the fingers so hard that the man's drink-flushed face turned ghastly white–but Ned smiled at the other members of the party as he said, with exaggerated softness: "I hope you have a good time, gentlemen."

He went directly to his bed, intending to be up early to make the trek to San Terenzo, to see what he could discover for himself about the group of like-minded men that seemed to be forming around the two English poets. Despite the remarks about consorting with *Carbonari* and fomenting revolution that the young gentlemen from Sussex had bandied about while laughing sardonically, Ned thought it perfectly possible that at least some of the men he had named in his report had come to Italy with none but literary interests in mind, and quite probable that all of them had far more interest in a potential scientific revolution than any petty political upheaval, but he knew that Gregory Temple would ex-pect more details in any case. Indeed, he felt sure that Temple and his superiors would be very grateful for any information he could provide on the potentially seditious activities of "Jacobin exiles," because it would soothe the suspicions of his Parliamentary masters that his and Ned's present endeavors might be entirely futile. He frowned as he wondered exactly how he could fabricate some such details without causing any difficulties for Byron and Shelley additional to those that already haunted them.

Once he was in his bed, Ned found that he could not sleep, and not because his encounter with the young men from Sussex had been slightly discomfiting. His sense of anticipation was too teasing. This was not merely because he ex-pected that his spying mission—which he so far proved rather dull—might sud-denly become more thrilling, or even because the prospect of "renewing his ac-quaintance" with one of the great minds of his generation was so delicious, but because certain implications were beginning to sink in of what it might signify if Byron and Shelley really were intimately involved in the project that seemed to be taking shape in Robert Walton's rented house.

Like every other man in England who considered himself a connoisseur of Gothic fiction, Ned had read *Frankenstein*, which purported to be based on let-ters sent by one Robert Walton to his sister and a manuscript transmitted with one of those letters. Because "Robert Walton" was such a common name, Ned had at first regarded the fact that he had been sent to watch a man of that name as insignificant, but the sight of the equipment that was being imported into the house, and his awareness of what it might be used for, had quickly convinced him otherwise. He had already guessed that Walton's mysterious companion must have been Victor Frankenstein—or the individual called by that name in the novel—before he had any inkling of Shelley's potential involvement, but he had also heard it rumored in London, long before Gregory Temple had sent him to Italy, that Shelley was the author of *Frankenstein*. He had dismissed the rumor at the time, because he was well used to the tactics employed by unscrupulous publishers to boost the marketability of works they published anonymously, but now he was forced to consider the matter anew.

Suppose, he thought, that there really as a connection between Shelley and Walton—that they had, in fact, known one another for some time, and that it was Shelley and Byron who had persuaded the inventor of the resurrection process to

221

resume his experiments. His first success had obviously proved traumatic for the Swiss scientist, who, if even part of the manuscript reproduced in the novel was authentic, might well have suffered some kind of delusional breakdown. In the meantime, the exploitation of his discovery had been continued by other hands–but now, it seemed, he was ready to begin again. How secure, though, was his return to sanity and resolution? And what had become of his first experimental subject: the very first "Grey Man?" These were the thoughts that buzzed in Ned's head as he twisted and turned on his pillow.

According to the gossip relayed with such relish by the young gentlemen, the rumors circulating in Pisa regarding the "Byronic conspiracy" were ridiculously wild. Some of the leaning tower's more credulous neighbors alleged that the recent brawl had been caused by their leading an armed insurrection, presumably on behalf of the *Carbonari*, against the city gate. That was certainly untrue, in Ned's judgment, but even the better-informed natives of Pisa seemed unprepared to accept that the gathering of the English company was what its members contended: a mere matter of assembling a company of literary men to found a new literary journal to provide a worthy showcase for their philosophically-inclined works. Given that Trelawny seemed to be an adventurer who had sought his fortune unsuccessfully in India, while Hay was an experienced military man, the explanation that Byron had put about did seem to be a trifle disingenuous.

Ned's Italian was still patchy, and he found it far easier to communicate with other English and French visitors than with the local population, so he was by no means ideally equipped to be a spy in these parts. His unsteady command of the tongue had, however, enabled him to understand that the gossips in Spezia devoted the greater part of their consideration to the imagined conspiracies of the Roman Church and the *Carbonari*, often mingling rumors of either sort with perennial whispers about notorious *banditti*. Despite San Terenzo's proximity to Spezia, and Lord Byron's frequent comings-and-goings in the *Bolivar*, no one in the immediate vicinity seemed to care a fig about Percy Shelley having taken up residence within comfortable walking distance of Spezia's harbor, and everyone seemed quite oblivious to the existence of Robert Walton–except for the other spy, who seemed to have been keeping watch on Walton's house as interestedly as Ned, albeit from the opposite side.

Spezia's "upper town" was much more generously distributed than the dense cluster of streets near the shore; it was arranged on a series of natural terraces on the jagged slope. Walton's house was set in a covert of its own, isolated from any other by at least 100 paces. The ledge on which it stood had once been a hive of industry, accommodating a small olive grove, which curled around the house on the eastern and northern sides, and a healthy herb garden as well as a rank of vines set against the wooded face of the hill, which reared up almost vertically 30 yards or so in rear of the building, but the war had put an end to its cultivation and the tiny estate had run wild while the house had stood empty for almost a decade. It was now very overgrown, the hedge along the road that ran past it having grown to more than seven feet in height. Ned's natural approach to the house from the hotel was on the eastern side, so he usually stationed himself in a gap in the hedge, from which he could see through the olive-trees. The other spy, by contrast, set himself up to the west, often positioning himself high on the slope at a point where it was not so steep, hiding behind a rock. Thus far, they had only caught glimpses of one another in the distance, but Ned was sure that the other man had marked his presence just as interestedly as he had marked the other man's.

Ned did not waste time wondering who his rival might be. Under the pressure of his insomnia, he did, however, waste time regretting that he did not have a copy of *Frankenstein* with him, and wishing that he had read it more attentively when he had borrowed its three volumes, one by one, from the circulating library. He had read the volumes swiftly and returned them quickly, in order to make the most of his subscription. That had, alas, been two full years before Sawney Ross had wandered into Jenny Paddock's gin-shop, so Ned had not had the slightest grounds for suspecting that the novel might be based on fact. Now, he cursed himself for the haziness of his memory of the text.

In the story, he knew, Frankenstein had died on Walton's ship in the Arctic, but that was obviously not true of the actual person on whom the character was based. The real man of science had vanished from sight, but his research notes must have been taken to Paris, where they had come into the custody of German Patou, then to Portugal, where Patou and Henri had conducted a considerable series of experiments but had failed to restore more than the most meager mental facilities to the vast majority of their resurrectees; nor had they enjoyed much greater success in that regard when they had transferred their operation to Purfleet. Had Frankenstein made any significant progress in the meantime? His single experiment had apparently been more successful than most of Patou's, although it might also have gone seriously awry, if the accusations labeled at the Grey Man featured by the novel were actually true rather than the result of Frankenstein's delirium or some ghost writer's penchant for melodrama. Had the originator any grounds to expect, or at least to hope, that his new venture would produce far better results than Patou's? If so....

Suppose, Ned thought, as he continued to turn over and over in his bed, his thoughts becoming wilder all the while, that he were able to insinuate himself into the conspiracy of English exiles. Suppose that the conspiracy extended much further than its presently-visible members, to include such "Jacobin scientists" as Humphry Davy, Joseph Priestley and Erasmus Darwin. Suppose that he could get himself onto Lord Byron's payroll, reporting to the conspiracy on the activities of the English secret service and *Civitas Solis*. What a player he might then become, instead of the pawn his employers presently considered him to be! And why should he not prefer the conspiracy mounted by Walton and Trelawny to those to which he was currently affiliated, if they already had a better version of the secret of resurrection and the apparatus to begin a new series of successful experiments? They might, after all, be the destined custodians of a glorious future in which death's sting was comprehensively drawn...

The man who now styled himself "Mortdieu" had evidently wrestled with the problem that had confounded his own maker, but his insider's view of it had apparently given him no advantage. Now that he and Patou had joined forces, they might be able to succeed where each had separately failed, but that depended on the *Outremort* having found a haven safe from fearful and prying eyes, and the material means to continue their research. That could not have been easy, Ned judged–and in the meantime, the original discoverer of resurrection might well have laboring with all his might to make further improvements in his process. Even if the Swiss scientist really had been vengefully harassed, as the published narrative implied, by his first experimental subject, the fact remained that the subject in question had obviously recovered more intelligence than any of Patou's subjects, save Mortdieu, and might well have offered Frankenstein a valuable clue to the means of generalizing that achievement...

Chapter Two
An Alliance of Spies

Eventually, sheer exhaustion forced Ned to be still. He finally dozed off, but his sleep was very light–fortunately so, as it turned out. Some little while after he drifted off into a quiet state, he heard a slight noise from the direction of his window.

Instead of sitting up and parting the curtains of his alcove in order that he might look towards the window, Ned remained exactly as he was, carefully feigning unconsciousness. He used his ears to measure what was happening.

Although his room was on the second floor of the hotel, Ned knew that its balcony was not inaccessible to a skillful climber, and that the shutters securing the window would not be difficult to unlatch from without. He listened to the tripping of the catch and the faint creak of the hinges as one batten of the shutter was drawn back. He heard the unobtrusive scrape of cloth on painted wood as the intruder slipped through the unglazed window, and the almost-imperceptible tread of slippered feet on the wooden floor.

Ned took firm hold of the dagger hidden beneath his pillow. Its blade was short, but that would not be to his disadvantage in the circumstances; the weapon would be easy to draw clear with a single fluid motion, ready for use. He had no idea whether the intruder was holding a weapon of his own, but he had to assume, for safety's sake, that he was, and that it would be ready to thrust home at a moment's notice.

Ned was not afraid, not because he had no respect for deadly weapons, but because he knew how ready other men were to underestimate him. Because he was only five feet tall, people who did not know him invariably assumed that he was both awkward and puny, but he was neither.

When the time came for him to move, he moved with great speed and great skill. He swept the other man's legs out from under him and had him flat on the ground within a second. The intruder's right arm was firmly pinned to the ground, and the point of Ned's knife was pressed to his throat.

It was only then that Ned ascertained that the intruder had, indeed, been carrying a weapon: there was still a stiletto clutched in his right hand.

"Drop it!" Ned ordered, in crude Italian.

The captive obeyed, and Ned picked the weapon up.

In the wake of a single reflexive convulsion, the intruder had made no further attempt to resist, and now seemed disposed to be cooperative.

"You have the advantage of me, Monsieur Knob," the supine man observed, in French.

The comment was ironic, and Ned was as displeased by its tone as its content. The remark told Ned that the other spy he had observed watching Robert Walton's house had succeeded where he had so far failed, in identifying his rival. Not only did his adversary know Ned's name; he also knew that Ned could speak French. To judge by his accent, French was not the intruder's first language, but Ned–much to his chagrin–could not identify the man's nationality from the inflection.

"Did you come to kill or to steal?" Ned asked, gruffly, also speaking in French.

"I merely came to talk, my friend," the other assured him, implausibly. "The time has come to form an alliance. Since you showed no sign of approaching me, however discreetly, I decided..." He broke off as Ned's left hand began rummaging inside his jacket, and sighed when the little man pulled out a sheet of paper.

There was too little light filtering through the unshuttered window to illuminate the paper, but Ned only had to touch it to divine that it was one of his letters. His fingers sought the broken seal, and contrived to identify the broken half. It was the letter to Henri de Belcamp, which he had given to the courier on the approach to the quay. The other letter did not seem to be in the spy's possession.

"I did not hurt the man from whom I took it," the spy was quick to say, "although he was certainly annoyed to be relieved of it, and swore vengeance, as these Italians are ever-ready to do. I hoped that I might be able to read it, but I could not decipher it–the code must be a subtle one."

"So you came to ask me to translate it for you," Ned guessed, "bringing your stiletto to provide an incentive."

"No, no, my friend," his rival assured him. "I came to discuss a mutually advantageous division of labor. We are in the same business, after all. We cannot be everywhere at once, and while both of us are stuck watching Walton take delivery of everything he needs to furnish his bomb factory, who knows what Milord Byron and his Carbonarist friends are plotting? We need to find out where the bombs will be placed, and by whom. I am no more English than French, as you can surely tell, and I cannot speak to milord's associates as you can–but I have information that you do not, and there is much that might be gained by our working together."

"Who are you?" Ned growled.

"My name is Guido," his captive said. "It does not matter who sent me, any more than it matters who puts money in your purse. We are two of a kind–I know that because I know that you sent a second report by a different route, presumably to a different master, although I was not in a position to interrupt the galloping horse to make sure. If we are to sell what we know to the highest bidder, we would do better to combine forces and act together."

Ned made sure that Guido had no other weapons about his person before allowing him to get up. He gathered both knives and the stolen letter in his left hand in the meantime, then used his right to strike a match and light the candle by the bed. When he stood up, Guido towered over Ned by an entire foot. He was no weakling, despite his leanness, but he made no attempt to renew their brief struggle.

Given his black hair, olive complexion and pointed beard, Guido could easily have been taken for an Italian or a Spaniard, but Ned suspected that he might be from somewhere further east, perhaps as far as the bounds of the Ottoman Empire.

"What do you know that I do not?" Ned demanded, expecting that he might get a few nuggets of information by way of inducement to enter into a compact.

"I know all about the boat," Guido replied, shortly.

Ned knew better than to confess ignorance by saying: "What boat?" Instead, he said: "I know all about the *Bolivar*'s movements." In fact, all he knew was that *Bolivar* was the name of Byron's yacht, and that it sometime docked in Spezia.

"Not the *Bolivar*," Guido countered. "The *Don Juan*. She set out from Genoa on May 10, but was not delivered to Lerici until May 12, having been driven back by bad weather. Shelley and Williams sailed out to the Isola del Tino on May 18. Byron brought the *Bolivar* to Lerici to meet the *Don Juan* on the June 13, and fired six cannon-shots by way of salute. Both vessels then set sail for Leghorn, where the *Don Juan* was put in for modifications, including a false stem and stern. She was brought to San Terenzo today, very discreetly; she is moored within 100 yards of Casa Magni at this moment."

"All that may be true," Ned conceded, "but I cannot see its relevance."

"Can you not?" Guido asked, raising a dark eyebrow. "I don't know exactly how the boat has been modified, or for what purpose, but I do not think that Monsieur Shelley is any common smuggler. I would dearly like to know what cargo it is intended to carry, and to what destination–you might be better able to find that out than I am. In order to ascertain all this, I had to leave you to watch Walton's house by yourself for a considerable period. Only you can tell me if anything significant occurred during that time."

"Indeed," said Ned, in a neutral tone. "What, exactly, are you proposing?"

"I speak Italian better than you do, and I am far better equipped to obtain information from Walton's neighbors and anyone making deliveries to his house. You, on the other hand, speak English better than I do, and are thus better equipped to obtain information from the wives and servants Shelley and Williams brought with them. Shelley's wife is confined to her bed, having fallen victim to a fever in the wake of a miscarriage; Madame Williams and the servants are in state of anguish. If Shelley and Williams are planning another expedition, I suspect that they will not be able to depart without an argument. What I propose is that I prowl around the Walton house for the next day or two, while you make inquiries at Casa Magni, and that we pool the information we glean."

This fitted in very well with the plan Ned had already made, but he was careful to give the appearance of being dubious. "I have been ordered to keep close watch on Walton's house," he said. "I need to find out more about his guest."

"I know that," Guido retorted. "I know, too, that you have been given Trelawny's name. You know that the conspiracy in which Walton, Shelley and Trelawny are involved extends much further than Spezia. One or other of your masters might send help, once they know that–but one, at least, will not receive your report in good time. I am already here–also alone, for the time being. Why should we not help one another?"

"That depends who your master is," Ned said, bluntly.

"Have I asked you to name yours?" the other retorted. "What does it matter? Neither of us is a common soldier, and if either of us is bound by oath to a nation, he is not the kind of man to offer oaths with any great sincerity."

Ned did not bother to complain about that unflattering estimation. "You mentioned bomb-making," he said. "Is that what you imagine Walton and his companion to be doing in their laboratory?"

"If they are working for the *Carbonari*," Guido said, "that is what they are highly likely to be doing. Infernal machines have become an important, if direly unreliable, instrument of modern politics. There is a new chemistry in the making, thanks to Messieurs Lavoisier and Priestley, and a new science of electricity too, thanks to Messieurs Galvani and Volta. Masters of artillery and ordnance all over Europe are taking a very keen interest in these new sciences. There are revolutions in progress in Spain and Portugal, while wars of unification are bubbling up in Germany and Italy. The Ottoman Empire will likely unravel completely if the Greeks win their independence, and the Americas are already in turmoil. Any man who can manufacture a more powerful explosive, or one subject to safer and more reliable detonation, is in a position to make a vast fortune."

"And that is what Walton's companion is doing with his apparatus, in your opinion?"

"I do not pretend to know the composition of all the compounds he has been importing by the barrel," Guido said, "but I know that your Monsieur Davy has used electricity to isolate new elements, and that some of them are so volatile that they explode in sudden contact with water. As you must know, Monsieur Walton's friend has a great many Voltaic piles at his disposal."

"Do you know his name?" Ned asked.

"Perhaps," was the guarded reply. "Do you?"

"Not for certain," Ned parried.

"Well?" the other demanded, abruptly. "What do you have to say to my proposition?"

Ned shrugged his shoulders. "I say yes," he said, "while reserving my judgment as to what you might have done had I not disarmed you as you drew nigh to my bed."

"You did not stab me," was Guido's response to that, "for which I am duly grateful. You have my word that I shall not attempt any violence against you, and will defend you vigorously if anyone should attack us while we go about our work. I will swear a blood oath to that effect if you require it."

Ned handed back the stiletto, but kept the stolen letter. "I'll go to Casa Magni tomorrow," he said, "while you keep watch on Walton. I'll find you when I have information to exchange–but you had best have something solid to offer me, for everything you've told me thus far is mere vapor."

"Agreed," said the rival spy, promptly, apparently having no suspicion of the fact that he had received no concession at all. "*Bonsoir, mon ami.*" He moved swiftly back to the window, and made his exit the same way he had come in.

Ned closed the shutter and went back to bed, even though he knew that he would not find sleep again before it was time to rise.

Henri will not be pleased when he finds out that his courier has been robbed, he thought, as he began turning this way and that on his pillow for a second time. *That will serve to arouse his interest more fully than the actual message I had sent. I shall wait until the next scheduled rendezvous to repeat the information–by which time I might have a great deal more to say... or a great deal less.*

Chapter Three
At Casa Magni

The first thing Ned Knob did on reaching San Terenzo was to make his way down to the shoreline so that he might approach Casa Magni along the strand,

228

on the lookout for the *Don Juan*. There were dozens of small boats pulled up on to the shore, some with masts and some without, and a great many small huts built to contain fishing-tackle and apparatus for repairing timbers and canvas. These afforded him abundant cover as he approached the house that Shelley and Williams had rented.

Casa Magni was somewhat dilapidated, like many of the larger houses on the once-prosperous shore that had lost their former occupants to the effects of Napoleon's war. There had been no major battles fought in the vicinity, so Spezia and San Terenzo were unmarked by the scars of cannon-fire, which now pockmarked so many European towns and villages, but the lingering effects of the war were not entirely hidden beneath the surface. The absence of violent defacement only meant that the subtler ravages of long neglect became more evident, putting a face to the dispirited quality of post-war existence. Seven years after Bonaparte's fall, this region was still stunned, its convalescence hardly begun. The mere sight of Casa Magni would have made that obvious to the discerning eye, even had the mind behind the eye not known that the house had been rented to the English, whose tourist swarms had returned to their old haunts in greater numbers than before, exerting their strange cultural pressure with renewed force.

Ned had no difficulty at all identifying the *Don Juan* among the other boats berthed close to the house, although a tarpaulin had been placed to mask the place on her hull where the name had been painted. She was the only brand-new vessel to be seen on this relatively quiet stretch of shore. It was obvious that corrective work had been carried out on her hull, in spite of the fact that her timbers had scarcely been exposed to the sea. Even more remarkably, a large piece of canvas had been cut out of her brand new sail and replaced. Ned guessed that her name had been painted there by the boat-builder, but that Shelley had demanded its removal. If Guido knew that, it must have greatly increased his suspicion regarding the purpose for which the vessel was intended.

As Ned came close to the boat, moved by curiosity, three men emerged from her cabin on to the aft deck. Ned immediately recognized one of the three as Robert Walton, and took even greater care to remain hidden thereafter; he knew that Walton had had numerous opportunities to catch sight of him while he was watching the house through the olive grove. The second man in clear view was unknown to Ned, and the third man was partly obscured by the mast. Ned had seen Shelley in London more than once, but only from a moderate distance; he had to creep even closer and find a better angle before he could be sure that the third man was, indeed, the celebrated poet.

To judge by their gestures, the three were arguing, though not very violently. Their body language suggested that Shelley, at least might have raised his voice to emphasize his case, but the other two seemed very anxious that he should keep his voice as low as theirs–this despite the fact that they were in a land where few would understand them if they shouted in English, which was certainly their native tongue.

Ned could only make out fragmentary phrases, but he gathered quickly enough that Walton and the other man were allied against Shelley, but more in sorrow than in anger. They were, apparently, intent on rejecting some proposal he had put to them or some demand that he had made that was contrary to a previous agreement, but they seemed to be doing so on someone else's behalf rather than their own. They seemed sympathetic to his distress, but were nevertheless unable or undisposed to make concessions to his request. The poet seemed to be on the brink of losing his temper, although he was struggling to control himself. He made more than one reference to his wife being ill, but Ned was unable to judge the exact relevance of that fact to the argument. His opponents were quite obdurate, though, despite their determination to soothe him with apologies and sincere regrets. In the end, they appeared to win his reluctant consent to whatever it was had previously been agreed.

Shelley evidently felt badly enough about the outcome of the argument to remain on the boat when his two companions jumped down to the shore and marched off, although their triumph in their petty victory was distinctly muted. At first, the poet stood in the stern watching them go, but then he stepped back towards the mast, apparently feeling very weary. He reached out a hand and managed to support himself for a minute or so, while the other two Englishmen passed out of sight. Then he slowly folded to his knees, eventually collapsing entirely, out of Ned's sight.

Ned had been instructed by Gregory Temple not to reveal himself to Robert Walton and his companion, but he had received no specific order in respect of Percy Shelley. Even if he had, it would not have stopped him going to the poet's aid. He did not hesitate for a second before running forward. He clambered up on to the *Don Juan*'s deck and dropped to his knees beside the stricken man.

Shelley was still breathing, but he was unconscious. He had fallen face-forwards, and Ned could see that the scab on an old wound on the back of his head had been breached by internal pressure. The fluid leaking from the breach had more yellow in it than red. Ned felt the poet's neck, and found the flesh hot. Then he measured Shelley's pulse, which was rapid.

The argument upset him more than he would consent to reveal to his friends, Ned thought, *but he must already have been ill, and was striving to conceal that too. Is this the wound he sustained in the brawl in which Masi was hurt? If so, it should have healed long ago–but if it ever did, it has now taken a turn for the worse and has begun to fester.*

Ned put his arms under Shelley's body and braced himself. The poet would have been a featherweight to Ned's once-beloved Pretty Molly, but was quite a burden to a man of his own size. Even so, he lifted the inert body up and carried it to the side of the boat. It was not easy to maneuver it down to the ground, but he managed to do it, and then set off towards the house at a steady walk. He managed to ring the bell without having to set his burden down.

The door was opened soon enough by a female servant. The look of astonishment that crossed her face when she looked down at the top of Ned's battered hat turned to horror when she saw what the little man was carrying. She let loose a little scream, and cried for help.

The only help that arrived was a sullen manservant; Walton and his companion obviously had not come into the house.

"We need to get him to bed immediately," Ned declared, authoritatively. "If one of you will show me the way, the other must fetch a doctor. If you have a kettle on the boil, you might fill a bowl with hot water and bring it to me, with some carbolic soap. An old wound on his head has opened, and it needs cleaning."

The manservant immediately stiffened, resentful of Ned's commanding tone, but he could obviously see the necessity of following Ned's advice. "Show the boy where the master's bedroom is, Jenny," he said to the maidservant. "I'll saddle a horse and ride to Pisa to fetch Dr. Todd."

"Yes, Mr. Gregory," Jenny replied.

"Is there no one closer?" Ned was quick to ask. "Surely there's a doctor in Spezia, if there's none in San Terenzo itself–the matter may be too urgent to allow you to prefer an Englishman."

The manservant was about to deny that there was a doctor in Spezia, but the girl chipped in: "I've heard the master say that the man staying with Mr. Walton knows more than any mere physician."

Gregory's expression became even more clouded, but all he said was: "I'll do what I can." As he strode off, the maidservant beckoned Ned toward the stairway.

Ned frowned at the necessity of climbing the stairs, but he did as he was bid, and was eventually able to lay Shelley's body down on a bed in a large room whose thick curtains were still closed, keeping the daylight at bay.

"The mistress is sick abed," Jenny told him, plaintively, "and Mrs. Williams has gone to Pisa with her husband. There's no one to help you but me–but there's a kettle in the kitchen."

"Put it on to boil," Ned said. "In the meantime, fetch me a jug of cold water and a glass," Ned said, "I think we might be able to revive him."

The maidservant raced away.

In the event, Shelley began to stir even before the water-jug arrived, and when Ned put a glass to the poet's lips, he was able to sit up. The poet did not look at Ned, though–it was the fluttering maidservant who caught his eye. Shelley frowned, and murmured: "You were ordered not to leave Mary's side, Jenny." The effort was too much, though, and he sank back on to the pillow, closing his eyes. He seemed far younger than his years–hardly more than a child–and his near-feminine beauty was strangely exaggerated by his distress.

The girl retreated, babbling apologies.

"Boil the water first," Ned called after her, "and fetch the carbolic soap." Then he turned back to the poet. "She was not at fault, sir," he said. "For the moment, your need is even more urgent than your wife's. The wound on your head has turned bad."

Shelley was still confused, but he opened his eyes again and peered at Ned through the gloom. "Is that you, Patou?" he whispered.

Ned controlled his astonishment. The opening seemed too promising to be neglected. "I am not Germain Patou," he said, smoothly, "although I had the honor of meeting him once, and I understand how the confusion might have arisen."

"You've met Patou?" Shelley murmured, still battling with confusion. "Where?"

"In London," Ned replied. "I've seen you there too, Mr. Shelley, on three separate occasions, but we were never introduced."

Shelley raised himself up to take another sip of water, propping himself up on his elbow so that he could stare at Ned more intently. His brow was furrowed with concentration. The effort seemed to help him, and his gaze became clearer.

"The Royal Institution," he said, eventually. "At Mr. Davy's lectures—twice, I believe."

Ned was genuinely impressed. Men of his extraordinarily short stature were a rarity at the meetings in question, always likely to attract more attention than individuals of ordinary height; even so, he was immensely flattered by the fact that he had been noticed by Percy Shelley. "That's true, sir," he said. "I suppose you noticed my resemblance to Monsieur Patou, if you are acquainted with him. The third occasion was one of Mr. Coleridge's lectures."

Shelley was still concentrating hard, perhaps focusing his thoughts as a defense against falling unconscious again. "In that case," he whispered, "there was a fourth occasion, which you have forgotten. You were in court when Tom Wooler was prosecuted for seditious libel in 1817. I marked you then, as a bantam who seemed ready to tear that rogue Shepherd limb from limb, for all that he outweighed you by several stones."

That took Ned's breath away. "I did not see you, sir," he admitted. "The public gallery was crowded that day, and I was thrown out for heckling the prosecutor too loudly. I missed Tom's speech in his own defense."

"It was historic," Shelley said. "I'm pleased to make your acquaintance again, if we might be said to be acquainted when I have no idea what your name is."

"I'm Edward Knob, sir, at your service," Ned said, automatically.

Shelley looked around, as if noticing for the first time where he was. "Have I been here long?" he asked. "I seem to remember that I was on the boat with Walton and Taaffe."

"You fainted, sir," Ned said. "I happened to be passing, saw you fall and carried you to the nearest house–which, it seems, is your own."

"*You* carried me?" the poet whispered, and then apparently felt ashamed of his own incredulity. "Well, sir," he added, "I'm grateful to you. I received a blow to the head some months ago. It seemed to get better, but it was never entirely right. It became vaguely troublesome again a few days ago, but the pain did not flare up until I was on the boat. It was a silly thing, to begin with–some fool of an officer in the Tuscan Light Horse picked a quarrel, and it blew up out of all proportion. I was sure that the headache would fade away again, and I dared not claim that I was suffering–poor Mary in a much worse state than I am."

Ned did not trust that judgment, although he understood that Shelley might have had little or no idea how his wound was faring, positioned as it was. "Was your injury examined by a doctor, sir?" he asked.

"Todd glanced at it, but he was more concerned about one of my companions, who was slashed in the face and bled fearfully."

"He should have done more than glance, sir," Ned opined. "The fact that wound has become infected probably has nothing to do with his neglect, though. Have you suffered another blow more recently?"

"Yes," Shelley admitted. "I lost my balance when Williams and I took the boat out to a nearby islet. I'm not much of as sailor yet, I fear. It was nothing–or seemed so."

"It might have been, had it not been for the earlier wound. I can clean it myself, if you'll permit, but I took the liberty of sending your manservant for a doctor, and told him that the matter was urgent. I hope he will not go all the way to Pisa if there is a doctor nearer at hand. Your Dr. Todd certainly would not be able to get here before nightfall, and would likely be delayed until tomorrow."

Shelley felt the back of his had with the fingers of his right hand, and winced. "Damn," he said, softly. "On the other hand, this might change..." He stopped, and looked at Ned again, studying him carefully.

"You're right, sir, in your estimation of me," Ned said, cheerfully. "I'm not a gentleman, alas–but I'm a man bent on self-education, and this is the 19th century. There's no reason why a man like me can't take the Grand Tour in his own fashion, just as his betters have been doing for a century and more. And there's no reason, too, why a man who has knowingly been in the same lecture-hall as Percy Shelley on three different occasions wouldn't take an interest in his welfare as well as his work. When I said that I happened to be passing, I wasn't entirely honest. The fact is that I came to see Casa Magni because I heard that the author of *Prometheus Unbound* was here–but I swear to you, sir, that I would not have dreamed of disturbing you had I not seen that you needed succor. You are a great man, in my opinion, and I would have been well content to catch a glimpse of you in the distance." He laid on the flattery with the utmost care, because he was perfectly sincere in his judgment of Shelley's worth as a radical poet.

"If you know me by repute," Shelley murmured, "and have read my work, you know that you have no need to apologize to me for not having been born a gentleman. We seem to have interests and sentiments in common, Mr. Knob, and I am glad to meet you in person, so far from home. Are you staying in Spezia, at the English hotel?"

Ned smiled at the assumption. "Yes sir," he said. "That is the ritual, is it not? We all stay in the *English hotel*, in the space marked out for us. It makes it easier for the townspeople to pretend that we do not really exist–that we inhabit some parallel world whose dimensions overlap with theirs, but somehow fails to intersect with it." He cursed himself silently for trying too hard to impress, even though his listener was sick and weak.

Shelley did not seem to mind at all. "Even here," the poet said, mildly, "one cannot fall down without being picked up to be a philosopher. You mistake the people though. They do not pretend that we do not exist, nor do the resent our presence. They are reserved by nature, and the legacy of the war has made them very careful. You might appreciate their discretion, if..." He broke off then, but not because he was too weak to continue. After a momentary pause, he resumed: "Thank you for bringing me home, Mr. Knob. I am in your debt."

"Never, sir," Ned was quick to say. "I remain in yours, as will every thinking man for centuries to come."

"You're too kind," Shelley said, giving the phrase a more earnest emphasis than was usually applied to it.

"If I might ask..." Ned began–but he did not get a chance to formulate his question. The bedroom door burst open at that moment, and Robert Walton strode in.

Chapter Four
The Man of Science

Walton was alone. Ned deduced that the manservant had encountered him and his companion on their way up the hill, and that Walton had sent Taaffe on up the hill to his own house, while he returned to see to Shelley.

As soon as he caught sight of Ned, Walton stopped dead. Ned judged that his earlier anxieties had been well-founded; Walton had indeed caught glimpses of him in the vicinity of his house. He could not know for sure that Ned had been spying on him, but he certainly suspected it.

"I'm sorry, Robert," Shelley murmured, while Walton was still dumbstruck. "I didn't realize..."

"Don't try to talk," Walton cut in, speaking more harshly than the ostensible sentiment of his words demanded. "Who is this man?"

"Edward Knob, sir, at your service," Ned was quick to say. "I know Mr. Shelley slightly, from brief acquaintance in London as well as admiration for his work. I'm staying at the English hotel in Spezia..."

"I've seen you there," Walton said, interrupting brusquely.

"Yes," Ned said, calmly. "You're the gentleman who lives in the house behind the olive grove. It's a shame, isn't it, that the terrace has been neglected of late. Perhaps you intend to restore its fortunes?"

"That's none of your business," Walton said, "and I'd be obliged if you'd keep away in future. I took that house in order to avoid all contact with tourists and locals alike."

"Don't be so harsh, Robert," Shelley said. "The man helped me. I know him–I saw him at Tom Wooler's trial, and he attends Davy's lectures."

The latter item of information did not diminish Walton's suspicions in the least. "You do not know him well enough to be sure of what he is doing here," Walton said, bluntly. "I do not accuse him of being a spy, but..."

Knowing that he was about to be more-or-less politely dismissed, and that Walton would try to make quite sure that he was never readmitted to Casa Magni, Ned decided to take a gamble.

"In fact, sir," he said, addressing himself to Shelley, "I suppose I *am* a spy, of sorts, although I am not here to spy on you. Everything I have told you is true, but I omitted to mention that I am in the employ of the government, directly answerable to Gregory Temple, of whom you might have heard."

"Temple!" Shelley exclaimed. "Isn't that..."

"The man who traveled with us on the night-coach to Dover some little while ago," Walton finished for him. "If he was watching us then, he put on a very good performance of utter disinterest." He frowned deeply. Ned was startled by the news that Gregory Temple had traveled on a coach with Shelley and Walton, but he had more urgent concerns on his mind than wondering whether the detective had really been as uninterested in his fellow passengers as he had seemed. The seafarer's mind was obviously working hard on the calculation of that probability, though.

Ned had to follow up on his decision. There seemed to be only one course of action open to him that might lead to considerable profit, and the knowledge that there was another spy interested in Walton and Shelley's project increased his sense of urgency. "There are some things you need to know, sir," he said, still speaking to the poet rather than the adventurer. "I mentioned to you just now that I met Germain Patou in London. I did not mention that I met him in the company of a *Grey Man*. I subsequently observed him in the process of resurrecting a man from the dead, and had the privilege thereafter of a brief interview with General Mortdieu. Mr. Walton has observed me taking an interest in his house, but he may not have observed the other man doing likewise. I cannot be sure, but it is possible that the other man is in the employ of the Sultan of Turkey; at any rate, he seems to believe that the research in which Mr. Walton's colleague is engaged is directed to the manufacture of some new explosive. I, of course, think differently."

The effect of this speech was, as Ned had anticipated, quite electrifying. Both men looked at him in frank amazement, mingled with desperate anxiety.

"Gregory Temple knows all this?" Walton whispered, his face having become very pallid. "And the English Parliament is sending spies to watch on us!"

Shelley's face was still flushed, and his eyes, already bright with fever, took on a new fire. "The Turks are watching us?" he said, incredulously. "They think we are manufacturing infernal machines?"

"I cannot be sure that the Turks sent him," Ned said, scrupulously, "but if not..."

"More likely the Italians," Walton growled. "I *knew* that Tuscan cavalryman was acting under orders..."

Shelley had already moved on. "Where is Patou now?" he demanded, excitedly, reaching out as if to grab Ned's sleeve, although he checked the impulse as soon as he realized what he was doing.

"I don't know," Ned told him. Looking up at Walton, he added: "Gregory Temple knows what Patou has accomplished and has seen the other Grey Men who were revived in London, but he knows little more than that. He sent me here to investigate a rumor, but I doubt that Parliament knows anything about it." He turned back to Shelley, thinking it more urgently necessary to elaborate his earlier reply. "I don't know where Patou and Mortdieu went when the *Outremort* sailed away from England, but their intention was to seek a quiet haven where they might establish a small colony. They probably headed for the Caribbean, but they might have decided to make their way to the Pacific."

"If the English police and the Turks are both on our track..." Shelley began.

Walton cut him off again. "Say no more, Percy," the seafarer instructed him, gruffly. "We must keep what secrets we still have."

"It is too late for that," Ned told him, gently. "Whoever sent the other spy may not know the truth, although it is entirely possible that his talk of bombs is deliberately deceptive, but Gregory Temple is not the only one who knows what your collaborator has accomplished. If the publication of a garish version of his apologia in the form of a Gothic novel was intended to deflect suspicion, the ploy failed. Any hope you might have cherished of resuming experiments in resurrection secretly was probably doomed from the start."

"We have to get away from here," Shelley said, in a low voice. "No matter how direly unsatisfactory the *Don Juan* and my sailing skills may be, or how much more time and equipment our volatile friend thinks he needs, we must act without delay. Byron must be told to bring the *Bolivar*."

"Say no more!" Walton repeated. "I will show this man out." He took a step forward, apparently more intent on throwing Ned out than showing him out.

Ned instinctively braced himself, although he had no intention of putting up a fight.

"You shall not lay a finger on him, Robert," Shelley said, with a slight hiss of anger in his voice. "This is my house, and the man came to my aid. I know him. I am prepared to swear that he was not at Tom Wooler's trial as a government agent. He may be in Temple's employ now, but he is not our enemy, else he would not have told us all this."

"I am certainly not your enemy, sir," Ned said, eager to confirm the fact, "and I think that you might find more friends than you know, if you care to stay here."

"Alas," Shelley said, in a low voice, "we already have more enemies than *you* know. Suspicious Turks fearful of Lord Byron's intentions are the least of our worries. Can you be certain that the *Outremort* did not head for the Mediterranean?"

"No, I can't," Ned admitted. "That was not Patou's intention, but if General Mortdieu is the man I took him to be..."

"No Grey Man is the man his dearest friends once took him to be, it seems," Shelley said mournfully. "Did you, by any chance, encounter one in London named John?"

"This is foolish," Walton complained. The expression on his face implied that it was not Shelley's question that had upset him, but some other thought or expectation. Ned had guessed what his particular anxiety must be before the door opened again, to admit Shelley's manservant and a second man. The manservant was carrying the bowl of hot water that Ned had requested, but he made no move to give it to Ned; indeed, he seemed determined to hold on to it.

Ned had only caught fleeting glimpses of Walton's mysterious houseguest, but he had no doubt at all as to the identity of the man who came in behind the servant. This, he knew, was the greatest inventor of the 19th century: the modern Prometheus who had begun the conquest of death. The modern Prometheus was not, however, an imposing sight at present. It was obvious that he had once been handsome, and Ned knew that he could not be more than 30 years old, but his features had been rough-hewn by strain and he was showing signs of premature aging. He was the very image of a man not yet recovered from some long and taxing illness or some profound and enduring anguish. There was a touch of Bedlam about him; his eyes were haunted and his hands tremulous.

The man of science seemed more anxious about Shelley's condition than Shelley was–but not, Ned judged, because he feared the imminent loss to the world of a great poet. The modern Prometheus seemed to be anxious for himself, afraid of the pressure that Shelley's illness, if it were serious, might bring to bear on him. He seemed, to Ned's curious eyes, to be *extremely* anxious about the possibility of being forced to action by Shelley's misfortune.

If Robert Walton, Lord Byron and their co-conspirators believed that Victor Frankenstein was yet ready to resume his experiments with due mental objectivity and clinical efficiency, Ned concluded, they were reckless optimists. This seemed to Ned to be a man unready for anything at all: a man still firmly in the grip of an ongoing nervous complaint that had just taken the latest of many turns for the worse.

The newcomer barely glanced at Ned as he went to the bed and attempted to put on a show of examining his patient. The tremulous hands made a tentative gesture towards Shelley's head, and the poet obligingly turned round to display the renewed wound–but the man who knew more than any mere physician barely glanced at it before stepping away, biting his lip. "If that infection should spread to your brain," he muttered, in faintly-accented English, "the consequences would be serious. If the skull is actually fractured...."

"I do not think the skull is fractured, sir," Ned said, quietly. "The infection needs to be contained, though, if possible. The wound must be properly cleaned and dressed, and the patient must rest thereafter."

"It's not serious, Victor," Shelley put in, addressing the nervous man of science. "I wish you would go to see Mary, though. I fear that her condition may be considerably worse than worse than mine. That's why..."

"I told Walton and Taaffe that I cannot do anything more for your wife," Frankenstein said, petulantly, "and certainly cannot do anything for her if... but yes, when I've cleaned and dressed your injury, I'll look in on Mary, although I'm certain that she won't be glad to see me, and I'll do whatever I can to make her more comfortable. That's all I can do, for the time being, no matter what happens. I can make no promises to you, either, on your own behalf. Patou went at the business with all the reckless force of a steam engine, it seems, and it did far more harm than good. I need to be careful."

"There comes a point," Shelley stated, quietly, "when there is no more harm to be done, saved by pusillanimous inaction."

Ned had deduced by now what the argument on the boat had been about. "If you will pardon me for continuing to play the spy, gentlemen," he said, "there is a question I still need to ask you. It's evident that you are all perfectly familiar with Monsieur Patou, but do you know the man who brought him to London, and directed his operation there?"

All three pairs of eyes were turned to him, although Ned was convinced that the thoughts behind them were still elsewhere. "Are you referring to the Comte?" Shelley said.

"Yes," Ned replied. "He is usually a Comte in Paris, although he is not always the same one. In London, he plays a different part, and he has other guises for use in Germany and Australia. I know that he is not involved in your own project, but I firmly believe that he would be more than ready to take an interest in it. If you need a useful friend, he..." He left the sentence dangling.

"The reckless force of a steam engine," Frankenstein repeated, grimly. "Patou, I think, was merely caught up in the toils of the mechanism. Lord Byron..."

"*Say no more, God damn it!*" This time, Walton barked the phrase as an order, with all the force of a ship's master. "Whether this wretched dwarf is the King's spy or some mischief-making imp strayed from Satan's kingdom, he has sown abundant seeds of worry and potential discord in our midst. Whatever we are to do, we must first get rid of him."

Shelley seemed disposed to disagree fervently, but Ned raised a hand to forestall his intervention. "Captain Walton is right, sir, at least for the moment," he said, politely. "You cannot trust me fully, since I am admittedly in the employ of Gregory Temple. I can understand, too, why you might be unready to trust our mutual friend the Comte–but if, as you say, you have more enemies than I know, you might be well advised to seek further assistance from those most sympathetic to your cause. I shall go now, but I will come back, if you will grant me permission, when your wound has been properly dressed and you have had a chance to discuss the matter."

He paused until Shelley nodded to give him the permission he had requested, and then continued: "In the meantime, I might be able to do you one small service by removing the Turks from the list of your potential enemies. The other spy who has been watching your house may well have followed your friend here from Walton's house. If so, I shall seek him out. I'll do my very best to persuade him that you are not, in fact, engaged in the manufacture of explosives, and that you have no hostile intentions in respect of the Ottoman masters of Greece or anyone else."

Walton and Frankenstein were still looking at Ned with alarm and frank distrust. Shelley, on the other hand, seemed to be clinging stubbornly to the good opinion he had formed in advance of the unexpected cataract of revelations. "Thank you for your kind assistance, Mr. Knob," the poet said, formally. "I shall look forward to seeing you again. Gregory will show you out."

Gregory scowled, but set down the bowl and gestured towards the door.

Ned went lightly down the stairs ahead of the manservant, and allowed himself to be ushered out of the door that let out on to the road behind the house. He went unreluctantly, feeling that he had set the stage well enough for another, hopefully more productive, encounter.

Chapter Five
The Skirmish on the Strand

Ned had little difficulty locating the man who called himself Guido, who had indeed followed the man of science from Walton's house, and was now inspecting the *Don Juan* very carefully. He saw Ned coming towards him, and made no particular attempt to hide himself. On the slope that led down to the strand, however, 100 yards behind Guido, another person was trying as best he could to conceal himself, although the cover offered by the desiccated bushes was not quite adequate to the task. Ned did his best to hide the fact that he had seen this new spy from both Guido and the man in question.

"They should not have hired a fool like Roberts to build her," Guido observed, as Ned drew near. "The English are so stupid, always preferring their own countrymen, however inept, to local craftsmen. This vessel is not suitable for pleasure-trips within the gulf, let alone for carrying armaments all the way around the boot of Italy to the Greek islands."

"That is not her purpose," Ned said. "I have spoken to Shelley, and I am certain that he has no intention of doing anything so silly. If ever Lord Byron decides to lend material aid to the Greeks in their war of independence, he will take a more direct route. For the moment, he has other concerns in mind."

"The *Carbonari*, you mean?" Guido guessed, giving the impression that he would not mind at all if Byron's mind were focused on Italy's domestic problems.

The bright daylight gave Ned a much better opportunity to measure his adversary than he had had the previous night, but he could not find any tell-tale sign to indicate whether his inference that Guido was a Turkish spy was correct. It remained possible that he had been sent by the Spanish authorities, who had cause enough to be anxious about their own revolutionaries and the possibility of their gaining foreign support, but Ned still suspected that he had come from the east rather than the west. "No," Ned said. "Shelley and his friends are not involved in anything of immediate interest to the *Carbonari*. What concerns them at present is a private and personal matter, with no political implications." That was not entirely true, of course, but Ned felt perfectly justified in giving a narrow meaning to the "political implications" of the project in which Shelley and Byron had involved themselves.

"You're telling me that I'm wasting my time here," Guido said, skeptically. "You know that I can't take your word for that. We're pooling information, remember. I need to hear something useful, something new, if we're to continue our friendly association."

"I don't know who you're working for," Ned said, in a neutral tone, "but I feel confident that I don't have anything to tell you that would be useful to them."

"Why don't you let me be the judge of that?" Guido said, instead of responding to Ned's tacit information to name his employers.

Ned sighed. "You were right about the boat having been modified," he said, nodding his head in the direction of the *Don Juan* "but you must have seen enough by now to know that it was a mere matter of correcting faults of construction. The boat has not been adapted for smuggling anything."

"To speak of correction is overgenerous," Guido said, gesturing contemptuously at the *Don Juan*. "The vessel is a death-trap. The Mediterranean has the

240

reputation of being placid, by comparison with the Atlantic, but the Ligurian Sea can be exceedingly treacherous. I agree with you, though–the adaptations were not made with the purpose I suspected."

"Shelley is not in need of any further death-traps at present," Ned told him. "He and his wife are both ill. Whatever plans he and his friends had in hand this morning will have to be shelved for the time being. The cavalry officer who was sent by the authorities in Pisa to put a spoke in their wheel succeeded all to well–the wound he inflicted on Shelley has been reopened and the injury has become serious."

"He seems likely to die himself," Guido observed. "These Italian hot-heads always take such projects a little too far. It would be amusing if the affair were to escalate into a vendetta, but this is not Sicily, and Masi was, as you say, act-ing under orders–however ineptly. Will Walton's associate be able to save Shelley's life, do you think?"

That, Ned knew, was the crux of the matter. What he did not know was whether Guido knew, or suspected, how exactly crucial it was. He glanced sur-reptitiously at the bushes on the slope, but he could not make out any detail of the person watching them, save that he was dressed in drab grey clothes, with a broad-brimmed hat pulled down over his brows and a scarf masking the lower part of his face. Given the scarf, and the gaucherie of his attempt to hide himself, the big man might as well have been carrying a flag bearing the word SPY, but there was something about him that unsettled Ned.

"They told me that they had more enemies than I knew," Ned told his im-mediate rival, risking one more small revelation in the hope of obtaining some-thing in return. "Do you, perchance, know of any enemies they have, apart from you?"

"I am no one's enemy, my friend," was the reply he got. "But I do know of at least other party which might be ill-disposed toward Walton's companion. Circumstances sometimes conspire to set the most virtuous of men at one an-other's throats. Do *you*, perchance, know who the man on the slope might be, who is watching us at this moment? His presence seems to be disturbing you."

Ned cursed his own carelessness silently, but contented himself with re-plying: "I don't believe that I've ever seen him before, although it's difficult to be sure while he's muffled up like that–but there is something disconcerting about him, is there not?"

"Yes, there is," Guido agreed. "He followed me from Walton's house, as furtively as he could, but he's far too awkward to be unobtrusive. Even had he been a tiny mouse like you, I'd have seen him easily enough. Given that he's so bulky as well as so clumsy, and so carefully wrapped up in spite of the summer heat, I would have had to be blind and stupid not to be aware of his proximity. Is *he* one of the enemies of whom your countrymen are fearful, do you suppose?"

"I don't know," Ned said. "Shall we follow him home and sneak into his bedroom tonight, daggers in hand, to propose that we all join forces?"

Guido laughed. "I like you, my friend," he said, "despite your reluctance to share what you know."

"This business is becoming far too complicated for my simple tastes," Ned told him. "When too many spies become involved in a matter, they're bound to waste their time fencing with one another, as we are doing now." So saying, he turned round, intending to march straight towards the bushes on the hillside where the third would-be spy was attempting to conceal himself.

Ned's primary objective was to get a closer look at the man, in order to assuage the nagging suspicion that had taken hold of him, for no reason of which he was conscious. Hardly had he taken two strides, however, when he saw that a number of other men were now heading towards the crouching man's hiding-place from the top of the slope. They were moving stealthily, and they were armed. Some had poniards in their hands, others pistols.

If the situation had seemed complicated before, it now seemed utterly chaotic. Ned looked to his right and left along the shore. There were several other people visible within 100 yards, all of whom seemed innocently busy about their boats, but none had yet taken alarm. He did not know whether he ought to resist the temptation to call out a warning to the tall man, but his hesitation in that regard was momentary. No warning was necessary.

The man who had been hiding in the bushes stood up suddenly, having realized that there were people behind him. To Ned's astonishment, it was the big man who called out a warning to him.

"Take cover," the masked man shouted, in French, just before the first shot was fired.

Ned was astonished that the big man's pursuers were prepared to fire their guns in broad daylight, for they were certainly not policemen or militiamen; they looked for all the world like a gang of bandits. Tuscany had no shortage of such robber bands, but they were very rarely seen this close to a town as large as Spezia. Although the shore of San Terenzo was relatively quiet, save for the hours at which the fishermen habitually set sail and returned, it was unusual in the extreme for bandits to call attention to themselves in such a location. The other men on the strand had all taken alarm now, and several had begun to run along the shoreline in one direction or the other.

Now that the man who had been hiding was out in the open, running down the hill with great leaping strides, it was possible to make a much better estimation of his size, build and gait–but Ned observed, with a slight sinking feeling, that it was still impossible to judge the color of his skin. His waving hands were gloved.

Because he was coming down the slope as fast as he could the fugitive was, perforce, heading almost directly towards Ned and Guido, putting them both in the line of fire. Only three pistol-shots had been released, but Guido needed no further provocation; he dived behind the stern of a fishing-smack drawn up on the strand parallel to the *Don Juan*, ducking low as he passed out of

Ned's sight. Ned ran the other way, into the shelter of the *Don Juan*'s prow, but he remained on his feet and went right around the boat to the stern, eager to keep track of the fleeing man.

More men had already appeared at the top of the slope, some of whom were already raising muskets–but they did not fire, perhaps because they were fearful that too many detonations would be sure to attract attention and perhaps because they were fearful of hitting their fellows instead of their intended target. Ned could not tell where the three pistol-shots had gone–for all he knew, they might have been fired into the air by way of warning rather than aimed to kill– but the pursuers chasing the big man certainly seemed determined, and were evidently not afraid to use their weapons.

Once he was on the level ground of the strand, the hunted man turned aside, running in the opposite direction to Casa Magni, towards Spezia's harbor. The boats drawn up on the shore provided far better shelter than the bushes on the slope, and he was soon lost to sight. No more shots had been fired after him, perhaps because the pistoliers thought that he was too far away to permit them to take aim, but perhaps also because they feared that a stray shot might hit some innocent party, and did not want that to happen. Ned glanced back at Casa Magni, and saw a face–almost certainly Walton's–at one of the first floor windows, staring out anxiously. The spectacle seemed sure to excite the conspirators' anxieties even further.

The men who were chasing the fugitive were all in plain view now. They were at least a dozen in number. Their well-worn clothes might have marked them as peasants had it not been for their weapons, but they were obviously well-used to bearing arms. Although the war had, in theory, been over for seven years, Ned knew that the desultory fighting in these parts was unlikely to have been stilled immediately by news of Waterloo. He knew, too, that many of the *banditti* in the northern provinces of Italy had joined forces with anti-Bonapartist resistance-fighters, rebranding themselves as patriots, and had thus obtained far greater license to steal and kill than they had ever enjoyed before. It was possible that these men still enjoyed a local reputation as heroes, and thus felt free to parade themselves, but Ned could not believe that the man they were chasing was merely a left-over Bonapartist who might be considered fair game by the townsfolk of San Terenzo and Spezia.

Within five minutes, the hunt and its quarry had passed out of sight and hearing. The bandits if such they were, had paid no more attention to Ned than to any of the fishermen they had briefly disturbed.

"This is a madhouse," Ned muttered, as he went to look for his rival.

Guido was lying down where he had taken cover, but he was not about to get up. His head was bleeding. For a second or two, Ned thought that he might have been grazed by a stray pistol-shot, but then a head appeared over the side of the fishing-boat, its face wearing a broad grin. A hand appeared, still clutching the short club with which the spy had been struck down. Ned recognized the courier to whom he had given the coded letter destined for Henri de Belcamp–the man that Guido had robbed on the previous evening, and who had sworn vengeance in the customary Italian style.

The courier jumped down and began to rummage through Guido's pockets, expectantly. Ned took the letter out of his own jacket, but paused before handing it over in case the courier found anything else of interest while searching for it. Eventually, though, the courier looked up and shook his head.

Ned handed him the folded paper with the broken seal. "I've no time to write out a supplementary report and encode it," he said. "Have you enough English to take and transmit a verbal report?"

"Yes," said the courier, "but..."

"No buts," Ned said, "unless you can tell me who that man was who fled just now, and why the others are hunting him."

The courier shook his head, but grinned again. The chase had provided him with the distraction he needed to get close to his own quarry, but he had no idea what it was about.

"In that case," Ned went on, "I must make shift to find out. Do you know who *this* man is?" He pointed at the unconscious Guido, expecting another shake of the head.

"Dirty magyar," the courier supplied, spitting on the sand beside the bleeding head.

"In the pay of the Turks, you think?" Ned said.

The courier shook his head. "No Turks here," he said, confidently. "Vampire's minion."

Ned looked at the courier in amazement. "You can't mean that literally," he said.

The courier shrugged. "Dirty magyar," he repeated. "Be careful. Great danger, if vampire comes. Strange things. I make report too."

"By all means do so," Ned said. "Make sure, though, that you keep it distinct from mine, which is this: *Shelley is injured, perhaps mortally. His wife is ill. Frankenstein is ill too, in a different way. He is extremely hesitant in the matter of resuming his experiments. Shelley and his companions know that I am here in the name of the English crown, but they know nothing of my other master. They are afraid of some enemy, but are reluctant to seek the help they may need.* That will do–can you repeat all that when you pass on the letter?"

"Yes," said the courier, "but..."

"He will not approve. I know that–but the time for codes and ciphers is past; events are moving too rapidly. If he decides to take a hand in this, he had best come quickly. Now go."

The courier made no further objection. He moved off rapidly along the shore, in the same direction that the fugitive had taken. Ned looked down briefly at the unconscious man, then shrugged his own shoulders and followed the courier at a slower pace, looking for signs of the pursuit.

The trail was very evident, and easy to follow whle the hunters and their quarry were moving along the shore towards Spezia. When the tracks turned inland again, however, they became more difficult to follow, and they twisted and turned as the hunted man attempted to evade his pursuers. They finally evaporated on the hard and busy pavements of the town.

After searching for some time, Ned eventually caught sight of eight of the hunters outside a tavern. They had evidently abandoned the chase, at least until one of their scouts could obtain another sighting of their prey. They had put their weapons away, but they were making no attempt to hide themselves from the eyes of passers-by. On the contrary, they often offered salutes that implied recognition, although not all the greetings were returned. The eight men seemed to be adopting a swaggering attitude, whose bravado did not seem to be exaggerated by insecurity. *Banditti* though they presumably were, the men were evidently familiar to the port's inhabitants, and had no fear of arrest or molestation. The day when they could pass for heroic veterans of a fierce guerilla war against Bonaparte's allies was evidently not yet done. There was no sign of any uniform whose wearer might be duty-bound to object to their armed presence.

Ned began to make his weary way back to his hotel, deep in thought. His priority now had to be to make contact with Shelley again as soon as possible, if possible in confidence, in order to build on the sympathy that had sprung into being between them.

He had to insinuate himself into the conspiracy, if he possibly could. If he could not convince its members that he was a friend–and they seemed far too mistrustful, at present, for that–then he had to persuade them that he could be useful to them in some way. They knew now that he knew the bare bones of their secret, but they did not know how much he knew.

Perhaps, he thought, he could persuade them that he knew more, and that he might be a useful assistant if the man of science were, indeed, forced by circumstance to use his new apparatus before he was ready, on Percy Shelley or his wife.

Chapter Six
Science's Adam

Deep in thought as he was, Ned was not long unaware of the fact when someone began following him. Nor had he any doubt as to the identity of his tracker. He was not in the least worried for his own safety, but he was anxious for the safety of his follower. Guido must have recovered consciousness by this time, and the *banditti* must still have scouts scouring the town. The man who was taking so much trouble to hide his face was only drawing attention to himself by so doing.

Fortunately, the Sun was past its zenith now, and the inhabitants of Spezia tended to be as strict in their observance of the *siesta* as any Catalonian. The streets were not yet deserted, but the people who were still about were mostly in a hurry to be elsewhere, and they walked with their heads bowed. Everyone sought the available shade, averting their eyes from the brightly-lit paving stones.

Ned hurried his paces, not because he was trying to evade the pursuit but because he wanted to draw the other man into a safer vicinity as soon as was humanly possible. He took as roundabout a route as the hill would permit back to the hotel, taking time to make sure, as best he could, that there was no one dogging his immediate pursuer's footsteps. When he reached the hotel, he was glad to find it silent, with no sign of anyone moving within. When he turned the corner of the stone arch that formed its coaching entrance, he stopped dead and waited for his pursuer to catch up.

As soon as the tall man with the muffled face turned the corner, Ned raised a hand. "We'd best hurry up to my room," he said. "You should be safe there, if no one has seen us. Fortunately, the *banditti* cannot have many friends in this part of town, no matter how many they have about the docks."

The other stared down at him, evidently surprised by this matter-of-fact greeting. The Sun was high and the big man's broad-brimmed hat cast a black shadow over his partly-veiled face, but Ned was almost certain now that the man's skin was grey. General Mortdieu was obviously not the only Grey Man ever made who had retained all or most of his mental faculties.

"Who are you?" growled the reanimated man, speaking English with a guttural accent that might have been Switzer-Deutsch.

"I believe that's the question I ought to be asking you," Ned said. "Either way, let's get out of sight first. This way–and be as careful as you can, in case any of the servants is still on the prowl."

Ned and his companion took the back staircase up to his room. They met no one as they climbed, and Ned sighed with relief as he shut the door behind them. The water jug on the dressing-table had been refilled since he had gone out; he filled two cups, offering one to his guest and drinking deeply from the other. The morning's exertions had given him a fearful thirst.

"You can remove the layers of protective clothing now," Ned said. "I've seen your kind before, and talked to them. I didn't get much out of poor Sawney Ross, but General Mortdieu was much more forthcoming, though not very polite to begin with."

The Grey Man took off his hat and headband, and then unwound the silk scarf that covered the lower part of his face. His movements were deliberate, but not particularly awkward. The resurrected man seemed to be challenging Ned, measuring his face to see if he were really as brave and well-prepared as he pretended.

Eventually, seemingly satisfied by Ned's composure, the Grey Man sat down into the armchair, accepted the proffered cup and drank even more thirstily than Ned had done. Ned filled both cups again, while he studied his guest carefully.

His heart had begun to race as he accustomed himself to the idea of who this man must be. In *Frankenstein*, he remembered, the man of science had called his subject a "daemon" or a "creature," never a *man*. Ned knew that much of what was said about the creature there must be the pure product of madness or the literary imagination, but it would be foolish to assume that it was all false. After all, General Mortdieu had given the impression of being a wrathful and violent individual, and it seemed not unlikely that waking up from the sleep of death to find oneself reincarnate as a slate-grey walking corpse might be a intrinsically embittering experience.

"Since you asked first," Ned said, as he continued to study the grey features anxiously, "I'm Edward Knob, an Englishman. I thank you for the warning you shouted to me on the shore, but I wonder why you were watching me from hiding before your pursuers chased you away."

"Do you really know what I am?" the Grey Man asked. "I was about to assure you that you had no need to be afraid, but perhaps there is no need. Have you seen many others of my kind?"

"Yes, I know what you are and how you were brought back from the dead," Ned said. "I am certainly willing to assume, until I have evidence to the contrary, that I do not need to be afraid of you. I have seen several dozen others of your kind, but I fear that all but a few were imbeciles, and only one seemed as articulate as you. May I take my turn to ask some questions now?"

"You were in that house on the shore," the Grey Man stated, guardedly. "You must, therefore, know... my maker."

"Ah," said Ned. "You were following *him*, of course, although that also obliged you to follow Guido, who was also following him. You are his first subject, then–the infamous *daemon* of *Frankenstein*?"

The Grey Man's dull eyes did not flare up at that, but his broad mouth curled in distaste. "My maker should not have described me thus," he said, softly, "if, in fact, he did. Nor should he have written his memoirs while he was still sick enough to mistake his fears and delusions for reality. In either case, Walton's sister should not have given the letters and the manuscript to a publisher. All of that has done us both a severe disservice. Walton was very angry with her, I think, when he found out–but it was too late."

"In all probability," Ned said, currying favor shamelessly, "the worst of the horrors supplying the story with a plot were grafted on to the original by some hired hack instructed to bring out the tale's inherent melodrama–I cannot believe the rumor that Shelley was responsible, but, whatever the truth of the matter, I agree with you it would have been better for everyone concerned had the book not appeared."

"I am entitled to compensation for that, if nothing else," the Grey Man murmured. "I am certainly not eight feet tall, as the text alleged, and I was certainly not patched together from the refuse of slaughterhouses, although I presume that my body was plucked intact from a fresh grave. However ugly I may seem, I am certainly not a demon."

"You're not so very ugly," Ned assured his visitor. "Your color is a little unusual, but it's preferable to the hideous yellow that was if my memory serves me rightly, cited in the published text. Actually, I'm not personally acquainted with your maker, although I knew *of* him before meeting him for the first time this morning. He is quietly famous, in his way, quite apart from what I feel sure is a gross misrepresentation of his character in the pages of the novel named after him. Germain Patou's continuation of his clandestine work has not provided the best of supplementary advertisements, but it has served to attract a good deal of fascinated attention from various interested parties. Why were the *banditti* trying to kill you?"

The Grey Man shook his head slightly. "I'm not sure," he murmured. "I've encountered their kind before, in a quarrelsome fashion, but I had hoped that the disagreement was long-forgotten, given that it dates back to the years when men of that sort fancied themselves revolutionaries–but Italians hold grudges. It was their fellows who attacked me all those years ago; I merely defended myself a little too well for their liking. Coming back to the region was always a risk for me, I suppose–that fact might have figured in my maker's calculations when he decided to establish himself in Spezia. It was a risk I needed to take, though. If my maker is about to resume his work, at last, then I am entitled to play my part. He owes me that–and his fears are groundless."

"What fears?" Ned demanded.

"He wants to reserve the privilege of educating his subjects and directing their lives to himself. He would have guarded the privilege of supervising my own education very jealously had he not fallen victim to illness and dire anxiety, and he bitterly resents the fact that he lost control of me–but once I had recovered self-consciousness, I was my own man; we were bound to quarrel. He fears, I think, that I might have more ready-made moral authority over other people of my kind than he would be able to retain for himself. That is true, or so I hope and believe–but he need have no fear of what I might do with that authority. My intentions are benign."

"In the novel," Ned observed, "the so-called creature demands that Frankenstein make him a bride, and becomes murderous when thwarted."

"Melodramatic embellishment," said the Grey Man, sipping water from his cup with affected delicacy. "My maker always intended to repeat his experiment, when he was well enough, and tried more than once. I was his natural partner–but he rejected me, as he lost his grip on reality, and fled from me. If I have pursued him ever since, it is only with the determination to make my peace with him. I have never murdered anyone. He might have loved his little cousin, I suppose, but he certainly never married her, and I certainly did not kill her, any more than I killed his brother or his friend Clerval."

Ned nodded, anxious to give every visible indication that he believed what the Grey Man was telling him, no matter what private reservations he was careful to make. In fact, he was perfectly prepared to believe that the Grey Man was no Hellish fiend, but he was a spy now, and it was his duty to withhold his judgment. "Your maker might be forced to resume his work sooner than he wanted to, if Shelley has his way," Ned observed. "He seems reluctant to press forward, but he might have no choice if he wishes to retain the good opinion of his friends."

"Is one of them dying, then?" the Grey Man guessed.

"Shelley is worried about his wife," Ned said. "I am worried about him. Do you know Shelley?"

"We have met," the Grey Man said, a trifle guardedly.

"As I said, I mistrust the rumor that he wrote the published version of Walton's story," Ned said, in case that was the reason for the other's caution. "It was probably falsely credited to him by a rumor put about by the publisher. Lord Byron was once said to have written a famous tale about vampires, but that ascription turned out to be false."

"I have met Byron too," the Grey Man said, mildly. "I know more of vampires now than he ever did."

Ned frowned at that. "Do you, indeed?" he murmured. "The man you followed from Walton's house is rumored to be a vampire's minion, it seems. Is that likely, do you think?"

"Quite likely," said the Grey Man, casually–but he was not unobservant, for he immediately added: "You did not believe it when you heard it, I suppose? You were testing me–but vampires are not what you think, if you have taken your notion of them from Polidori's tale."

"What are they, then?" Ned asked.

"Nature's Grey Men," his guest replied. "The accidentally reanimated dead. Most are mere brutes, even if decay leaves them relatively unravaged, but on occasion... I am not alone, you see, even though I was the first of my kind to be deliberately made. A new Adam I may be, but the world beyond my meager Eden was not empty. There are more avid hunters looking out for me than the ones you saw today. Is Shelley really in danger of dying? I had thought Byron far the more reckless of the two, and hence more likely to die first."

"He was injured in a brawl, it seems," Ned said. "The wound was not serious at first, but it was aggravated by an accident on his boat and it has become infected."

"Did he aggravate it deliberately, do you think?" the Grey Man asked, surprising Ned yet again.

This time, Ned did not attempt to hide his surprise. "I cannot believe that," he said. "Do you really think that he might be courting death deliberately, in order to force your maker's hand? I don't think so–although I do believe that he

249

tried to win an agreement from his friends to subject his wife to the treatment, should she fail to recover from her present fever."

"Is she very ill?" the Grey Man asked.

"I haven't seen her, but Shelley was obviously very anxious."

"*She* would not have endangered herself deliberately," the Grey Man said, bleakly. "She did not like me at all, although I was never anything but courteous to her, and she did not take to my maker either, although he was still handsome when they first met. She could almost have believed that farrago of nonsense that the publisher put out–her nightmares were worse than my maker's."

"Where did you meet her?" Ned asked, curiously.

"At the Villa Diodati, on the shore of Lake Geneva, six years ago. My maker had a house not far from Cologny; Byron and Shelley became acquainted with him there. He and I were on better terms in those days, but he was still de-termined to hide me away. Inevitably, his secrecy only piqued their curiosity, and they persuaded him to let them in on his secret, swearing to keep it. He probably did not take much persuading–he was still proud of his accomplish-ment, as much in the process of my initial education as my reanimation. It was shortly thereafter that he fell prey to the delirious fever that induced his panic and caused our estrangement. That was not entirely a disaster for me, though, for it forced me to take charge of my own education–not in the bizarre fashion rep-resented in that silly romance, but with far greater success."

"I'm a self-educated man myself," Ned told him. "I pride myself on having made a better job of it than many schools would have done–but I suppose that men like us are bound to think that."

Grey Men did not, in Ned's experience, have expressive faces, but the Adam of the New Grey Men did his best to demonstrate his surprise at that. "*Men like us*," he repeated, softly. "Thank you for that, my friend. No one has ever gone out of his way to pronounce such a phrase before."

It was at that moment that the sheer bizarrerie of the occasion struck Ned with some force. He had been face-to-face with Grey Men before, but those oc-casions had seemed to be the substance of pure melodrama even at the time. Now, he was sitting in a hotel's bed-alcove while a reanimated corpse was re-laxing in a nearby armchair, and the two of them were talking, as if engaged in the most natural conversation in the world, about great poets and vampires.

What an adventurer I have become! Ned thought–but then he broke out into a half-smile as he realized that he really did feel more at ease with this strange creature than he had felt during his first interview with the glowering Gregory Temple.

"May we talk about these others of my kind you have seen?" the Grey Adam asked, with scrupulous politeness, after a brief pause. "I had heard that they existed, but I have not yet had the privilege of meeting one. Do you know how many there are altogether?"

"I don't know whether Patou has been able to make any more since leaving England," Ned replied, "but even if he has, I doubt that any them have retained as much presence of mind as you. He has hit a snag there, it seem, that your own maker contrived to avoid."

"It's a common problem, it seems," murmured the other. "I've heard rumor of more than one so-called vampire who can pass for human, but I'm far from sure that I can trust the second account, even if the first is true. There are a great many who are less than beasts."

"Patou certainly had not given up hope of restoring more of his patients to full self-awareness and ordinary intelligence," Ned observed. "Had he not been trying so hard to facilitate their re-education, I would never have run into Sawney and become entangled in this business. Given time to experiment, and improve his methods, who knows what he might achieve? In time, it might be possible to replenish all the lost humanity of the reanimated dead."

"In time," the Grey Adam said, equably, "it might be possible to do far better than that—if we are only given the chance."

That possibility had not occurred to Ned. He chided himself silently; he had, after all, met General Mortdieu and seen evidence of *his* vaulting ambition. "Who are you, my friend?" he asked. "Or should I ask who you *were*, when you were alive?"

"I was no one when I was alive," the Grey Man retorted, "and I'm no one now—but I'm not a monster now, any more than the tenant of this body was when he was alive. I wish I could tell you that my predecessor had been a man of note, but he died too young to make his mark."

Ned took careful note of the fact that the Grey Adam now saw himself as a person distinct and different from the one he had been before his death, but took leave to wonder how that could really be the case. "You must have had a name, though," he objected.

"I did—but I gave it up when I died, and never troubled to invent another. I certainly never thought to call myself Mortdieu, or the Vampire King. If you need a name by which to think of me, though, you might call me Lazarus—I dare say that some such analogy has already cropped up in your private thoughts."

"Of course," Ned murmured. "It was too much to hope, I dare say, that you might have been someone renowned, who would have been at or near the head of any list of those deserving to be brought back from the dead—Tom Paine, for example."

"It's not the rights of man that concern me," the new Lazarus replied, seemingly conscious of taking a risk, "but the rights of the undead."

"You'll not achieve the second without first establishing the first, my dear Lazarus," Ned said. "If you and I are to be allies, that must be understood and agreed."

"I have not asked for an alliance," the Grey Man pointed out. "It was you who invited me to your room and made me welcome. Do you really want to be my friend, given that I am being hunted by men with pistols and muskets, who seem to be prepared to shoot on sight even in a law-abiding town like Spezia?"

"Of course," Ned said. "In my youth, in St. Giles's, all my friends and almost all my acquaintances were hunted men, endangered by the rope if not by bullets. I've lost more than I can count, including those I loved most dearly of all. I made a new friend today, who seems very likely to go the way of all the rest. Death and I are far from strangers–and whatever Ned Knob can do to assist in the war of science against death, you can be very certain that he will not hesitate. You have not asked for an alliance, it's true–but you were following me, were you not, in the hope that I might be useful to you?"

The new Lazarus did not deny it. "I hope and trust that a reconciliation with my maker might be possible," he said, "but it might be better if the initial approach were made through an intermediary. I dare not approach Walton, because I'm far from sure what his attitude to me might be. I would have risked an interview with Shelley, despite his wife's opinion, if that had been the best course–but when I saw you come from the house, not long after my maker had gone in, I thought there might be another opportunity worth investigating. I was still wary, as you saw, but I'm glad now that I followed my impulse. You might want to be wary too, though–as you've seen, I'm not without enemies."

"Your maker told me that he and his conspirators have enemies of whom I knew nothing," Ned observed. "In retrospect, though, it's possible that he might have been thinking of you."

"It's possible," the Grey Man conceded, sadly. "I'm not his enemy, though. I'm determined to make my peace with him if I can–but it might not be easy, if he has not entirely recovered from the legacy of his delirium. Are you willing to help me, Mr. Knob?"

"As it happens," Ned said, "it would suit me very well to become your ambassador. It wouldn't be fair to let you think that I am agreeing to your request for purely altruistic reasons."

"I had taken it for granted that you have your own reasons for being here," the new Lazarus replied, graciously. "That is your business–always provided that you mean no harm to my maker or his friends."

"I mean no harm to anyone, at present," Ned assured him. "Although I might want to make some exception to the rule in future. If the mysterious Guido really is a vampire's minion... but perhaps I'm jumping to conclusions. Perhaps vampires are no more deserving of the reputation that Gothic fiction has given them than the reanimate dead."

"I must reserve my own judgment on that score," the Grey Man said. "The term *vampire* appears to be local, though. In the Caribbean, I'm told, the reanimated dead are called *zombis*. The rumors are unclear as to whether they're natural or artificial, although they're said to be very stupid, without exception. You'll go to my maker on my behalf, then?"

"Yes I will, this very afternoon," Ned said. "You had best stay here, for the time being, but if one of the hotel servants comes in, or Guido decides to pay me another surreptitious visit, you might find it diplomatic to leave in a hurry. If so, try to make your way to San Terenzo again, and hide within view of the *Don Juan*–the boat I hid behind when you shouted your warning. I'll look for you there."

"Thank you, Mr. Knob," said Lazarus, extending his hand to be shaken. "You're a true gentleman."

Ned shook the hand willingly. "I had such pretensions once," he said, with a sigh, "but I'm a hardened radical now, who deem all men to be strictly equal, in terms of their innate quality."

Chapter Seven
Wheels Within Wheels

When Ned set out for the house he had been watching for the last few days, the Sun was still some way above the western horizon, reddening in hue but shining very fiercely. The atmosphere was thick and heavy, more somnolent than it had been during the siesta hour, and the world seemed very still and perfectly content.

Ned walked with a confident and satisfied step, thinking furiously about what he ought to say to the new Adam's maker and Robert Walton, and any other conspirators who might be with them. Shelley, he knew, would not be there unless he had taken a turn for the worse, so he would probably meet a wall of hostility–but he had an ace up his sleeve now.

As he approached the house, he looked up at the vantage point where Guido had placed himself on previous days, but found it empty. That put him slightly on his guard, but wariness was not enough to prevent misfortune. He was within ten yards of the gate into the grounds when a man stepped out of the shadows to his right, moving swiftly to block his way.

Ned did not recognize the man, but his costume and the way he moved– like a man accustomed to moving stealthily and to combat–strongly suggested that he must be one of the *banditti* who had been hunting the Grey Man earlier in the day. He had no weapon in his hand, but he had a dagger in his belt and he placed his hand on its hilt suggestively.

"You will come with me, please," he said, in Italian.

The relative mildness of the request suggested that the *banditti* were now showing a certain circumspection, at least while operating in this respectable neighborhood, but Ned had no reason think that help would arrive swiftly if he called for it.

"I think not," Ned said, continuing to move forward, with his hands ready to grapple the bandit's wrist if the knife were drawn. Instead, the other man fell back two paces–but that was a tactical move, for Ned heard footsteps running up

behind him. He turned round, and then leapt forward to meet his second assailant, who was wielding a cudgel. He managed to deflect the first thrust of the
cudgel, and kicked backwards in anticipation of the other man's closing movement. Had his leg been a handspan longer the maneuver might just have worked,
but for once his short stature was his undoing. He put himself off balance without striking a wounding blow at either of his attackers.

He screamed for help then, with all his might, but–as he had anticipated–no
help came, at least not swiftly enough to lend him any useful assistance. He hit
out with both fists, and tried another kick in the Parisian style, but his opponents
were accomplished brawlers. Had they been intent on killing him, they would
have slit his throat within five seconds, but they were not. The fact that they
only intended to knock him out gave him a full quarter-minute to make his displeasure felt, but he knew before the last blow landed that he had not hurt either
one of them significantly.

When he woke up with a roaring headache, he could not estimate how
much time had elapsed. It was quite dark, but that told him nothing, since he
seemed to be in an enclosed space, with his body lying on a thick carpet and his
head on bare boards. His hands were tied behind him, and his ankles were bound
too.

As he began struggling against his bonds, Ned tripped a cord attached to a
little bell. As soon as it rang,he suspended his struggle, realizing that someone
would undoubtedly come in response to the summons. He wanted to compose
himself for the confrontation.

A door opened somewhere to his left and two men came in, one of them
carrying a tray on which a lighted candle was mounted. It was a tallow candle of
no great dimension, and it was held at arm's length, but Ned would have been
able to recognize either face by its light, had he ever seen it before. He had not–
but neither man was dressed in the manner of the *banditti* who had chased the
new Lazarus and kidnapped Ned. Their clothing was simple and severe, but not
cheap or well-worn.

While they stared down at him, Ned took the opportunity to look around
the room. There was no furniture, although indentations in the carpet suggested
that there had once been a sofa, a sideboard and several chairs. The walls had
been cleared of pictures, whose outlines still showed there in the stains on the
surface. The empty bed-alcove was now home to a large crucifix, though, and
there was a slab of slate set beneath it as a kneeling-platform.

The man holding the candle had obviously followed the flicker of his gaze.
"Have you a religion, Monsieur Knob?" he asked, quietly, in French.

Ned ignored the question. "It seems that I am the only person involved in
this business who readily owns up to his true name," he observed, instead. "In
consequence, everyone seems to know it, while I languish in ignorance as to
theirs."

"An embarrassing situation, for a spy," the man said. He seemed to be very old and exceedingly thin, but also quite fit and strong—a near-paradoxical combination that Ned had observed before in men of a certain kind. "I am not at all reluctant to tell you my true name. I am Malo de Treguern, of the Order of St. John of Jerusalem."

"The Hospitaller knights?" Ned retorted, skeptically, trying unsuccessfully to squirm into a sitting position. "That Order was disbanded, I believe, when Napoleon captured Malta more than 20 years ago."

"Many of Bonaparte's commands have been reversed in recent years," the warrior monk replied. "Some less ostentatiously than others. If you had come peacefully, as you were asked to do, you would not have been hurt. You were fortunate that we had given our assistants such strict instructions—they are the kind of men who would not normally hesitate to kill someone who attacked them."

"It was they who attacked me, when they blocked my way," Ned said. "If you intend to engage a man in polite conversation, you should not have your invitation delivered by bandits—even bandits who represent themselves as resistance fighters against non-existent oppression."

Malo de Treguern set the candle down beside Ned and stepped back, as if to appraise his condition. "You may have a point," he conceded, "but we are only two, and far from home. It was necessary for us to find local allies, and we selected the men we bought because they already had a grievance against the individual we were seeking, and have been fortunate enough to find. Now, alas, the opportunity for politeness seems to have passed. If you will oblige me by answering my questions honestly, we might yet be friends. If not... Well, let us not get sidetracked."

Treguern knelt down then, to help Ned assume a sitting position, with his back to the wall. This allowed the old man to look Ned more fully in the face, while his younger companion remained standing. "*Have* you a religion?" Treguern repeated. The question seemed genuinely important to him.

"I'm no Calvinist," Ned answered, warily, "if that's what concerns you." Frankenstein, he knew, was Genevese, and hence reckonable as a Calvinist no matter what his actual beliefs might be. Shelley was reputed to be an atheist. Neither persuasion was likely to be congenial to an ex-Knight of Malta.

"But have you a religion?" Malo de Treguern repeated.

"No," Ned finally consented to answer. "I have not."

His interrogator nodded, as if he had merely wanted to make certain of his suspicion. "Is that why the demon came to you?" he asked.

"He's not a demon but a man," Ned said, bluntly. "He has been dead, and is alive again, but he is a man regardless. He followed me because he hoped to find a friend. He did. Why were your hirelings attempting to kill him?"

"How can a man who is already dead be *killed*?" the self-supposed Hospitaller countered. "No more banter, please. Was it on the demon's behalf that you were going to the necromancer's house?"

"Ostensibly," Ned said, deciding that it was hardly worth the bother of protesting that Victor Frankenstein was a man of science, not a necromancer. "But it was on my own behalf as much as his. I wanted news of my countryman, Percy Shelley. He fell ill this morning on his boat, the *Don Juan*, and I carried him back to his house. Walton's colleague came to attend him there, because there was no doctor close at hand. I was interested to know the result of his examination."

Malo de Treguern's weathered face gave not the slightest hint of any reaction to this statement, although he undoubtedly suspected that Ned had more reasons to make contact with Walton than the one he had specified. "Who was the man with you when the demon ran towards you this morning?" the Churchman asked.

Ned took leave to regret that the dutiful Lazarus had shouted out his well-meant warning. If only the Adam of the Grey Race had kept quiet, the *banditti* might not have leapt to the conclusion that there was a link between Ned and his rival spy. "He calls himself Guido," he replied, shaking his head in a vain attempt to clear it, "but I doubt that it is his real name."

"Are you working together?"

"No."

"Who are you working for?"

"The King of England," Ned replied, with a certain emphasis.

His interlocutor laughed dryly, although he did not accompany the laugh with a smile. "That will win you no credit in these parts," he said. "There's no lingering love for Bonaparte's lackeys in this region, but that does not make the appalling George more popular than any other foreign king. Is Guido in the employ of His Majesty too?"

"No," Ned said. He almost stopped at that, but could not resist the temptation to make one more attempt to stir a reaction from those wrinkled features, which seemed as hard and polished as teak. "I took him for a Turkish spy at first," he added, "but it seems that he's a magyar, minion of some vampire king."

Ned half-expected another dry laugh, perhaps slightly more vitriolic than the first, but none came.

"That's an awkward complication," muttered the standing man.

"Please be quiet, Simeon!" said Malo de Treguern. To Ned, he said: "Will the necromancer attempt to bring Shelley back to life if he dies?"

"I'd dearly like to know the answer to that myself," Ned said. "Unfortunately, your bully-boys stopped me as I was on my way to find out."

"You talked to Shelley, though," the questioner pointed out. "Is he determined to be brought back, if he should die?"

256

"He didn't mention the possibility," Ned said, "but I can't imagine that he would prefer to remain dead, if there's a chance that he might not. Did Masi try to kill him in order to provide the man of science with a suitable subject with which to resume his work?"

"You'd have to ask Masi's masters that," the Hospitaller consented to reply, in a neutral tone, after a slight hesitation. "You might ask the boat-builder Roberts the same question—nor would I very confident in trusting the Irishman, Taaffe, if I were your friend Shelley. Someone there is, it seems, who imagines that poets and atheists are ideal subjects for this kind of devilry."

"You might be stretching the imagined conspiracy too far," Ned said, "although I can understand how you might, given the circumstances. Is the reborn Order of St. John commissioned as a new Inquisition, then, hot on the trail of a new breed of heretics? Have you news of *Civitas Solis*?"

That was a chance shot, and a reckless one, but it struck home. For a moment, his interrogator's previously-expressionless face showed such blatant alarm that Ned could easily have believed that the man really was an inquisitor terrified by the imagined threat of legendary heresy. "What do you know of *Civitas Solis*?" the kneeling man asked, sharply.

"What does anyone know of *Civitas Solis*?" Ned countered, blandly. "It's a phantom, the stuff of superstition—like vampires, zombis and poor fugitive Lazarus."

"If we were like the inquisitors of old," Malo de Treguern told him, "we would doubtless feel entitled to use less tender methods to discipline your sarcastic tongue. Perhaps we are, but we still feel obliged to give you the opportunity to make a free confession before we begin heating the irons and crushing your fingers. At any rate, as you have obviously deduced from my questions, we do not approve of atheism or of necromancy. Given that you seem to be involved with known advocates of both, you might want to be a little more wary of offending us."

"I have nothing against true Christians," Ned told him, sincerely, "but I would not count any torturer, however pious he might pretend to be, as a true Christian. You didn't bring me here to hurt me, or your tame *banditti* wouldn't have been so careful, and you certainly didn't bring me here to instruct me to beware of atheism or necromancy. Why not proceed directly to the matter of bribery? I'm a spy, after all, ever ready to work for hire."

"Will you sell us the demon, then? Do you know where he is?"

"How much is he worth?" Ned countered. "I'll need more than the traditional 30 pieces of silver, mind. Gold is more in my line."

"Fifty sovereigns," said the kneeling man, promptly. Inquisitors, Ned remembered, were reputed to be specially licensed to lie to their victims.

"Done," said Ned. "He's in my room at the hotel, waiting for my return." This too was a chance shot, but he felt quite certain that if these supposed Hospitallers had sent two *banditti* to intercept him, they must also have sent others to his room. What he wanted was confirmation that his ally had escaped them.

"Where did you arrange to meet him?" the kneeling man countered, harshly, tacitly providing the desired confirmation.

"Has he already escaped, then?" Ned asked, insouciantly. "Your *banditti* are by no means the cream of the crop, are they? Fra Diavolo must be weeping tears of shame in his Corsican grave, if rumors of his death have not been exaggerated."

"Leave him here, Malo," the standing man advised. "He won't tell us anything useful, even if he knows anything, which I doubt. In two days, it will all be over and we can let him go. He's harmless enough. We ought to provide him with a little company, though, if this Guido really is working for the vampire."

Ned took due note of the fact that the man his interrogator had called Simeon had said "*the* vampire," not "*a* vampire." These gentle inquisitors seemed to be demon-hunters rather than heresy-hunters, and might well have been badly misled as to the manner of creature they were chasing. Perhaps, he thought, they too had read *Frankenstein*. The *banditti* evidently knew Lazarus of old, though, well enough to harbor a long-held grudge against him. They must know that he was no wild beast or imp of Hell.

"We'd better make room for more company than that, if that's the way we intend to go," Malo de Treguern replied, with a hint of annoyance. As he turned to speak to the standing ma, he looked up, thus tilting his head back and allowing Ned to glimpse his tonsure.

He really is a monk of sorts, then, Ned thought, scrupulously. *Perhaps he really was a member of the Order of St. John, and perhaps some relic of the Order really does survive, just as relics of* Civitas Solis *survive. It may well be, though, that the ex-Knights of Malta are, and perhaps always were, affiliates of* Civitas Solis. *Even if Henri has succeeded in infiltrating that Order, he might have provoked grave mistrust as well as keen interest among its factions.*

"You should have answered our request and our questions politely," Malo de Treguern said to Ned, again–although Ned took some slight offense at that, having thought his responses reasonably polite as well as reasonably honest. "That way, we might have been prepared to let you go."

In a pig's eye, Ned thought. Aloud, he said: "I'm no man's enemy, and I don't bear grudges after the fashion of your local hirelings. I can do you no harm, in any case, although I'll have to be careful now that I don't lead you to my friend–unless, of course, you can come up with the 50 sovereigns."

Malo de Treguern stood up, picking up the candle-tray as he did so. Looking down at his captive, he said: "I'm glad to hear that you'll bear no grudge. I'll let you go in two days, as Simeon suggests, provided that we've succeeded in our mission by then. I'll send you water and food when I have time to spare. I'm sorry to have inconvenienced you–you're a mere fly, after all, whose buzz is no more than a tiny nuisance–but matters are already moving too quickly for my liking, and the last thing I need is another loose cannon rolling around the deck. In case you're minded to try to escape, I must warn you that I shall instruct my hirelings that they need not handle you so tenderly if you get in our way again."

"If one of the great minds of his era were to die an untimely death," Ned said, making no attempt to hide his annoyance in the face of this sententious threat, "and your intention were to prevent his being resurrected, and his intelligence preserved to the extent that can be contrived, I might bear a grudge for that."

"Our intentions go a great deal further than that," the aged warrior monk told him, with more than a hint of renewed threat in his voice, as he and his companion moved towards the door, "and we are not to be intimidated by the grudges of dwarfs. Be grateful that we have removed you from the game–it's now a field of play where not-so-innocent bystanders are very likely to get hurt."

The door closed, plunging Ned into total darkness again.

He immediately began to worry the cords binding his wrists, hopeful that he could get free, given time. He rather liked the idea of being a loose cannon rolling around the deck, albeit one that wanted to prevent injury rather than inflicting it. At any rate, he liked the analogy far better than the one that had likened him to a fly whose buzz was only a tiny nuisance.

Chapter Eight
The Necromancer's Den

Ned struggled for an hour in pitch darkness, attempting to extricate his wrists from the tightly-knotted cords, but whoever had tied them knew his business, and Ned was coming close to despair when the door swung open again and faint candlelight poured through it.

The man who entered, bearing a candlestick, was Guido, the "vampire's minion." He looked down at Ned with a wry smile on his face.

"You trapped me very neatly by the shore," he said, in a low voice, "but it seems that you've run into trouble yourself."

Ned did not bother to correct the other's slight misapprehension. "Have you come to taunt me or to set me free?" he asked, keeping his own voice low.

"To set you free," said Guido, with the slightest of sighs, setting the candlestick down and starting work on the knots binding Ned's ankles, "although you don't entirely deserve such generous treatment. We still have enemies in common, Monsieur Knob, and ought to make what alliances we can."

"How did you know where to find me?" Ned asked.

"I have not been idle since I woke up with a sore head. I thought that I had every chance of making friends with the *banditti*, if I were to dispense a little coin; I hardly thought to find them in the employ of Mother Church, avid to do violence to her enemies. We live in strange times, my friend. Anyhow, I found out easily enough where the bandits' masters were lodged, and I saw you carried in unconscious. We're only a few hundred meters from Walton's house, in another covert on the same irregular terrace. I would have come to you sooner, but I had to make perfectly certain that the coast was clear. There are only two Churchmen, it seems, but they have more than a dozen bandits at their beck and call. One party is watching Walton's house, while a larger one has gone to San Terenzo, perhaps hoping to find the demon there—not that he is actually a demon, of course, as you must know as well as I do."

"Any more than your own master is a actually a vampire, I suppose," Ned retorted, rolling over so that Guido could get a better purchase on the cords securing his wrists.

"Did the Churchmen tell you that?" Guido asked.

"Everyone seems to have known it but me," Ned admitted. "I'd assumed that you were in the pay of the Turks, but it seems that I was naive."

"My master would be amused to hear that," Guido said. "The Sultan hates vampires even more virulently than the Pope—mercifully, neither has much say in Hungary nowadays. The last relic of the Holy Roman Empire is neither very holy nor very Roman. There!"

Ned sat up and rubbed his wrists to restore the circulation to his numb hands.

"Do you know who the Churchmen are?" Guido asked.

Ned hesitated, but decided that he owed the other that much. "They claim to be members of the Order of St. John of Jerusalem," he said, "reformed in secret since the fall of Malta. One calls himself Malo de Treguern; he addressed the other as Simeon. Do you know them?"

Guido shrugged. "The name means nothing," he said, "but there are rumors a-plenty of a new crusade against so-called necromancy. Thus far, its operations are clandestine—but if they were able to capture a man returned from the dead, of whatever sort, they might elect to put him on show in order to rouse mobs to continue their work. They would not dare put Frankenstein on trial, given that he is a Swiss citizen with a magistrate for a father, but few people know that he is here, or even that he is alive and nearly sane; if he were to vanish, I doubt that anyone in authority would exert themselves overmuch to find him. We need to prevent that, if we can."

Ned was duly grateful for the fact that his supposed ally really did seem disposed now to share what information he had. There would be no more nonsense about bomb-factories. "Shelley and Byron know that he is here," he pointed out, "and they are famous men."

"For which reason the Hospitallers will not lay a finger on them," Guido said. "But that will not mean that anyone will take them seriously if they were bold enough to tell their story. Their discretion thus far suggests that they are keenly aware of that—genius has the reputation of being perilously close to madness and I doubt that they would be able to win support from the likes of Davy and Darwin without incontrovertible proof of the contention that the dead may return. Frankenstein and Patou have been very wise, I think, to try their hardest to perfect the process before granting it any publicity, given that they want to inspire hope rather than horror. We need to leave now, and must be careful. There was no one downstairs when I came in, but they might send someone back at any moment to make sure that you are safe."

Ned nodded, and followed Guido through the door and along a corridor to a flight of wooden steps. There was no light in the house save for Guido's candle, and they made their way outside without any difficulty. Once they were outside, Guido extinguished the candle, although the Moon was far from full and the stars were partly obscured by drifting clouds.

Ned did not recognize the street, but they were high enough on the hill for him to estimate their location within the town; Guido had been reasonably accurate in his estimate of its distance from Walton's house. Guido started walking in that direction.

"What do you intend to do?" Ned asked him.

"If Walton has any sense, he must have sent a messenger to Pisa to summon as many of the conspirators as possible. If you did not scare them sufficiently by barging into Casa Magni this morning, the sight of that pursuit down the hill and along the strand will certainly have brought them to a fine pitch of alarm. If Walton recognized the demon, as he might well have done, they will know that all hope of proceeding in secret is now gone. They'll probably take flight, but they'll gather at the house first. If there's to be a siege or a pitched battle, it will be as well for us to weigh in before the larger party returns from San Terenzo. If we can help Frankenstein to get away while there's still time..."

"They can't take flight," Ned objected. "Shelley and his wife aren't well enough to travel."

"Then they'll be left behind," Guido said, simply. "Williams and his wife might stay to care for them, but the rest will have to go, and go quickly. I can help, especially in the matter of finding a new place of safety."

"I don't think..." Ned began. He had several objections to raise, and strong reservations to express regarding the wisdom of accepting guarantees of safe conduct from the minion of a vampire, but Guido cut him off and silenced him with an abrupt gesture. They were coming close to Walton's house now, and had to complete their approach silently. Ned wondered briefly whether he ought to have passed on Malo de Treguern's warning about giving the bandits permission to use any and all violent means, but decided that it was unnecessary. Guido did not seem the type to be squeamish in such matters himself.

Ned had no weapon, and Guido only had his stiletto–that being why he had had to untie Ned rather than simply slicing through the cords that bound him– but Ned had no hesitation about going forward regardless. He was not afraid. If the *banditti* were widely scattered, as they probably were, given the size of the tract of land they had to surround, it might well be possible to take them one by one and appropriate their arms. Ned still had questions that he wanted to ask his currently-obliging informant, especially concerning his mysterious vampire rently-obliging informant, especially concerning his mysterious vampire master, but that would have to wait.

They found the first bandit easily enough, on the very spot where Guido had stationed himself to watch the house–an understandable coincidence, given that it was a natural coign of vantage. The bandit was not standing up, though– he was laid out flat on his back, unconscious, and he had already been deprived of his weapons.

Guido let out his breath with a slight sigh of delight. Ned, too, was more delighted than surprised. If this was not the work of one of Frankenstein's more muscular friends–Trelawny, perhaps–than it could only be the work of the new Lazarus. Either way, it suggested that the battle had already been joined, and that the right side had seized an early advantage.

The second bandit they contrived to locate was, however, awake and alert. Guido crept up behind him and used one of the cords that he had taken from Ned's wrists as a garrote, preventing him from calling out. Whether he released the strangling-cord before the man had choked to death, Ned could not tell, and he could not afford to care overmuch. Guido took the man's pistol for himself, and handed his poniard to Ned.

Then the silence was broken by an alarm call–not occasioned by Guido or Ned–and there was a sudden flurry of movement all around the house. Ned and Guido separated, hurrying to assist in the burgeoning conflict. Ned had evidently chosen a bad direction, for he found his path suddenly blocked by one man, while another immediately tried to circle behind him. This time, they were obviously not acting under orders to be discreet.

One of the attackers fired a pistol, whose ball whirred above Ned's head, while the other tried to stab him in the throat. Ned avoided the knife-thrust, rather to narrowly for comfort, and hurled himself forward to butt his nearer assailant in the midriff. They went down in an untidy heap, but Ned was able to get a grip on the hand that held the knife and force it away from his body.

He heard a dull thud as the other bandit fell, struck from behind. No more than a second elapsed before strong hands reached down to push him out of the way, before a heavy boot came down on the knife-wielder's throat, crushing the bandit's Adam's apple.

"Into the house, quickly!" said a voice he recognized readily enough as that of Lazarus.

Ned allowed himself to be bundled toward the main entrance of Walton's house and through the open doorway. The corridor within was dark, but he was hurried along it, then pushed up against a wall and told to be still. Others were now hastening through the door, which was abruptly slammed. Then a light was struck and a candle lit.

There were seven men gathered in the corridor, counting Ned and Lazarus. Walton was there, and John Taaffe; Ned also recognized Edward Trelawny, who had visited the house on several occasions, and a man with a terrible wound on his face, whom he took to be Captain Hay. The seventh man was a prisoner, who had evidently been seized by Taaffe and Hay; it was Malo de Treguern.

"Guido's still out there!" Ned was quick to say. "He's no Turkish spy, but a friend–he took care of at least one of the *banditti* for you."

"He'll come to no harm," Lazarus was quick to say. "If he wants to come in, he may–but one of the bandits, at least, ran away down the hill. He'll be in San Terenzo within the hour, and the whole gang may well be back within two. We've no time to waste."

Malo de Treguern looked at Ned, with a steely glint in his eye, which suggested that he might be regretting his clemency. He had seemed perfectly reasonable on his own ground, when all was going according to his plan, but there was a wildness about him now. "The fact that you have a hostage will not deter them from attacking," the Hospitaller said. "They will rely on God to protect me–and rightly so."

The Churchman was not the center of the group's attention, however. The others–Walton and Trelawny in particular–were staring at Lazarus mistrustfully, although they had to know that he had helped them in the skirmish.

"It was *you* who brought down this swarm of hornets upon us," Walton said, angrily. "If you knew how hard we have struggled to avoid any possibility of being thought to be in league with demons, you would surely have stayed away."

"I am not a demon," Lazaruis repeated, yet again. "If the work is to begin again, I have more right to interest myself in its progress than any one of you."

"We have no time for this," said Trelawny, putting his hand on Walton's arm. "Bring them both into the laboratory. Hay, guard the door–and watch out for the man who is not, after all, a Turkish spy, since he seems to be on our side. Let him in if he asks to come in–we may yet need every man and every weapon we can muster."

In the absence of any specific instruction, Ned followed as Trelawny and Taaffe hustled Malo de Treguern into a room at the rear of the house, where the equipment that Victor Frankenstein had been gathering was accumulated, much of it not yet removed from its packaging, Ned's heart sank as he realized how very unready Frankenstein was to resume his experiments, even in the simplest terms. No wonder Shelley had become alarmed by the danger threatening his wife–and so much the worse for him, if the wound in his head could not be healed.

Victor Frankenstein was there, perched on a stool. Malo de Treguern shook off Trelawny's arm and immediately stepped forward to confront him, although Ned could see that the confrontation would be futile. Frankenstein's eyes were glued to his "creature," and his face showed a bewildering confusion of emotions. The man of science clearly did not have the slightest idea what he ought to think or feel about his "creation," let alone what to say to him.

"Vile necromancer!" said the warrior monk, in English, for all the world as if his curse might have real injurious power. "Blasphemous maker of demons! You shall rue this day!" He seemed mad with frustrated rage, having lost every vestige of the calmness and method that he had brought to his earlier examination.

Frankenstein continued staring at his "daemon," who stepped forward and offered his hand. "*Bonjour*, Victor," he said, pausing slightly before withdrawing the unaccepted hand and continuing, in French: "It's good to see you again, and to find you better than before. I came to help you with your work, but I seem to have arrived at the same time as your enemies. It's too late to hide, I fear–in mainland Europe, at least. Will you let me help you find a safer refuge, and assist you in your work?"

Malo de Treguern was amazed, and seemed to have taken great offense at being ignored. He took hold of the small wooden crucifix he wore suspended about his neck and brandished it, as if he were about to attempt an exorcism.

It was, Ned thought, purely because Victor Frankenstein could no longer bear to meet his creature's calm eyes that the man of science turned his gaze aside momentarily to look his angry accuser up and down, with frank disdain–as John Calvin himself might have studied a Romanist friar. Then the alleged necromancer turned to look at Lazarus again, with tears welling in his eyes. "You should have let me alone," he said, in a voice hardly above a whisper. "How many times have I begged you to stay away?"

"I tended you when you first fell ill, Victor," the Adam of the new race replied, quietly. "I was kind, and faithful, although I had recovered but half my wits. Would you rather I had been the monster your delirium proclaimed me to be? Was it so very hard to bear that you found yourself helpless in my arms, like a child? Was it such a terrible blow to your godlike pride? Do you really believe that your future subjects will be more thankful and more docile than me?"

"We have no time for this," Trelawny said, in an anguished tone. "We must act, and quickly. We must leave Spezia–the only question is, where shall we go? Even if Byron brings the *Bolivar* tonight, it may be too risky to go down to the shore, given that the remaining *banditti* are scouring San Terenzo for this fellow. We have a chance to strike inland and make our way to Pisa–I say that we should take it."

"We'd have to hire horses," Walton said, "and carriages too, if we intend to save any of this apparatus. If we can defend ourselves until daylight..."

"We'll get no help from the authorities," Taaffe said. "They sent Masi to deliver that message in brutal fashion. They had no idea what we were planning to do, but they simply didn't want us here. If we fight the *banditti* we'll do it alone, and if anyone's to pay the law for the blood that's shed, it's likely to be us."

"Patou might have been wise to set sail for some remote island," Frankenstein muttered. "I tried to do the same myself, once, but Scotland was not remote enough."

"It's your decision, Victor," Trelawny said. "If you say the word, we'll fight."

"Going inland wouldn't save us," Walton said. "Pisa is full of Churchmen. This one may be a rogue element, but..."

"There's not a man in Italy whose hand would not be raised against you if he knew what you were about," Malo de Treguern shouted, insistently. "The Church has its reasons for discretion, but if you force its hand, anathema will be declared against you."

"What about Shelley?" Ned put in, although he knew that his intervention might be far from welcome. "Do you propose to abandon him?"

"Byron's bringing the *Bolivar*," Walton said. "He and Williams can take ship if they wish, with their wives and servants. If not, they'll still have the *Don Juan*."

"Setting to sea too soon might be the death of Shelley and his wife," Ned objected. "What hope will there be for them, if Frankenstein is not on hand to intervene?"

The man of science turned to look at Ned then, his tearful and bloodshot eyes full of anguish. "I am not ready!" he said, hoarsely. "I wish to God that I were, but *I am not ready*."

"He's talking about his state of mind, not his apparatus," Lazarus put in. "We could get that ready in a matter of hours–except that we don't seem to have hours to spare. *I* am ready, though, Mr. Knob–will you follow my lead, no matter what these men decide to do?"

Ned was astonished by this, but he tried not to show it. "If Shelley grows worse," he said, "and there's a chance of saving him, then I'll seize it–no matter what the risks might be."

"Even a man with no religion ought not ally himself with the Devil," said Malo de Treguern, sententiously.

"It might be General Mortdieu who had the right of it, after all," Ned murmured, distinctly enough to be heard. In a louder voice, he added: "But we are here, and must make our stand in Spezia or San Terenzo. I'll gladly follow Lazarus, if he has a plan, and I'm sure that the vampire's minion will do likewise. With four more men to support us, with or without a hostage, I'll wager that we can put the *banditti* to flight–and we can certainly defend Casa Magni thereafter, even if the *Bolivar* takes several days to come to our aid. If the worst comes to the worst, we'd still have the *Don Juan*. I say that we should make a stand, win the fight, and then take the equipment down to Casa Magni–if we can."

Trelawny snorted at the mention of Shelley's boat, suggesting that his opinion of the *Don Juan*'s seaworthiness was no higher than Guido's, but he did not protest against the whole of Ned's speech, despite having been the proponent of the opposite plan. It was Frankenstein who took exception to the notion of following his creature's lead.

"Am I cursed to be haunted forever?" the man of science demanded. "I'm for Pisa, and thence to God knows where–the East, perhaps. India, or the Ile de France."

"You'll never replace and replenish your apparatus there," Walton objected. "We are bound to civilization, if only by technical necessity. Best to head north, don't you think? To Protestant lands where warrior monks will find no sympathy at all. The most important thing is not to be divided. The dwarf's right about one thing–together, we might force the bandits to retreat. If we split up, we'll surely play into their hands."

"To Casa Magni, then!" Ned said. "Lock up the laboratory, so that we can recover the equipment later, but let's be on our way, while we still have a chance of taking the enemy unawares and driving them down the hill into the sea." Lazarus made no objection to Ned voicing this plan, having presumably recognized that his own voice roused reflexive opposition.

"Victor?" said Trelawny, again deferring to the scientist, but with an edge in his voice that testified to his change of mind.

Frankenstein looked at Lazarus, with an eerie dread in his eyes–but in the end, he said: "Very well. We should not desert Shelley, however meager the help might be that we can offer him..."

He would certainly have said more, but the door to the laboratory opened at that moment to reveal John Hay, in a state of high anxiety. "You'd best come immediately," he said. "We're surrounded–and they seem to be demanding a parley."

Chapter Nine
The Power of Desire

When John Hay declared that the house was "surrounded," Ned took the inference–as everyone else presumably did–that the remainder of Malo de Treguern's hirelings had returned from the shore. The Hospitaller certainly jumped to that conclusion, for he was seized by a visible thrill of excitement and triumph. It was he who led the charge to the main door, and no one sought to hold him back, preferring to shelter behind him for the moment–but when he arrived at the door and flung it wide open, Treguern stopped in confusion just beyond the threshold, utterly nonplussed by the sight that met his eyes.

Frankenstein and Walton hung back warily, while Lazarus maintained his usual careful discretion, but Hay had already stepped outdoors and Ned had to step out too in order to see what was happening–with the result that he and Malo de Treguern ended up side by side, while Trelawny moved tentatively out on one flank and Hay on the other.

The house did, indeed, appear to be literally surrounded—but not by any mere dozen bandits strung out along the hedge and lurking in the olive grove. Ned could not count the crowd, but it looked to be at least a hundred strong. Many, but not all, of its members were armed with guns or blades, but there were women and children there as well as men, and the attitude of the whole did not seem to be menacing. In the immediate instance, at least, they seemed quite content to watch and wait.

The townspeople of Spezia, Ned realized—or a substantial fraction of their number—had abandoned their habitual reserve, and had stopped pretending that they and their English guests were living in parallel worlds. For a moment or two, he assumed that they had simply become impatient with the armed *banditti* running through their streets, and wanted to put an end to the private battle that had flared up on the edge of their town—but then he realized that he was quite mistaken, and that the truth was far more complicated.

There was a moment's pause before Malo de Treguern seized the initiative, and began haranguing the crowd in what seemed to Ned to be very fluent Italian. Ned could not understand that language well enough to follow every detail of what the warrior monk was saying, but he knew that Treguern was calling them to action, appealing to them as loyal Catholics. The former Knight of Malta demanded that the people of Spezia should seize the demon, the necromancer and their English lackeys, and deliver them, bound and helpless, into the care of the Church's designated representatives.

It took at least three minutes for the rant to falter, but Treguern finally realized that he was not getting any response.

Someone stepped forward then from the group clustered about the gate. He spoke too rapidly for Ned to be able to grasp all of what he was saying, but there were others in Walton's party who knew even less Italian than he, and they looked at one another in anxious bewilderment until Trelawny took it upon himself to translate.

"They're demanding to see the man who has been raised from the dead," Trelawny said, uncertainly. "I don't understand..."

"I believe that I do," said Lazarus, mildly. He had to step past Walton and Frankenstein as well as the advance party, but no one attempted to interrupt him as he moved forward. "Bring me a lantern," he ordered.

Ned ran back into the house in search of the brightest lantern he could find, and hurried back with it. The Grey Man was now standing three paces ahead of Malo de Treguern, and Ned went to stand beside him, holding the lantern as high as he could.

Lazarus did not say anything, at first, but merely removed his hat. He was no longer wearing his scarf over the lower part of his face, but he unwound it from his neck, and opened his shirt to display his torso. He held up his gloveless hands, fingers widespread. After displaying himself for a few seconds, he began to speak, in a calm and measured fashion. His Italian seemed to be almost as fluent as Treguern's.

Ned understood that the Grey Man was telling the crowd something of his history, and that he was referring repeatedly to Victor Frankenstein as a great man: not a necromancer but a miracle-worker. He understood, too, that the principal reason for the speech was to assure the crowd that a man returned from the dead could, in fact, speak, with all the intelligence that might be expected of a cultured person. The Grey Man did, however, take the trouble to warn them that he was not representative of those who had so far returned from the dead, and that many of the others were stupid and confused.

It was at that moment that Malo de Treguern realized, belatedly, what was happening. The Churchman began shouting again, but Ned knew that the argument was already lost. At first, that seemed astounding—but he immediately began to see the logic of the situation. In the gloom, he picked out the three men beside the gate who were carrying dead bodies in their arms—three *banditti*, who had been struck down in the ferocious struggle that had take place half an hour before. Bandits, he realized, were no different from other men in having mothers and grandmothers, brothers and cousins. Outlaws the dead men might have become, unable to return wholly to the bosom of society following the years they had spent as guerillas, but they had been born in the neighborhood and it was not simply their reputation as heroes that kept them safe when they came into town. Few of their former neighbors returned their salutes nowadays, but everyone who had known them as children felt entitled to take an interest in their deaths—and Malo de Treguern had made certain when he first employed them that everyone would come to know the cause for which they had recklessly given their lives.

Ned did not doubt for a moment that the people in the crowd were good Catholics—as good, in their own quiet fashion, as Malo de Treguern—but they were also veterans, again in their own quiet fashion, of the war into which Napoleon Bonaparte had plunged the whole of Europe. Although Spezia bore no obvious cannon-scars, the order of these people's lives had been rudely overturned, and peace had not restored it to its former clarity. They were, as Ned had earlier observed, still *stunned* by the experience, uncertain as to what the future might hold, and what they ought to expect or demand of it.

In simple terms, the people of Spezia—or those among them who has taken the trouble to put a stop to the latest battle waged by foreigners on their soil—had withheld the judgment that Malo de Treguern found so easy to make. They believed in God, in the Devil, and in necromancy and miracles too, but the idea that there was a man in their midst who had raised the dead, and was eager to repeat the experiment, had not aroused in them the kind of reflexive horror that it struck into men like Treguern. They had dead men of their own on hand, and they wanted to put Frankenstein to the test. They were not about to descend upon his house like a mad mob, to put its inhabitants to the sword and its furniture to the torch. They were in a very different mood. They wanted to know whether Victor Frankenstein really could do what was claimed–and, if so, they wanted him to do it *for them*.

"We have all been too fearful," Ned murmured, addressing himself primarily to Lazarus, although the others were able to hear him now that Treguern's tirade was dissolving into inarticulate confusion for a second time. "The world is already changed. Whatever people in authority might dread, common people are not so foolish."

"I am not ready," Frankenstein said, fretfully. "I cannot do as they ask."

"You certainly cannot refuse them," Lazarus said. "They will be patient if they see that we are making what effort we can, but we must certainly make what effort we can. Ready or not, we must attempt to resurrect those three men. The crowd may well be tolerant if we are not wholly successful, but they will not brook cowardice and will be direly disappointed by total failure. We must all work together, as hard as we can, and our many hands must make swift progress. These people will protect us while we work from any further interference– and that is a security to be treasured, however brief it might prove to be."

Frankenstein opened his mouth again, but did not speak. After a pause, he nodded his head. He knew that he had no alternative.

Lazarus spoke to the crowd again. He asked them to bring the three dead men into the house, and he went on to ask a great deal more than that. Ned did not even try to follow the details. Instead, he confronted Malo de Treguern, and said to him, in French: "You must not waste time in further protest, my friend. You must seize this chance, even if you cannot yet see it as anything more than a chance to see necromancy in action. You need not help us, and cannot hinder us, but you have an opportunity now that has not been granted to any man since the first Lazarus rose and walked."

The Churchman looked at him bleakly. "I have spent more time in the company of revenants than you can know," he said.

"Perhaps you have," Ned said, "but even you, aged and wizened as you are, might live long enough to see a world in which revenants are familiar to everyone, and death has lost its dominion on Earth, as well as in Heaven."

Malo de Treguern stared at the crowd again, as if he were now beginning to absorb the implications of its gathering and its attitude. All of humankind was there, in microcosm, and the understanding seemed for a moment to be dawning in him that the mass of men, faced by a real possibility, would welcome a new way to defy death. Then his expression changed, though. "This is the Devil's work," he told Ned, stubbornly. "No good can come of it, and much evil must. You have no notion of what you are doing, boy. Had you a religion, and a mind unperverted by silly lies, you would have recognized this Victor Frankenstein as the prophesied Antichrist, and you would have shielded your eyes against his seductions."

"Be that as it may," Ned said, with a sigh, "you would do well to observe what happens. Now, I have work to do and no time to waste. In the past, I have only witnessed a resurrection; now I must help to contrive a whole series on them. I am very glad to have the opportunity."

"Imp of Satan!" was the warrior monk's reply to that. "Hell shall claim you all!"

Given that the bulk of the equipment that Frankenstein had gathered was not even unpacked, there was a great deal of work to be done, and it had to be admitted that the many hands available to help him did not make such light work as Lazarus has hoped. Indeed, the presence of so many inexperienced hands in a restricted space led to a good deal of clumsiness and confusion. The lack of clear and efficient leadership made the problem worse.

Initially, everyone looked to Frankenstein to take the lead in imposing order upon the chaos, determining what had to be done, by whom, and according to what timetable, but Frankenstein was too distracted to play the general. When Lazarus took it upon himself to assume command, Frankenstein was not the only one who seemed unready to obey him, but Ned weighed in again, taking the Grey Man's orders and relaying them. The Englishmen, at least, seemed willing to do as he said, perhaps telling themselves that he was, after all, an agent of their King.

Once the work was well underway, in a reasonably disciplined fashion, Frankenstein began to lose his hectic manner and warm to the task in hand. Gradually, and without opposition, he took back his stolen authority. He had to send the townspeople scurrying to their homes and workplaces to bring him tin baths and various household implements, and to plunder more electrical cells from the ships in dock, but they were ready enough to help. The laboratory gradually filled up with apparatus that was carefully assembled into intricate networks. The assemblies looked untidy and rather precarious, but there was a stern order within the makeshift, and Ned felt confident that the delicately-poised towers of acid-filled batteries were fit for purpose.

For the first few hours, everyone involved in the project toiled together, but Walton eventually had to devise a shift pattern that prevented Frankenstein's helpers from getting in one another's way and allowed them time to rest. For the whole of the night and most of the morning the breaks, they took were short, but as the *siesta* hour approached it became obvious that everyone was in need of sleep. Taaffe, Hay, Walton and Trelawny were dispatched by turns to the villa's bedrooms, and in mid-afternoon Ned finally consented to be sent back to the hotel, with instructions not to return for at least four hours. Ned was quite ready by then to obey this command in letter and spirit alike, and he was not best pleased to find Guido waiting for him in his room.

"This," Guido said, shaking is head slowly to signify his incredulity, "is not a situation that my master could ever have anticipated. Had it really been the case, I suppose, that a vampire's bite could confer a kind of conditional immortality, his kind might not have been forced by idiot superstition to lurk in the shadows, but the Age of Enlightenment has not yet begun to penetrate the mysteries surrounding them. If only you could have persuaded Frankenstein to come with me..."

"You would have had to persuade me first," Ned said, grimly. "Your master does not seem to lack friends and loyal servants, who do not seem to fear him any more than servants usually fear an exacting master."

"You should not judge me as typical," Guido replied. "If I appear uncommonly cheerful and content, that's partly because I am so far away from him. If I like my work, that's because it so often takes me away. You are not mistaken, though–because I know what he really is, I am not prey to the same exaggerated dread as the greater number of my fellows. I know that he does not really feed on blood, any more than the South Sea islanders are really cannibals... but he is not a noble and innocently virtuous individual, either, as Rousseau would have us believe that men unspoiled by civilization would be."

"He will be able to step into the daylight soon enough," Ned said. "The Grey Men will not have to hide themselves away much longer."

"Don't be too optimistic," Guido said. "You have not yet seen the outcome of your current experiment. You know well enough, I think, how exceptional Frankenstein's Adam is."

"The process is in dire need of perfection," Ned agreed, "but once experiments can be carried out on a grand scale, in adequate security, progress will be swift."

"And within two or three generations," Guido said, skeptically, "the reanimated dead will outnumber the living, and will set the world to rights. We've a great deal of trouble to endure, my friend, before the empires of the living will condescend to live alongside the empires of the dead. These Tuscan craftsmen may want their beloved stray sheep back, but do you really believe that they would rejoice in the news that Bonaparte and all his hawkish generals might return? Not, you understand, that I am making the mistake of assuming that your General Mortdieu *is* Bonaparte, merely because he is dwelling in Bonaparte's dead body."

"It seems that our alliance has been a modest success after all," Ned observed, mildly, "despite its shaky start. We are scattering our secrets recklessly now–but I'd like to know a good deal more about your master before I agree to act as his emissary and spokesman."

"I dare say that we still have a few secrets in reserve," Guido said. "We are spies after all. I'd like to know a good deal more about *your* second paymaster, before I make him an offer of amity on my master's behalf."

"I don't even know the name of your vampire," Ned pointed out, feeling obliged to play the careful diplomat, in spite of his physical exhaustion.

"He calls himself Szandor, and poses as a Count–but I do not suppose that the name and the title were his before he died. That does not matter–you must have discovered by now that men successfully resurrected from the dead do not consider themselves to be the same men they were when they were alive."

Ned had, in fact, taken due note of the fact that "Lazarus" preferred a obvious pseudonym to the name he had owned in life. "The world is overfull of imaginary Counts," he said, still dutifully beating around the bush. "What the French Revolutionaries began, Bonaparte completed–the old aristocracy is gone, and the new one is open to anyone who can make his claim persuasive. I do want to open negotiations with you, on behalf of Comte Henri de Belcamp–which is only one of my own employer's many names–but I wonder whether it can wait until I've had a few hours' sleep. My first priority is to be able to work as hard and efficiently as I can to make Frankenstein's new experiment a success. May we postpone the remainder of this conversation until tomorrow?"

"Yes, if that's your wish. You do seem very tired. If the Tuscan army puts in an appearance, though, I might be forced to retreat. If so, tell Frankenstein, his Grey Adam and your Comte that my Count would be very interested in a meeting, to discuss matters of mutual interest. Paris might be the most suitable venue. I'll find you again, when I can."

"Do you think the Tuscan army is likely to intervene?" Ned asked.

"They are a good deal more likely to do so now that half of Spezia has taken up arms," Guido told him. "A few foreigners dabbling in conspiracy can be regarded as a matter of marginal concern, but local populations forming associations of self-interest is something else. Don't get carried away by your enthusiasm, Monsieur Knob. You might be full of optimism just now, because of the strange turn that events have taken here, but the Church has sharper blades than Malo de Treguern, and the many political wounds inflicted by the war are still very sore. The individuals we represent must make what alliances they can against the new crusade. You and I must try to keep in touch."

"I'll do my best," Ned agreed. "Is your Count Szandor also interested in meeting Gregory Temple, then?"

"I suspect that Temple and his political masters will be more ready to align themselves with Treguern, for all that they are Protestants. For the time being, it will surely be sufficient to bring the parties I named together."

"Do you know how Shelley is?" Ned asked, abruptly.

"Bearing up, I believe. No worse, at any rate. His wife is said to be improving too–but it's too soon to tell whether or not they'll need Frankenstein's services, as it's too soon to tell whether he'll still be able to offer them this time tomorrow. You'd better sleep now–I'll try to find out what the other Hospitaller is doing, and hinder him if I can."

The rival spy left by means of the door, his slippered feet making hardly any noise on the wooden stairway as he went downstairs. Ned drank a cupful of water and then lay down on his bed, fully dressed. Exhaustion sent him to sleep without delay, in spite of the fact that he had not eaten for more than 24 hours.

Chapter Ten
Between Death and Life

By the time Ned was able to return to Walton's house, dusk was falling. The crowd surrounding the grounds parted silently to let him through. He found Malo de Treguern sitting on the step of the main door, haggard and dispirited. The warrior monk did not reply to Ned's polite greeting.

The stove in Frankenstein's laboratory was blazing, and the room was exceedingly hot, although the French windows opening to the rear of the house had been thrown open to the light breeze that drifted down the steep hillside towards the cooling waters of the Ligurian Sea. Trelawny, Walton and Hay were all in the garden outside, talking in low voices.

All the carefully-stacked supportive apparatus had now been established around the three large enameled bathtubs in the center of the room. The wires carrying the electrical fluid had been gathered into clumps and tied in bundles, but still seemed to be running back and forth in chaotic confusion. Only a few of them were attached to the arrays electrodes immersed in the liquid that each bath contained. Lazarus and Frankenstein were working steadily to put the final touches on this phase of the labor, apparently in perfect harmony.

Ned was delighted to see the Grey Man and his maker united in their purpose. The man of science no longer seemed haunted or unready for anything; he was fully absorbed in his quest again, working with calm determination. Lazarus was at ease too, as if this were his vocation too–as well it might be, Ned supposed, given that he was bravely working for the better future of his own kind in a hostile world.

The apparatus Ned had seen in Patou's cellar in Purfleet had seemed makeshift enough, but the many polished relics of James Graham's pretentious "Temples of Health and Hygiene" that Patou had acquired had given the ensemble a certain style and grandeur, and the cellar itself had been large enough to allow the individual units to be sensibly spaced out. There was no style or grandeur here; all the equipment communicated an impression of hasty improvisation, and the sitting-room that had adapted for use as a laboratory seemed decidedly cramped and inappropriately overcrowded now that so much metal and so many ponderous ceramic vessels had been accumulated within it.

The viscous liquid in the baths was conspicuously darker in hue than the fluid Ned had seen in Patou's baths, but it did not seem, as yet, to be alive in its own right. Patou's life-endowing fluid had resembled brightly streaming protoplasm observed with the assistance of strong light and a magnifying lens, but this was more like sullen molasses accumulated in the gutters of a sugar refinery.

The three dead bodies had not yet been immersed in the baths; they were still laid out on a table adjacent to the wall opposite the French windows. Their congealed blood had been re-liquefied and drained from their bodies into huge jars; while Ned watched, waiting to discover whether there was anything his hands and mind could usefully contribute, Frankenstein set about replacing it with a different fluid, whose function was not to embalm the bodies but to assist in their revitalization.

Lazarus stood up and nodded to Ned. "It looks ugly," he said, "but I believe that it will work." The Grey Man's voice now had a tremor of anxious excitement in it, but there was none of the nervous agitation that possessed Frankenstein.

"What do you want me to do?" Ned asked.

"Help Frankenstein with the injections," Lazarus said. "Your fingers are nimbler than mine, and he's almost ready to drop."

Ned moved to do as he was asked. The bodies were largely unmarked. Ned recognized the one Guido had strangled and the one whose throat Lazarus had crushed. The third man had been stabbed in the heart, but the wound was not gaping, and seemed as if might disappear altogether if its edges were carefully placed together.

Frankenstein looked up as Ned appeared by his side. "This requires expert hands," the scientist said. "Thank you, but I'd better do it myself." In the end, though, once Ned had watched him subject the first body to the necessary preparations, he reluctantly accepted that his weariness was beginning to get the better of him, and contented himself with watching Ned repeat the operation twice more under his instruction.

I am a resurrectionist now! Ned thought, exultantly. *I am a true collaborator in the great work. I have surely seen and understood enough, now, to direct such an operation myself, when the need and opportunity arise.* He knew that he was assuming and claiming a little too much, but his spirit was over-full of enthusiasm and ambition.

"When you're done," Frankenstein told him, "we must place the bodies in the fluid. After that, there'll be little to do but wait, and hope. With luck, at least one or two of them will recover some semblance of life–and we shall have to pray that the crowd outside find enough to satisfy them in that appearance." His voice became noticeably less robust as this speech was concluded; the man of science seemed to be faltering in his resolve again now that his work was almost complete. When Ned finally set the last syringe down and turned to look at his instructor, he saw a slight flash of resentment in Frankenstein's bloodshot eyes. It was as if Frankenstein saw something in Ned's fervent determination to carry the resurrectionist cause forward that made him jealous.

Ned went back to Lazarus, who was testing the tangled wiring. "Will there be sufficient electrical fluid?" Ned asked.

"We must hope so," the Grey Man replied, in a low voice. "Frankenstein's provision in that regard was barely adequate, but the extra batteries the townspeople secured should give us a margin for error. My maker has concentrated his recent research on the chemical aspects of the revivifying process, as is only to be expected."

"Why is that?" Ned asked.

The Grey Man hesitated momentarily, but then said: "Because the resurrection of the dead can only be a preliminary and partial goal, so far as he is concerned. His ultimate objective has always been the preservation of the living against the possibility of death, to the extent that such preservation might be possible."

"The discovery of an elixir of life, you mean?"

"Yes—or, perhaps, an elixir of metamorphosis, which would permit a living body to remake its own substance, greatly augmenting its resilience in respect of disease and injury."

"Alchemists and magicians sought such a device in vain for centuries," Ned reminded him.

"Their chemistry was fatally flawed. They had not even begun to understand the chemistry of life. We have only made a beginning, even now, but at least we have begun. I am the living proof of the rewards that may flow from progress yet to be made. Let us hope that we can show the people outside a little more, while they are still hungry for it. They have opened a window of opportunity for us, and it will be a tragedy if we cannot keep it open. If Frankenstein were able to continue to work here in peace, under the protection of his neighbors, it would be very advantageous to our cause."

"I admire your optimism," murmured a newcomer to their conversation, "but conspicuous success in this endeavor might prove more disastrous than total failure."

Ned looked round, and found himself looking up into Robert Walton's anxious eyes. "In what way?" he asked.

"As King George's spy, you should understand that quite well," Walton told him, bitterly. "If Victor's method demonstrates its worth publicly, at this relatively early stage in his research, the Church's objections to necromancy will be the least of our problems. Do you think that the Tuscan authorities, or any other government, will be content to let us be, so that we may revive bandits and the poor? What do you think the fate would have been of any alchemist who actually discovered the rudiments of a method of making gold or the elements of a technique that might deliver immortality? It was not for fear of madmen like Treguern that we set out to operate in secret, but for fear of possessive monopolists who might fight for our custody like starving dogs over a joint of meat, in order to reserve the proceeds of our further progress for their own profit. Whatever the result of this experiment is, we need to get out of here and vanish as soon as we can." The last remark was aimed at Lazarus, who could not now be excluded from Walton's narrow conception of "we."

"Guido seems to be thinking along the same lines," Ned said, uneasily.

"We can surely deal with properly constituted authorities by diplomatic means," Lazarus said to Walton. "We may yet have cause to be thankful that we have a representative of His Majesty's government here."

Remembering what Guido had said about the side that Gregory Temple and his political masters might take, Ned was not so sure that His Majesty's government would be behind him, or even that it would be as readily amenable to diplomacy as the Grey Man naively assumed–but he did not say so.

"Time is on our side now," Lazarus said, "provided that Treguern's companion cannot summon reinforcements."

"The Tuscan Light Horse is a greater danger by far," Walton opined. "A detachment could ride from Pisa in a matter of hours. They already have a score to settle with us, and might not be in a mood to negotiate. If they do come, Trelawny, Taaffe and Hay agree with me that the vital thing is to spirit you and Frankenstein away–on the *Bolivar* if that is possible, the *Don Juan* if not."

"San Terenzo is conveniently close," Ned observed, addressing himself to Lazarus, "for a man who can walk freely and at his leisure. In a chase or a hunt, as you've already had occasion to notice, the same distance might seem a very long way."

"It's the only escape route we have," Walton stated, baldly. "What's King George's position on the matter, Mr. Knob? Would he rather we surrendered to the local authorities, or that we killed a few in making good our escape?" He spoke the King's name with a contemptuous curl of his lip. Ned knew that the King and Lord Byron had once been on good terms, in the days when the Prince had not yet surrendered himself completely to a life of idle debauchery, but no one seemed to like him now that he had ascended to the throne.

"In His Majesty's absence," Ned said, airily, "I must obviously act on my own initiative. I'll help you, to the extent that I can–but I'd rather we didn't have to kill anyone, if that's possible, even if we are forced to run."

"Good," said Walton. "I'll pass the word along." He turned and strode back through the open French windows, leaving Lazarus and Ned to assist Frankenstein in moving the bodies into the tanks. Walton brought his companions in from the garden while the three bodies were being carefully immersed and the electrodes connected. Lazarus and Frankenstein made the final adjustments, and then there was nothing to do but wait.

Lazarus went out to tell the crowd that everything had been done that needed to be done, but that no result could be expected for at least 12 hours, and perhaps 24.

The crowd began to disperse, but left a cohort behind that was more than sufficient to form a cordon around the house. These guardians did not prevent John Taaffe from leaving, in order to carry news to Casa Magni, but they grew far more attentive when Frankenstein stepped out for a breath of air, and Ned deduced that they knew exactly what the value of each of their hostages was.

Ned felt duty-bound to go to Frankenstein and say: "If you care to come to England, sir, I can guarantee you the protection of Gregory Temple, who is a man of considerable influence and ability."

"Perhaps you could," Frankenstein said. "The government of Switzerland would probably do more, given that I'm a citizen of Geneva, and I'd be sure of a welcome in Prussia, too–but I'm too much a Calvinist to tolerate overseers of my conscience, whoever they might be."

"I'm a radical myself, sir, despite my profession," Ned said, "and I sympathize with your position."

When Lazarus came back indoors, Ned went to sit with him, and asked the Grey Adam to tell him the true story behind the melodrama of *Frankenstein*. Lazarus did so, and also undertook to complete Ned's practical education in the art and science of resurrection by telling him everything he knew and supposed about the process by which Grey Men were made. All this took several hours, but the new Adam did not pause or hesitate–nor, seemingly, did he hold any anything in reserve. "Take all that to England, if you will," he said, when he had finished. "Make a full report to Gregory Temple, by all means–but if anything should happen to my maker and myself as this particular affair proceeds to its culmination, make sure the information reaches Humphry Davy and Erasmus Darwin. I don't know whether the Royal Society or the Lunar Society will be the better motivated to use it, but one of them must."

"I'll do that," Ned promised.

As with Walton and Trelawny, no move was made to stop Ned when he went back to the hotel again to get something more to eat. He was not so lucky, though, when he tried to leave the dining-room to go back to his bed, for the young men from Sussex were there, making merry before yet another whoring expedition. They knew that something very strange was afoot in the town, and had found out that he was caught up in it.

He told them the truth, in synoptic form, but they laughed uproariously and called him a fine romancer. They, at least, were still trapped within the narrow span of their own limited dimension, which hardly touched the world through which they moved as idle tourists.

"Have you seen Master Shelley at Casa Magni?" one of them asked him. "He could probably make a fine epic poem out of a story like that."

"Where do you suppose the little man got it from?" scoffed another of the good companions. "It's all borrowed from that garish horror tale he published anonymously back in '18."

"No, that was Byron," said yet another, "and it was in '19, in *Blackwood's*."

"The tale of the vampire is another story," Ned said, apologetically, "which I have yet to learn in full. In time, though, lads, in time..." And with that, he contrived to extricate himself from their company, and went back to bed.

Chapter Eleven
The Tuscan Light Horse

Ned did not intend to sleep late, but exhaustion got the better of him again, and the morning sunlight was streaming through his window when he finally staggered out of bed. He bathed and ate a hearty breakfast before making his way yet again to the house behind the olive grove under the harsh light of a blazing Sun that was no more than two hours from its zenith.

He found Frankenstein poring over one of the three corpses, vibrant with excitement, while Walton and Lazarus looked on. "It's definitely working!" the man of science said. "The fluid is beginning to flow in his veins, albeit sluggishly and his flesh is maintaining its consistency remarkably well. Decay had hardly set in, so there's less work to be done..."

"Can you wake him?" Walton asked, impatiently.

"Not yet," said the Grey Man, answering for his maker. "For his sake, it will be better not to hurry."

"I don't care about the bandit," Walton said, brutally. "The point is to satisfy that mob, and get out of here while we can. It might be better if he doesn't recover his wits, in my opinion. How soon will he be in a fit state to put on parade?"

Frankenstein pursed his lips, but made no comment on Walton's attitude. He pushed his right hand into the slimy liquid again to test the flesh of the dead man's arm.

"The signs of life he's showing won't be sustainable outside the fluid for six hours, at least," the man of science opined. "Even then, he might not be able to walk or talk if we hauled him out. We have to leave him immersed until dusk, at least."

Walton consulted his watch. Dusk, Ned knew, was a full nine hours away. "Time for a division of the infantry to arrive in force," Walton muttered, "let alone a detachment of cavalry–but we wouldn't be wise to make a move before nightfall, unless it's absolutely necessary. I can't stand all this *waiting*, though."

"Go to Casa Magni, then," said Frankenstein. "The crowd won't bar your way. Change the dressing on Shelley's wound. Comfort Mary–and tell Williams to be ready to put to sea at a moment's notice."

Walton shook his head. He was determined to stay. If trouble did materialize, that would be the time for him to assume command.

Once the night became dark, Ned knew, Gregory Temple's courier would return to the hotel, expecting to collect another report. At the same time–or a little beforehand, if his ship had caught a favorable wind–Henri de Belcamp's courier would station himself on the approach to the quay at much the same time. The thought of encoding everything he had to write, twice over, was distinctly tiresome, although he knew that he ought to send some word, in case he did not get the chance again. Assuming that he still had time in hand, though, he went out of the main door into the sunlight. Malo de Treguern was still sitting on the step, as if he were hoping that God might somehow contrive to send down a lightning-bolt from the cloudless sky, to obliterate the Antichrist's lair.

"Have you had anything to eat, Brother Malo?" Ned asked him, sitting down beside him.

"I have fasted for 40 days and 40 nights in my time," the ex-Knight of Malta informed him, stiffly.

"They will let you leave, I think," Ned said. "It's only Frankenstein and the Grey Man they're holding prisoner, and Walton won't try to hold you any longer against your will. You'll probably find your friend waiting for you in San Terenzo–although I'm surprised that he hasn't come here to make sure that you're unhurt."

"You will not obtain any advantage by pretended amity," Treguern told him, bluntly.

Ned ignored the rebuke. "You think he's gone for help, then," he said, as if thinking aloud. "But where to? Not to Rome, that's for sure. *Civitas Solis* had convents within a day's ride of Paris, but I doubt that the same is true of any Italian city."

Mention of *Civitas Solis* made Treguern turn his head slightly to look more sharply at his interlocutor, but the warrior monk was as good as his word, and gave nothing away.

"It would not be unprecedented for two orders of the Church to be at loggerheads," Ned went on, "especially when one, at least, could easily be deemed heretical. On the other hand, you seem to me to be every inch the scholar, probably as conscientiously esoteric in his chosen fields of study as Victor Frankenstein. If I were to guess, I'd guess that the relic of the Order of St. John is now under the protection and supervision of the revitalized *Civitas Solis*–unlike my old friend John Devil, whose application for membership was probably rejected, although a certain Jesuitical caution might have prevented your masters from telling him outright. On the other hand, *Civitas Solis* may be a mere myth, like vampires and the elixir of life, unworthy of serious consideration by intelligent men."

Treguern deigned to comment at last. "A buzzing fly," he said. "The slightest irritation imaginable."

"You are entitled to your opinion of me," Ned said, equably, "but I'm not an unreasonable man, Brother Malo. Even though I have no religion, I'm also a passably virtuous one. If and when you find out where the *Outremort* has made landfall, I have information to trade that might make it worth your while to let me in on the secret. I'm usually in London or Paris, and will not be too hard to find in either city for a man with your resources."

"I have spent more time than I deserved in the company of revenants, working patiently for the fulfillment of prophecies," Treguern said, enigmatically but with perfect equanimity. "I'm an old man, and my time of rest cannot be long delayed–but if God still has work for me to do, then he will succor me. You'd do well to be wary, if you're as easy to find as you say."

"I'm sure that the Lord will lend you the assistance you need," Ned told him. "Remember, though, that He works in mysterious ways. Given the company you've been keeping of late, death might be no more than a punctuation mark in the ongoing story of your life, and you might be required to do the Lord's work for a long time thereafter. The road to Heavenly indolence might not be as easy to negotiate as you presently suppose."

That finally got an emotional reaction from the Churchman. "Vile korrigan!" he exclaimed–but then the expression in his fiery eyes changed from wrath to exultation as he saw something beyond the hedge. Ned immediately stood up to see what it was.

It was as if a flock of birds with impossibly ornate tails were fluttering in the unkempt branches at the crown of the hedge. It required two seconds and an anxious murmur from the waiting crowd for Ned to realize that they were actually the plumes of military helmets.

The Tuscan Light Horse had arrived.

Ned promptly turned back to Malo de Treguern, and contrived to pronounce the single syllable "Don't..." before he realized how futile any such plea would be.

Having lost the loyalty of his hirelings and failed to sway the Spezian mob, the soldier in God's Army still had high hopes of claiming the loyal support of a secular military unit. He had already come to his feet and was drawing in a deep breath.

Ned did not linger, but darted inside the house, calling for Walton and Trelawny. This time, he knew, the Grey Man would not be the right spokesman to represent the conspiracy.

By the time Walton had run outside, though, followed by Trelawny, Malo de Treguern had already embarked upon his new clarion call–and he was more in control of himself now than he had been when he had ranted at the sullen crowd in the gloom.

The officer in charge of the cavalry detachment had been followed through the gate by three other riders, but once he had come to a halt, there was no room on the path for any more, so the others were grouping in the narrow lane beyond the hedge. The members of the loosely-knit crowd, somewhat circumspect in the presence of bright uniforms and sturdy sabers, had hesitated between pressing forward and retreating into the shadows; they had already sacrificed the opportunity to seem intimidatingly resolute.

Malo de Treguern pointed a bony finger at Walton, rattling out a string of accusations that had nothing to do with necromancy. Ned knew that the cavalrymen were already ill-disposed towards the Englishmen, even though it had been their own man who had picked the quarrel some weeks before. In all probability, none of these riders knew that Masi had been acting under orders, and they very probably had their own ideas as to what had happened and why. Malo de Treguern knew all of that too, and know how to make his pitch to the mind of officialdom.

Walton ran forward and began to shout as loudly as Treguern, denying the accusations leveled against him and demanding to be left in peace. Ned had enormous difficulty following the overlapping tirades, but he understood well enough when Treguern set off on a new tack, complaining about the desecration of the bodies of good Italians and good Catholics, and demanding that the corpses be recovered for proper burial. Walton immediately launched into a stream of protest, but Ned could see that the pre-emptive strike had taken effect on both the officer and his men.

The crowd realized that too, and its ringleaders made a belated decision to exercise its power–but the artisans had delayed too long to make any effective attempt to demonstrate conclusively that they were the superior force and the ultimate arbiters of the situation, and thus deter the soldiers from any belligerence. When the Spezians attempted to gather in a tentatively threatening manner, the Pisan calvarymen were quick to draw their sabers and muster a formation.

There was a brief moment when the crowd's ringleaders might have drawn back, to form their own men up in quasi-military ranks and put on a countervailing display of potential strength, which might have made the officer pause to reflect–but the moment was lost. The mounted soldiers urged their horses forward, as they had probably done a dozen times before when breaking up crowds in Pisa, fully expecting the men on foot to scatter and run. The Spezians were, however, made of sterner stuff.

Ned wanted to join in the shouting, in order to beg the men of Spezia to mass by the door of the house and block the entrance, but his Italian was not up to the task, and he could not have made himself heard even if they had been willing and able to listen to him. The Tuscan Light Horse had evidently been given grounds for a grudge or two in their time, and as soon as the impression was created that they were actually attacking the common people, with no good reason and without sufficient numbers to be sure of victory, the incipient conflict turned into a disorderly riot.

The officer's reaction–natural enough, on tactical grounds–was to look for a defense. The door of the house stood wide open, with no one to defend it but a handful of unarmed men. The officer yelled an order at his men, and charged straight for it.

It was, unfortunately, a capacious doorway; there was plenty of room for a horse and rider to pass through it, without the rider having to duck too low. Walton was bowled over by the officer's horse. Ned had no alternative but to imitate Trelawny and dive sideways to avoid his thrusting saber and the iron-shod hooves of his mount.

Ned got to his feet as quickly as he could, but there was nothing he could do as five more horses swept past him, one by one. They galloped straight along the corridor towards Victor Frankenstein's laboratory.

Ned had to imagine what would happen when they arrived there, but it was not hard. In his mind's eye, he saw the sturdy but delicately-balanced equipment tumbling, its brittler elements smashing on the tiled floor, and also saw the multitudinous wires dragged hither and yon, ripped from their connections. The baths would not be upset; nor, in all probability, would the calvarymen pause to drag the men who were suspended between death and new life from their fluid in which they were immersed—but all hope of their eventual resurrection was lost now.

The remainder of the cavalry troop was caught up in the seething crowd, whose members were now agitated to fear and fury. There were few screams, and Ned could see that both sides in the battle were exercising a measure of restraint; the horsemen still considered themselves to be engaged in crowd control rather than a massacre, and the men fighting from the crowd were trying to unhorse the soldiers rather than hack them to pieces. Far more bruises were being inflicted than cuts—but even so, the situation was completely out of control. The riot could not be stopped.

Walton barked an order, in English, instructing his own people to execute the emergency scheme he had hatched. There was no alternative. There seemed to be little chance, though, that Frankenstein's friends could form a coherent group in order to protect one another as they retreated in an orderly manner.

Ned ran into the house. The corridor leading to the laboratory was clear now, and there was nothing to obstruct his passage. As he had anticipated, though, the laboratory itself was in a very different state. The horses had passed right through and made their exit by the wide-open French windows, their riders apparently hoping that they might go around the house and tackle the crowd from the rear, but they had done enormous damage as they passed. In the event, three of their riders—including the officer—had been thrown or forced to dismount, and all three were waving their swords in near-panic, although no one was trying to engage them in combat.

Frankenstein, to his credit, had not only stood his ground bravely but was still doing everything he could to defend the baths where the dead men lay. He was screaming at the soldiers, with his empty hands held high to demonstrate that he was unarmed, but his Italian was not good enough for him to make his message clear; the cavalrymen were extremely unsympathetic to his attempts to block their way, even though they had no idea where they ought to be going, or why. The officer would have run the scientist through had Lazarus not snatched his maker away in the nick of time and dragged him towards the French windows.

Ned would have run to help them if he could have done so, but there was too much debris in the way, and his short legs could not bound over it with sufficient alacrity.

Lazarus caught sight of Ned as he was making good his escape, dragging Frankenstein with him. "Run, Ned!" he shouted. "Get clear as best you can!"

It was good advice, and Ned knew it. He turned on his heel and went back the way he had come. Once he was out of the front door, he put his head down and sprinted for the gate. Once he was out of the gate, he headed for the steepest part of the hill and he went down it with all possible speed.

He did not stop running until he reached the shore, by which time he was completely out of breath. He looked around, hoping that he might see Lazarus and Frankenstein, or any one of the others, running behind him—but he found himself alone. He took two or three leaden steps in the direction of San Terenzo, but paused as he realized that help might be available nearer at hand. He hesitated for a full minute—but then he did catch sight of other running men coming towards him, from the direction of Casa Magni. There were at least three, He cursed as he recognized more of Malo de Treguern's *banditti*. He did not suppose that the orders Treguern had given them two nights before had been countermanded.

Mercifully, he had time to give the bandits the slip.

Fortunately, it also turned out that the boat that had brought Henri de Belcamp's courier to collect his latest report had arrived early.

Unfortunately, that was the last stroke of luck he had for quite some time.

Epilogue
At Sea

Ned intended, once the courier's vessel had cleared the harbor, to sail directly to Casa Magni. That did not happen quickly, though, because the harbormaster insisted on delaying the vessel's departure until it had been cleared by customs officers.

The customs officers were not acting on anyone else's orders, and had not the slightest inkling of what had been happening on the hill above Spezia, far beyond their sphere of interest and influence, but simply by carrying out their ordinary functions in their customary manner, they contrived to hold Ned back for several hours. During that interval, the weather changed drastically.

A violent squall blew up—so violent that the boat's master evoked his privilege and refused to put to sea once he was cleared to do so. Ned had authority enough and anger enough to overrule him, but his insistence turned out to be worse than futile—once out of the harbor, the vessel could make no headway at all towards Casa Magni, even though it was a mere mile away, and was blown out to sea instead. By the time the storm had died, as rapidly as it had been born, it was too late. Ned returned to Casa Magni to find the *Don Juan* gone and the house deserted. He lingered for a while, hoping that Guido might be lurking in the vicinity, but in the end, he consented to be borne away westwards.

At Genoa, Ned wrote his report and translated it into code—once only—for the benefit of Gregory Temple. He took it to a dispatch office in the city which handled large volumes of material sent to England by tourists, and entrusted it to the mail-coach. By that time, 48 hours had passed since the vessel had left Spezia, having been forced to put into Riomaggiore to pick up supplies that the captain had not had time to load upon departure. That particular delay proved something of a small blessing, though. The Italian courier, who was no stranger to waterfront inns, was able to collect rumors regarding the sensational events in Spezia in Riomaggiore that would not have troubled the more urbane gossips of Genoa. Once the more flagrant fantasies had been discarded, those rumors had allowed him to amend and augment his report to a judicious degree.

What Ned wrote to Gregory Temple, in the clear version, was: *VF forced to abandon new experiment and flee following arrest attempt by Tuscan cavalry, urged on by Malo de Treguern, once Knight of Malta—please investigate. VF's first resurrectee joined company; fled with his maker. No reported English casualties.* Bolivar *and* Don Juan *both put out to sea, carrying most or all of conspirators, but all their equipment lost. Destination unknown, but should be possible to identify if enough spies alerted. VF will certainly resume work if possible.* Ned was by no means entirely content with this narrative, but he resisted the temptation to embellish it further. There were some things that he would have to confide to Temple in person.

By the time Ned finally reached London, a full two weeks later, more news had caught up with him, arriving through the orthodox medium of the French daily newspapers.

Percy Shelley and John Williams, in company with one Charles Vivian, it was reported, had set sail in the *Don Juan* from Leghorn on July 8, intending to take the vessel to San Terenzo. Edward Trelawny had intended to accompany them in the *Bolivar*, but had been retained there by the harbormaster. A storm had blown up that afternoon, and Trelawny had been forced to wait until it cleared to set out after his friends. The *Don Juan* had not arrived at San Terenzo, and the boat's dinghy had been washed up at Viareggio, with other debris. Three days later, two bodies had come ashore, one near the tower of Migliarino and the other near Viareggio. Both had been badly damaged and were partly decomposed; they had been buried in quicklime. One of them had been identified as Shelley's by means of a book of poems by John Keats, contained in the pocket of his jacket; the other was assumed to be Williams. A third body was subsequently found, and buried at the mouth of the Serchio. The body identified as Shelley's was subsequently burned on a pyre, although Trelawny was said to have recovered a heart, miraculously unburnt, from the ashes and had preserved it in brandy.

284

Ned felt perfectly sure that these reports were false from beginning to end, and he told Gregory Temple that when he finally came face to face with him in his office in Whitehall.

"For one thing," Ned said, "the *Don Juan* was at San Terenzo on the morning of July 8, not Leghorn, and the *Bolivar* was almost certainly there too. If the two boats encountered the storm, as my own did, they probably encountered it together. Mary Shelley and Jane Williams were in Spezia when I arrived at Casa Magni, having presumably been sent there for safety's sake. Having been entirely uninvolved in the events at Walton's house, it is possible that Percy Shelley and Williams remained there with them, but I feel certain that they would have gone with their companions.

"Assuming that they did put out to sea with Frankenstein and the other members of the company, they must have been taken aboard the *Bolivar* if the *Don Juan* really did run into difficulties, but it seems equally probable to me that the debris was thrown overboard deliberately, to give the impression of a catastrophe that did not, in fact, take place. The intention may well have been to persuade the Tuscan authorities, and Malo de Treguern, that Victor Frankenstein and his first subject had drowned in the storm–although the authorities could hardly be expected to publicize that, whether they believed it or not

"I cannot guess whose the three bodies actually were, but I am sure in my own mind that Shelley, Williams and Frankenstein are all alive. This manifest nonsense about the heart being recovered from the funeral pyre must have been put about for the purposes of dissimulation. Even if they are not alive–even if Shelley had already succumbed to the unfortunate reopening of the wound that Masi had inflicted–I feel sure that his body is safe in Frankenstein's custody, not burned on some Italian beach. Whatever Trelawny has in that jar of brandy, it is certainly not Shelley's heart. It cannot be."

"You're an utter fool, Master Knob," Temple told him. "A spy cannot think like that. He must deal in facts, not Romantic fancies and delusions. In any case, there is no need for us to worry about some miserable poet. The point is to determine whether Frankenstein and his creature are alive. If they do contrive to resume their work, even after some delay, when they have made a discreet landfall, we need to know about it. You made a bad mess of this mission, and I'm sorely disappointed in you. You should have discovered where Frankenstein was bound, even if you had to stow away on the vessel that carried him away from Spezia in order to do it. Now we have to find him all over again. It might not be so easy to stop him in his new location as it would have been in Tuscany."

"Stop him?" Ned queried. "Is that the policy of the King and Parliament? Are they so jealous of their petty privileges that they would preserve death's empire in order not upset their own?"

"No more of that radical talk, imbecile!" Temple told him, sternly. "You work for me now, although you're so ridiculously incompetent that I ought to send you back to play the fool in Jenny Paddock's gin-palace until you rot. The King's desires are your desires, and you'd better not forget that."

"I won't forget it," Ned promised. "Did you investigate Treguern, as I suggested?"

"I've obtained reports on your former Knight of Malta from his native Brittany," Temple told him. "They're agreed that he's a good and heroic man, albeit a little crazed. We can work with him, I think, despite his being a Romanist."

Ned shook his head, slowly, but made no verbal protest. He knew that Henri de Belcamp would not have understood, either, why it was so important that Percy Shelley should not have been lost forever, whether he were dead or alive. Nor would Guido, the vampire's minion, have understood it. None of them understood that it was the poets who were the true legislators of the world. None of them was a true Romantic.

Ned had not included any mention of Guido's vampire master in the report he had sent to Gregory Temple from Genoa, and he renewed his decision not to mention it in Whitehall. This was not because he particularly wanted to keep the vampire's existence secret, but because he did not want to damage his credulity and further than it had already been damaged. He had, however, told Henri de Belcamp about the alleged vampire's request for a meeting, on the grounds that John Devil was a man of far more liberal imagination than his former arch-enemy.

I am on no one's side but my own, now, Ned told himself, when Gregory Temple finally dismissed him from the dingy office, after suggesting disdainfully that he might as well go back to his work with Jenny Paddock's petty theater while awaiting further instructions. *No one's side, that is, but that of the unbound Prometheus. If Shelley is really dead, and there is no one left but me who understands how the world ought to be changed, and must be changed, then I must be the one to direct its metamorphosis.*

END OF PART THREE

Part Four of The Empire of the Necromancers, *"The Vampire in Paris," will appear in* Tales of the Shadowmen 5.

Credits

Captain Future and the Lunar Peril

Starring:	**Created by:**
St. Menoux	René Barjavel
Daniel Crewe	Edmond Hamilton
Erik John Stark	Leigh Brackett
Simon Wright (The Brain)	Edmond Hamilton
Curt Newton (Captain Future)	Edmond Hamilton
Halk Anders	Edmond Hamilton
Grag	Edmond Hamilton
Otho	Edmond Hamilton
Northwest Smith	Catherine L. Moore
Yarol	Catherine L. Moore
Gerry Carlisle	Arthur K. Barnes
Tara of Helium	Edgar Rice Burroughs
Annette Essaillon	René Barjavel
Also Starring:	
Noël Essaillon	René Barjavel
Madame Atomos	André Caroff
The Planets:	
Vulcan	Edmond Hamilton
Mercury	Leigh Brackett
Sha-ardol (Venus)	Catherine L. Moore
Barsoom (Mars)	Edgar Rice Burroughs
Eurobus (Jupiter)	Edgar Rice Burroughs
Cykranosh (Saturn)	Clark Ashton Smith
L'gy'hx (Uranus)	Ramsey Campbell
Yaksh (Neptune)	Clark Ashton Smith
Yuggoth (Pluto)	H.P. Lovecraft
Rhea	Jean de La Hire
Mongo	Alex Raymond
The Moon:	
Michel Ardan	Jules Verne
Selwyn Cavor	H.G. Wells
Baloise, Ingala, Nial	Catherine L. Moore
Moon wolves	Edmond Hamilton
Mars:	
Jekkara	Leigh Brackett

Helium	Edgar Rice Burroughs
The Ahai	Clark Ashton Smith
The Macrocephales	Arnould Galopin

Written by:
Matthew BAUGH is a 43-year-old ordained minister who lives and works in Sedona, Arizona, with his wife Mary and two cats. He is a longtime fan of pulp fiction, cliffhanger serials, old time radio, and is the proud owner of the silent *Judex* serial on DVD. He has written a number of articles on lesser known pop-culture characters like Dr. Syn, Jules de Grandin and Sailor Steve Costigan for the Wold-Newton Universe Internet website. His article on Zorro was published in *Myths for the Modern Age* (2005). He is a regular contributor to *Tales of the Shadowmen.*

Fool Me Once...

Starring:	**Created by:**
Harry Dickson	Anonymous
"Hunter" (his alias)	James Mitchell
M	based on Ian Fleming
The Hautefeuilles	Anonymous
Fascinax	Anonymous
The New Lords of Chaos:	
Numa Pergyll	Anonymous
Leonid Zattan	Jean de La Hire
Dorje	Talbot Mundy
Benedict Stark	Theodore Tinsley
Dr. Natas (a.k.a. Fu Manchu)	Guy d'Armen
	& Sax Rohmer
Dr. Mabuse	Norbert Jacques
Roxor	Harry A. Earnshaw,
	Vera M. Oldham
	& R.R. Morgan

Written by:
Bill CUNNINGHAM is a pulp screenwriter-producer specializing in the DVD market and a regular contributor to *Tales of the Shadowmen*. A recognized authority and speaker on low-budget filmmaking, his website, www.D2DVD.blogspot.com, offers screenwriters and filmmakers useful tips and insight into the DVD industry. He is currently producing the motion pictures *Stainless* and *The Gore Gore Gore-met* with legendary exploitation filmmaker Herschell Gordon Lewis.

The Atomos Affair

Starring:	Created by:
Madame Atomos	André Caroff
Alexander Waverly	Norman Felton & Sam Rolfe
Napoleon Solo	Norman Felton & Sam Rolfe
Ilya Kuryakin	Norman Felton & Sam Rolfe

Written by:
Win Scott ECKERT holds a B.A. in Anthropology and a Juris Doctorate. In 1997, he posted the first site on the Internet devoted to expanding Philip José Farmer's concept of the Wold Newton Family. He is the editor of and contributor to *Myths for the Modern Age: Philip José Farmer's Wold Newton Universe* (2005) and a contributor to *Lance Star, Sky Ranger* (2006). His article "The Black Forest and the Wold Newton Universe" is included in *The Black Forest 2: Castle of Shadows* (2005), and he recently contributed the Foreword to the new edition of Farmer's seminal "fictional biography," *Tarzan Alive: A Definitive Biography of Lord Greystoke* (2006). He is a regular contributor to *Tales of the Shadowmen*.

The Anti-Pope of Avignon

Starring:	Created by:
Solomon Kane	Robert E. Howard
Fausta	Michel Zevaco
Gaston Rochefort	based on Alexandre Dumas
The Horla	Guy de Maupassant

Written by:
Micah HARRIS is the author (with artist Michael Gaydos) of the graphic novel *Heaven's War*, a historical fantasy pitting authors Charles Williams, C.S. Lewis and J.R.R. Tolkien against occultist Aleister Crowley. Micah teaches composition, literature and film at Pitt Community College in North Carolina. He is currently developing several comics and prose projects. His self-published novel, *The Eldritch New Adventures of Becky Sharp*, in which the villainess of *Vanity Fair* becomes the agent of a Lovecraftian alien race, will be available soon.

Three Men, A Martian and A Baby

Starring:	Created by:
Doctor Omega	Arnould Galopin
Denis Borel	Arnould Galopin
Fred	Arnould Galopin
Kal-L	Jerry Siegel & Joe Shuster
The Selenites	H.G. Wells

Written by:

Travis HILTZ started making up stories at a young age. Years later, he began writing them down. In high school, he discovered that some writers actually got paid and decided to give it a try. He has since gathered a modest collection of rejection letters and had a one-act play produced. Travis lives in the wilds of New Hampshire with his very loving and tolerant wife, two above average children and a staggering amount of comic books and *Doctor Who* novels.

Corridors of Deceit

Starring:	Created by:
The Black Coats	Paul Féval
Kaitlin de Winter	Arthur Conan Doyle
Baron Gruner	Arthur Conan Doyle
Catarina Koluchy (a. k. a. Mrs. Moriarty)	L.T. Meade & Robert Eustace
Count Corbucci	E. W. Hornung
Antonio Nikola	Guy Boothby
Josephine Balsamo	Maurice Leblanc
Marguerite Chavain	Narcisco Ibanez-Serrador & Juan Tebar
Maude North (a.k.a. Hendrika Pienaar)	based on Marcel Allain & Pierre Souvestre & John Buchan
Maud Beltham	Marcel Allain & Pierre Souvestre
Irene Chupin/Tupin (a.k.a. Irina Putine)	Narcisco Ibanez-Serrador & Juan Tebar
Victor Chupin	Emile Gaboriau
Rosette Trevor	based on Guy Boothby
Eva Relli	based on Dario Argento & Daria Nicolodi

Countess Yalta	Fortuné du Boisgobey
Purity Parker	based on Arthur Conan Doyle
The Pallid Mask (a.k.a. Juan	Robert W. Chambers,
North a.k.a. Fantômas)	Marcel Allain
	& Pierre Souvestre
Sebastian Medina	Richard Matheson
Roger Vollin	based on David Boehm
Anna Beringer	L.T. Meade & Robert Eustace
Porky Shinwell	Arthur Conan Doyle
Mary Holder	Arthur Conan Doyle
Dr. Mabuse	Norbert Jacques
Richard Vollin	David Boehm
Introducing:	
Berenice Fourneau (a. k. a.	Rick Lai
Blythe Furnace)	
And:	
Institution Bachelard	Emile Zola

Written by:
Rick LAI is a computer programmer living in Bethpage, New York. During the 1980s and 1990s, he wrote articles utilizing Philip José Farmer's Wold Newton Universe concepts for pulp magazine fanzines such as *Nemesis Inc*, *Echoes*, *Golden Perils*, *Pulp Vault* and *Pulp Collector*. Rick has also created chronologies of such heroes as Doc Savage and the Shadow. He is a regular contributor to *Tales of the Shadowmen*.

The Evils Against Which We Strive

Starring:	**Created by:**
Sâr Dubnotal	Anonymous
The Shadow	Walter Gibson
Ligeia	Edgar Allan Poe
Introducing:	
Nick	Roman Leary
Miss Nolan	Roman Leary

Written by:
Roman LEARY was eight years old when a family friend gave him an Ace paperback of *Conan* stories. He has been a devotee of pulp fiction ever since. Today, he is a librarian living in the small town of Washington, North Carolina, with his lovely wife Ana. *The Evils Against Which We Strive* is his first published story.

Madame Atomos' Christmas

Starring:
Madame Atomos
Also Starring:
Lee Harvey Oswald

Created by:
André Caroff

The Reluctant Princess

Starring:
Doc Ardan
Sleeping Beauty
Joseph Rouletabille
Introducing:
The Phantom Angel

Created by:
Guy d'Armen
Charles Perrault
Gaston Leroux

Randy Lofficier

Written by:
Jean-Marc & Randy LOFFICIER, the authors of the *Shadowmen* non-fiction series, have also collaborated on five screenplays, a dozen books and numerous comic books and translations, including *Arsène Lupin*, *Doc Ardan*, *Doctor Omega* and *The Phantom of the Opera*, all published by Black Coat Press. They have written a number of animation teleplays, including episodes of *Duck Tales* and *The Real Ghostbusters* and such popular comic book heroes as *Superman* and *Doctor Strange*. In 1999, in recognition of their distinguished career as comic book writers, editors and translators, they were presented with the Inkpot award for Outstanding Achievement in Comic Arts. Randy is a member of the Writers Guild of America, West and Mystery Writers of America.

A Wooster Christmas

Starring:
Jeeves
Bertie Wooster
Aunt Dahlia
Uncle Tom
Florence Craye
Arthur Hastings
Hercule Poirot
With:
Monsieur Anatole

Created by:
P.G. Wodehouse
P.G. Wodehouse
P.G. Wodehouse
P.G. Wodehouse
P.G. Wodehouse
Agatha Christie
Agatha Christie

P.G. Wodehouse

Written by:
Xavier MAUMÉJEAN won the renowned Gerardmer Award in 2000 for his psychological thriller *The Memoirs of the Elephant Man*. His other works include *Gotham* (2002), *The League of Heroes*, which won the 2003 Imaginaire Award of the City of Brussels and was translated by Black Coat Press (2005), *La Vénus Anatomique* (2004), which won the 2005 Rosny Award, and *Car je suis Légion* (2005). Xavier has a diploma in philosophy and the science of religions and works as a teacher in the North of France, where he resides, with his wife and his daughter, Zelda.

Red in Tooth and Claw

Starring:	Created by:
Rocambole	Pierre-Alexis Ponson du Terrail
Lord Speedicut (a.k.a. Speed)	George Macdonald Fraser
John Sinnat	S.B.H. Hurst
Coyle	Hugh Pentecost
Inspector Bucket	Charles Dickens
Sergeant Cuff	Wilkie Collins
Hunt	based on Chris Chibnall
Creegan	based on Paul Abbott
Fitzgerald	based on Jimmy McGovern
Tennison	based on Lynda La Plante
The Rats:	
Albanian Brown	Jess Nevins
Priory Rat	H.P. Lovecraft
Qwhglmian Rat	Neal Stephenson
Sumatran Rat	Arthur Conan Doyle
Also Starring:	
Jack Black	
Jemmy Shaw	

Written by:
Jess NEVINS is a reference librarian at Sam Houston State University in Huntsville, Texas. He is the author of two companion books on Alan Moore and Kevin O'Neill's *League of Extraordinary Gentlemen* and of *The Encyclopedia of Fantastic Victoriana*, a comprehensive guide to 19th century genre literature. Jess is currently working on *The Encyclopedia of Pulp Heroes*, an exhaustive list of series heroes, in numerous media, published around the world from 1902 to 1945. Jess lives outside of Houston with his wife Alicia and their menagerie of animals.

The Mark of Kane

Starring:	**Created by:**
Erik	Gaston Leroux
The Minister	based on Bruce Geller
Charles Foster Kane	Orson Welles
	& Herman J. Mankiewicz
Gilberte "Gigi" Lachaille	Colette
"Irma Vep" (her alias)	Louis Feuillade
The Persian	Gaston Leroux
Elizabeth Eynsford Hill *née*	George Bernard Shaw
Doolittle	
Riolama a.k.a. Rima	W.H. Hudson
Théophraste Lupin	Maurice Leblanc
Favraux	Louis Feuillade
	& Arthur Bernède
Haghi	Fritz Lang
	& Thea von Harbou
Perry Bennett	Arthur B. Reeve,
	Charles W. Goddard
	& George B. Seitz
Madame Sara	L. T. Meade & Robert Eustace
Dunston Gryme	Gustave Linbach
Simon Carne	Guy Boothby
Dr. Materialismus	Frederic J. Stimson
Abijah K. Jones	George Lippard
Wanda Stielman	Jean de La Hire
Ballmeyer	Gaston Leroux
Baron Maupertuis	Arthur Conan Doyle
Dr. Jack Quartz	Frederic van Rensselaer Dey
Wizard Whateley	H.P. Lovecraft
Professor Fate	Blake Edwards
	& Arthur A. Ross
Sir Cuthbert Ware-Armitage	Ken Annakin & Jack Davies
The Assassination Bureau,	Jack London
Ltd.	
The Black Coats	Paul Féval
Raymond Owen	Charles W. Goddard
	& George B. Seitz
Voltaire	John Kneubuhl
Henry F. Potter	Philip Van Doren Stern,
	Frances Goodrich,
	Albert Hackett, Jo Swerling

	& Frank Capra
William Boltyn	Gustave Le Rouge
Hattison	Gustave Le Rouge
Gurn	Pierre Souvestre
	& Marcel Allain
General Guy Sternwood	Raymond Chandler
Joseph Harrison Paine	Lewis R. Foster
	& Sidney Buchman
Julian Karswell	Montague Rhode James
Natasha Natasaevna di	George Chetwynd
Murska	& Griffith Jones
The Face	Donald Cotton
	& Richard Harris
	& Verity Lambert
Emeric Belasco	Richard Matheson
Johnny Barlowe	Ilya Surguchev
	& Frederick Albert Swan
Gaylord Ravenal	Edna Ferber, Jerome Kern
	& Oscar Hammerstein II
Sebastian Moran	Arthur Conan Doyle
Jimmy Valentine	O. Henry & Paul Armstrong
Freddy Eynsford Hill	George Bernard Shaw
Bret Maverick	Roy Huggins

The Former Angels:

Christine Daaé	Gaston Leroux
Irene Adler	Arthur Conan Doyle
Trilby O'Ferrall	George du Maurier
Loveday Brooke	Catherine Louisa Pirkis
Unorna	F. Marion Crawford
Grunya Constantine	Jack London
Marahuna	H.B. Mariott-Watson
Anna Franklyn	Anthony Hinds
Hagar Stanley	Fergus Hume
Geneviève Dieudonné	Kim Newman
Yuki Kashima	Kazuo Uemura
	& Kazuo Koike

Also Starring:
Kathleen Ruston
Edda van Heemstra
Jacob Epstein
(Elizabeth's aliases)
And:

Royale-les-Eaux	Ian Fleming

Written by:
Kim NEWMAN's literary career began as a film reviewer and critic. His first stories were published in *Interzone*. In 1985, he wrote two non-fiction books, *Ghastly Beyond Belief* (with Neil Gaiman) and *Nightmare Movies*. His first novels were *The Night Mayor* (1989) and *Bad Dreams* (1990). The publication of *Anno Dracula* (1992) established him as a major name in horror fiction. That series continued with *The Bloody Red Baron* (1995) and *Judgment of Tears* (1998). Other novels by Kim include *Jago* (1991), *The Quorum* (1994) and *Life's Lottery* (1999). Kim's short story collections include *The Original Dr. Shade* (1994), *Famous Monsters* (1995), *Seven Stars* (2000), *Where the Bodies are Buried* (2000) and *Unforgivable Stories* (2000).

Twenty Thousand Years Under the Sea

Starring:	Created by:
Professor Arronax	Jules Verne
Captain Nemo	Jules Verne
Suydam	H.P. Lovecraft
Cthulhu	H.P. Lovecraft

Written by:
John PEEL was born in Nottingham, England, and started writing stories at age 10. John moved to the U.S. in 1981 to marry his pen-pal. He, his wife ("Mrs. Peel") and their 13 dogs now live on Long Island, New York. John has written just over 100 books to date, mostly for young adults. He is the only author to have written novels based on both *Doctor Who* and *Star Trek*. His most popular work is *Diadem*, a fantasy series; he has written ten volumes to date.

Night's Children

Starring:	Created by:
Irma Vep	Louis Feuillade
Count Orlock	F.W. Murnau
	& Henrik Galeen
Introducing:	
Wilhelm Schmidt	Steven A. Roman

Written by:
Steven A. ROMAN is the writer/creator of the horror graphic novel *Lorelei: Building the Perfect Beast,* and the author of the novels *Final Destination: Dead*

Man's Hand and *X-Men: The Chaos Engine Trilogy*. His most recent short fiction appeared in the anthologies *Doctor Who: Short Trips: Farewells*, *If I Were an Evil Overlord*, and *The Dead Walk Again!* He lives in Queens, NY.

Cyrano and the Two Plumes

Starring:	Created by:
Alcandre	Jean de Rotrou
Cyrano de Bergerac	Edmond Rostand
Ragueneau	Edmond Rostand
D'Artagnan	Alexandre Dumas

Written by:
John SHIRLEY is the author of numerous novels and books of stories, including the novels *Cellars, Demons, Wetbones, City Come A-Walkin', Eclipse, A Splendid Chaos*, the collection *Black Butterflies* (which won the Bram Stoker award and which was chosen by PW as one of the best books of that year), and the collection *Really Really Really Really Weird Stories from Nightshade*. His new story collection is *Living Shadows* from Prime Books. He has had stories in two Year's Best collections, and his novels *City Come A Walkin'* and *Eclipse* are thought to be seminal in the cyberpunk movement. He was co-screenwriter of the film *The Crow*, has written scripts for television series and cable movies. He was lead singer and songwriter for various bands including the punk band SadoNation, the post-punk band Obsession (Celluloid records) and the post-cyberpunk band The Panther Moderns. He has also written nonfiction including the book *Gurdjieff: An Introduction To His Life And Ideas* (Penguin/Tarcher). Forthcoming are "the lost cyberpunk novel" *Black Glass* (from Elder Signs) and a new urban fantasy novel, *Bleak History*.

The Return of Frankenstein

Starring:	Created by:
Ned Knob	Paul Féval
"Guido"	Brian Stableford
Robert Walton	Mary Shelley
"Lazarus"	Mary Shelley
Victor Frankenstein	Mary Shelley
Malo de Treguern	Paul Féval
Simeon	Brian Stableford
Count Szandor	Paul Féval
Gregory Temple	Paul Féval

Henri de Belcamp (a.k.a.   Paul Féval
John Devil)
Also Starring:
Percy Bysshe Shelley
John Taaffe, Jr.
Edward John Trelawny
Capt. John Hay
Edward Williams

Written by:
Brian M. STABLEFORD has been a professional writer since 1965. He has published more than 50 novels and 200 short stories, as well as several non-fiction books, thousands of articles for periodicals and reference books and a number of anthologies. He is also a part-time Lecturer in Creative Writing at King Alfred's College Winchester. Brian's novels include *The Empire of Fear* (1988), *Young Blood* (1992), *The Wayward Muse* (2005), *The Stones of Camelot* (2006), *The New Faust at the Tragicomique* (2007) and his future history series comprising *Inherit the Earth* (1998), *Architects of Emortality* (1999), *The Fountains of Youth* (2000), *The Cassandra Complex* (2001), *Dark Ararat* (2002) and *The Omega Expedition* (2002). His non-fiction includes *Scientific Romance in Britain* (1985), *Teach Yourself Writing Fantasy and Science Fiction* (1997), *Yesterday's Bestsellers* (1998) and *Glorious Perversity: The Decline and Fall of Literary Decadence* (1998). Brian's translations for Black Coat Press include Paul Féval's *Anne of the Isles, John Devil, Knightshade, Revenants, Vampire City, The Vampire Countess, The Wandering Jew's Daughter, The Black Coats: 'Salem Street* and *The Black Coats: The Invisible Weapon*; Paul Féval fils' *Felifax the Tiger-Man*; Villiers de l'Isle-Adam's *The Scaffold* and *The Vampire Soul*; Jean de La Hire's *The Nyctalope vs. Lucifer*; Marie Nizet's *Captain Vampire*; Ponson du Terrail's *The Vampire and the Devil's Son* and the anthology *News from the Moon*.

TALES OF THE
SHADOWMEN

Volume 1: The Modern Babylon (2005)
Matthew Baugh: *Mask of the Monster* - Bill Cunningham: *Cadavres Exquis* - Terrance Dicks: *When Lemmy Met Jules* - Win Scott Eckert: *The Vanishing Devil* - Viviane Etrivert: *The Three Jewish Horsemen* - G.L. Gick: *The Werewolf of Rutherford Grange* (1) - Rick Lai: *The Last Vendetta* - Alain le Bussy: *The Sainte-Geneviève Caper* - Jean-Marc & Randy Lofficier: *Journey to the Center of Chaos* - Samuel T. Payne: *Lacunal Visions* - John Peel: *The Kind-Hearted Torturer* - Chris Roberson: *Penumbra* - Robert Sheckley: *The Paris-Ganymede Clock* - Brian Stableford: *The Titan Unwrecked; or, Futility Revisited*.

Volume 2: Gentlemen of the Night (2006)
Matthew Baugh: *Ex Calce Liberatus* - Bill Cunningham: *Trauma* - Win Scott Eckert: *The Eye of Oran* - G.L. Gick: *The Werewolf of Rutherford Grange* (2) - Rick Lai: *Dr. Cerral's Patient* - Serge Lehman: *The Mystery of the Yellow Renault*; *The Melons of Trafalmadore* - Jean-Marc Lofficier: *Arsène Lupin's Christmas; Figaro's Children; The Tarot of Fantômas; The Star Prince; Marguerite; Lost and Found* - Xavier Mauméjean: *Be Seeing You!* - Sylvie Miller & Philippe Ward: *The Vanishing Diamonds* - Jess Nevins: *A Jest, To Pass The Time* - Kim Newman: *Angels of Music* - John Peel: *The Incomplete Assassin* - Chris Roberson: *Annus Mirabilis* - Jean-Louis Trudel: *Legacies* - Brian Stableford: *The Empire of the Necromancers* (1)

Volume 3: Danse Macabre (2007)
Matthew Baugh: *The Heart of the Moon* - Alfredo Castelli: *Long Live Fantômas* - Bill Cunningham: *Next!* - François Darnaudet & J.-M. Lofficier: *Au Vent Mauvais...* - Paul DiFilippo: *Return to the 20th Century* - Win Scott Eckert: *Les Lèvres Rouges* - G.L. Gick: *Beware the Beasts* - Micah Harris: *The Ape Gigans* - Travis Hiltz: *A Dance of Night and Death* - Rick Lai: *The Lady in the Black Gloves* - Jean-Marc Lofficier: *The Murder of Randolph Carter* - Xavier Mauméjean: *A Day in the Life of Madame Atomos* - David A. McIntee: *Bullets Over Bombay* - Brad Mengel: *All's Fair...* - Michael Moorcock: *The Affair of the Bassin Les Hivers* - John Peel: *The Successful Failure* - Joseph Altairac & Jean-Luc Rivera: *The Butterfly Files* - Chris Roberson: *The Famous Ape* - Robert L. Robinson, Jr.: *Two Hunters* - Brian Stableford: *The Empire of the Necromancers* (2).